Book 1 of the Skalterra Duology

Written by M.T. Zimny

Paperback ISBN: 978-1-7356571-4-1
Hardcover ISBN: 978-1-7356571-7-2

Fonts used: Merriweather and Urbanist
Cover art and typography by: Maria Mondloch
Map Design by: M.T. Zimny
Editing by: Jessica C

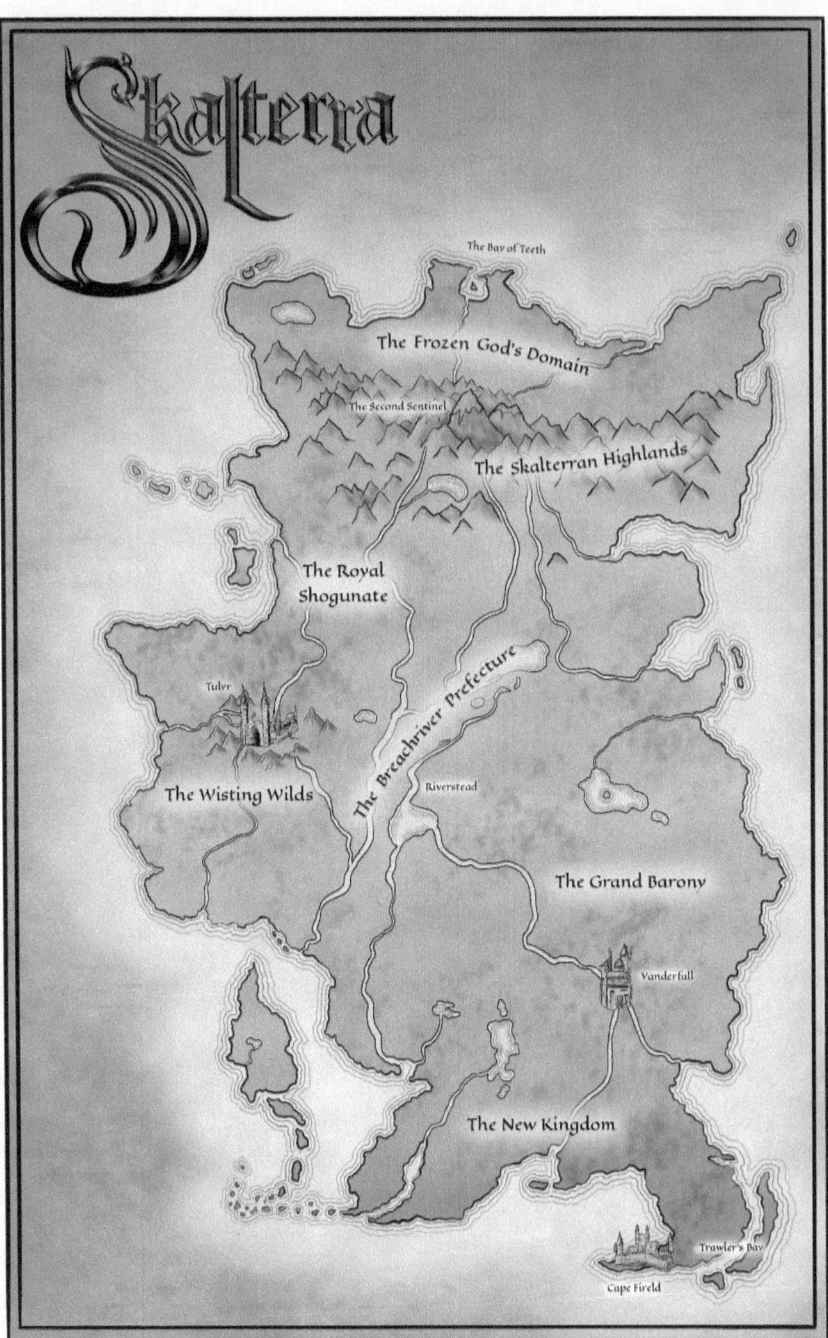

Skalterra
The Bay of Teeth
The Frozen God's Domain
The Second Sentinel
The Skalterran Highlands
The Royal Shogunate
Tulvr
The Breachriver Prefecture
The Wisting Wilds
Riverstead
The Grand Barony
Vanderfall
The New Kingdom
Trawler's Bay
Cape Fireld

To Gaga

You ruined your shirts to fix my stuffed animals. You leaped over live wires to help strangers. You gave everything to everyone and never asked for anything in return.

The least I can do is write a book with a badass grandma who loves the color blue and dedicate it to you.

Table of Contents

One
Intro to Siege Warfare

These were not my eyelashes.

Yes, I had bigger things to worry about, like the screams of falling soldiers, the quaking of the battlements, the fact that I was inexplicably on a battlement in the first place...

But these eyelashes! Long and lush and certainly not mine, yet there they were, fluttering at the edges of my vision, illuminated by the bright bursts of neon light that accompanied the blasts that shook the fort.

Right.

The fort.

At least, it seemed like a fort, with stone parapets strung between turrets to protect a mossy courtyard. It might've been peaceful if not for the soldiers swarming between its upright stones and gnarled, spindly trees.

An arcing ball of orange lit the sky from above, streaking against the inky black of night. A turret interrupted its path into the courtyard, and it burst in an explosion of light and rubble, rocking the stones beneath me.

I shrank back against the low wall of the battlement. Someone screamed something about a gate being breached, and heavy bootsteps clattered past, taking no notice of the girl huddled against her knees.

This was all wrong.

I screwed up my face, trying to remember how I'd gotten here, but only came up with snatches of foggy battles and muddied greaves. I was somewhere else before all that, though. Somewhere that definitely wasn't a battlefield.

More explosions. More yelling. The weight of chainmail pressing down on my shoulders.

And eyelashes that were not mine.

"Focus, Wren." My desperate whisper bounced against the metal of my helmet's faceplate. This was not the time to get distracted, especially as I was now alone on a crumbling wall that the other soldiers had all had the sense to abandon.

The stones ahead of me turned orange in the light of another bombardment, and the shimmering blaze blasted through the stone to my right.

Sparks and bits of rubble rained against me, and I stumbled to my feet as the cobbled flooring gave way. The parapet rocked and swayed, making it impossible for my heavy boots to gain purchase, and I fell forward.

I scrabbled at the stone as my legs slipped into the chasm left by the crumbling fort. My chainmail, heavy before, was damn near a death sentence now, and I screamed through gritted teeth with the effort of trying to hoist myself back up.

It was useless. With my helmeted face pressed against stone and every muscle locked, I couldn't see how far the drop was, but the clash of metal and yells of soldiers below were far enough away to tell me my prospects were less than great.

At least I'd die with fantastic eyelashes.

I squeezed my eyes shut. I could try to pull myself up again, but if my muscles gave out—

"Where is the Sovereign?" a voice growled above me. My helmet pulled at my hair, scraping against stone as it was pulled from my head. I opened my eyes to an orange glow bouncing off black boots inches from my face. My hair fell loose of the helmet, long, lush and blue.

Forget the eyelashes, whose *hair* was this?

Gloved hands yanked me to my feet and held me by the collar of my tunic and chainmail. Orange irises glowed bright at the center of dark pearlescent sclera, looking all the more black set against an alabaster face.

Sure, this stranger had saved me, but the way he glared over the dark cowl pulled up over his nose, I had enough sense to know that whoever he was, he was an enemy.

"The Sovereign." He raised a knife that glowed the same color as his eyes—the same color as the blasts that had taken out chunks of the parapet—to my throat. "I won't ask again, Blue."

"I don't know," I choked. The ragged cloak that hung off his shoulders whirled as he spun me around to throw me to the stones. Maybe it was my relief at escaping the orange knife or my new distance from the lip of the edge, but I added, "and my name's not Blue. That's stupid."

His scowl deepened, and the blade in his hand elongated into a scythe that had me regretting that last quip.

"Oh, no thanks." I tried to scramble away, but a heavy boot blocked my path as the man drew back his weapon. I tucked my face into my shoulder, thankful that this would be cleaner than falling to my death.

The curved blade whistled through the air, but was cut by a crash and a garbled shout. I opened my eyes in time to see the whip of tattered cloaks disappearing over the open edge, and the darkness swallowed the orange glow of my assailant's weapon as he hurtled to the courtyard ruins below.

"Stop wasting time, Nightmare!" A young woman pulled me to my feet, and she stared at the spot the cloaked figure had disappeared. At least, I was pretty sure that was where she was staring. It was hard to tell with the opaque, metal-rimmed goggles fixed over her eyes. The green fire that swathed the hand she held aloft cast shadows that carved valleys against her sharp cheekbones, making her appear older than her voice suggested.

"You killed him," I said blankly. Better him than me, but *still*.

"I wish." She twisted around, the movement made awkward by the leather armor strapped across her chest. "To the tower, pet! We need you with us down below!"

She spoke with an air of fake authority that I could tell she was forcing into her tone, but I wasn't in any position to disobey. Glowing bottles hung off the woman's belt, and they clinked against each other in time with her strides.

"Look, I don't know how I got here," I tried to explain. Green light from the fire in her hands danced ahead of us, illuminating the heavy, oaken door of a turret.

"Down the stairs, now. They're waiting." She threw the door open and watched over my shoulder as we disappeared inside.

The air inside the tower was dusty and stale, and the woman's firelight cast the claustrophobic stone walls in shades of emerald. I staggered down the steps, trying to see past the shadows.

The sounds of a door being blasted off its hinges echoed behind us, prompting a gentle prod between my shoulders.

"Usually you Nightmares are faster than this," the woman mused behind me. "I wonder if Galahad isn't feeling well."

"Please." I tried to go down the steps faster, but the chainmail on my shoulders was cumbersome and awkward. "I don't know what's going on. My name is

Wren Warrender, and I'm supposed to be at my grandmother's."

Yes, that was it. I had been at Gams's, but this war-torn fort looked nothing like the coastal town where she made her living. And while the memory of moving into the guest room above her gift shop had finally resurfaced, it did little to explain how I'd found myself in the middle of a battle on a castle.

"Orla, what's taking so long?" The dark head of a young man poked out of a trapdoor at the foot of the stairs. He shielded his goggled eyes as another tower-shaking blast shook dust loose overhead. I braced just in case the stone steps I'd just stumbled down came falling after me. "Ferrin and Caitria went ahead to clear a path, and if we're late to follow—"

"Sorry, Tiernan. Ran into a Grimguard." The woman, Orla, placed a hand on my shoulder to guide me to the trapdoor. "Careful, pet! It's a bit of a drop."

The young man ducked away as I stumbled through the trapdoor. The golden firelight in his hand caught the metal of the beads he wore at the end of short, twisted hair locks. While his goggles made his expression hard to read, I got the feeling he was glaring at me. He held a protective hand out to bar me from the cloaked girl who stood behind him.

"This one has blue hair!" Orla announced as she landed in the passageway. "Galahad, do you see this? Blue hair! You should do them all that way."

The room had a low ceiling, and its walls stretched into shadow so that I couldn't see where they ended. The little alcove where we stood was crowded, though there were only three people waiting for us here. The oldest of them pushed his way forward.

His white beard clashed with bronze skin, and, despite his age, he wore warrior's armor similar to Orla's under a knee-length leather duster that made him look like a steampunk motorcycle grandpa.

"Blue hair, you say?" He pushed metal-rimmed goggles up his forehead, revealing pale gray eyes that reflected the greens and golds of his companions' fires. I flinched away when he took a clump of my hair in his gnarled hand and let the tresses slide between his fingers. "Well, that is certainly different."

A shriek echoed from deep within the shadows ahead.

"Caitria!" The young man, Tiernan, looked towards the darkness. "That was Caitria!"

Muffled shouting ensued, and the others surged forward to leave me in the dark.

"Protect the Sovereign!" the old man bellowed back at me. I glanced around in the lengthening shadows and found the small girl who'd been hiding behind Tiernan. Her large brown eyes glittered in the fading light, and the carried fires of her comrades sent multi-colored shadows through her halo of dark hair.

"I don't—" I sputtered, then pulled the girl after the others by her wrist. "Wait, I don't have a light!"

"Make one!" the old man commanded without looking back. A crash overhead made me run faster still, and, to her credit, the girl kept up despite her thick robes and thin frame.

"You don't seem like a very good Nightmare," she whispered between labored breaths. I chased after the yellow and green fires of the others, not wanting to get left behind in the dark, still struggling to remember how I'd somehow gotten from Gams's apartment to a fort under siege.

The corridor bent and widened into a room, and I careened into Orla where she and the men had stopped to stare at the grisly scene ahead of us.

A man slumped against the far wall, and blood flecked the stones above his head. A woman lay in the center of the room at the feet of a man shrouded in dark cloaks. He looked up from the woman with eyes that glowed orange, just like those of the assailant Orla had blasted off the roof.

"Caitria!" Tiernan lunged forward, reaching for the woman on the floor, but Galahad grabbed him by the back of his cloaks and pulled him back. "If he hurt Caitria, I'll kill him!"

"Daithi, Grimguard of the Frozen God," the old man growled. "You're a bit far from home."

"Galahad." His voice was raspy and low, not unlike that of his friend on the parapet. "I'm here for the Sovereign."

"Send the Nightmare," Galahad said, and several hands shoved me forward to stand between them and Daithi. I staggered backwards under his orange gaze, but someone pushed me forward again.

"Oh, no," I said. "This isn't— I don't do *this*."

"This is what I made you for!" Galahad boomed. "Now defend the Sovereign!"

"I don't know what that means!" I hated the panicked whine in my voice, but none of this made sense. I had been at *Gams's*.

"It means fight!"

I stared at Daithi, and while he remained poised for an attack, he waited for me to make the first move.

He would be waiting a long time, I decided.

"Look, I don't know who you are, or what's happening, but—" I started to say to him, but then glanced down at the woman at his feet.

My stomach dropped. From here, in the center of the room, I could see that she wore goggles like the others, but one side had shattered out. Behind the frame of broken shards, her brown eye stared up at the ceiling, blank and unseeing.

"She's—she's dead?" I backpedaled from the man.

A cry went up behind me.

"No!" Tiernan tore away from Galahad to meet me in the middle of the cavern, staring down at the woman. He took in her parted lips, gray face, and the blood already drying in her dark hair. A broken gasp worked its way from deep in his throat. "You killed...you killed Caitria."

And then he threw himself at Daithi.

The gold fire in his hands lengthened into a sword, but Daithi deflected the attack with a blade of orange. I tripped over my leather boots in my haste to escape, and then Tiernan tripped backwards over me.

The yellow glow of Tiernan's sword sputtered out, and the weapon dissipated. Daithi stood over us and drew back to strike. Someone shrieked a too-late warning, but just as Tiernan was about to meet a quick end on the point of an orange blade, still tangled in my limbs, green light burst in Daithi's chest.

He staggered backwards, staring blankly ahead as blood trickled from his nose and mouth, and then he tripped over the dead woman at his feet to join her in the dust.

A tentative silence fell over the cavern, and I stared at the dead man and woman on the floor just feet away from me.

"I want..." I whispered through a shaky breath, "I want to go home now."

"Your Nightmare seems defective, Galahad." The previously unconscious man at the far wall was upright now, and he leaned against the stone, bleeding from the head with one eye swollen shut over a neatly trimmed beard. Green flames danced at his fingertips. "You're lucky I've got a good aim."

"Uncle Ferrin!" Orla broke free of the group to rush to the side of the injured man. "What happened? Is Caitria really—"

"He was waiting for us." Ferrin glared at the dead Grimguard. Tiernan shoved me aside so he could crawl to the woman on the ground and extricate her out from under Daithi. "Tiernan, I'm sorry. I tried, but—"

He cut off to shake his head. Tiernan brushed the hair from the dead woman's face. She was older than Tiernan, older than me, but looked as if she'd still had so much life left to live.

"Caitria always told you that you're too hotheaded, Tiernan." Galahad hobbled forward and bent down to gently remove Caitria's broken goggles from her face. "She may be gone, but that doesn't mean you need to rush to join her."

None of this was right, and bile worked its way up my throat. I needed to find my way back to Gams. If people were being attacked here, wherever here was, I needed to make sure she was safe.

But I couldn't move. I stared at the two dead bodies in front of me. The orange light in the Grimguard's eyes had died when he had, and he stared unseeing at the cavern ceiling.

"Now what?" the girl in the golden robes asked in a tiny voice. She clung to Galahad's leather duster, hiding behind him.

"We need to keep moving." Galahad straightened up. "The other Grimguard is behind us, and when he finds his friend, he'll be out for blood as well as the Sovereign."

Tiernan wrapped his arms around the dead woman and glanced around, as if expecting someone to help him lift her. No one did.

"Tiernan," Ferrin murmured.

"We'll come back for her, right?" Tiernan said. Galahad shook his head.

"Cape Fireld has fallen. There is no coming back, but this is her home. It's a better resting place than any."

"But this is my home too." The young girl knelt next to Tiernan. Her thin fingers brushed hair from the dead woman's ashen face. "Where will I go?"

"The Second Sentinel," Ferrin asserted.

"Who's the Second Sentinel?" I asked.

Ferrin looked at me with a brow knit in confusion.

"It's a where, not a who. Galahad, your Nightmare, she—"

"The Second Sentinel is out of the question," the old man cut him off.

"It's the safest place." Ferrin leaned on Orla, but the steel in his one open eye said he'd been expecting this fight.

"It's too close to the Frozen God," the old man said. "You may as well deliver the Sovereign to his doorstep."

"The Second Sentinel is protected! And the Grimguards don't know it's there! What does proximity matter when they've come this far south, anyway?"

"It's clear across the continent." Galahad remained resolute.

"Then where?" Ferrin asked. "Tulyr?"

Galahad's wrinkled face darkened.

"You've made your point. But if the Second Sentinel goes the way of Tulyr by the end of this, it'll be your doing."

"And the Nightmare?" Ferrin asked, his face glowing green in the light of Orla's flame. "She's defective, but now she knows where we're going."

"Feed her to a rotsbane," Tiernan spat from where he still knelt with Caitria's body. I recoiled away, stumbling to my feet. I didn't know what a rotsbane was, but I was sure I didn't want to be eaten by one.

Every face in the room turned towards me.

"Oh," I said, my voice too high. "No, actually, if someone could just point me in the direction of Keel Watch Harbor. I'm supposed to be at my Gams's house, but—"

"Orla, where did you say you picked this one up, again?" Galahad strode forward, studying me, and I backpedaled until I found the edge of the room.

"She was on the parapet," Orla chirped. "The other Grimguard was about to ash her, but I thought it'd be handy to have a Nightmare with us."

Galahad cocked his head at me, and I stepped back, bumping up against the cavern wall.

"Girl, do you have a name?"

"Wren." Finally, we were getting somewhere. Someone was going to help me. "Wren Warrender."

A stunned silence buzzed around the room.

"She knows her name," Ferrin hissed.

"She's lucid." Galahad's face turned stony, as if every wrinkle had been carved there on purpose. "I know."

"But Nightmares aren't supposed—"

"I *know*." He pulled a vial of glowing liquid from his belt and downed the contents in a single gulp. He slipped his goggles down over his eyes with one hand as silver firelight sparked in the other. "Tiernan, cover Fana's eyes."

"Oh, Galahad." Disgust laced Ferrin's tone. "Not here."

The firelight at Galahad's fingers lengthened into a blade. I pressed against the cold, ungiving stones at my back.

"She's a liability, Ferrin," Galahad growled. "She's lucid, and she's heard too much. Tiernan's right. She'll only slow us down, but if the other Grimguard finds her and interrogates her—"

"No!" I threw my hands up in surrender. "I promise, I'm very dumb! I have no idea what you've all been saying! I'd be horrible in an interrogation."

"Galahad," Ferrin warned. The old man looked at him and shrugged.

"She's my Nightmare, Ferrin," he said. "And she's mine to dispose of as I see fit. Tiernan, Fana's eyes are closed, yes?"

And the silver blade dug into my chest.

Two

Diagnostic Evaluation

Sharp fire in my belly brought me to the waking world, upright and with one arm outstretched in a desperate attempt at self-defense. For a moment, the searing, gut-wrenching pain lingered, but then it dissipated into nothing more than the ghost of a dull ache.

A sleepy hiss issued from the foot of my bed, and I strained against the early morning dark to make out the shapeless form of Jonquil where she curled up in the folds of my quilt.

It had been a dream.

A weird, terrible dream that I couldn't quite shake but had escaped all the same.

I fell back against my pillow in shaky relief, but jolted up when I found my sheets wet with cool sweat.

Nice. Night sweats. An early sign of leukemia.

"You don't have leukemia," I mumbled to myself as one hand fumbled for my phone. I needed to check the internet if obnoxiously vivid dreams about blue hair and Grimguards, whatever a Grimguard might be, were also signs of blood cancer.

My free hand found its familiar resting place on my cheek as I waited for the search results to populate the screen. The feeling of eyelashes between my fingertips usually helped to calm my nerves, but the memory of the long lashes I'd had in my dream stayed my wandering fingers. I knew I'd pulled them out far too many times to ever hope to achieve that kind of length again, but still. I could dream.

After the internet assured me that I was probably okay, I swung my legs over the side of the bed to stretch. It was only just past three AM, but maybe I'd get a head start on chores in the shop. Even if I *could* fall back asleep, I definitely didn't want to risk falling back into the same nightmare.

Jonquil's flat face was fixed in what looked like a permanent glare, but the look she gave me when I flicked on the lights was extra icy. The poor thing wasn't yet used to sharing the guest room above the shop, and she clearly saw being awake before sunrise to be an affront to her Persian nature.

"Can cats smell cancer?" I asked her, pulling my hair into a bun and exposing the undercut at the base of my head. Disguising my neurotic hair pulling habit as a trendy haircut was one of my more recent strokes of genius. "You would tell me if I had cancer, wouldn't you?"

Jonquil jumped off the bed to hide in the dark shadows beneath it.

"That's fine," I called after her. "Let me rot. We both know you want the room to yourself again."

I tiptoed across uneven floorboards in the hall, trying not to wake Gams. I'd thought getting out of the dusty bedroom might make me feel farther from the dream, but its remnants hung off me. The distant orange glow of the rising sun through the windows that overlooked the street looked too much like the arcing balls of orange that had destroyed the parapet. The dark, narrow staircase that led down to the shop felt too much like the spiraling steps of the turret.

And the light spilling out from under the door to the shop looked too much like I wasn't the first one awake.

"Gams?" I asked the empty shop aisles as I pushed my way inside. The lights of early morning fishermen twinkled out in the harbor through the massive windows that Gams refused to replace—no matter how much they drove up heating and cooling costs.

Knick-knacks and bare-essential groceries lined the shelves, and as I traipsed through them, I noticed Gams had added to the growing collection of painted ceramic chickens that she kept front and center near the entrance. Near the back of the shop, meanwhile, the glow under the basement door told me she was busy in her workshop, toiling away to bring even more chickens to the shelves.

"Gams?" I asked again, pushing open the basement door.

"Did you sleep in again?" Gams called back. She appeared from around the corner at the base of the wooden staircase. Her silver and gray hair was pulled back, and her massive glasses magnified her eyes. The blue glaze on her hands confirmed she'd been painting more chickens.

"It's not even four yet," I laughed.

"Like I said," she tutted. "Sleeping in. Stay there, I'm coming up."

I stepped aside as she hurried up the steps with surprising agility for a woman her age. The fly-away hairs from her bun caught the glow of the workshop lights behind her, and she grinned wide, pushing the shoebox she carried into my arms.

"Add those to the shelf, please."

"All blue?" I stared down at the ceramic chickens in the box, each painted in different shades and patterns of blue.

"Von Leer colors! For luck!" She beamed, going to wash her hands in the sink behind the ice-cream station. "Speaking of, any news yet?"

I looked at the chickens with new, bitter distaste. I'd rather be back on the exploding parapet in my dream than talk about school.

"I wouldn't know. Your wifi is so bad they could've emailed me a week ago, and it still won't have loaded in my inbox."

Gams looked at me with scandal in her eyes.

"My wifi is fine. Your phone is the problem."

"I would show you your online reviews of customers saying otherwise, but they won't load for some reason." I set the last chicken on the shelf by the front door. "But no, I haven't heard from Von Leer."

Graduation had only been two weeks ago. Summer was still young. There was still time for Von Leer University to take me off the waitlist, but my hopes weren't high. With every passing day of continued silence from the admissions office, they sunk ever lower.

Mom and Gams had both insisted on me accepting the offer my safety school had sent me, but I'd rather take the year off and reapply. I only got to go to college once, and Von Leer had the best biochemistry program on the west coast.

More importantly, they also had the best geophysics program, which was what I was *actually* interested in, but geophysicists were something of a taboo in our tiny family thanks to my father.

"Their loss," Gams sniffed, now restocking the cereal selection. It was a favorite aisle of the touring families who came through Keel Watch Harbor. "Though I suppose if you don't get in, that's an extra year of free labor I get from you."

That was a joke. I hoped. Gams had told me I was getting paid, though I felt bad taking money from my grandmother.

"I don't know how they wouldn't take me." I grabbed the broom from behind the register. "My application essay was textbook."

"The 'absentee father' bit doesn't work, dear, when the school is on said absentee father's lecture circuit."

"Then that rules out just about every college of any caliber!" I growled.

"Maybe, but he's only an alumnus of one of them, and that's the one you're trying to impress."

"And maybe it was my bravado at calling him out on being a deadbeat dad that got me waitlisted instead of going straight into their reject pile."

Gams sighed and beckoned for me to stoop lower so she could kiss my cheek.

"Absentee father or no, they're missing out on a bright student like you. If I ran a school, I'd admit you for sure. Even if you do sleep in."

I looked at the clock behind the register. It still wasn't four.

"Are you usually up this early?" I asked.

"Prime chicken painting time." Gams winked. "Plus, Teddy will be by with bagels soon. I made sure to tell him to bring you one. He's such a nice young man."

I snorted. Teddy was well into his forties, if not fifties, already.

"Thanks." I leaned against the register, checking my email again.

It was no wonder I'd had weird dreams last night. The stress of waiting to hear from Von Leer was weighing on me, and after everything that had happened graduation night, I was in need of some good news.

Teddy did eventually come by with spare bagels from his shop down the street, and while the man would never dream of charging Gams, she tipped him with her newest favorite chicken. He took it happily, pocketing it in his puffy vest. I wondered how many of her chickens he already had in his bagel shop.

It was a slow morning, but Tuesdays usually were, since most tourists came through on weekends. Of course, we still got the occasional stragglers searching for Keel Watch Harbor hoodies. The cool ocean air tended to catch tourists off guard, and they were always happy to shell out a few extra bucks if it meant staying warm.

I was refreshing my email again, hoping that maybe it *was* an issue of wifi and not the Von Leer University admissions team. It gave me something to focus on, at least. The lingering feelings of doom and stress from my nightmare had faded a bit with the rising sun, but I rubbed the spot below my sternum where the old man had run me through.

"Wren Warrender, are you there?"

I looked up at the sound of my name, but the only people in the shop were a young, pregnant couple poking through the hoodie selection on the far wall.

"Gams?" I asked, but she'd long since returned to her workshop in the basement. Jonquil came bounding down the apartment staircase, chirping with each step. She peeked out at me from the stairwell. "You're not Gams."

She meowed, as if offended I didn't see her as an equally important figure of authority in the shop, and went to find Gams in the basement.

"Blue?"

I jumped at the voice, thinking back to the Grimguard and his dumb nickname for me on battlements.

But it wasn't a Grimguard standing in the doorway of the shop. It was a young man, roughly my age, holding a ceramic chicken in his hand.

"Can I help you?"

His smile was crooked and boyish and stupid under his messy blond hair. My eyes narrowed at his hoodie with "Von Leer University" plastered over the university's coat of arms on his chest.

"I'm looking for Ethel. Is she downstairs?" He set the chicken back on the shelf.

"Basement is for employees only." I was being difficult on purpose, if only to punish him for his offensive attire. "She might be up in a bit, or I can give her a message for you."

"That's okay." He pulled his hoodie off as he crossed to the ice-cream station. "I'll let her paint in peace. She'll see me when she comes up."

He went to stand behind the ice-cream station, and my warning of "employees only" died on my lips when he pulled on an apron with an embroidered name tag.

I didn't even have an apron with my name embroidered on it.

The pregnant couple brought a couple of hoodies and a small collection of chickens up to the counter. I tried to smile as I wrapped them in tissue paper, but the young man, my apparent *coworker*, grinned at me with an impish smile from behind the couple.

Neither Gams nor Mom had warned me about a coworker.

The young couple left, leaving me alone with the boy.

"I take it Ethel didn't tell you I was starting today?"

"That's Miss Warrender to you." I pressed my lips together, suddenly a bit more sympathetic to Jonquil's plight of having me invade her living space. "And if it's your first day, how'd you get that apron?"

"She hasn't been Miss Warrender to me in years." The boy laughed. He was laughing at *me*. He was mocking *me*. "And this apron is old. I've worked for Ethel the last three summers."

"Fan of Von Leer?" My eyes darted to his hoodie hanging on the wall hook behind him.

"Student. Just wrapped up freshman year. Go Vikings."

Of course he was a student. It was a good school. It attracted all kinds of kids, but why did it seem the only ones to get in were the people I actively disliked? The geophysicist father I'd never met, Linsey Harper, and now this guy...

Not that Linsey Harper would be going there in the fall, and I didn't really have any grounds to hate my surprise coworker other than the fact that it was easier to dislike new people and rob them of the chance of disliking me first.

"You'll mess up your make-up if you do that." Gams came out of the basement, drying freshly washed hands on her apron. My hand snapped away from my face where my fingers had been inching towards my eyelashes.

"I wasn't touching them." It was a lie. I knew it. She knew it. She nodded approvingly anyways.

"And you!" The grin that broke across her face deepened the wrinkles around her eyes and mouth yet somehow made her look younger. "Returned after all these months! Are you smarter yet? And when's that lazy cousin of yours getting in?"

"Don't worry, Riley's on his way. I know he's your favorite." The young man with the stupid smile stepped out from behind his ice-cream barricade to hug Gams, and my dislike for him grew. I wasn't just an only child, but an only grandchild too. I didn't like suddenly having to share my grandmother.

Even Jonquil seemed to like him, trotting after Gams with her fluffy tail held high.

"I take it you've introduced yourself to Wren already." Gams released him, and he turned that infuriating, quirked smile back to me.

"Sort of." He dipped his head. "It's Liam."

"Teddy's nephew." Gams patted Liam's shoulder, which was eye-level for her. "Why scoop bagels when you can scoop ice-cream?"

"You shouldn't be scooping bagels at all." I scoffed. "If you're going to spoon all the bread out of a bagel to make room for more cream cheese, just eat cream cheese."

"Exactly." Liam nodded, and I fumed inwardly. I pretended to recount the cash in the register while Liam recounted his freshman year to an enraptured Gams. As much as I loved my grandmother, I was secretly relieved when she disappeared back to her basement.

I couldn't stand the absolute betrayal of it all. Jonquil took pity on me, and brushed up against my calf in a rare display of affection.

I would have to learn to stomach Liam. It wasn't like I could stay at home alone while Mom traveled abroad. Not after what Linsey had done.

My palms turned sweaty, and my chest tightened.

Linsey was far away. I was never going to see her again, even if I did make it off the waitlist. I'd seen to that personally, whether that had been my intention or not.

"Wren Warrender." It was that voice again. Gravely, old, and familiar, but not in a good way.

"What?" I blurted, scanning the empty shop for the source of the voice. Liam looked back at me, confused.

"Is something wrong?" he asked.

I knew I'd heard it this time, the voice saying my name. Maybe I was overtired from my night of poor sleep, but I didn't like the concern on Liam's face.

"It's nothing, I—"

My phone screen lit up next to the register, and it was as if the uneven floorboards had dropped away, leaving me suspended in the salty, dusty air of the shop.

I had an email from the admissions office of Von Leer University.

"Wren Warrender, I know you're there."

"Wren?" Liam asked, just as the voice said my full name a third time.

"Leave me alone!" I snapped, more at the voice in my head than Liam.

"Ah," it replied. "I knew I'd found you."

The last thing I saw was Liam lunging across the shop floor to catch me.

Three
Advanced Botany

I didn't like waking up in a standing position. My knees buckled, and firm hands rushed to steady me. The world blurred and shifted until shapes and colors that made sense locked into place.

The grove where I stood was sunken, and a ring of towering trees stood guard at the lip of the embankment. Their roots cut out of the dirt before dipping back into the small hillside, leaving me in the middle of a tangle of bark and shadow.

"Welcome back to Skalterra, little Nightmare." It was that voice again, the one that called for me in the shop. The old man from my dream stood in front of me, his hair more white than silver in the mottled green shadows of day. His goggles perched on top of his head, and he had his hands jammed in the pockets of his leather duster. "I'm sure you have questions, and so do we."

"No," I gasped and stumbled away, ripping myself from the hands that held my shoulders.

"We don't want to hurt you," a new voice said in my ear. The swelling in Ferrin's face had gone down since I'd seen him in the tunnel under the fort. His leather shoulder armor wrinkled the edges of the vest he wore over a simple white shirt, and the thick, metal-rimmed goggles pushed up his forehead made his hair stick up like a cockatoo's feathers. He looked like a steampunk professor, but he'd killed the Grimguard. He was dangerous.

But he also wasn't real. This was another dream. It had to be.

Behind him, the old man, Galahad, drew a hand out of his pocket, alight with silver fire, and I turned heel.

Nope. Absolutely not. Dream or real, I wasn't getting stabbed again.

"Grab her!" Galahad yelled. Ferrin's fingers scratched at my back, but I was already sprinting for the embankment.

I grabbed onto gnarled roots for extra purchase as I heaved myself out of Ferrin's reach. Blue hair fell in my face, obscuring my vision, and I suddenly missed my usual haircut as I fought to push thick tresses out of my way.

"Orla! Tiernan!" Ferrin shouted just as I pulled myself up over the embankment lip. A river rushed up ahead, and maroon tents stood between the trees to my left, so I banked right, sprinting between tree trunks and over roots.

I thought I might actually get away, but then pain exploded in my flank. I collapsed in the dirt, howling.

"Oh, no, I'm sorry!" The short-haired woman leaned overhead, her forehead creased with guilt.

"Ferrin said to *catch* her, not *ash* her!" Tiernan appeared next to the woman. "She's not coming back from that. Put her out of her misery."

The woman bit her lip, shifting in and out of focus overhead me as I writhed in agony, unable to escape the burning in my side.

"Orla," Tiernan warned. Orla gulped and pulled round goggles down over her eyes in sudden resolve.

"Wait!" I lifted a hand, but the woman was already raising a blazing knife of emerald green.

"I'm sorry!" she wailed, and the forest dissipated with a blinding cut that slashed across my throat.

"No!" My hand flew to my neck as I jolted awake, trying to make sense of the slatted ceiling overhead and the arms that held me. I craned my head back to lock eyes with Liam, who stared down at me with a pale face and wide eyes. "Oh, *god* no!"

I scrambled away, trying to regain my dignity as best I could with my short forest sprint still replaying in my mind.

"You need to lie still," Liam said. "I called for Ethel, but—"

"She can't hear you from downstairs." I clawed my way to my feet. Jonquil sat next to the register with my phone between her paws. The email notification was still bright on my screen, so I couldn't have been out for too long.

Oh, god. Von Leer Admissions.

"Wren Warrender, come back." Galahad's voice echoed in my head, and I winced.

"Careful!" Liam tried to put an arm around me, but I shoved him away.

"I'm fine." Sleep beckoned for me to return to its embrace, wrapping around my brain like tendrils as Galahad's voice became louder.

"Wren Warrender, I command you to return to Skalterra."

Hell. No.

I shooed Jonquil off my phone. I needed to escape. If I passed out again, Liam would make sure to alert Gams properly this time. If he got Gams worried, she'd call Mom, and Mom would fly home, and her book tour abroad that she'd been so excited for would be ruined. And I'd already almost ruined it once.

"I just need to lie down." I stumbled for the door that led to the apartment staircase and hurried up the creaky steps.

"Are you sure you should be alone?" Liam called after me.

"I'm fine!" I spun around on the top step to shake my phone at him threateningly. "And if you tell my grandmother, I'll find a way to make sure you spend the rest of your life scooping bagels."

I whisked down the hall.

"Orla wants to apologize, Wren Warrender," Galahad said as I staggered into my bedroom.

"And I need to check my email," I snapped back.

"So you *can* hear me."

My room twisted as I reached my bed, but before I could slump forward onto the mattress, I turned upright, back in the same clearing as before.

Orla tried to hide behind Galahad and Ferrin, but she was taller than both men, so her forehead stuck out behind Ferrin's cockatoo hair.

Graduation night must've stressed me out more than I'd realized. Recurring dreams couldn't be a good sign, though this was admittedly more of a continuation than a proper recurrence.

"Wren Warrender, we only want to talk," Galahad said.

"It's just Wren, and you aren't real." I tried to step away, but it was as if my legs were fused together and rooted to the spot. I looked down, and my stomach lurched. It wasn't that they were fused together, it was that I didn't have legs at all, and "rooted" was a far more appropriate word than I would've liked.

I had on leather armor over a simple brown tunic, but the hem of my shirt fluttered loosely over not my waist, but the sturdy trunk of a tree.

"What the *hell*—"

"It's okay!" Ferrin stepped forward. "It's so we can talk without you running."

"I'm a *tree!*" I screamed.

This wasn't real. This wasn't real. This wasn't real.

So why did it all feel so vivid?

"No, you're a Nightmare," Galahad said. "I constructed you this way for your own safety."

He glared at Orla, who blushed.

"You're the nightmare," I shot back. "*My* nightmare. This isn't real."

Ferrin laughed.

"In a way, yes. We are your nightmare, but we're sorry to say that we are just as real as you."

"I'm a tree!" I twisted my torso, trying to break free of the bark.

"A birch, by the looks of things," Orla piped up, peering at me from behind Ferrin. "Interesting choice, though we shouldn't be surprised considering the hair."

I thought she was taking a dig at my undercut, and my hand slapped to the base of my neck in defense of the hairstyle. However, the undercut was gone, replaced by thick blue tresses.

"I did not *choose* to be a tree!" I snarled.

"No, but you chose to be a birch, and the blue hair was your choice too, whether you realize it or not. That's what Nightmares do. They take on their ideal form, so your ideal tree must be a birch, the same way your ideal hair is blue. Nightmares taking on their ideal forms makes for faster, stronger soldiers!"

I had never considered dying my hair, but I remembered Gams beaming over her blue chickens earlier that morning. *"Von Leer colors!"* she'd proudly explained.

"Why do you keep calling me a nightmare?" I demanded.

Galahad pulled his goggles down over his eyes. His hand glowed silver, and dirt pooled itself at his feet, growing taller and taller, until it had surpassed him in height. Clay hardened into skin and chainmail, and a person stood before us, his face blank and passive.

"This is a Nightmare." Galahad pushed his goggles back up to better survey his creation. "They're made of dust, Skal, and the sleeping consciousnesses of the people in your world. We use them as soldiers to cut back on bloodshed."

There was something off-putting and vaguely horrible about the man in front of me.

"What's wrong with him?" I asked. He hadn't so much as blinked yet. Granted, he at least wasn't half-tree, so he was doing better than I was.

"This is how they're supposed to be, trapped in a dream-state. Pliable, easy to control, and immune to pain." Galahad gave the man a shove. He wavered under the hit, but remained passive and ready. "The real question is, what's wrong with *you*?"

"His mind is asleep?" I waved a hand in front of his face. "And mine isn't? Even though my real body is?"

"Nightmares aren't fully aware of what's happening. It makes them obedient and fearless. Good things to have in a soldier."

"Until they end up lucid!" Orla interjected. "Like you!"

"And in seventy-two years, I've only ever seen one before now," Galahad added. "It's not supposed to happen."

I frowned, wondering if I'd also been a blank-faced golem before I'd woken up on top of that fort.

No.

No, I couldn't have been, because this wasn't real. It was all made up. I was stressed. It had been a matter of time before all my anxiety caught up to me like this.

"How do they get back to their bodies?" I asked, staring at the glassy-eyed soldier.

There was a flash of silver fire as Galahad procured a short blade from the air and dug it into the soldier's chest. The man gave a gentle gasp, then dissipated into ash, clothing and all.

"Oh," I said simply.

"It's not always so violent," Ferrin assured me. "A nocturmancer like Galahad is able to passively release all their existing Nightmares at once, but then you'd wake up too."

Galahad's hand glowed silver again, and a shiver ran up my legs as tree bark gave way to pants, boots, and legs.

"Please don't run," Orla begged.

I stepped forward, testing my reformed legs, and peered at the neat pile of ash where the Nightmare had stood. When I raised my eyes to Galahad's, he smiled, but the way the expression pulled at the wrinkles on his face told me it was forced.

"Right," I said. "I'd love to hear more, but I really do need to check my email."

I grabbed Galahad's grizzled hand and shoved his silver blade into my own gut.

I woke up face down on my quilt with my knees digging into the wooden floor. Worried knocking echoed behind me, accompanied by Liam's nervous voice on the other side of my bedroom door.

"Wren? Come on, just say something so I know—"

"Why are you up here?" I wiped drool off my cheek as I shouted through the door.

"I was worried!"

"Who's watching the shop?"

"Jonquil, I think."

My phone was still in my hand, but I'd barely read the email header when Galahad's voice boomed at me from inside my head.

"Wren Warrender, you will not play games with me!"

"I just—" Liam said from the hall.

"Go away!" I snarled at them both.

The phone slipped from my hand, and the wooden floorboards rushed towards my face as sleep reclaimed me.

I was a tree again.

Galahad's face was ruddy behind his white beard, and a muscle jumped in Ferrin's jaw. Orla wrung her hands and glanced up the embankment. Tiernan and the girl in yellow robes from the night before watched us from between the trees that lined our clearing.

"I was trying to read my email," I growled. I knew Von Leer didn't expect me to email them back right away, but it was killing me not knowing what was waiting in my inbox.

"And I'm trying to save both our realms," Galahad retorted. "You can have your legs back after you've listened."

"This is a dream!" I snapped. "My brain is broken because of Linsey Harper and Von Leer and that stupid bagel boy, and now I'm stuck here!"

Silver flames lit in Galahad's hand, and he procured a glowing staff from the air. He dragged it in the dirt between us to draw two circles.

"I could've fetched you a stick," Ferrin sighed. "You shouldn't waste your Skal."

"We'll refuel in Tulyr." Galahad stepped back. "Skalterra and Keldori. Two worlds. Ours and yours."

"I'm from Earth."

It sounded stupid to say out loud, and they must've thought so too, because they laughed.

"Skalterra and Keldori are both Earth," Ferrin said simply. "If that makes sense."

It didn't.

"And this is Skalterra?" I looked up at the tree canopies. They looked an awful lot like the ones at home.

Of course they do, I told myself. *I made them up. This is my dream.*

"We used to be one world," Galahad said. "Magicians and non-Magicians living together before the Rift.

Unfortunately, magical warfare is particularly volatile, and the Skal Wars of 1616 nearly ripped reality apart. To protect everyone, four sorcerers came together to sequester the Magicians in their own realm. That new realm, that new reality is what became Skalterra. And that is where you are now."

"And the Skal remained in Keldori, your realm." Ferrin tapped the glowing bottles of liquid at his belt. "It's the source of our creation magick. It bleeds through to Skalterra in the cracks between our worlds, and we harvest it at springs. The limited supply has been enough to keep the Skal Wars from returning"

"Mmhmm." What if Von Leer *did* need me to respond right away? What if the longer I was trapped in this nightmare, the less likely the school was to accept me? "Sounds very real and very important."

"She doesn't believe us," Orla whispered.

"Orla, Tiernan is calling you," Ferrin said.

"I don't hear him."

"Leave, Orla." Galahad's voice boomed, and Orla scurried to join the two figures on the embankment. Galahad narrowed his eyes at me. "It doesn't matter if you believe us or not, Keldorian. You told me your name and answered my call. The only way to escape my employ is to wait for me to permanently release you. Otherwise, I'll keep dragging you back."

I focused on my legs. Orla had said Galahad had made me a tree, but I had chosen the type, which meant I had some degree of control over myself. That made sense, considering this was all happening inside *my* head.

The bark where my knees should've been snapped and creaked, but the two men didn't notice.

"And why have you employed me?" I asked in an effort to keep them distracted while I concentrated on my ankles. I tried to imagine them there, contained in the wood of the tree. "What do you need from me?"

"The Four Magicians separated our worlds over four centuries ago," Galahad said, "but it wasn't long before one of the four, a Magician named Saergrim, broke from the others. He wanted the Skal we'd left in Keldori, and sought to re-merge our worlds and sow chaos that he alone would have control over. The other three stopped Saergrim by binding him in a glacier with a curse that lives as long as their descendants still walk Skalterra."

A splintering snap signaled my freedom. My freed legs weren't quite *legs*, though. They were made of rigid wood and awkward joints, like a poorly crafted marionette puppet.

But they did what I needed them to do.

I bowled between Galahad and Ferrin, running on my makeshift legs towards the embankment. Perhaps jumping in that river I'd seen before would be enough to wake me. I just needed to make it up—

"I've got her!" one of the watching figures yelled.

"Tiernan, don't!"

To his credit, Tiernan's aim was much better than Orla's. I didn't feel any pain this time as the blazing ball of golden fire exploded against my back.

I opened my eyes to the dusty floor beneath my bed. A groan worked its way up my chest as I pushed myself into a sitting position

"And then in the fourth grade, I finally caught my first fish, but Riley—"

"What are you talking about?" I snapped at Liam, who was talking on the other side of the door.

"I don't know. You haven't said anything, so I figured I'd just keep talking to make you feel better. Is it working?"

"I can do this all day, Wren Warrender," Galahad growled in my head. I ignored him, searching for my phone.

Von Leer was waiting. I needed to know—

Hands gripped me at my shoulder and wrists, but at least Galahad had let me have my legs back this time. I was on my knees in the clearing, looking up at Galahad and Ferrin while Tiernan and Orla kept me still.

"It's not my fault," Galahad was saying to Ferrin. "It's not the same when they're lucid."

"Then figure it out fast," Ferrin said in a hushed tone. "If we can't control her—"

"It's not about control." Galahad turned back to me. "Wren Warrender, you'll listen carefully this time, because both our realms depend on it."

I tried to jerk my arms away from Tiernan and Orla, but their grips tightened, and Orla whispered an apology. Galahad bent down to look me in the eyes.

"I don't care about your Saergrim," I said. "I don't care if you are real or not. I just want to read my email."

Galahad stepped to the side, revealing the young girl from the night before. She lingered at the edge of the clearing and hid the bottom half of her face behind giant sleeves that hung past her fingertips. Shifting golden sunlight danced between the green shadows of the forest canopy, catching the golden details of the girl's robes in a way that made me think she was more suited to this forest than she had been to the stuffy fort she'd been fleeing.

"That girl is Fana the Divine Sovereign Fireld, and she is the last living descendant of the Three Magicians," Galahad explained. "Saergrim's most loyal followers, the Grimguards, have hunted down the rest, while we, the Riftkeepers, have tried to defend them. The other two bloodlines have already fallen. Fana is all that's left. If she dies, Saergrim is released. Both our worlds will crumble."

"And the Grimguard—" I said.

"Will kill her."

"Right."

"You don't seem too perturbed by the fact that the fate of existence as you know it depends on keeping a ten-year-old alive," Galahad said.

"Because Orla was right. She doesn't believe us." Ferrin's laugh undercut the direness of the situation that Galahad was trying to sell. "It's useless. If she doesn't believe us, what good is she?"

The girl, Fana, stared at me from where she continued to lurk. She reminded me of a sunflower with her yellow hood pulled up over her hair, framing her dark face.

"You want me to protect her?" I asked. "I can't. I can't just *sleep* all day. I have a life. I have a job. I have an email—"

"We only need you until we can get her to Ferrin's stronghold in the mountains." Galahad pulled at his white beard. "And Grimguards are nocturnal. We don't need you during the day."

I laughed. This was ridiculous. Terrifying, but ridiculous. And definitely not real.

Ferrin clicked his tongue.

"I'm with the Nightmare. It's a bad idea."

"She can't die. She's lucid enough to understand more complex commands. She can keep coming back with the previous night's memories and aid us until we get to the Second Sentinel."

"She'll get in the way."

"I'll make sure she doesn't." Galahad's tone carried a foreboding growl. "Tiernan, Orla. Go with Ferrin back to the tents. Take Fana. You should eat."

"But—" Tiernan tightened his grip on my arm and shoulder, and I tried to shake him free.

"She won't run." Galahad narrowed his pale eyes at me, and I smirked. "I'm releasing her soon, which will be much less painful for her than running."

Tiernan and Orla let me go, and I staggered to my feet, rubbing my wrists.

"Wren Warrender," Galahad continued as the others retreated up the embankment, "I shall call upon you at the same time every night. I recommend you make yourself comfortable before I do."

I pushed blue hair back over my shoulder.

"You aren't real," I asserted.

"The fate of your world rests on you. If Saergrim is released from his prison, there is no telling the chaos he will wreak. Both Keldori and Skalterra—"

"I know."

"No," he said darkly. He was still holding the blade I'd used to stab myself with several deaths ago. "You don't. And if you don't think this is real, then let me give you something a bit more material to encourage you."

He grabbed my left hand with an agility I didn't know old men capable of, and the blade cut across my palm in the shape of a "T". I braced for blood, but instead, silver light glowed from the cut before resealing the skin together.

"What did you do?" I yanked my hand away. A silver "T" of puckered skin scarred my left palm.

It's not real, I told myself. Except that it freaking felt real as hell. I hissed through my teeth, trying to will the sharp sting away.

"That's the Curse of Tulyr," he said simply. "Lucid Nightmares are too few and too useful to let go to waste, but you've made it clear you have no intention of aiding us. I can't have you killing yourself every time I summon you, so I've limited the amount of times you'll be able to die here."

I blanched.

It's not real.

"What does that mean?"

"If you die five times in Skalterra as a Nightmare, then Wren Warrender dies in her sleep in Keldori. Five lives are plenty to last you until the Second Sentinel, but if at any point you try to save yourself over Fana, I will end you myself then and there."

"But that's stupid! I thought you needed me. How am I supposed to protect anyone if I'm dead?"

"You're useless if you keep killing yourself to escape. Consider it motivation. And best to keep this our secret. The others are soft, and I don't need them putting themselves in danger if they think your life might be on the line."

"You'd really kill me?"

"To save both our worlds? In a heartbeat, Wren Warrender. I'll see you tonight. I release you from service. For now."

The forest and Galahad dissolved, and I woke up face-down on my floor. My hand that still reached for my discarded phone smarted, but when I pushed myself up out of a puddle of my own drool, it wasn't the email that had my attention, but the puckered silver skin on my left palm in the shape of a "T".

Four
Psychology 101

It was a trick. It had to be. I must have hurt my hand on something in my hurry to escape the shop, and then subconsciously incorporated the injury into my dream.

Yes. That was it. That made sense.

Except the scarring on the skin looked years old, despite the fresh sting the faint lines carried with them, and I knew they hadn't been there before I'd last passed out.

Skalterra couldn't be real, as real as the memory of it felt in my head. It was a dream. A very vivid dream brought on by stress. But the scars on my hand made my heart beat faster and harder in my chest, and I couldn't tear my eyes away from the "T" they formed on my palm.

"Wren?" Gams knocked on my door, and I jumped, curling my hand into a fist. "What's wrong? Liam said you weren't feeling well. Was it the bagel? I can yell at Teddy if you like."

"No!" I said a tad too aggressively. My head spun with the speed at which I stood to open the door. "I mean, no. The bagel was fine. I just—"

Gams stood in the hall with her fist raised to knock again.

"What? What is it?" Gams's eyebrows shot up at the look on my face. I pointed at my phone on the floor behind me. Usually, the nerves that accompanied such an email from Von Leer would be unwelcome, but now they served an important distraction.

"Von Leer?" Gams asked in a hushed tone. I nodded, and she cranked her volume up several decibels to demand, "Well? What'd they say? Are you in?"

"I don't know! I haven't checked!"

She hurried into the room and snatched my phone up to check for herself. The more she tapped the screen, the more her face screwed up in frustration.

"These damn things don't make any sense. Open it!" She pressed the phone back into my hands, and I hoped she didn't notice my shaking fingers.

"'Hello, Ms. Warrender'," I read aloud. "'We received your letter of continued interest as well as your finalized GPA and would like to schedule a phone interview to discuss possible fall admission to Von—!'"

That was as far as I could read before Gams tackled me from the side.

"Another Von Leer Viking in the family!" she squealed. "I knew the chickens would bring good luck! I knew you'd get in!"

"They didn't say I'm accepted." I extracted my arms from her embrace to read the rest of the email. A half-hour ago, I might've been excited about this email, but I couldn't shake the feeling of dread that had followed me back from Skalterra. "It says 'possible' admission."

"It's a phone interview. You know how to talk on the phone. Mention your mother. She's an alumnus. And she's well-known!"

"Oh, yes. My mother the smut author. They'll take me for sure."

"I heard yelling." Liam appeared in the doorway, out of breath and red in the face. "Is everything okay?"

Jonquil wove between his ankles, glaring at me. Her pale eyes reminded me of Galahad's, and I suppressed a shudder. It wasn't as if Galahad was *real*, even if the scar on my hand suggested otherwise.

"Wren got into Von Leer!" Gams cheered. Liam perked up, but I shook my head.

"I didn't *get in*. I have an interview."

"That's great!" Liam smiled wide and genuine.

God, he was annoying.

"It's *something*," I admitted, "but it's nothing for sure, and I don't want to jinx it."

I wiped my hands on my jeans, hoping that I might remove not only the nervous sweat but also the strange scars on my left palm.

"I've got to call Teddy and tell him," Gams announced. "He'll be so excited. Maybe you two and Riley can carpool in the fall! Wouldn't that be fun?"

She kissed me on the cheek and hurried out of the room.

"Another one for Von Leer!" she cheered in the hallway, and Jonquil chased after her.

Liam and I stood staring at each other. His jovial smile fell from his face, and his brow furrowed. I tucked my scarred palm behind my back.

"You aren't going to tell her?" he asked.

"About what?"

"Passing out downstairs. And then sulking in here about it. You look sweaty too."

"I didn't pass out, and I wasn't sulking." I rolled my eyes and shooed him into the hallway, closing my bedroom door behind us. "I fell asleep. I'm fine."

"Narcolepsy?" His eyebrow hitched upwards.

"Just tired," I growled, leading the way back down to the shop. "And I told you not to get Gams."

"Just got the email!" Gams's voice echoed up the stairwell. "Call Siobhan. I want everyone there. No, it's not for sure, but be real, Teddy. They'd be stupid not to admit her!"

I groaned and quickened my step.

"Gams, what are you doing?" I demanded. She hung up the phone as I came through the door, and she threw her hands up in a show of innocence.

"Nothing. Thinking I might paint another chicken. To celebrate, you know."

I glanced back at the shelf of ceramic chickens. Someone must have come in and bought another while I was sleeping, or maybe Gams had given one away, because they were lacking in numbers.

Liam turned sideways to shuffle past me on his way back to the ice-cream station.

"Dinner tonight," Gams snapped at him. "Siobhan's. You and Teddy are both coming. Riley too, when he gets in."

"Gams," I hissed. She patted my shoulder.

"You'll be fine." Her tone was gentle, and more assuring than dismissive. "We'll call it Liam and Riley's homecoming dinner if that makes you feel better."

It did make me feel better, but only a little.

Gams left the shop early that afternoon. She insisted that anytime after 4:30 PM was too late for dinner and shuffled out the door, still barking closing instructions as it swung shut.

The scars on my hand continued to tingle, and I avoided Liam's eyes as we cleaned in silence. He hadn't brought up my sleeping spells anymore, but I knew he was worried by the way he watched me when he thought I wasn't paying attention. He tracked my movements as I paced across the floor with the broom, and when it was finally time to pack up and head to Siobhan's Tavern, he offered me the blue Von Leer hoodie he'd come to work in.

"You want me to jinx it, don't you?" I accused.

"You aren't feeling well today, and I don't want Ethel to yell at me when you show up at your dinner with a cold."

The early summer sun was still high above the rooftops of the shops that lined Main Street.

"Oh, yeah. It's positively chilly out. The elements will surely make quick work of my frail, womanly physique."

He snorted and threw the hoodie over one shoulder while I locked the front door. Jonquil stared at us through the glass, her tail swishing angrily, though I wasn't sure what for.

Keel Watch Harbor was a quaint town. Iron-wrought street lamps lined the single road that cut parallel to the water, making up Main Street. This time of year, though, as we headed into long summer days, the lamps were seldom lit as the sun shined down on bright rooftops and a humble marina from the early morning until late at night.

I wrinkled my nose as we started down the sidewalk. It must've been low tide judging by the sulphuric scent of kelp baking in the sun, but I welcomed the stink. It was so real, so tangible, that it forced Skalterra to the back of my mind. *This* was reality. Walking in the warm sun and the sea breeze, I knew it had to be.

And as thoughts of Skalterra melted away, I finally found the room in my chest to be just a tiny bit excited about Von Leer.

"You'll get in, you know," Liam said. Seagulls cried overhead, and I caught glimpses of the glittering harbor between the bakeries, shops, and restaurants. Many of them had already locked up for the day. I hoped it wasn't so the owners could go to Siobhan's.

"Stop," I said.

"What?"

"Jinxing it!" I waved a dismissive hand at him. "And being nice."

"You'd rather I be mean?"

"I'd rather you be honest."

His steps faltered, and I forged ahead, hoping I remembered where Siobhan's Tavern was located.

"Oh, I can be honest if you like." Liam recovered with a laugh.

"Please."

"I think you're trying to be unlikeable on purpose."

"And what are you? A psych major?"

"Architecture, actually."

"I'm not a building, so you can go analyze literally anything else, please."

He laughed louder this time, though I couldn't tell if it was at me or with me. Best to err on the side of "at me". I scowled.

"No?" he teased. "Then what are you?"

I stopped walking to look at him, and I hated that he was several inches taller than me. I would've preferred him to be shorter.

"I'm an amalgamation of good grades and participation points in clubs I never cared to join in the first place, all so I could look good on paper for the university that passed on me in the first round."

"Amalgamation?" He smirked.

"It means combination or a fusion."

"I know what it means." There it was again. That infuriating laugh. "I just don't know why you used it."

"Because it's a good word."

"Spoken like an author's daughter."

"I promise, the books my mother writes aren't using words like 'amalgamation'."

I didn't know that for sure, of course. I hadn't been allowed to read them until I was eighteen, and even now, I wasn't sure I wanted to know what lurked in the pages of Eliza Warrender's twenty-plus-books-and-counting erotica series.

"What is it, then?" Liam continued. "What makes you so determined to be disliked?"

I bristled at the question. I didn't want to be disliked, that was obviously stupid. So why did it bother me that he had asked it?

"Most people end up disliking me one way or another," I said simply. "Maybe I like to speed up the process so we don't have to linger on the fake niceties for too long."

"You've never had friends, then?"

"I've had friends!" I snapped.

"And they must like you."

I swallowed, focusing on the sound of two gulls squabbling over something tasty in the tidal flats.

"They did. Until they didn't."

"Very insightful."

"I don't owe you my life story."

"I'm not asking for it." His tone was genuine and gentle. What a farce.

Ugh, he'd probably make fun of me for using the word "farce".

"I had friends," I repeated. "Or I thought I did. And we were all in the same Advanced Physics class. It was the last test of the year, and Linsey Harper had gotten her hands on the answer key. She said it didn't matter if she cheated because she'd already gotten into Von Leer, and we were all graduating soon. High school was over. But it *wasn't* over. I needed a good grade. I was getting ready to send my finalized GPA to Von Leer. I needed to be perfect."

"You cheated?"

"Never." I gritted my teeth. "*Linsey* cheated. She gave the answers out to all her other friends. She admitted later she'd only left me out because she wanted to be the only one from our high school to get into Von Leer."

"And what does it matter to your GPA if everyone else cheated?" Liam frowned.

"The test was on a curve. My B+ could've been an A. So I told the teacher."

Liam ran a hand over his face.

"You didn't."

"Of course I did!" I knew he wouldn't understand. I could tell he was probably perfect in every regard. He'd never had to claw his way to the top. "I needed that A! And I got it. Only four of us didn't cheat, and my B+ was the top score. Automatic one hundred percent."

"And then all your classmates collectively decided to hate you?" Liam asked.

"Not yet." My stomach twisted thinking back on it. It hadn't been my intention. I didn't know our teacher had a connection at Von Leer. I didn't know he'd report Linsey to her new school before she even had a chance to start there. "The teacher called Von Leer and got Linsey's offer of admission rescinded."

"Shit."

"Yeah." I ran my hand over the buzzed hair at the base of my neck. "And only four of us didn't have our test thrown out. It was easy for her to figure out who had snitched. And then, they—"

I cut off. I didn't want to think about it. A thrill of panic sent of a rush of adrenaline through my chest, and I took a deep breath to calm the fluttering of my heart.

"They shaved your head?" Liam asked in a hushed voice. I shot him a look of pure loathing.

"No, *I* did that myself, thanks, and I like how it looks."

His cheeks flared red.

"Oh. No, it's nice, I just assumed—"

I held up a hand to silence him and put us both out of our misery at his floundering for an apology.

"We're here." I looked up at the carved sign that read "Siobhan's Tavern". The wooden building jutted out over the marina, and at high tide, it was fun to look down at the crabs scuttling under the water. Now, however, it reeked of exposed seaweed.

"Look, your hair—"

"It's fine." I gave Liam an insincere smile and swung the heavy door open.

A cheer went up, and I had half a mind to walk backwards straight into traffic. Not that there was any traffic on a Tuesday in Keel Watch Harbor, but maybe I'd get lucky.

Liam, however, put a hand between my shoulder blades, hovering it there, respectful enough not to touch me, but still barring me from a quick retreat.

"Welcome back, Liam!" A tall woman with a blonde bob forced her way to the front of the crowd. I hadn't seen Siobhan since I'd last visited three years ago, but she looked just the same. "First year down at Von Leer! What an accomplishment. It's a great school."

She winked at me as she said it, and I knew Gams had warned everyone not to congratulate me outright on tentatively moving off the waitlist.

"Liam, sit with us!" A group of kids ran up to Liam to take his hands in theirs and drag him towards the back window. Like the window in Gams's shop, it stretched clear across the room, providing diners and drinkers as good a view of the harbor as one could get in Keel Watch. The low ceilings kept the atmosphere dark but cozy, even while the sun shined outside.

Gams beamed at me from the center of her gaggle of friends, all with graying hair and long sleeved shirts that the summer weather probably didn't warrant this late in the day, even with the sea breeze that kept the town cool and comfortable.

"You remembered to put food out for Jonquil, right?" Gams asked as I got closer.

"Of course," I lied. I'd have to feed her later when Gams wasn't looking.

"Excellent! And you all remember Wren?" Gams turned to her friends with a proud hand on my shoulder. I always felt like a giant standing next to her. My height had to have come from my biological father, though as searchable as Maxwell Brenton, PhD, was on the internet, his accomplishments weren't notable enough for his basic body metrics to be readily available online.

"Wren!" The nearest woman pulled me into a hug that smelled of old perfume and hairspray. "It's about time you visited Keel Watch! I hear we get the whole month with you?"

"Whole summer, actually." I blushed, and Gams's friends squealed in delight.

"And was that Liam Glass you walked in with?" The woman next to me gave me an animated nudge with her elbow. "Now that's a smart match, isn't it?"

The women erupted into laughter, and Gams shushed them.

"No, no, Sarah. Don't say that. Wren can't keep a boyfriend, and I don't want to lose the best ice-cream scooper in all of Keel Watch when it falls apart."

"Joke's on you." I forced a laugh. "I'm not really the dating type, so who knows if I can keep a boyfriend or not."

"Not the dating type?" the perfumed woman repeated. "Maybe you're looking in the wrong places. Siobhan's got a daughter, and I think you might be her type."

When Siobhan announced to the room that the burger bar she'd prepared for the occasion was ready, I found a seat by the window, planning to wait out the line. However, when Gams came to join my table, she'd already prepared a burger for me.

"Don't mind Gladys and Sarah," she said. "They're happy you're here, and Keel Watch gets boring without young blood like yours."

"They're okay," I assured her, and I meant it. Mom and I lived five hours down the coast by car so that Mom could be near her publishing house's main office. She'd helped build it after all, and Keel Watch Harbor was too remote for that line of business. However, we were also the only family Gams had. Her friends were a lot, sure, but I was thankful she had them.

The city was no place for Gams, anyway. She was spry enough to keep up with the fast pace of a city, and street smart enough to make her way, but I couldn't imagine her without her shop and her basement where she painted and fired ceramic chickens.

Maybe the city was no place for me either, at least not in the suburbs I grew up in. Not anymore. Not after graduation. Gams lived closer to Von Leer University, anyway. Maybe it would make sense for me to make the move into the guest room a more permanent arrangement.

Or maybe I was getting my hopes up prematurely.

Gams's friends and favorite neighbors settled into the tables and booth seats, and I got the impression it wouldn't have mattered if I'd received an email from Von Leer or not. The community gathering seemed familiar to them, like they did this often. The local baker had several cakes ready for the occasion that he couldn't have whipped up at such a late notice. The children of Von Leer strutted up to the lemonade table, hastily constructed by everyone's favorite coffeehouse owner, with a confidence that said they'd been looking forward to this.

They carried overflowing cups back to their table where they kept Liam hostage, now also joined by a young woman with the same blonde ringlets as Siobhan.

The two extra seats at my table with Gams were a rotating roulette of vaguely familiar faces, each commenting on how tall I'd grown and how they weren't surprised Von Leer was interested in me.

"No one from Keel Watch stays on the waitlist," Gladys said on her third rotation through the seat opposite mine. "If Liam Glass could wiggle his way off it, you're a no-brainer from what Ethel has told me about you."

"Liam was waitlisted?" I sat up straighter and looked for him across the room, but Teddy had pulled him aside to talk in a corner.

"Of course! Wanted to follow in his cousin's footsteps. Riley got in on early admission, but he was always an overachiever. Captain of just about every sports team. Valedictorian. Homecoming King. Did you ever meet him on your visits here?"

I shook my head and stared at Liam with a newfound respect where he spoke with his uncle. I still didn't like him— it was easier this way— but it did make him a little more relatable. I'd thought everything must come so easy to him, but it sounded like that was his cousin, Riley.

Liam's brow furrowed, and Teddy frowned. It looked like something had upset them both, but then my hand started to burn.

It was just a tickle at first, hardly noticeable. Then it grew stronger until it seared across my palm.

"Ouch!" I startled, grabbing my hand at the wrist as if that might help stem the pain. I turned my palm over to reveal the scars Galahad had left there were angry and red.

"What's wrong?" Gams asked with sudden concern.

"Nothing," I lied, standing up.

"Wren Warrender, I hope you're ready," Galahad's voice echoed in my head.

You aren't real, I tried to tell it back.

"I'm just—" I glanced around at the room of smiling faces. "I'm tired. This was nice. Tell Siobhan thank you."

My chair clattered to the floor behind me.

"Wren!" Gams made to move after me, but Teddy was there to stop her.

"Ethel, a word, please. It's about Riley."

She glanced between me and Teddy, and I took the chance to bolt.

"Wren Warrender, I demand you answer me." Galahad's voice chased me out the tavern door.

"Give me two minutes!" I said between gritted teeth as I hit the sidewalk outside running. "I have to feed my grandma's cat!"

Maybe he was just a fiction after all, because he remained silent in my head until I'd made it back to the apartment over the shop and filled Jonquil's bowl next to my dresser.

"Wren Warrender—"

"I told you!" I snapped, standing in my bedroom. "It's just Wren!"

And my bedroom fell away.

Five

Intro to Medieval Weaponry

The thick trees that had stood bright and resolute in my dreams earlier that day now cast dark shadows that criss-crossed through the gold of a setting sun. I blinked, trying to orient myself as the stinging in my palm died.

"Welcome back, Just-Wren." Ferrin clapped me on the back as he passed by and handed a bulging pack off to a blank-faced Nightmare.

"You're not going to kill yourself again, are you?" Orla appeared next to me, juggling green light between her long fingers.

"Stop playing with the Skal," Ferrin chided. He clipped a set of glowing bottles to his belt. "You're wasting it."

Orla flashed an apologetic grin, and the green fire in her hands danced into darkness.

"Sorry, Uncle."

"Where is he?" I demanded, searching the clearing for the old man in the duster.

"Who?" Orla asked, but Ferrin gave a bruised grin.

"The—the…" I gestured wildly at my chin, trying to pantomime a beard. "You know!"

"Galahad is getting the other Nightmares ready," Ferrin said through a low laugh. He jerked a thumb over his shoulder. "You'll find him that way."

The old man's silhouette stood out against the river through the trees where he was busy giving instructions to a line-up of pack-laden Nightmares. Tiernan and Fana stood nearby in robes of yellow and red that caught the setting sun.

I shoved Ferrin out of my way to march towards Galahad.

"At least she's not running away," Orla mumbled behind me as she and Ferrin followed towards the riverbank.

"Hey!"

Galahad turned at the sound of my shout, and his wrinkled face worked into a scowl.

"Wren Warrender, I told you to be ready when I called—"

"You said you'd only need me at night!" I stopped inches from his face and pointed at the sinking sun that peered between the tree trunks. "It's still daytime. I barely finished dinner!"

"We need to put extra distance between us and Cape Fireld before the Grimguard wakes and continues his hunt." Galahad's beard was braided into a simple plait that rested on the chest of his leather armor, and I resisted the urge to yank on it.

"You said nighttime!"

"Should I take this arguing as a sign that you finally believe me to be real?"

I froze, mulling over the words. He made a good point. Why *was* I arguing with him? I curled my fingers over the scar on my palm. I was arguing because he felt real, but that didn't mean that he was more than a dream.

"No," I finally shot back. Galahad smirked and turned back to his line of Nightmares.

"Real or not, I *am* curious. You have to feed the cats in Keldori?"

My face warmed. "Just the ones that live inside."

"They don't feed themselves? Are there no mice?"

"There's mice, but we still have to feed the cats."

"Strange," Orla whispered. "What is the cat's primary function if not to eat the mice?"

"Companionship?" I was far from Jonquil's biggest fan, and I didn't like the sudden defensiveness that rose in my chest on her behalf. "Or so I've been told. Mostly she gets in the way."

"Then the cats are as useless as the people." Tiernan helped Fana onto the back of the beefiest Nightmare in Galahad's line-up.

"Yeah, well," I muttered so he couldn't hear me, "you're not even real."

"Orla! Wren Warrender!" Galahad barked. His Nightmares, each in leather and chainmail, formed a circle around him, Fana, and the Nightmare who carried her. "Take the rear guard. Ferrin will go on ahead to make sure the path is clear. Tiernan, with us."

Ferrin gave Orla's shoulder a pat and pulled his goggles down over his eyes.

"I'll see you in Trawler's Bay." An emerald longsword formed in his hand. "Take care of Just-Wren. Don't take it personally when she says you don't exist."

"Of course, Uncle."

He gave the side of her face a fatherly peck, and then surged forward to lead the way into the darkening forest. Orla gave his back an ostentatious salute, but her mouth turned downwards in a slight frown.

"Is something wrong?" I asked.

"No." She shook her head, watching Ferrin disappear into the lengthening shadows. Galahad's team followed at a slower pace while Orla and I stayed put on the riverbank. The gentle rush of the river whispered behind us, and a frog croaked to a steady beat nearby. The level of detail in this dream really was astounding. "It's just, last time Ferrin went ahead with someone..."

Orla hugged herself around her shoulders, and I remembered Ferrin slumped unconscious against a wall flecked with his blood and the woman dead on the floor.

"Her name was Caitria, right?" I asked. Real or not, my heart dipped at the sad smile on Orla's face. "Were you close?"

"Of course. I spent the last several years in Cape Fireld. She and Tiernan were in charge of keeping Fana and her family safe there." She nodded at Tiernan's leather-armored back as he sank into the forest ahead. "The other two Divine Families are gone, along with the rest of Fana's family. Since Fana's the last living Divine Sovereign, Caitria was sort of the unofficial leader for all of us."

"Even though Galahad's the oldest?"

The silver glow of Galahad's magick had nearly disappeared between the tree trunks ahead, but glimpses of it continued to flit in and out of sight.

"Galahad's a Lyrian!" Orla snorted. She pulled her goggles down over her eyes and lit a green flame in her hand to stave off the growing dark. "He's a talented Magician, but the last Tulyr died ages ago, so he hasn't been officially employed in decades."

"I thought you were all in charge of Fana." The rapidly sinking sun set my nerves on edge, and I reminded myself that this place wasn't real. The dark woods couldn't hurt me. There was no danger lurking in the trees. Not anything that wasn't just my imagination, anyway.

"Yes," Orla said slowly, "but only by default. There were three Divine Families sworn to keep the Frozen God locked away, and each family had an Order of Riftkeepers to guard them and their children. Galahad was in the order assigned to the Tulyrs."

"And you and Ferrin?" I asked. If I kept asking questions, maybe I would find the limit to my imagination and definitively prove that this was all in my head. Orla lit up again.

"We are the last two members of the order assigned to protect the Quills. My mother was a Riftkeeper before me, but she died protecting the last one before I joined the guard, so really, it's only Fana that I've been protecting. Do you think the others are far enough ahead yet?"

She adjusted her goggles, and mimicked the motion Ferrin had made to create her own sword of blazing green out of the fire in her hand. She arced the blade through air with a test swing, and it hissed and sizzled. The gravel of the riverbank crunched under her shin-high boots as she strode forward.

Meanwhile, I took a step back.

"Just-Wren?" The green light of Orla's sword glittered off the rim of her round goggles.

"I don't have to follow you," I said quietly. "If you're not real—"

"But what if we are?" she asked. "I understand why you think we're not, but have you considered what it means if you're wrong?"

"If you're real, then I'm screwed," I laughed. "And so are you, because I can't help you protect Fana."

A strong breeze rolled in over the river, ruffling Orla's cloak and making the trees behind her shift and bow.

"Is that why you've opted to believe us to be a dream? Because it's less frightening?"

I didn't have an answer, and I hugged myself around my leather armor as the breeze twisted through my blue hair.

Orla's sly smile glowed green in the light of her sword, and she pivoted on her heel to continue towards the shadows of the trees.

"Quick question." I chased after the safety of Orla's green light, realizing I didn't want to be left behind in the dark. "Where is it we're going, and how long will we be in the woods?"

"Trawler's Bay!" she chirped. "It's a cute port city. I think. I've not actually been there before. But there's a steamcart station that will take us north towards the Second Sentinel. It won't go the whole way, though."

"A steamcart?" I looked up as dark tree cover swallowed the star-spotted sky. I'd been okay with the trees in the daylight, but now it felt too much like graduation night.

It's not real, I reminded myself. *Linsey isn't here.*

I balled my fingers into fists.

"Right! I forgot! You probably don't have steamcarts in Keldori." Orla gnawed on her lip, thinking hard. "It's like a bunch of carriages strung together, but instead of being pulled by horses like you're used to, steamed Skal powers the cart at the front. That cart pulls the rest of the carts along a track from one destination to another. It's very advanced technology. You're going to love it."

"Like a train?" I asked.

"I suppose you could describe it that way!" She brightened. "Because the carts all train behind each other! You're catching on quick."

Even if Orla wasn't real, I didn't have the heart to explain to her that trains were very old news to me. Nor did we still rely on horses as our main mode for transportation.

"I'm assuming it's been a while since anyone from here has been to—what did you call it?" I asked.

"Keldori? Your home? Not since the Rift, no. And that was centuries ago." She sighed wistfully. "I'd love to go someday. I bet it's so quaint, with your useless cats."

"Can't Galahad make a Nightmare on the Keldori side of things and then stick your consciousness in it from here?" I asked. I chanced a glance back the way we'd come, but the night had already swallowed the trees there.

Orla shook her head.

"Galahad knows all the most complex Skalmagick, but not even he could project a Nightmare across the Rift."

A splintering snap pulled my attention behind us again.

"Did you hear that?" I whispered.

"It was probably just a deer," Orla whispered back. "You have deer, right?"

"Yes, we have deer."

"Do you have to feed them too?"

Another crack silenced us both. I swiveled forward, trying to find Galahad's light on the path ahead, but it had disappeared between the trees a while ago. I hoped Orla knew the way without his help.

"We should split up," she suggested. "I'll flank Galahad's team on the left, and you go to the right."

"But I don't have a light."

"Make one."

"How? I don't have any of that magic liquid." I glanced at the glowing bottles attached at her waist.

Orla's gentle laugh was a quiet hiss in the night.

"Of course you have Skal. It's what you're made of. That's what makes you so well equipped to fight the Grimguard."

"What if I don't want to fight the Grimguard?"

Her laugh was louder this time.

"Then tell Galahad to send you home! But I doubt he'll oblige." She stepped closer to me and held out a hand. "Try to concentrate your Skal in your palm. It should burn a bit, but not so much that it hurts."

I wasn't sure exactly what she meant by "concentrate my Skal", but I stared at my hand, trying to imagine energy buzzing there. This was a dream, after all. If it was all in my head, then of course I should be able to will superpowers into existence in the palm of my hand.

I thought I was imagining the gentle tingle at first, but then it grew hotter, until it felt as if I were pressing my hand against a hot lightbulb.

A small silver flame burst in the middle of my curled fingers.

"That's it! That's the Skal! See, it's silver like Galahad's because your magick comes from him!"

"Okay, great." I held the fire at arm's length. My long blue hair might have been fiction, but I still wasn't keen on the idea of burning it. "Now what?"

"You can hold it like that if all you need is a light. It won't burn you, or Galahad for that matter, but you could still use it against an enemy. It'll be more useful as a weapon, though, so try to shape it into something more substantial."

A weapon. I needed a weapon. I tried to imagine a sword like the one Orla wielded. The Skal flickered and grew heavier in my hand, and the sudden weight surprised me.

"Grab it!" Orla yelped.

I clamped my hand around a warm silver handle. The blade of my sword, however, dropped and elongated in a way I didn't expect, reminding me of not a sword at all, but rather—

"A flail?" Orla stepped away. "That's a choice, but alright."

Chain links made of silver light clicked together. A heavy, spiked ball swung on the end of the chain, and I was once again standing with my arm outstretched as far as I could reach.

"Do I need goggles?" I asked, watching Orla's green light glint off the rim of her eyewear.

"Your retinas will be rebuilt tomorrow night when Galahad summons you again. We're stuck with ours, and too much Skal-light exposure at close proximity like this can cause blindness. One night won't hurt you."

A coyote laughed in the dark, much closer than I would like. Hopefully the silver light of my flail would be enough to keep the wildlife at bay, because I absolutely had no idea how to otherwise use the weapon.

"Alright. Me to the left, you to the right! Galahad is that way." Orla pointed into the dark. "Again, the Grimguard is far behind us, so he shouldn't be a problem. Best to keep an eye out, though!"

She turned on her heel and stepped between two trees. The shadows were already cutting across the light of her blade, leaving me in a circle of silver.

I didn't want her to go. The forest had been bright and welcoming during the day, but now, oppressive shadows loomed, hiding who knew what and who knew who.

"It's not real," I said to myself, stepping off on my own into the dark.

"Yes, it is!" Orla called at me from the shadows. I scowled and tightened my grip on my weapon.

"That's exactly what someone who isn't real would say." I kept my voice low so that Orla wouldn't hear me this time.

The forest at least felt different from the one in the mountains near my high school. For one, these woods weren't real, unlike the woods where I'd been lost in the dark. That had been all too real. Not only that, but here the tree trunks were thicker and their roots more exposed and gnarled, making for tricky footwork in the dark, but the undergrowth was sparse. I didn't have to fight my way through brambles and thickets like I had graduation night, and instead focused on crawling over roots and dirt mounds while I kept the distant green light of Orla flickering between trees to my left.

As far as nightmares went, this one was tame. It was vivid and the amount of detail and continuity my brain had managed to fit over the course of several different dreams was alarming, sure, but I wasn't *scared*.

Or, at least, not as scared as I was used to feeling. If this was all Galahad needed from me for the next however many nights, I could probably manage that. And then, hopefully, my subconscious would set me free.

A branch snapped, and I turned too quickly, bringing my flail swinging around. I dropped it to avoid the spike ball smacking me in the leg, and it fell in a tangle of roots, casting a mosaic of silver shadows upwards against tree trunks and distant canopies.

I swore under my breath and reached my arm down into the jumbled roots.

It was then, with my face pressed against a root and my fingers scrabbling at the handle of a weapon just out of reach, that a man's voice spoke.

"Hello, again, Blue."

Six

Ballroom Dance I

The Grimguard's steel-toed boot stood so close that I could smell the dirt and loam that clung to its tread. I craned my head away from the tree root to better see the Grimguard towering over me. The light from my discarded weapon cast deep shadows up his body and face, but he looked just as he had the night before, all dark clothes and glowing orange irises. Pale Skal-light from the bottles at his belt peeked out from beneath a tattered cloak that hung down his frame.

Orange light sparked to life in his hands, and I abandoned my flail in the roots, rolling away to avoid the spear that skewered the space I'd just been lying.

I backpedaled away, scooting through dirt and dust, keeping my eyes on the Grimguard as he yanked the spear out of the root.

"Were you there?" His voice was an icy growl. "Did you help them kill Daithi?"

I scrambled to my feet. The spear sizzled as it flew through the air, and I ducked in time to hear the dull *thunk* of it embedding itself in the tree trunk.

"I'm not with them." I put my hands up. I still wasn't convinced this was real, but if it were? Galahad and his pals were the ones who'd dragged me into this

58

nightmare. I wasn't prepared to take a spear to the skull for them.

"No?" The Grimguard stepped off the tangled roots, looking all the more sinister with the silver light of my flail at his back. "I thought you were a Nightmare last night. You reek of dirt and used-up Skal. But you're back. Nightmares don't come back."

"Maybe I'm not a Nightmare." I puffed my chest out, trying to look tougher than I felt. The hiss that sounded from beneath the man's cowl resembled something like a laugh.

"That's Galahad's Skalmagick, Blue. I don't know how you're lucid, but since you are, maybe you can tell me, which of those cowards killed Daithi?"

Another spear formed in his hands, and he held the point just beneath my chin. The weapon's orange glow bounced off the black sclera of his eyes. I wondered if that's what Orla and the others' eyes would look like if they didn't wear their goggles.

Orla.

I searched for her green beacon through the trees to my left, but the only lights were my silver and the Grimguard's orange.

The Grimguard tensed, as if preparing to lunge forward and drive the point of his spear through my neck, and I grabbed the staff of the weapon with both hands before he could make his move.

White-hot pain seared across both my palms, but I kept my grip and swung the spear. The Grimguard stumbled to the side, and I released the staff, unable to bear the burning in my hands any longer. I curled burnt fingers over my welted palms and cradled them against my chest.

The spear sizzled against air resistance, and I managed to avoid the attack, but the Grimguard already had a new weapon in hand. He brought a massive orange broadsword down swinging over my head.

Some ancient instinct took over, maybe something Galahad had programmed into my Nightmare body, and I pulled a new weapon from the air.

Sword! I need a sword! I told myself, trying to imagine the weight of a sword in my hand.

Nope. Another flail.

Damn. It.

I rolled out of the way of the broadsword attack, swinging my flail feebly in response. The Grimguard stepped back, and though half his face was covered by his cowl, something about the look in his eyes and the set of jaw told me he was smirking.

"If you kill me," I panted, "how will I tell you who killed Daithi?"

"I'll just have to ask you again tomorrow night when Galahad drags you back to fight his fights for him."

He swung again, but I was proving adept at dodging. He buried the edge of the sword in the side of a tree, and pulled on the handle. When it didn't budge, I saw my opportunity and brought my flail arcing downwards.

He abandoned the sword to dodge my attack, and when he tried to form a new weapon, the orange light sputtered and died in his hands.

"Ha!" I yelled. He was out of Skalmagick. For the first time since I'd gotten Linsey Harper expelled from Von Leer, I had the upper hand in something.

A muscle in my back spasmed with the effort of swinging my flail as hard as I could. The spiked ball hurtled towards the Grimguard's head, crackling with silver fire and energy.

I had him. I *had* him.

He stepped back, out of my range, and the flail ripped itself from my grip, sending the weapon careening between the trees.

We both paused to watch its light get farther and farther, until a gentle thud told us it had found a resting place in the dirt.

The Grimguard's hands shot to the bottles of Skal that hung from his belt, but I already had a new flail in hand. It wasn't quite the throwing knife I'd been trying to form, but it would do.

His spear had burnt my hands. I was certain any weapon of mine would do the same to him.

I hurled the flail at the Grimguard, making no effort to keep a hold of it this time. He danced away, but I was ready with a new weapon to rain flail after flail down on the Grimguard.

Because it didn't matter that I didn't want to fight him. If he managed to get to the bottles of Skal at his belt, he'd make sure I died, and, yeah, I was mostly sure Galahad and the scar he'd left on my hand weren't real, but I wasn't keen to prove it with another dream that ended with me skewered.

Each flail I threw was heavier than the last, and the Grimguard saw an opening in my attacks as they slowed. He tackled me around the middle, pulling us both to the forest floor. He pinned my arms to my side under his legs, and leaned in towards my face as he panted for air.

"Your methods are..." He paused for breath.

"Inspired?" I quipped. I arched my neck, trying to wiggle free, and he placed a leather-clad hand over my sternum to keep me still in the dirt.

"I was going to say questionable." He removed a bottle from his belt, deftly uncorking it before pulling his cowl down. He was clean-shaven, and his pale skin glowed white in the light of my many discarded flails. The neat line of his nose matched the sharp cut of his jaw, and I was struck by how young he appeared. "You're bleeding yourself dry of Skal. You'll be nothing but dust if you keep this up."

He shook loose hair back from his face and downed the bottle of Skal in a single gulp. Light sparked in his hands.

I doubled my efforts to escape, trying to buck the Grimguard off me, but he leaned in closer, so that his forearm was a heavy weight across my chest as an orange sword formed in his free hand.

"Now. Back to my question. Did you help them kill Daithi?" The sword tip seared beneath my chin.

"No," I spat.

"Then who did it?"

I remembered Galahad turning me into a tree, and I remembered forcing my trunk to break into two legs. This was *my* dream. *I* had control.

I ignored the Grimguard's sword and instead focused on my arms slowly going numb under the weight of the Grimguard's legs. I imagined what it might feel like to grow boney spikes, and sharp agony erupted across both my forearms.

My cry of pain mingled with that of the Grimguard, and I finally bucked him away. I staggered to my feet, staring at the four serrated spikes of bone that stuck out from each of my arms like knives. Dark blood dripped off their points, and my eyes darted to the Grimguard, who hurried to use his cloaks to hide the gauge marks my improvised anatomy had left in his thighs.

"It wasn't the old man." His voice was haggard with pain, and he pulled a second sword from the air. "He can make Nightmares, sure, but he's otherwise useless, as much as he pretends he isn't."

He launched at me, his swords melting into twin blurs as he twirled them ahead of himself. I threw my forearms up in defense, but he cut through the bone spikes like they were nothing.

The pain was blinding, and the Grimguard pressed me against the gnarled trunk of a tree, pinning my hands up over my head and holding me there with the weight of his body. His chest heaved against mine as we both fought for air.

His orange irises glinted and shined brighter while his eyebrows drew together.

"Was it the Quillguard maybe? What's his name again? Ferrin?" he whispered. "Or perhaps Caitria?"

"Caitria is dead." The venom in my voice surprised even me. The face of the dead woman with blood matting her hair haunted me. Even if she'd never existed, the memory of her corpse felt real.

I tried to procure a sword, knife, flail, anything in my pinned hands, but drew only silver smoke that flickered feebly between my fingers. Whatever Skal Galahad had used to create me must have been running low.

The Grimguard smiled. It was a shame lips as pretty as his had to share a face with such horrifying eyes.

"Caitria? Dead? Well, that's wonderful news. Then it must've been Ferrin. I hear he and Caitria were..." he paused and licked his lips as he searched for the next word, "...close."

I glared back at him, which he must've taken as confirmation that it had indeed been Ferrin who'd killed the other Grimguard because his smile darkened.

"Fine. Kill me," I spat. He had the information he wanted. I might as well get the gory bit over with so I could wake up and escape this nightmare. "You aren't real anyway."

The Grimguard twirled one of my dismembered bone spikes in his free hand and leaned in to plant a tiny, soft kiss on the tip of my nose.

"If you say so."

His wrist flicked, and the silver lights of my many flails were swallowed by the dark of the forest as pain erupted below my chin.

Wood flooring pressed against my cheek, and I opened my eyes to the space beneath my bed. Jonquil lurked in its depths, her blue eyes glinting in the dark. She looked very much like she was trying to be menacing, but her fluffy coat and pushed-in face made her look more like an angry slipper.

"Crap." I groaned, pushing myself up off the floor of my bedroom. Night had fallen outside, and the light from my digital clock spilled across the floor. My head pounded where I must've hit it when I fell asleep, and the cut of the Grimguard's killing blow still stung beneath my chin, but both maladies paled in comparison to the cutting pain that suddenly seared across my palm. "*Crap!*"

I grabbed my wrist and forced my fingers to unfurl. The T-shaped scar of my left palm caught the edges of green light from my digital clock, but a new, angry line cut its way across the trunk of the T. It was shorter than the line that ran perpendicular to the trunk, and I thought it glowed a faint silver for just a moment, but it must've been a trick of the moonlight streaming in from my window.

I stared at my palm, my heart thundering in my ears. Then red droplets fell on the pale skin of my arm, sticky and thick.

I swallowed and raised a shaking hand to my neck where the Grimguard had cut me. My fingers came away wet with my own blood.

No. *No.*

No, no, no, no, *no.*

This was worse than Linsey. This was worse than being waitlisted.

Because I knew what the new line was. It was a notch. It was a countdown. It was a confirmation of something I hadn't wanted to consider.

Skalterra wasn't a dream, and neither was the limit Galahad had placed on how many times I could die while I was there.

I'd lost one life, represented by the new mark on my scarred hand. I only had four more.

The gravity of the mess I was in had only just started to dawn on me when Galahad's voice echoed at the back of my head.

"I hope you didn't think dying while the evening was still young would give you the rest of the night off. We aren't finished with you yet."

Jonquil meowed at me as I slumped forward yet again.

Seven

Ballroom Dance II

This was the first time I'd come into consciousness in Skalterra in a full sprint. I stumbled as my feet formed beneath me, but I caught myself mid-step and managed to remain upright. Silver and gold light emanated from Galahad and Tiernan's swords, illuminating the ring of Nightmares that surrounded us in formation as we ran.

The largest of the Nightmares carried Fana on his back between Galahad and Tiernan.

"Is Orla alright?" Galahad asked. It was all he could muster before falling into a coughing fit.

"I *died*. Your stupid Grimguard killed me!" I seethed. I kept pace with Galahad's running stride but shoved my palm in his bearded face so he could see the fresh scar there. "What the hell is this? What *is this*?"

"Is Orla alive?" Galahad demanded.

"She should be fine, which must be nice, because *I* was murdered!"

"Where's the Grimguard?"

"Galahad!" I grabbed his arm, bringing his faltering sprint to a stumbling halt. The Nightmares surrounding us followed suit, and Tiernan was several paces ahead before he realized we'd stopped.

"Let go of him!" Tiernan charged back to rip my hand away from Galahad. "If the Grimguard catches up—"

But Galahad held up a staying hand from where he stood doubled over, fighting for air. The Grimguard had warned me the old man wasn't good for much more than creating Nightmares, but whatever pity I might've felt was eclipsed by anger and panic at having woken up in my bedroom with blood dripping from my neck and a new scar to mark my most recent death.

"There's a new mark." I shoved my palm in Galahad's face. "It's there in the real world too."

"The real world?" A bushy gray eyebrow quirked above Galahad's goggles.

"Keldori," I hissed. "The scar is still there in Keldori when I wake up. You're going to kill me."

"The Grimguard is going to kill us all if he catches up!" Tiernan watched the shadows behind us, tensed and ready.

"You fought him," Galahad panted. "Where?"

I oriented myself for a moment, thinking back to when Orla had forked left, and I had gone right.

"That way." It was hard to see the trees beyond the yellow and silver glows of Galahad and Tiernan's weapons, but I was fairly certain I was pointing in the right direction. Galahad nodded and every Nightmare except for the one carrying Fana on his broad back rushed into the forest shadows.

"They were carrying all our supplies," Tiernan growled.

Galahad straightened up, having somewhat caught his breath.

"We'll restock in Trawler's Bay." He took my hand in his to inspect the scar the night had added. "I hope you gave him a good fight at least."

"Send her with the other Nightmares," Tiernan said through clenched teeth. He was the tallest of the group, matching height with the remaining Nightmare. "We don't need her."

"We are a young girl, an old man, and a rash, untrained warrior too eager to prove himself," Galahad said. "The lucid Nightmare stays."

"I'm not untrained!"

"Then you agree you are rash and too eager?"

"You can't keep me here." My voice quaked as I cut between the two men. This *was* real. I could die. "It's- it's inhumane!"

"This is nothing compared to what the Frozen God will reap if he is freed." A burst of orange light in the distance flashed across Galahad's face, but he ignored it. "Do you feel it yet? The gravity of the situation? You faced the Grimguard. Is that who you want unleashed on your world?"

"I—"

"And I wish I could say the Grimguard is the worst thing to exist in Skalterra, but I fear there is far worse, probably here in these woods with us right now. Last night you mentioned a 'Gams'. Do you think she'll be spared if our worlds are forced to collide? There was a reason the Four Magicians banished our kind here. There is a reason that here is where we must remain."

The dark of the forest pressed in on our ring of light, and I wanted nothing more than to dissolve into dust like the Nightmare I was.

"I can't help you." I shook my head and stepped away. I glanced between Galahad and Tiernan before meeting Fana's wide brown eyes. She stared at me from over her Nightmare's shoulder. She looked so tiny on his back, and so horribly breakable.

"You can—" Galahad started.

"I'm just Wren!" I shouted.

"Do you want the Grimguard to find us faster?" Tiernan clapped a gloved hand over my mouth. The muscles in my arm rippled with strength I wasn't used to, and my fist flew, smashing into his jaw. He fell back in the dirt with his goggles askew, staring up at me with shock and loathing.

"Maybe you're just Wren in Keldori," Galahad conceded, "but here you are a lucid Nightmare, and there is no weapon more powerful than a lucid Nightmare."

He nodded at Tiernan where he sat sprawled in the dirt, rubbing his jaw.

Green light flashed through the trees ahead, shooting upwards to arc over the forest.

"That's Ferrin." Galahad offered Tiernan a hand up, but he batted it away and climbed to his feet on his own. "We're near the edge of the forest then."

Orange flashed behind us, and the screams of Galahad's Nightmares had me second-guessing what he'd said about non-lucid Nightmares and their immunity to pain.

"Then move!" Tiernan grabbed Galahad's elbow and pulled him towards Fana and her Nightmare. "I'll buy you time if he catches up."

Galahad adjusted his goggles and procured a silver staff to lean against.

"Keep Wren with you. She might prove useful." He turned his head towards me. "And try not to die. You know what's on the line now."

His silver light faded behind us as he led Fana and her last remaining Nightmare bodyguard deeper into the trees.

Tiernan's golden light, meanwhile, simmered and hissed, catching the rim of his protective goggles. The golden rapier flickered as it crackled with the energy of the Skal that made it.

Right. I probably needed a weapon too. Or else I'd die again.

But worse than the thought of dying a second time tonight, the image Galahad had put in my head of the Grimguard hunting Gams had stuck with me.

I didn't even bother trying to draw a sword and settled for the inevitable, pulling a silver flail out of the air.

"Do you know how to use that?" Tiernan kept his eyes trained on the shadows of the forest, scanning for signs of the Grimguard.

"I was using it just fine earlier." That was, at best, a stretch of the truth. Lobbing flail after useless flail at the Grimguard had only kept him dancing for so long.

Tiernan stood ready, staring into the shadows. He might've looked stoic had I not noticed him gulp in the light of another orange burst.

"Look," I started, "I'm sorry about punching you, but—"

"You will not speak to me, Nightmare."

"Excuse you?"

"You will not speak to me." He said it slower this time. He kept his gaze trained on the trees. "And you will not speak to Fana. The others think you can help, and unfortunately for me, I'm outvoted. But from here until we reach the Second Sentinel, you will not address me."

"*Excuse* you?" Pain registered as shards of bone erupted from beneath my skin to form three lethal blades. Blood dripped off their tips to dot the dirt at my feet. "And what makes you so much better than me? Both our worlds are at stake, aren't they? At least you *chose* to be here!"

Tiernan ignored me and grabbed his rapier handle with both hands. The gold light crackled and split to morph into two curved picks, and Tiernan launched himself at the nearest tree. He clambered up it with ease, sinking the barbed points of his picks into the soft wood one after the other as he hoisted himself upwards.

"I don't think I'm able—"

"What did I just say about speaking to me?" he growled down from where he perched on a thick tree branch.

I took a steadying breath, suddenly very much missing Orla. I grabbed my flail handle the way he'd grabbed his rapier and tried to apply what Orla had taught me earlier in the night. The Skal buzzed in my hands, and when I ended up with two flails instead of two picks, I looked up at Tiernan helplessly.

The orange bursts of light were growing closer.

"I can't get up there!" I called after Tiernan. He turned his back to me, balancing on his branch with a hand braced against the trunk.

My cheeks burned with indignant rage.

"I'm here against my will, remember?" I hissed up at the twisted locks gathered at the back of his head. The trees had gone still, and there were no more orange bursts of light to disturb the shadows. "You can hate me all you want, but I promise—"

A twig snapped, and my attention fell from Tiernan to the shadows beyond his tree. I held my breath, waiting, and just when I decided I must have imagined the sound, two glowing eyes of orange emerged from the darkness.

The Grimguard took shape, stepping into the halo of silver light cast by my flails. His cowl was back over his mouth and nose, but he stood bowlegged, and blood dripped from the wounds I'd left in his thighs.

I gave one of my flails a swing, trying to look intimidating, but the Grimguard raised a condescending eyebrow at me.

"I'll kill you all night if I have to, Blue." A sword of orange sizzled to life in his hand.

He charged, and I side-stepped his first attack before fending him off with a sloppy flail swing.

"Nightmare!" Tiernan called down to me, and a ball of glowing gold formed in his arms like a miniature sun. He lobbed it into the air. "Catch!"

I stumbled to catch it, desperate for anything that might help me survive another round against the Grimguard. The tiny sun fell into my arms, searing against my skin.

"Squeeze it!" Tiernan's command echoed overhead, and as the Grimguard bore down on me again, I had no choice but to obey.

I squeezed the orb, fighting through the burning pain, and waited for whatever it was to deploy and save me and—

Searing golden light ripped through my every molecule, and I was back on my bedroom floor, dripping sweat and wide awake.

Eight
Information Dissemination

The shop was busy for a Wednesday, which wasn't to say that it was bustling by any means. Rather, it was just busy enough to annoy me that Liam Glass was late for work.

Gams had abandoned her workshop to help me in the store and was recommending Mom's books to what appeared to be a Bachelorette Party passing through town on their way to the real festivities in a bigger city. They giggled and blushed as they poured through pages, giving me time to stare at the two new scars the night's events had added to my hand.

The throat wound had luckily sealed itself shut during my second bout in Skalterra, but the blast Tiernan had subjected me to had left me sore and bruised.

My ribs and arms had taken the brunt of the explosion when I'd unknowingly detonated Tiernan's Skal bomb. My forearms were painted in yellow bruises that looked weeks old, and my ribs were a mottled green and purple that had made pulling on my clothes that morning more painful than I cared to admit.

Luckily, the morning was cooler than usual, so Gams didn't question the Keel Watch Harbor hoodie I wore to hide the injuries.

Worse than the physical remnants of Tiernan's explosion, however, was the gentle panic broiling inside me. Skalterra was real, and not only was something evil trying to break through from there to here, but somehow I was the person to keep that from happening.

We were screwed.

Unless, of course, my sacrifice last night had been worth it and the Grimguard was already dead. He'd nearly been on top of me when the explosive had detonated. I hadn't survived it. It wouldn't be a surprise if the Grimguard hadn't either.

The young women shopping in their matching "Laurel's Bride Tribe" t-shirts carried two complete sets of Mom's books to the register, along with three Keel Watch Harbor hoodies, and enough wine to last the week.

I stared at their haul for a moment, blinking slowly, before one of them cleared her throat and pushed the items closer to me from across the counter.

"Oh!" I shook my head. "Right. Sorry."

I hurried to ring up their things, and the bell over the door chimed. Liam shuffled into the shop with his head down and his blue Von Leer hood up. I wanted to be angry at his tardiness, but something about his hunched shoulders and the bags under his eyes softened my edge.

Gams abandoned the shelves she was restocking to pull him into a hug that crushed his bag of bagels between them, but it was hard to feel jealous at the familiarity of their embrace when Liam looked so terrible.

The bachelorette party paid and went on their way, and I strained to listen to Gams and Liam's hushed conversation as I rang up the ceramic chickens the next customer had picked out. Gams patted Liam's shoulder, took a squashed bagel, and retreated to her workshop.

"Back for more chickens, Stanley?" she called as she crossed to the workshop door.

"As long as you keep making them, Miss Ethel." The customer, a bespectacled man with a weak chin and a stiff button-up, raised a hand to her, took his chickens, and left.

Liam pulled his hood back as he came to meet me at the counter. He pulled another misshapen bagel from the bag and tried to smile.

"I promise it's not scooped."

I took the bagel even though it was nearing lunch time.

"Did something happen?" I hadn't planned on asking it, but the words tumbled forth. Maybe I was looking for an excuse to think about anything other than my fight with the Grimguard, Tiernan blowing me up, or the fact that our entire reality really was teetering on the edge of collapse. Or maybe I was actually concerned about Liam, despite his stupid smile and perfect hair.

He sighed and ruffled said perfect hair, somehow making it look stupider and perfecter.

"My cousin Riley," he said. "He was supposed to come back from grad school yesterday, but no one's heard from him in two days. He hasn't called, and he's not responding to texts."

"Oh." I remembered Teddy's pallid, worried face at the tavern the evening before. Riley would be his son. "Your uncle didn't have to make us bagels."

"He needs to keep busy." Liam shrugged and took up his spot behind the ice-cream just in time for a young family to rush in. A small boy led the way to the ice-cream station and pressed his face against the glass to survey the flavors. "And you need to keep fed."

I looked up to see Liam still watching me from over the heads of the family.

"What's that supposed to mean?" I demanded.

"You won't pass out if you have enough food," he reminded me. "Eat that bagel. I don't want to have to catch you anymore."

My face bloomed with embarrassed warmth, and I considered not eating the bagel out of principle. However, it was still warm in my hands, despite its squished form, and I'd never been able to resist a pairing of bacon and guacamole. I unwrapped the bagel sandwich with stinging pride as well as gratitude.

Gams made an effort to pop out of her workshop more often, checking in with Liam each time she did. Anyone else might have felt suffocated by her fussing, but Liam smiled every time she came by, even accepting the little blue chicken that she brought to him a while after lunch.

She handed a second blue chicken to me, beaming. This particular chicken had careful white lines cross-hatched across the blue body, and while it wasn't a very intricate pattern, the tiny details and careful lines must've taken Gams forever.

"Does this one go on the shelf too?" I asked, looking at the shelf of ceramic chickens for sale by the door.

"This one is for you!" She goggled at me with eyes magnified behind her work glasses. "For getting into Von Leer!"

"I didn't get in yet," I murmured, though I closed my fingers around the chicken all the same.

"We've been over this," she sang. "With a phone interview, you're as good as in."

The chicken's glazed paint was smooth under my fingers, and I held it tighter, as if its cool touch might erase the scars Galahad had left on my palm.

"Wren?" Gams stared at me from behind her giant spectacles, and concern doused her usual fire.

"What?" I loosened my grip on the tiny statue and tried to blink away thoughts of Galahad. I avoided her gaze, worried if she looked too closely at me, she might see the midnight forest of Skalterra rushing past behind my eyes.

"You've been distracted today." She raised a hand to my forehead, but I ducked away and smiled.

"I'm okay. Promise," I insisted softly. Gams was a wild spirit, but she and Mom had both become quick to worry over me in the last few weeks.

The bell over the door jingled, and the young woman who'd sat with Liam at Siobhan's Tavern the night before walked in. Her curly hair glowed strawberry in the light that streamed through the back wall windows, and she forced a smile through her grim demeanor.

"Hot off the presses." Her smile faltered as she held up a stack of papers. "Mr. Lane let me use the library printer for free, since it's for a good cause."

Gams took the top paper, somehow managing to work a chicken into the woman's hands as she did so. She nodded approvingly and passed me the paper over the counter.

"It's a good picture of him. Thank you, Sabrina," she said. "Wren, put that on the bulletin board."

A black and white face stared back at me from the paper, grinning the same stupid grin that Liam liked to flash. His hair might've been darker than Liam's, but it was hard to tell without color, and he wore an identical Von Leer hoodie. It looked like a picture that might've been snapped between classes or on a school weekend while out with friends.

I'd been sad for Liam before seeing a picture of Riley, but putting a face to the name brought a new, more profound sadness. I didn't want this young man to be missing, not when he looked so friendly and so much like Liam.

Not that I cared for Liam, but he *had* brought me a bagel, and that counted for something.

I pinned Riley's poster to the bulletin behind the register, trying to put it to the side so that I wouldn't block customers' view of it as I rang them up.

"Mom's letting me use the car to drive these up the coast. I was going to post them as far north as Dunningham," Sabrina said. Liam shot Gams a pleading look.

She nodded.

"Absolutely. I've got things handled here." She waved me out from behind the register. "Wren, go with them. They'll appreciate the help."

I faltered, hunkering down in my safe haven behind the counter.

"But what about the shop?"

Gams laughed and side-stepped around me to take up my post at the register. Jonquil jumped onto the counter to greet her with a chirp.

"What do you think I do the rest of the year when neither of you are here to help? I'm perfectly adept at running my own store. Besides, you've been staring at the far wall all day without blinking. You need a break. Get a move on. The highway is going to get crowded soon."

The air outside was uncomfortably warm, but I pretended it didn't bother me. If Liam worried about my tendency to take sudden and aggressive naps, he'd panic if he saw the bruises on my arms.

Sabrina introduced herself properly as we walked to her mom's tavern. Like Liam, she'd grown up in the town. Unlike Liam, she attended the community college in the next town over.

"Von Leer is the most popular school in the area," she admitted with a shrug, "but I'm not nearly pretentious enough to go there. Even if they did admit me, I'd die living on a campus full of people just like Liam."

Liam rolled his eyes at her ribbing, but smiled.

"That's great news for Wren," he said. "She uses words like 'amalgamation' in casual conversation. She's perfectly pretentious enough for us."

He took the stack of posters as we approached a black sedan, and Sabrina climbed into the driver's seat. Liam paused with his hand on the passenger door.

"Are you okay?" he asked under his breath.

"I'm fine. Why?"

"Yesterday you would've thrown me in the harbor for calling you pretentious. Today you seem... I don't know. Off."

"Maybe because you don't know me?" I raised an eyebrow at him.

His cheeks tinged pink, and he opened the passenger door.

"Would you like the front seat?" Liam asked. I stopped myself from scowling at him, remembering that we were only climbing into a car together in search of his missing cousin.

"I'm fine," I repeated, taking the backseat, and then forced out, "Thanks."

The inside of the car was sweltering. I risked pushing my sleeves up, trusting that Liam wouldn't look back and see my bruises. They'd faded slightly since morning, but were still dark and mottled enough that I was sure he would worry.

The coastline blurred past outside as we headed north on the two lane highway that wound through trees and along the lips of cliffs. I relaxed against the window while Sabrina and Liam talked in the front seat about small things that didn't matter. I figured she was trying to distract him. However, the way Keel Watch Harbor was, she was probably close with Riley too.

I tried to focus on what they were saying. I wanted to think about anything that wasn't Galahad and Grimguards, but the trees that passed outside the car reminded me too much of the forest from my dreams.

My fingers inched to the back of my head, but my undercut served as a reminder to not pull hair there. Heat rose in my face, thinking about how Liam had thought my classmates had shaved my hair in retribution for narcing about the physics test.

Instead, I leaned my head against my hand and gave in to the urge to pull at my eyelashes. I'd stop after just a couple. I would force myself to stop. In the meantime, it helped. When my thoughts raced faster than I could keep up with, the act of plucking hair from follicle *always* helped.

I'd pulled my first eyelash back when I was only nine-years-old, but it didn't get bad enough for Mom to notice until I was fourteen. That was when I'd raised my hand to play with my eyelashes and found none left on my right eye. So, I moved to the back of my head.

The first doctor Mom took me to said I was depressed, that the hair pulling was a form of self-harm. She'd been so smug in her assessment, so self-assured, that I didn't know how to speak up and say otherwise. I wasn't depressed. I knew I wasn't. I was an anxious mess, and had been since a small age, but I was an otherwise happy kid.

Luckily, Mom didn't think much of the first doctor's assessment either. The second doctor wasn't much better in my opinion, but Mom liked what he had to say a lot more.

"It's because she's gifted," he had explained through a neatly-trimmed white beard. He probably should've retired a long time ago. "I see this all the time in smart kids."

Mom liked that. *Gifted.* Her kid wasn't defective after all. No, it was the opposite. Her kid was smarter, better, more advanced than the other children! And somehow that translated to a compulsion to remove the hair from my face and head one strand at a time.

That doctor's solutions weren't great—fidget toys to busy my hands, gloves to render my fingers useless at pulling out hair.

But gloves are easy to remove, and fidget toys don't get the nervous energy out quite as well. Besides, no one wants to be the kid with the fidget block in class. It's an easy way to get labeled *different*.

"Smart" felt like a lazy diagnosis to me, but Mom was satisfied, so that was all the help I was going to get.

And here I was, four years later, pulling out eyelashes to deal with the weight of keeping reality from collapsing while helping Liam look for his lost cousin.

Partway through the drive, Liam rolled his window down. He stuck a hand out to play with the current of salty sea air, and when he asked if it was too much wind on me, I lied and said no. Maybe feeling the air rush between his fingers did the same thing for him that pulling my hair out did for me. Maybe he needed the distraction.

It was hard not to notice him checking his phone every minute. I knew he was waiting for Riley to text him, or for his Uncle Teddy to call with good news. He was still flashing Sabrina that stupid smile as they talked, and there had to still be some semblance of hope behind it.

Riley had only been missing forty-eight hours after all.

The first town we stopped in had a community board at a marina similar to the one I'd seen in Keel Watch Harbor. I felt like an intruder as I followed Sabrina and Liam out of the sedan. They clung to Riley's posters as they assessed the board to determine best placement.

"There." Liam pressed the flyer against the board at eye level and drove a push pin into the paper just above Riley's picture. "One down."

Sabrina leaned in towards the poster and lifted onto her tiptoes to give the corner a swift kiss.

"For luck," she asserted. She rubbed her thumb over the red lipstick mark she'd left on the paper. "Sorry about that."

Liam clapped her on the shoulder and forced a laugh. "He'll think it's funny."

They made to move towards the line of shops that overlooked the marina, more posters in hand, but my phone buzzing in my pocket held me back. I pulled it out, and my heart soared at the sight of the caller ID.

Liam looked back at me expectantly, but I shook my head at him.

"I'll catch up," I promised, fumbling my phone in excitement as I rushed to answer. "Mom! Mom, are you there?"

"Wren!" Mom cheered on the other line. I had missed her voice, and the sound of my name reverberating through my phone speaker was enough to dispel every thought of Skalterra. "Your Gams told me the news! My baby's going to be a Von Leer Viking!"

The heat that rushed to my face made the hoodie a bit too warm for comfort.

"No, I only have a phone interview and not for another two weeks."

"If they're making you wait that long, they've already made their decision. You're in. Otherwise, why waste everyone's time?"

I pulled my phone away to glance at the clock.

"Wait, where are you?" I asked, doing quick timezone math in my head.

"Lisbon! Oh, Wren, you'd love it! Maybe next summer we can come here together. Call it a late graduation gift!"

"Lisbon? It's got to be past midnight in Portugal." I scanned the street for Liam and Sabrina, but they had already disappeared into one of the shops.

"Book reading went late." I could hear the shrug in her voice. "Plus, there's no event scheduled for tomorrow, so I get to sleep in. Is Gams there? I wanted to talk to her, but she never answers her own phone."

"No, I'm out with Liam Glass and Siobhan's daughter. I guess no one has heard from Teddy's son in a few days, so we're posting missing flyers in the neighboring towns."

Silence buzzed on the other end of the call for a moment before Mom broke it.

"Teddy's son is missing?" she asked, her tone suddenly tight and careful. "Riley?"

"Yeah, but he's probably okay, right? It's only been two days."

"And you're putting up posters?" She said it in a way that implied the answer better be no, even though she knew it wasn't.

"The librarian printed them. Gams gave Liam and me the rest of the afternoon off to help Sabrina post them and—"

"Take them down. Wren, do *not* let those posters stay up long enough for anyone to see them."

Nine
Ethics

I acted instinctively, pulling down Riley's flyer without questioning my mother. Then I hesitated, and the paper wrinkled in my grip.

"Why?" I asked, and the phone line crackled as Mom sighed heavily into the receiver on her end.

"Just do it. It's too much to explain right now, and I'm tired. But Keel Watch Harbor is a small, quiet town, and missing posters bring the wrong kind of people sniffing around."

"The wrong kind of people?" I scoffed. "Like the kind of people who might find Riley?"

"Riley's gone, Wren." Mom's voice was hard and final. My stomach dipped. How could she be so certain from across the world, and after only a couple of days? "He was a good kid, but if he's missing, then—"

She cut off, and the silence that followed was strained.

"Mom?" I prompted.

"Please." She was urgent now, and pleading. "I'll explain later, but I need you to take down those flyers. Your grandmother never should've let you go to put them up. She knows better."

She spat out those last three words, angry and frustrated. I gulped and hoped I hadn't landed Gams in hot water.

"She's only trying to help," I mumbled.

"Listen to me. If the wrong people come snooping around Keel Watch Harbor, it could be the end of the town. Everything will be gone, including your grandmother's entire livelihood."

That didn't make sense. Keel Watch Harbor was a peaceful place. There wasn't anything dark or sinister hiding behind the bright storefronts. Everyone at Siobhan's Tavern the night before had been so lovely and so *normal.*

"But that's—"

"Wren. There will be no more Keel Watch Harbor. Your grandmother will have nothing. Take down the posters. Promise me."

"I—"

"Promise me, or I'm coming home to do it myself."

She'd already considered canceling the book tour after graduation. The waver in her voice told me she'd just as easily cancel it now.

"I'll take them down," I promised. Riley's crinkled face looked back at me from the paper in my hands, but I squashed the guilt that gnashed in my belly.

If anyone else had asked, I would've said no. Even if it had been Gams asking me to remove the posters, I probably would've left them up. But Mom was supposed to be light and gentle and unserious. If I had to sum her up in a single word, it would be "fun". That wasn't a bad thing. In fact, it was something I loved about her.

This dark tone and her new, serious edge scared me enough to fold up the poster and push it into the pocket of my hoodie.

"I'm serious, Wren," Mom said. The quiver of fear that laced her words felt out of place on the sunny marina. She'd only sounded like that once before, when she'd begged me to tell her what had happened when I'd gone to that party after graduation. "Make sure those papers come down."

I'd hoped the first phone call I'd had with my mother all week would've been more cheerful. It had at least started that way, but now I scanned the shops as I pocketed my phone. There was no way Sabrina and Liam wouldn't continue to put the pictures up. I'd have to follow them and remove any they'd already posted.

My cheeks burned as I picked a shop at random and trudged inside.

Riley's face stared at me from the register of a bakery. I was able to pull it down and run back to the sidewalk before the baker came out from the back kitchen.

The next shop was trickier. The old woman at the counter smiled at me with Riley's poster on the wall behind her.

"Hi!" I pushed as much fake cheeriness into my voice as I could muster. "Sorry, my friends were just in here posting these, but there's a mistake on them."

I held up the poster I'd stolen from the bakery and forced a sheepish shrug.

"Oh, dear," the woman tutted, pulling the poster down to hand it to me. "Come back with the new one. It makes my heart sick to think about that poor boy."

I ran out before she could see the guilt on my face.

Maybe Mom was wrong to ask this of me, but she'd never been wrong before. She wouldn't ask me to do something so horrible without good reason.

There was definitely something she wasn't telling me, though. I wasn't naive enough to let that go unnoticed. My resentment for it grew with each shop I ducked into, until I had a hearty stack of flyers in my hands. I shoved them into a trashcan, hoping Liam wouldn't pass by and see them.

"Wren!" Liam called from across the street. I jumped at his voice, but his kind smile told me he hadn't seen me throwing away his hard work. "Over here!"

I bounded across the road to meet with him and Sabrina. Their stack of flyers was considerably lighter than it had been when they'd set off without me. I tried to gauge my memory of how many they'd started with against how many I'd just shoved in the trash, hoping I got most, if not all of them.

"I already did the shops down that way." I jerked a thumb over my shoulder. "I think we've papered the whole town."

Liam cocked his head at me, and I tried to tone down my enthusiasm just a touch. I was overcompensating.

"That's great." Sabrina smiled, flashing white teeth behind red lipstick that stood out against pale, smooth skin. "On to the next town?"

I kept my smile in place. The next town. I'd have to chase after them all afternoon, pulling down posters when they weren't looking.

I wondered if they knew what secrets Mom was so scared of being discovered. At least the drive gave me an excuse to poke for answers.

The car had heated up again in the sun, but I ignored the sweat beading under my hoodie as I leaned between the driver and passenger seat.

"Tell me about Keel Watch Harbor," I said, straight to the point. I'd never been a tactful person.

Sabrina laughed.

"You know just about everything there is to know already," she said. "And to be honest, after you ran out of dinner last night, I wasn't left with the impression that Keel Watch is somewhere you care about that much. "

She pulled back onto the two-lane highway. Liam kept his window up this time, sitting instead with his head turned precariously, so I knew he was watching me without looking at me straight on.

"I care." I shrugged defensively. "If I get into Von Leer, I might live with Gams during the school breaks. It's closer to campus and the train station connects directly to the university town."

"I think Keel Watch would like that." Sabrina smiled at me in the mirror. "Everyone loves Ethel, but we all worry about her living alone like she does."

"She's got Jonquil," Liam reminded her.

"That old bag?" Sabrina snorted, and I cracked a tentative smile. I wasn't Jonquil's only enemy.

"She's a precious baby." Liam *would* be Team Jonquil. "But, yes. Ethel needs more than a cat and ceramic chickens to keep her company."

"Those chickens keep us all company." The car swerved as Sabrina leaned over to pull open the glove compartment. A purple chicken fell out into Liam's lap. "I think I'm nearing my tenth one."

"Oof, she must not like you very much, then," Liam retorted. "I've got twenty-two."

I thought back to the cross-hatched chicken Gams had brought me earlier that day. It was the only chicken she'd given me, and suddenly I felt very much like Mom had robbed me of a happy, close-knit upbringing in Keel Watch Harbor.

I'd always thought her publishing career had been what dragged us away from her hometown and away from Gams, but after that phone call, I wondered if there was another reason.

"So everyone in Keel Watch is nice, then?" I pressed. "There's no town weirdo lurking somewhere?"

Sabrina and Liam shared a bemused look.

"I guess Gladys is a bit overly enthusiastic about most things, and she likes to lurk in other people's business," Sabrina offered.

"But she's not a weirdo," Liam said with just a touch of defensiveness.

"No, the only weirdo in Keel Watch is that loser Liam Glass." Sabrina laughed as Liam struck a face.

Maybe this was the wrong way to go about it. Sabrina and Liam loved Keel Watch Harbor as far as I could tell. They'd never air out its dirty laundry.

"It's a quiet town, isn't it?" I continued. "Nice and peaceful, right?"

Liam cracked his window, and my ears popped.

"Last night at Siobhan's was as wild as it gets." His brow furrowed in the mirror. Riley's disappearance really was out of the ordinary then. So why was Mom so worked up about the missing posters?

The crumpled poster in my hoodie pocket crinkled as I adjusted in my seat. I could figure out Mom's reasons later. For now, I had no reason to not believe her, and I didn't want to give her a reason to cut her big European tour short. Besides, Riley hadn't been gone long. He was probably fine. I wasn't hurting anyone by taking the posters down.

We drove to two more towns, and I followed behind Liam and Sabrina, reversing their hard work and removing as many of the Riley flyers as possible. I was able to slip most of them into the trash, but a few joined the crumpled poster in my pocket, folded tightly enough that they wouldn't crinkle with my every movement and give me away.

When Liam insisted on paying for my dinner in the last town, my guilt nearly brought a confession to my lips. I swallowed it, letting it fester in my stomach instead. I picked at the skin around my thumbnails to keep from pulling out any hair or eyelashes. Skin healed much faster than hair grew.

I stayed quiet through our dinner of burgers and fries. Not only did I feel guilty about sabotaging all our efforts this afternoon, but it was hard not to feel like a third wheel with Liam and Sabrina.

It wasn't that they seemed romantically involved. Far from it. No, they were more like siblings. They ate the food on each other's plates without asking, and each time Liam's smile faded as thoughts of Riley returned, Sabrina knew all the right things to say to distract him again.

I wondered if either of them had actual siblings, or if this was it. I had neither biological relatives or friends close enough to consider family, and usually this was where I'd let jealousy get the better of me. Instead, I felt something like growing curiosity. They'd let me tag along on their mission today. That had to mean something. As annoying as Liam was, maybe he wouldn't be so bad if we were friends.

Of course, if they found out I actively worked against the fight to find Riley, any chance at friendship would be over, so maybe it was best to not get my hopes up.

The drive home was long, and the sun was setting over the ocean horizon. I leaned my head against the car window, resenting Mom, resenting Riley, resenting what I'd done today, but hoping it had been the right thing to do, and that it would make sense after Mom explained.

I'd been so worked up over the fliers, that I had forgotten to be worried about the sound of Galahad's voice in my head. Maybe I'd killed the Grimguard after all. Or maybe it *had* been just a dream.

I drifted to sleep to the sound of the sedan rumbling down the highway, not worried about where I might wake up.

Ten

Transportation Engineering

The low roar of tires on pavement shifted into something harsher and faster, and the jostling of the cab jolted me awake.

I blinked in the dusky light, expecting to see the back of Liam's headrest but instead found Orla's face inches from mine. Her green eyes grew wider as I gathered my bearings.

"Wow!" she breathed. I could see my reflection in her tinted goggles where they rested on top of her head. "That's so cool every time you do it, Galahad."

I was sitting on a wooden bench, facing Orla. Tiernan sat next to her, but kept his eyes on Fana next to me. A darkening forest rushed past through the rattling window on my right, though it was hard to make out much thanks to the shifting white light that lit our small cabin. Steam hissed somewhere out of sight, and I realized I was on a train.

"We'll get to Vanderfall by morning." Galahad stood at the doorway to our train cabin. On the other side of the frosted glass, Ferrin's back pressed against the door. He must've been standing watch. "Should be a quiet night, but stay alert. No one leaves this cabin without me knowing. And Wren Warrender?"

I gulped as he locked eyes with me. I would much rather be sabotaging Riley's search efforts than be back in Skalterra under Galahad's command.

"Yes?"

"No one is to know that you are a Nightmare."

"Why?"

His bushy eyebrows furrowed.

"Lucid Nightmares aren't legal, but before you get any ideas on using that to escape your employ here, you should know that they'll punish you just as much as they'll punish me. Save yourself the trouble, and if anyone asks, you're a dish maid from Trawler's Bay."

He gave a tiny nod, and then stepped out to join Ferrin in the hall.

"Welcome back!" Orla spread her arms wide, smacking Tiernan in the face. "It's okay if you feel overwhelmed by our advanced technology. Take your time getting oriented. This is a steamcart, like I was telling you about!"

"Right." I glanced around the cramped cabin, looking for the source of the shifting light. I found it in the glass pipes that ran along the ceiling from our cabin into the next. Their insides swirled with white, glowing mist. "You have electricity?"

Orla and Tiernan followed my gaze to the ceiling.

"Electricity?" Orla repeated. "This is a Keldorian word."

"No, it's not." Tiernan grunted. His gold tunic and leather armor hid under a yellow cloak, and he wore the hood up. A couple of twisted hair locks hung in his eyes, which he kept resolutely trained on the wood paneling just above Fana's head. "She means lightning."

"Is it storming?" Orla looked out the window, but the night was clear. Two full moons washed the passing forest canopy in shifting shades of silver. I gave them a double-take. Skalterra was real. I knew that now, and somehow the idea was easier to swallow while sitting safe on a train instead of dodging magic blasts on a parapet or running through a forest.

Still, the double moons took me a moment to accept.

I had really thought for a moment that Galahad wasn't going to summon me back. In the back of Sabrina's car, I'd been stupid enough to think this was all over.

Crap.

Sabrina's car. That's where my body was, asleep and unable to wake up unless I died here or if Galahad released me. It wouldn't be long before Sabrina and Liam would be trying to shake me awake.

Maybe, if I was lucky, Sabrina would let me sleep there, and they wouldn't ask any questions.

"I actually meant your lights." I pulled myself back to the electricity conversation.

"Our lights!" Orla stood to better point at the pipes that ran along the ceiling. "These are steam-lamps! Diluted Skal is heated into steam and then pumped through the pipes to create light. Why did you think it was lightning?"

"I didn't. Tiernan misunderstood what I meant." I took special delight in calling out Tiernan. My blue-haired Nightmare body didn't have any of the bruises I'd sustained from the previous night, but I hadn't forgotten how he'd blown me up. "We have lights in Keldori too. We make them with electricity."

The others stared back at me with varying degrees of confusion. Only Fana seemed to take what I'd said at face value, nodding solemnly and looking much too serious for a ten-year-old.

"You trap little storms in glass without magick?" Tiernan raised a dubious eyebrow.

"Not exactly, no. We use things like batteries to create, um, little lightning. And then it runs through wires to power things like lightbulbs."

"Lightbulbs," Orla repeated, relishing the word. "And what's a battery?"

"By the Three Magicians, Orla, don't be so dense." Tiernan glared at her from under his hood. "You can't *make* little lightning, not without Magicians. It's a lie."

I stood up and motioned for Fana to swap seats with me so I could sit across from Tiernan. He leaned back against the wood paneling of the cabin in apprehension while I bent over to unlace the boots I'd woken up in, revealing wool socks.

"What are you doing?" Tiernan asked. I pulled my feet free of the boots in response and placed them on the dusty, wooden floor.

"Give me your cloak," I said. Tiernan recoiled, but Fana rushed to pull hers off over her head and offer it to me. I threw the thick material to the floor.

With a grin, I rubbed the soles of my feet back and forth on the cloak.

The others watched in quiet anticipation, and Tiernan's shoulders relaxed with a roll of his eyes.

"You're getting the Divine Sovereign's cloak dirty. This is stupid," he said, and I reached a hand towards him to offer my pointer finger.

"Touch it," I goaded.

"No." His nose wrinkled in disgust.

"Coward."

He scowled and crossed his arms.

"I'm not being—"

I leaned forward to tap his nose.

An electric zap tickled the tip of my finger, and Tiernan swatted my hand away. Orla laughed at his scandalized face, and Fana allowed herself a timid giggle that made her black curls bounce.

"Electricity." I smirked. "Or 'little lightning'."

"It's magick," Tiernan insisted.

"It's physics."

"Do it again!" Fana extended her head forward as if to offer me her nose.

Tiernan stood to rip the cloak from the floorboards, and he pressed Fana back in her seat with a protective hand.

"The Sovereign needs food and rest," Tiernan growled. "Orla, take the Nightmare to the dining cart to find us something to eat."

"Galahad said to—"

"Galahad is an old windbag who can't even scrounge up a decent Nightmare anymore, and as the only guard of a living Sovereign, I outrank all of you." Tiernan glared at me as he said it. He fell back into his seat and tapped his boot against my leather greaves. "Now go."

"I can go get food," Orla conceded with a frown, "but Wren should stay with you. She's here to protect—"

"I don't need its help," Tiernan grunted.

"Oh?" I narrowed my eyes at him. "That surprises me. You found '*it*' plenty useful last night."

Orla paused at the door.

"How *did* you stop the Grimguard last night?" Orla asked. Tiernan kicked his boots up onto Orla's abandoned seat by the window. He stared out at the passing forest instead of answering.

"He blew me up," I said.

"You did not!" Orla swatted at Tiernan's head. He ducked ruefully, but otherwise took the punishment. "Just—Wren is our friend. We don't blow up our friends."

"It's a Nightmare, Orla, no different than the ones that fight and die for us any other night. Don't get attached."

Orla pressed her lips together, but whirled away from Tiernan. She grabbed me by the elbow and dragged me to my feet and out the hall.

"My shoes—" I tried to say, but when I scanned the floor for my boots, they'd been replaced by a small pile of ash. Orla marched me into the rattling corridor that smelled of dust and iron before I could better investigate what had become of my footwear.

Windows and wood panels made up the wall to our left, and doors of frosted glass lined our right. Beneath my wool socks, the carpet was worn and faded. It was remarkably similar to the trains I'd been on at home, even if it did feel a bit dated.

Galahad stood at the cart exit, and he raised a threatening, bushy eyebrow at us.

"The Sovereign is back the way you came."

"Tiernan's mood will keep the Grimguard away," Orla sniffed. "Also, he told us to go to the dining cart and that he outranks you."

Galahad's eye twitched, but Tiernan's assertion of rank must've held some merit because he didn't protest.

"Be kind to Tiernan," he said through clenched teeth. "He's mourning Caitria."

"Then what was his excuse before she died? Did you know he blew up Just-Wren last night?"

Galahad locked eyes with me, and I clenched my left hand, curling my fingers in over the scars he'd left there. He knew I was down to three lives. His eyes flickered over my wool socks, and his eyebrows furrowed.

"If Tiernan decided the best course of action to fight the Grimguard was to blow up the Nightmare, then so be it. That's what she's here for," he said simply, and my stomach knotted.

He really would let me die and feel no remorse over it.

"Then at least let her enjoy some pastries while she's stuck here getting blown up." Orla wrapped her arm around my elbow and pulled me to her side in a show of solidarity.

"She's getting blown up for her own world too, don't forget." It felt like a reminder to me rather than Orla. "And she isn't your pet. You shouldn't waste your money on pastries for a person that isn't real."

"Then let me waste *my* money." A firm hand landed on my shoulder as Ferrin appeared behind us. "We have a long road ahead. Let them enjoy the dining cart."

Galahad narrowed his eyes, but he stepped aside, letting us pass into the open air between passenger carts. The rumbling of the train and the howling of the dark wind that rushed passed were louder out here. My cloak and blue hair whipped around me in a flurry of fabric.

"Believe we're real yet, Just-Wren?" Ferrin grinned at me as Orla opened the door into the next passenger cart.

"Unfortunately." I had to yell over the wind to hear myself, but Ferrin's grin widened beneath his fluttering cockatoo hair.

"Excellent. Then do try not to stare."

With his hand on my shoulder, he steered me through the open door into the bright light of the passenger cart, and I immediately found myself disobeying his directive.

Some of the passengers' cloaks looked like those of Tiernan and Fana, ranging from brown and torn to ornate and embroidered. Others dressed more like Ferrin, Galahad, and Orla, with vests, leather, and unnecessarily complex belts and garters. Long tailcoats and longer skirts dominated the scene, though plenty of women wore leather pants and tunics. A couple sat together in traditional kimonos. Everyone had goggles pushed up into their hair.

One old woman wore her goggles over her eyes as she heated a metal mug of steaming liquid with a fistful of magenta skalflames. A ticket-taker in a red uniform and leather baldric reminded her this was a Skalflame-Free cart, and she let her fire flicker out as she mumbled about the good old days when she could light a flame wherever she liked.

"You're staring." Ferrin leaned in to murmur in my ear. "Remember, lucid Nightmares aren't exactly legal, so try to look less like you just woke up in an alternate reality."

I blushed and snapped my eyes to the back of Orla's pixie cut. She turned around to give me a smile.

"Told you," she whispered. "Steamcarts! Very cool, right?"

"Orla," Ferrin warned in a low voice, and she spun back around.

"It is very cool," I assured her, and Ferrin patted my shoulder with a heavy hand.

"Don't worry," Ferrin continued as we entered the next cart. The lights were dimmer in this one, and most of the passengers slumped in their seats, trying to sleep. "You'll have plenty of time to stare and meet our people once we reach the Second Sentinel. For now, let's focus on pastries."

The dining cart was easy to identify by its smell alone when we arrived, and I relished the scent of freshly baked dough and something savory that I couldn't name. Orla led the way through the door to reveal a cart lined with wooden tables that overlooked the windows. Pipes of steamed Skal ran across the ceiling and spilled shifting, dull light over the booths and the far counter where a man stood in a vest like Ferrin's.

"What sort of sweet pastries do you have available?" Orla pressed against the counter, and the man stared past us with an unfocused look.

"Sweet cream, peach, cinnamon apple—"

"Oh, peach!" Orla cut off his droning voice. "We'll have a half-dozen of peach!"

"And a pint of whatever is strongest," Ferrin added. He pushed forward to place a few large coins on the counter.

"I can pay for myself," Orla said, but Ferrin shook his head.

"Your mother would haunt me from this life into the next if I let you do that."

The man took the money without looking at Ferrin, and an uncomfortable prickle worked its way down my spine.

"He's a Nightmare," I realized out loud. "I thought we just fought your battles."

Ferrin put a finger to his lips and cast an anxious glance at a nearby table of cloaked men.

"And serving pastries to travelers is worse than fighting on a battlefield?" He motioned to a nearby wooden table. I took a reluctant seat across from Ferrin while Orla waited at the counter for her pastries.

"No," I admitted, watching the Nightmare disappear through a sliding door behind the counter. "But it's wrong. We don't have a say. We don't get paid. It's free labor."

Ferrin sighed and looked out the window. I followed his gaze, but the lights of the dining cart made it impossible to see outside. Instead, our reflections were thrown back at us, and I startled at the sight of the young woman sitting across from Ferrin in the window.

A sleek jawline accentuated her delicate chin and slender neck. Her cheeks were smooth, though that might've been courtesy of the dark night behind the window washing out her reflection. And her hair...

I ran a hand through the blue tresses, half-convinced my reflection wouldn't follow suit because the woman in the window couldn't be me. But her hand tracked mine, and her eyes widened in surprise just as I felt mine do the same.

They'd told me Nightmares took on their own idealized versions of themselves, but I hadn't realized until now that it had affected me beyond my hair and eyelashes.

"It's not really labor," Ferrin said, bringing me back to our conversation about the Nightmare behind the counter. "Not for normal Nightmares, anyway. The Skal and the will of the nocturmancer in charge of it do most of the work. The sleeping consciousnesses inside are just unwitting pilots."

"It's still wrong." I tore my gaze away from the window.

"Maybe." Ferrin shrugged, then looked away from the window to smile at me. "Help us get Fana to safety, and perhaps we can bring you back to campaign for Nightmares' rights across the Seven Provinces."

"Seven Provinces?" I repeated. Ferrin settled back on his bench with a coy smile and dragged his finger in a circle on the table between us. A thin stream of green flame danced in his finger's wake until he'd drawn out the rough outline of a continent.

"There's Skalterra." He drew criss-crossing lines through his picture. "You've got the New Kingdom, where we currently are, the Grand Barony, which is where we'll be by morning, then the Breachriver Prefecture, the Wisting Wilds, the Royal Shogunate, the Skalterran Highlands, and finally, the Frozen God Saergrim's domain in the north."

I studied the map as it flickered and burned in front of me.

"And where is the Second Sentinel?" I asked.

Ferrin drew a zig-zagging mountain range across the north end of the continent.

"In the Skalterran Highlands, hiding in the highest peak."

"Mountains?" I leaned over the drawing now, holding my blue hair away from the flames. "What kind?"

Ferrin laughed.

"The tall kind?"

"I mean are they volcanic?" I couldn't help it. I wondered if the magma and lava here would be as magical as the water my new comrades kept in flasks at their hips.

"The First and Third Sentinel have been known to kick ash into the sky, but not within my lifetime. Why do you ask?"

"Geology is cool." I shrugged.

Ferrin made room for Orla on his bench. She slid in next to him with a platter of flakey pastries, each decorated in white drizzle and peach slices. Ferrin's map of green dissipated, leaving behind an untarnished tabletop.

"So!" Orla beamed at me. "Steamcarts! Amazing, right?"

I laughed and felt my cheeks warm.

"They are, but I meant to tell you, we have these in Keldori."

Orla's face fell.

"Why didn't you say so last night?"

"I tried to," I admitted. "We don't call them steamcarts. In Keldori, we say 'trains'."

I frowned as a new question clouded my thoughts. I looked to Ferrin.

"Yes?" He smiled as if he knew the question I was about to ask.

"If I'm from a different reality, why do we speak the same language? Even if some of our names for things, like steamcarts, are different?"

"A very astute observation, Just-Wren."

"It's—"

"Wren. Just Wren. We know." His smile quirked. "I'm afraid Just-Wren has stuck. But your question, it's a good one. Do you have any theories?"

I felt like I was back in class, being asked to find the answer before being handed it. It was a familiar feeling, and I suddenly wanted very much to impress Ferrin. As much as Galahad seemed to enjoy pretending his age made him the group leader, and even if Tiernan claimed his guard-status over Fana meant he outranked everyone, I could tell Ferrin held an authority that neither Galahad nor Tiernan could compete with.

"We were all one world at one point," I said slowly. "Our language bases would still be the same, but that doesn't explain how easily we communicate after centuries apart."

Something clicked in my brain.

"And?" Ferrin prompted, folding his hands together neatly in front of him.

"And we haven't actually *been* apart, have we? Not if Skalterra has been pulling sleeping Keldorians in every night for hundreds of years. So our language developed alongside each other, rather than separate of each other."

Ferrin nodded approvingly, but a man ordering at the nearby counter interrupted us before he could reply.

"Is that how the kids are doing their hair these days?" he grumbled. "*Blue?*"

Skalterra and Keldori were still very much alike in more than what languages we spoke.

I took a pastry at Orla's urging and picked at the peach slices.

"You said there have been other lucid Nightmares?" I spoke low enough that the judgmental man at the counter wouldn't hear me.

Ferrin's smile faded.

"Yes, but it's been a while." His words were slow and careful.

"Then why does it happen? Why am I different?"

"We have theories. The Rift wasn't a perfect split between our worlds. Families that had both Magicians and normal humans were torn between Skalterra and Keldori. It's possible your family line goes back to those few who were left behind."

If that were the case, I'd reach a dead end fast. Gams had been adopted. She knew nothing of her birth family, and she refused to speak about Mom's biological father. As for my *own* biological father, Maxwell Brenton, PhD, was as much a stranger to me as anyone.

"Okay, and what are your other theories?" I pressed.

"Skal leaks from Keldori to Skalterra. It's possible you have spent an unusual amount of time near one of those schisms. Your proximity to Skal and to Skalterra could make you more connected to our world than others."

I thought back to the suburban neighborhood I'd grown up in. Linsey had only lived a few streets away. Hopefully I didn't come across her in Skalterra. I pushed away the thought. I'd rather face the Grimguard again than some Nightmare version of Linsey.

"It doesn't really matter, though, does it?" Orla smiled through a mouthful of pastry. "You're here now!"

"I have a life back on Keldori. Even after we get Fana to the Second Sentinel, I have things at home to worry about. I don't want to keep coming back to Skalterra."

However, I stared at the spot on the table where Ferrin's map had burned out. I hadn't seen much of Skalterra outside of dark forests and the train we now rode, but that map, along with the eclectic outfits of the other passengers, held a promise of an entire world to explore and discover.

"Uncle?" Orla said, suddenly serious. I turned my attention to Ferrin where he stared at the window, fighting to see past our reflections and into the passing forest outside.

"I thought I saw something," he murmured. "It's too bright in here."

He stood and pushed his way behind the counter.

"Sir—" the Nightmare worker protested. Ferrin held a hand up, and the Nightmare didn't have the wherewithal to argue. He stood back and continued to survey the dining cart with a faraway look as Ferrin forced his way through the sliding door and into the kitchen.

I tripped in my haste to follow Orla after Ferrin. Two cooks stood over a stove that burned with red skalflames. They regarded us with the same blank stare the counter-worker had donned, and I faltered as I realized they were also Nightmares.

Ferrin threw open the far door, and rushing wind ripped through the kitchen cart. The cooks swayed in the torrent, but otherwise stayed put as Orla and I followed Ferrin out into an open air cart. A tangle of pipes ran along either side of us, presumably transporting Skal to the rest of the steamcart from the massive, black engine that whistled and hissed ahead. Steam that glowed a soft ruby color billowed from the head of the engine, staining the star-streaked sky.

Wind ripped at my blue hair, and I steadied myself against a low railing.

The twin moons glittered in an ocean of foreign stars, washing the trees in the valley below us in silver. Beyond the forest, a massive lake reflected the moons back up at the sky, and the distant silhouette of a mountain range cut jagged shapes into the night. Three peaks stood taller than the rest, and I wondered if those were the First, Second, and Third Sentinels.

"There!" Ferrin leaned over the railing to point through the tangle of pipes. "Did you see that?"

The wind snatched at his voice, and I struggled to hear him over the whistling of the engine. Orla peered out into the forest, but we were moving so quickly, I doubted she'd be able to see anything.

But then I saw it too.

At first, I thought it was a trick of the double moons, casting dual shadows through the woods. However, the shadow twisted, nimble and lithe, through the nearest trees, and seemed to exist in spite of the moonlight rather than because of it.

Orla yelped in surprise and pulled her goggles down over her eyes. She lit green fire that danced between her fingertips, ready to draw forth whatever weapon she deemed best fit to fight the dark shape.

"Orla, no!" Ferrin howled. "It's a rotsbane!"

Ferrin lunged for Orla, trying to extinguish the green fire, but the dark shape seemed to have taken notice.

It shifted across its moonlit path, keeping pace with the steamcart, before leaping into the air, extending hooked claws of shadow that were easily the length of my forearm.

"Move!" Ferrin pushed us back towards the kitchen, and the cart lurched as the monster clawed up and over the pipes to land on our walkway.

It towered over us, shadows rolling over its hunched, colossal form. The metal beneath its animal-like feet bent under its weight, despite that the beast seemed to be built of nothing more than bones, shadow, and claws. Four hands that floated on the ends of shadow-wisp arms dug their talons into the engine pipes. Glowing steam screamed as it escaped before being sucked into the blackhole that sat where the monster's mouth should have been.

Then the kitchen lights faded with a hiss, leaving us in total darkness with the monster.

Eleven
Wildlife Biology

The only light was that of the escaping steam. It highlighted the contours of the rotsbane's skull-like face in shades of red and shimmered through the gossamer shadows that hung off its frame. The monster howled as it sucked steam into its gaping maw, and the sound was less animal and more like a screaming gale.

My knees shook, but I couldn't run. I couldn't move. I couldn't breathe. I was trapped in my own body as I watched the ghoulish beast rip at the pipes and suck down the steam.

A flash of green to my right accompanied Ferrin's warning shout. The flame in his hands solidified into a massive hammer that he brought swinging through the open kitchen door. It rang out as it crunched against the connection between our cart and the monster. A second swing of the hammer finished the job.

Metal groaned as the pipe connections burst and broke. The engine continued full-steam ahead with the monster still on board, while our cart, as well as the rest of the train behind us, rumbled to a stop. Ferrin let his hammer evaporate, and he pushed his goggles up his forehead to watch the monster get farther away.

"What was that?" I dared to whisper.

"Rotsbane," Ferrin growled. "Soulless monsters that feed on Skal. They're getting bolder if they're attacking steamcarts now, but it shouldn't come back as long as we don't ignite anymore Skal."

The engine was just getting far enough ahead to put me at ease when the rotsbane lifted its head from where it feasted on the pipes. Shadows hung off it like liquid cloaks, from which its four, skeletal arms extended. Even at this distance, I could see its eyes, deepset behind a hollow black skull and bright with the embers of ruby Skal, lock with mine.

"Wren." Ferrin's voice was a shaky breath. "Wren, *run*. It's done with the engine, but you and the cooks are made of Skal."

"But they can't die," Orla said.

"If the rotsbane catches her, it'll devour more than her Skal, but her consciousness too." Ferrin cast a panicked glance between me and the two cooks. "Wren, why aren't you running?"

The rotsbane cocked its head, still getting farther and farther, but then it pounced, bounding at us from down the tracks.

"Wren!" Ferrin yelled.

My legs still didn't want to work. I stumbled back on them, feeling like I was trying to walk through mud while on stilts. I hadn't replaced my boots after they'd turned to dust in Fana's passenger cabin, and my wool socks slipped on the kitchen floor. I fell, and the rotsbane descended upon our cart. It ripped the wall away, and it took one of the cooks first.

It dug long claws into her sides, and its jaw unhinged. A dull red light emanated from the cook's chest, and she blinked, as if coming to, but before she could scream, her eyelids fluttered and she dissolved into ash as the rotsbane sucked down the last bit of red Skal from the air between them.

"Wren!" Ferrin's scream somehow made it through the buzzing in my ears. He reignited his sword of blazing green, and ran it through the remaining cook. The cook disintegrated, but he would at least wake up, unlike his counterpart. To my horror, Ferrin turned the blade towards me next. He was going to kill me, to spare me a more certain death in the mouth of the rotsbane, but just as the blade came arcing down, it evaporated, sucked into the rotsbane. Its empty eyes flashed green, and then the monster fixed its gaze on me.

Its four sets of claws reached forward, but a metallic clang rang out as Orla attacked the monster, armed with nothing but a stove pot and a kitchen knife that she drove into its back.

"Find Galahad!" Ferrin yelled, pulling Orla away just as the rotsbane swiped at her with its claws.

My legs finally found their bearing, and I staggered to my feet and slid into the dining cart. It was empty, but screams echoed from the next cart over.

"It's a rotsbane!" someone shrieked, and chaos greeted me on the other side of the door. People fought against each other to find the exit, and in the light of the skalflames held aloft by passengers to light the way, I saw a silver-bearded face fighting against the tide of bodies.

"Galahad!" I screamed just as the sound of ripping metal echoed behind me. I pushed against the bodies at the back of the crowd, trying to reach the Magician. I didn't want to die. I didn't want to disappear in a cloud of dust and light like the cook had. I hadn't gotten into Von Leer yet. I hadn't done *anything* yet. "Galahad, please!"

Four sets of claws sank into my flank, but they felt cold instead of sharp. The rotsbane lifted me and turned me around so we were eye-to-eye. I fought against its grip, but it was no use. The rotsbane's jaw unhinged, so that all I could see was the dizzying nothingness of its insides.

This was it. This was how I died.

The cold nothing of rotsbane sucked at my warmth, my energy, my everything, and—

"Wren Warrender!" A voice, deep, desperate and, for once, welcome, boomed over the clamor behind me. "I release you from my service!"

And the rotsbane disappeared.

The summer heat of my bedroom was too warm and too disorienting after being inside the rotsbane's mouth. I stumbled out of bed, sweating profusely, and staggered to my window. A single moon hung over the quiet harbor.

I was still in my hoodie from earlier in the day, and Riley's missing flyer from the first marina crinkled in the front pocket. I pulled it out, trying to orient myself, trying to remember where I was and how I'd gotten here.

Had I died? Ferrin had said the rotsbane would kill me for real if it ate me. I flicked my bedroom lights on, much to Jonquil's ire, but I ignored the cat as I inspected my palm.

There were still only two slashes through the "T". I still had three lives left.

Then that must've been Galahad's voice there at the dream's end, releasing me from my Nightmare form to avoid being devoured.

I shoved the flyer into my nearby backpack and pulled the hoodie off, still breathing hard, still mentally replaying the rotsbane unhinging its humanoid jaw as it descended on me.

Taking the hoodie off wasn't enough. I needed air. Or water. Or anything.

I slipped into the apartment hall, passing the stairwell that led to the shop and tip-toeing to the tiny kitchen and living room.

The full moon lit the space through the open curtains, and I kept the lights off as I fumbled for a drinking glass in the kitchen cupboards. A row of ceramic chickens, painted all different colors, stared at me from the windowsill, and I stared back as I filled my cup at the sink. Jonquil must've been on the counters again, because one of them had a crack along its wing.

"What's happening?" a groggy voice asked behind me.

I jumped, and my cup fell from my hand, shattering in the sink.

"What the hell?!" I spun around, ignoring the broken glass, to see a shape pushing itself into a sitting position on Gams's old couch. The moonlight tinged Liam's dirty-blond hair, and his mouth drew downwards in a confused frown. "What are you doing here?"

He extricated himself from the sagging cushions with a groan, and tried to stretch out a kink in his neck by pushing on his chin.

"Trying to sleep," he mumbled. "Unsuccessfully. Maybe you have some pointers for me. Not only do you drop dead asleep without warning, but you're impossible to wake up."

I groaned and leaned against the counter, running a hand over my face. I'd fallen asleep in Sabrina's car but had woken up in my own bed. Gams definitely wasn't strong enough to carry me up the rickety flight of steps to our apartment.

"You..." I pointed at Liam, and he blushed in the moonlight. "Because I was..."

"Asleep." He nodded in confirmation. "I should thank you. It was a real ego-boost learning I could carry an entire person up a flight of stairs."

My cheeks warmed, and I turned around so he wouldn't see the heat rising in my face. I tried to busy myself with pulling the chunks of broken glass from the sink, but he came up behind me.

"Let me." He pulled an empty cup down from the cupboard and filled it before handing it to me. I stepped to the side, drinking the water, as he cleaned the glass from the sink.

I watched him work for a moment, letting the cool water calm the last of my nerves after my encounter with the rotsbane. I finally spoke as he rinsed the sink out.

"Why are you so nice to me? Did Gams put you up to it?"

He laughed softly, throwing away the last of the larger glass chunks.

"What if she did?"

"It would make sense."

His brown eyes looked black in the dim light as he turned to study me in the dark.

"Why's that?"

"She thinks I can't make friends."

"You told me you had friends, but they sucked."

"Fine. She thinks I can't make *good* friends. Is she paying you extra to be nice?"

"Is that an option? I should ask her about that in the morning."

His smile was playful, but his eyes sad. He pulled another glass down to fill for himself. He treated the apartment with more familiarity than I felt with it, even after two weeks. Jonquil waltzed from my room to twist around Liam's ankles.

The pang of jealousy came back, accompanied with a new feeling—bitter resentment, not towards Liam, but towards Mom. I could've grown up here too, if not for her book career.

The thought wasn't fair, and I shook it away.

"You said you couldn't sleep," I said, trying to turn the conversation away from myself. "Is it because of Riley?"

The last remnants of Liam's brave attempt at smiling slipped away, and he sighed.

"I hate being home without him, not knowing where he is. I thought I might sleep better here. It works for you, anyways." The smile returned.

I gave a half-hearted shrug as I finished my water.

"I sleep hard, but not well."

"What's that mean?"

"Nightmares." I smirked at my own double meaning.

"Is that why you're out here at one in the morning?"

I crossed to the living room window so he couldn't read my face. Sure, he was annoying, but he was proving better than Jonquil at calming my nerves after another misadventure in Skalterra.

"Yeah."

"Do you want to talk about it?" He followed me to the window, staring out at the single moon with me.

"There's nothing to talk about. It's not real." I felt bad about the words as soon as they left my mouth. Even though my nightmare *had* been all too real, Liam didn't know that. He'd probably give anything to have his biggest worries be not real too. He'd love it if Riley's disappearance was just a bad dream. "It was a monster."

"Spooky." He leaned his head against the window to look sideways at me.

"You laugh, but it was."

"I'm not laughing."

I studied him an extra moment, waiting for his mirth to give itself away. When he stayed deadly serious, I continued.

"It felt real. I thought I was dying."

"I'm sorry." He frowned, then gave a tentative smile. "Let's blame Sabrina. She chose dinner last night. Maybe it was those burgers that gave you nightmares."

I tried to smile at the joke, but was stuck staring out at the moon. Its reflection in the harbor made me think of Skalterra's night sky.

I hoped the rotsbane had left after Galahad had released me for the night. If Skal weapons really were useless against it, my friends were defenseless.

Friends.

That wasn't quite the word I meant, but I didn't know how else to describe Orla, Ferrin, and Fana. Galahad and Tiernan I could do without, but I didn't want any of them to be devoured by the rotsbane.

"You should go back to bed." Liam sighed. "Jonquil and I will keep watch and make sure the monsters stay away. Won't we, Jonky?"

He bent down to scoop the cat into his arms. Persians don't smile, but I could've sworn I saw her flat cheeks inch upwards.

"Thanks." Hopefully, Galahad would leave me alone. Hopefully, I could enjoy the dark void of unconsciousness without being dragged into another fight. I tip-toed to the hall and looked back at Liam where he still stood at the window, cradling Jonquil.

I wanted to say something, anything, to make him feel better about Riley, but the thought of the crumpled flyers in my bedroom turned my empty placations to ash in my mouth.

While Galahad had given me a break for the rest of the night, Liam didn't look like he'd slept at all by the time we were both up for work the next morning. He stumbled around the shop with a broom, sweeping up dirt that wasn't there. When his uncle brought us bagel sandwiches, Liam avoided him. I wondered if he was afraid Teddy's sadness might compound his own.

Gams missed Teddy's visit, but when she shuffled out of her workshop with more trinkets to sell to tourists, she stopped by my station at the register to pick up the bagel I'd saved her.

"You were tired last night," she commented, unwrapping the bagel. She looked like a bug, as short as she was and with her magnified eyes behind her work glasses. "Didn't even wake up when Liam carried you upstairs."

The shop was busier today. The weekend was approaching and more tourists were on the road. Liam was busy helping a family, and I took the opportunity to lean over the counter and whisper to Gams.

"Mom called yesterday while we were putting up posters."

Gams nodded, but didn't meet my eye.

"I told her to. I thought you might want to let her know about Von Leer." Her tone had gone flat and dismissive, as if she knew what I was about to say.

"Why did she tell me to take down Riley's posters?"

Gams's eyes darted up from her bagel to meet mine, and she frowned tightly.

"Did you?"

"Yes," I said, shame blooming hot in my cheeks, "but—"

"Good girl." She turned away, as if to escape back to her workshop.

"Gams!" I hissed.

"Wren!" She mimicked my tone.

"Did you know she'd tell me to do that?" When she didn't respond, I continued. "Is that why you sent me to help yesterday? To do your dirty work?"

"I knew you'd do what needed to be done." It wasn't like my grandmother to sound so serious and callous. "The posters will only bring the wrong sorts of people into town, and nothing good ever comes from outsiders poking around Keel Watch Harbor. Riley is a good boy, but if he's missing, he's not coming back. Liam and Teddy will move on. The town always moves on."

She spun around with a finality I didn't dare question, and she took the rest of her bagel with her to the workshop stairs, dropping a bit of salmon lox for Jonquil as she went.

Her words echoed what Mom had said on the phone, but neither seemed willing to explain themselves.

The Riley business should've been the least of my worries, especially after my run-in with the rotsbane. I still didn't know why I was a lucid Nightmare, and as much as I wanted to believe it was simply because I was *better* than everyone else, I knew that couldn't be it.

Ferrin's theories on the matter bounced around my head as the day wore on, but one stood out among the others. He'd mentioned genetics might play a role, so between customers, I pulled out my phone to search "Maxwell Brenton, PhD".

Celebrated geophysicist, Von Leer University alumnus, and my estranged father.

Mom had shown me pictures of them together from when they were college, but I'd never met him. He wasn't even on my birth certificate, and we'd never received a single penny from him. But I knew he was my father. Tall and willowy, just like me, while Gams and Mom were both short. I had his pointed chin, his passion for geophysics— though I would never dare admit that to Mom—and I saw a bit of me in his creased brow.

If the answer to my Nightmare question wasn't hiding in a water supply, then maybe it was hiding in my genetics.

I stared at him on my little screen and memorized the dates listed under his picture on the Von Leer site.

His summer lecture circuit would take him through Von Leer in just over a month. All I had to do was nail my phone interview in two weeks, secure my spot at the school, and convince Gams to let me take the train to the campus.

I would tell her it was to get acquainted with the school, take a tour with the admissions team, decide which dorm to apply for.

And maybe while I was there, I would pay a visit to a certain lecturer. And maybe, just maybe, I would get the answers I needed about Nightmares and Skalterra and how I'd ended up at the crux of it all.

Twelve
Library Science

Galahad didn't call me that night. I made sure to be in bed, determined to be ready this time, but after drifting to sleep without help from any other-worldly summons, my dreams remained my own. They were still stressful, of course, full of teeth falling out of my mouth and chasing after a faceless figure who I knew was Riley, even if I couldn't get a good look at him.

When I woke and realized I hadn't been to Skalterra, I was surprised at the knot of worry that lumped in my stomach. A few nights ago, I'd been sure they were all imaginary. Now, I hated the thought of the rotsbane hurting them.

Around lunchtime, the day got worse.

The Friday tourists had kept me busy enough that morning to not have a chance to say hello to Liam, but the strained smile he put on for the customers told me there was still no word from Riley.

He'd just clocked out for his lunch break when Sabrina burst into the shop, her strawberry blonde curls wild and her cheeks red with anger.

"They're gone!" she thundered, drawing the attention of every customer. Liam froze where he was hanging his apron on the hook behind the ice-cream bar.

"What're gone?" he asked.

"Riley's posters!" Angry and indignant tears streamed down her cheeks. "I was up in Port Fletcherton, because Mom likes the bakery there, and I wanted to surprise her, so I took the car up north to see if they still had her favorites—"

"You're rambling." Liam took her by the shoulders as gently as her wild gesticulating would allow. "What do you mean Riley's posters are gone?"

Sabrina tried to explain through hiccups.

"The bakery! We put a poster there! But I noticed it wasn't there anymore, so I checked the marina! And that one was gone! Then I checked the other shops, and all the posters are missing!"

"Okay." Liam shot me a side-glance, and I hoped he didn't see the guilt etched across my face. "It's alright. Someone from City Hall probably took them down because we didn't get approval. You know, dumb bureaucratic stuff."

Sabrina pushed him away, shoving him hard against his chest. Gams hurried out of the basement and to Sabrina's side. Sabrina, despite her agitated state, allowed Gams to pull her into a hug.

"No, Liam," she hiccuped into Gams hair. "They're *all* gone. I drove up north to the other towns and checked. One of the storekeepers said some girl took them down."

"It's alright, come upstairs." Gams took Sabrina by the elbow to lead her behind the register to the apartment stairs. Jonquil chirped her support, bounding up the steps ahead of them. "Tell you what, I'll send Wren in my car to replace the posters. They'll be back up before you know it."

I loved Gams, but I knew there were no new flyers for me to post. I was doing her dirty work again.

Liam looked as if he'd aged another ten years since Sabrina had run in, like gravity and grief alike weighed on his handsome face just a little more than it had before. He waved a hand towards the street.

"I've got it covered here," he said. "You remember where the library is, right? Mr. Lane should have the posters on file still. If he wants to charge you to print more, have him put it on my account."

I nodded, unsure of what else to say, what I even *could* say. However, the library wasn't a bad idea. I'd happily go anywhere where I wouldn't have to look Liam in the eye.

Mr. Lane was a friendly old man in a plaid newsie hat that hid the bald spot I knew shined bright in the center of his scalp. He was older than Gams, though he walked with the same spritely step. I'd always liked Mr. Lane when Mom and I would visit Gams for holidays, and after dealing with Galahad, it was nice to be reminded that not all old men were ornery grouches.

"Shame about Riley, it really is," he said as we stood over the library printer. While Gams's shop had been full of tourists, the library was nearly empty. Wood beams ran across the slanted ceiling, giving way to large windows that looked over main street at the base of the hill the library stood upon. I could see the roof of the shop from here, and beyond that, the harbor.

Mr. Lane beamed as he handed me the new stack of missing flyers. I wasn't sure if his face or Riley's, printed in black and white ink, did more to work my stomach into knots of fetid guilt.

The papers were warm, and I slipped them into the backpack I'd brought with me. It was a shame to waste so much ink, paper, and time, but I knew Gams had given me this task to make sure no one saw the new flyers.

"What do I owe you?" I asked, zipping up my backpack. Liam had said to put the printing cost on his library account, but I'd never let him pay when I knew these flyers were destined for the trashcan. I wouldn't have printed them at all if I didn't think Sabrina might ask Mr. Lane about it later.

Mr. Lane patted my shoulder, and a gentle grimace flitted across his wrinkled face.

"It's on the house," he assured me.

A contemptuous snort echoed from a nearby armchair, and a bespectacled face framed by frizzing white hair popped up from the other side of the seat to glare at us.

"You'll run the library into the ground like that, Ronald," the woman croaked.

A new wrinkled face, laden with heavy blush and blue eyeshadow, peeked out from behind the chair back next to the first woman's.

"Don't listen to Sarah. You know she's a harpy." Gladys, Gams's friend from the other night, winked at me.

"And you know that boy is dead," Sarah snapped back. Gladys swatted at Sarah with a magazine, and I clutched the backpack of flyers closer to my chest.

"What do you mean?" I came around the chairs to look at the women straight on. Both had bright magazines in hand and heavy shawls to stave off the library's air conditioning.

Sarah adjusted her glasses and pressed her lips into a thin, stern line.

"Everybody who's been in Keel Watch long enough knows it." She shrugged. "They're just all too afraid to admit it."

"Sarah," Gladys warned under her breath.

"People go missing, and they don't come back. It's cruel to pretend that they will."

"The only cruel thing here is you, you old bat." Mr. Lane pulled the magazine from Sarah's hands, but she was already reaching for a new one from the stack that sat on the table between her and Gladys.

"Oh, I'm the old bat?" Sarah's near-translucent eyebrows shot up over the rims of her glasses. "You're older than I am, Lane!"

"Then respect your elders. I won't have you talking about that poor boy like that in my library."

"My tax dollars pay for this library, so I'll talk how I like."

"We all pay taxes!"

"Then what are you doing spending your own tax dollars on flyers for a dead boy?"

I jammed my hand into my pockets, fishing for change.

"How much?" I asked.

"What?" Mr. Lane blinked at me, and Sarah blew a frizzy white curl out of her face as she settled back into her armchair.

"For printing." I found a few crumpled dollars in my back pocket. "This should cover it, right? I don't mind."

Mr. Lane reached forward to fold my hand back over the money.

"It costs nothing," he insisted.

Sarah grunted from behind her magazine.

"You don't know that he's dead," I snapped.

"Pardon?" Sarah glared at me over the magazine cover.

"Riley might not be dead," I repeated. "He's just missing, and even if you're right, you don't have to be such a hag about it."

Gladys and Mr. Lane shot each other a look of surprise while Sarah slowly lowered her magazine.

"So," she said coolly, "there's a bit of Ethel in there after all. Good. I thought maybe there'd been a mix-up at the hospital."

My cheeks burned.

"What's that supposed to mean?"

Sarah laughed, and while the sound was genuine, it wasn't quite kind either.

"It's a compliment. Your grandmother is a good woman. You could stand to be more like her."

"Maybe you could too," I retorted. "I don't think she'd like to hear you talking about Riley the way you have been."

"Please!" Sarah guffawed. "She knows he's dead, even if she won't admit it."

"She sent me to print these—"

"She's humoring poor Liam," Sarah said. "No one who goes missing in Keel Watch is ever seen again, and life goes on. It's sad, but it happens."

The library air conditioning chose that moment to shut off, throwing an unsettling silence over the room.

"This has happened before?" I asked.

"Well, sure," Gladys interjected. She leaned over their shared stack of magazines to rifle through the titles until she found one she wanted. "Every town has disappearances, but it's more noticeable when it's a small town like ours."

"Like Margaret." Mr. Lane nodded.

"Like Margaret!" Gladys agreed.

"She was always trouble," Sarah said.

Gladys glared at her friend, but continued.

"And Rusty and Hank Tracewell about fifteen years after that. They were brothers. That one hurt."

"Not as much as Sophie and Henry Glass," Mr. Lane said.

"Glass?" My heart dropped. That was Liam's name.

"Liam got over his parents. He'll get over his cousin too." Sarah shrugged. "Where'd the magazine you just had go? I wanted that one."

"Did he get over them?" Gladys asked, helping Sarah to the discarded magazine. "Or does he not want to listen to harpies like you tell him that he should?"

Sarah replied with another shrug and licked her finger before thumbing through the magazine pages.

"How old was Liam?" I'd assumed just because he was friendly and mildly attractive, he must've had it easy, and I'd been such a dick. Worse than that, I'd been a dick to an *orphan*.

The flyers in the backpack felt heavier than before.

"I think Liam was in middle school?" Mr. Lane guessed. Sarah shook her head.

"It was more recent than that. It was the same year Gladys was a ginger." Sarah gave Gladys's gray hair a pat without looking up from her magazine.

"It wasn't ginger, it was a warm chestnut."

"It was an eyesore."

"Anyway," Mr. Lane cut in, "it wasn't that long ago. Maybe a few years. Liam came home from school one day, and no one was waiting. We never figured out what happened."

"But life goes on." Sarah dropped her magazine again to look at me from behind her giant glasses. "We're used to it by now. People go missing, we wait a little bit, we hold a memorial, and then we carry on. It doesn't do anyone any good to linger on things we can't fix."

I clutched the backpack tighter. I had half a mind to repost the flyers against Gams and Mom's wishes, just to prove Sarah wrong. Riley would come back. There was no need to be so cynical.

"Thanks for the posters, Mr. Lane," I clipped. "I know Liam will appreciate it too."

I made sure to glare at Sarah as I spun on my heel and bolted for the doors, moving fast enough that I wouldn't hear whatever nasty thing she said next. The last time I'd wanted to spite someone as badly as I wanted to spite Sarah, I'd gotten Linsey's Von Leer admission revoked.

I tossed my backpack into the front seat of the car, and Riley's posters spilled out on the floor. They were still warm from the printer as I shoved them back into place, threw Gams's car into drive, and started the journey north.

I didn't have time to hang all of the new posters, but I managed to replace most of the ones I'd removed in the first town. Sarah had pissed me off just enough to disobey Gams and Mom, but what did they know either? I probably shouldn't have listened to them in the first place. Riley deserved a chance to be found, and Liam deserved my help in finding him.

As for their fears about unwanted attention coming to Keel Watch Harbor? Surely the town's reputation wasn't worth the life of one of its own.

I returned to the shop well after closing. Gams raised an eyebrow from where she counted money at the register when I came in, and I scowled in response.

"Your friend Sarah sucks." I shuffled past her towards the stairs.

"Welcome to Keel Watch Harbor. You aren't an official resident until Sarah's offended you in some way."

Dinner was the first normal meal we'd had together in the last few days, and I held my questions about Keel Watch Harbor's sordid history of missing persons at bay. I must've been pulling at my eyelashes at some point because as I let Gams blather on about Von Leer and my upcoming phone interview, I found my fingertips grasping at empty space where I was certain eyelashes had been that morning. The black remnants of my mascara under my fingernails confirmed my suspicions.

"When is that again?" Gams asked, gathering our salad bowls to take to the sink. If she had noticed the broken glassware in the trash from the night before, she didn't say anything.

"The phone interview? Two weeks from yesterday. I'll need that morning off."

"Consider it done." She winked at me, then noticed the broken ceramic chicken on the windowsill. She picked it up to turn it over in her hand and inspect the crack. "Shame. I really liked that one."

She tutted and slipped it into her cardigan pocket.

"And if the interview goes well—"

"It will," Gams interrupted with a kind of ferocity that suggested she believed she could get me into Von Leer through sheer willpower.

"Right. *When* the interview goes well, I'm thinking about taking a long weekend next month to tour the campus."

Gams lit up at the idea, which would've made me feel guilty about my ulterior motives to corner my biological father and interrogate him about Skalterra if it weren't for her dragging me into her plot to sabotage the search for Riley.

"Just tell me when, and I'll give you both a few days off."

I faltered.

"Both?" I repeated.

"You and Liam."

No, that wouldn't work for me.

"I don't need Liam." My cheeks warmed at Gams's ensuing laughter.

"No? Then who is going to show you around campus? How were you planning on getting there?"

"There's a train—"

"Perfect. I'll pay for both of your tickets and a hotel room."

"Hotel room?" I blanched. "No, that's not—"

"The train schedule isn't day-trip friendly. Don't worry, it'll be a double room. And *I* won't worry because I know Liam is a good boy and that *you* aren't into those sorts of things."

"But—"

"That poor thing needs the distraction, Wren. You'd be doing him a favor by taking him."

I swung my backpack onto the small, two-person table that stood in the center of the kitchen. Riley's remaining posters slipped from the open zipper and scattered across the linoleum.

"I'd be doing him a favor by actually helping him find his cousin, instead of actively working against him."

Gams narrowed her eyes at me, pausing in her scrubbing of our dinner bowls.

"We've been over this. Riley is gone."

"Right." I nodded. "Just like Margaret, and the Tracewell brothers, and Liam's parents."

Gams's face paled, and her neck bobbed with a nervous gulp. Then, she turned stony, any sign that I'd caught her off guard squashed.

"What've you been up to today, Wren Warrender?" she demanded. "I told you, nothing good comes from outsiders poking around Keel Watch Harbor, and that includes you."

The word "outsider" stung in an unexpected way, but I could sense Gams was running defense, which meant I held more power in this conversation than I had initially realized.

"I don't need to poke around when your friends are giant gossips."

"Sarah?" Gams hissed.

"Gladys too."

Gams grimaced.

"This isn't some puzzle for you to solve. There's no big conspiracy here."

"No?" I sang, fanning myself with the paper. "Then why are you using me to cover up Riley's disappearance?"

"I'm covering up nothing."

"Then why—"

"Keel Watch is small, Wren. Smaller scandals than a missing boy have ruined towns like ours." Gams turned back to the dishes so I couldn't see her face. "And the Glass family has a complicated past. I'd go into it more, but quite frankly, their business is not mine to tell and it does you no good to be nosy. I'm keeping us from becoming a spectacle. I'm keeping Liam safe from people who would see him as a tragic story to gawk at and package up for their Real Crime podcasts."

"It's not called 'Real Crime', it's 'True Crime'," I mumbled, trying to tame the sudden shame rising in my cheeks. Maybe I shouldn't have reposted the flyers after all. "And it should be Liam's decision if he becomes a spectacle or not."

"He's young. He wouldn't understand that I'm trying to protect him."

"But Margaret and the Tracewell brothers, they disappeared too."

"Years apart! Margaret was a sad story. We get a lot of people through town, and not all of them are well-intentioned. As for Rusty and Hank, they were avid fishermen. One day they sailed out, and they didn't come back. It doesn't take a detective to figure out what happened."

I hated to admit that her words made sense, though there was still one important detail bothering me.

"Then how do you know Riley is gone for good?"

"Riley was a good boy." Gams stared into the sink, but her eyes were unfocused. "If he were alive, he would've checked in by now. He'd never do this to his parents and Liam on purpose."

She cleared her throat and turned back to look at me. Her magnified eyes glistened behind her glasses. I'd been so focused on fighting her that I had forgotten she would be just as upset by Riley's appearance as anyone.

But it didn't mean I wasn't upset too.

"I don't want to do *this* anymore," I said, gesturing at the scattered flyers. "It doesn't feel good, and it's not fair."

"You're right" Gams's face softened, and she opened her arms in apology. I accepted the hug, reluctant at first, but then melted into her embrace as I always did. "That wasn't right of us to ask you to do this, and moving forward, you don't have to help anymore."

I nodded, my chin bumping against her head as I did.

"The fourteenth," I said. She pulled away from the hug.

"What?"

"That's when I'd like to visit Von Leer. It's a Thursday. I can have that day off, right?"

She grinned.

"Of course. You and Liam both."

Thirteen
Intro to Criminology

For the second night in a row, Galahad failed to summon me. I remained braced for his call, ready in my head, while Jonquil watched me from my dresser top. The ceiling darkened as the sun sank below the horizon outside my window, and I dared to close my eyes.

When I opened them again, it was to sunlight streaming in through my curtains. It felt like a sick joke. They'd finally convinced me that Skalterra was real, and now I'd been stood up two nights in a row.

At the register that morning, I curled my fist around the T-shaped scar on my palm. As much as I resented the marking, it was the only indicator that Skalterra *had* been real.

Maybe the rotsbane had hurt the others. Maybe it had killed Ferrin, Galahad, and Orla on that train.

No evil Magicians had come bursting through the fabric of reality yet, so the Frozen God's glacial prison had to still be in place. At the very least, Fana was probably alive.

But the others?

The bell over the front door rang as Liam walked in. My stomach clenched at the sight of him. I was worried about people I'd barely known for four days. It must be so much worse for him to be in the same boat but with his cousin.

And his parents.

"What?" Liam's lips cocked into a confused smile as he handed me my morning bagel.

"I didn't say anything."

"No, but you've got a look on your face."

"What, am I not allowed—" I cut off, remembering his assumed dead parents and probably dead cousin.

Liam laughed and pulled his apron on over his t-shirt.

"That face! Right there. You're still making it."

"I'm just listening to the rain," I tried to cover. The steady beat of rain on the roof had followed me from the upstairs apartment to the shop. There was a cozy comfort in the pattering sound after so many days of sunshine.

Liam turned to look out at the street, and his brow furrowed.

"The rain?" His confused smile returned. I followed his gaze to the cloudless sky that shined down on the dry pavement.

My stomach clenched, and I strained my ears, focusing on the patter of rain that I could still hear tapping out a disjointed rhythm overhead.

I took a bite of bagel to keep from having to answer Liam about the weather. Unfortunately, it left the door open for him to keep talking.

"How did yesterday go with the posters?"

"Oh!" My cheeks burned hot, and I glanced towards Gams's workshop door. "Mr. Lane says not to worry about the printing cost. He covered it."

Liam nodded, and his brow furrowed.

"That's good. And you were able to get them posted okay?"

"Um—" I hesitated. "Yeah. It was—"

"All this talk and no working!" Gams burst through the door to the basement, laden with more blue chickens. "What am I paying you both for?"

"For bagels." Liam held up the brown bag. Gams gave him a grateful smile as she traded her armful of chickens for her bagel.

"You don't need to keep painting them blue," I said, watching Liam arrange the chickens on the front shelf. "I got the interview with Von Leer."

"The blue chickens have gotten you this far. I'm not changing the color until I'm sure you are a Von Leer Viking," Gams said as the front door swung open.

I recognized the weak-chinned man who'd bought a chicken a few days ago, and he gave Gams a jovial wave.

"What've you got for me this time?" he asked, crossing to the chicken shelf.

"Weren't you just in here buying chickens the other day, Stanley?" Gams laughed through a mouthful of bagel. "Are you trying to deplete my stock?"

"One of my client's kids saw it on my desk, and I let him take it." Stanley plucked a new chicken off the shelf and crossed to the register to hand it to me. I tilted my head to the side, certain I could still hear rain pattering against the roof.

"And here I thought bankers were supposed to be heartless," Gams chuckled as I wrapped the chicken in paper and took Stanley's payment.

"Maybe in Keel Watch, but not up in Dunningham! If you shipped chickens to one of the shops in town, I wouldn't have to drive all this way for new ones."

"And run myself out of business?" Gams patted Stanley on the back. "My chickens will stay here, thanks. Supply and demand! Surely they taught you that at your fancy banker school?"

Stanley shook his head as he laughed, thanked me for the chicken, and headed back out the door.

Gams returned to her workshop, and Liam didn't ask anymore about Riley's posters, but that might've been thanks to the steady stream of customers keeping his ice-cream scoop busy. The invisible rain let up around noon, just in time for me to go enjoy my lunch break in the sun of the back deck. I convinced myself it must've been the sound of Gams's air conditioning I'd heard, or maybe Jonquil was running laps upstairs.

Whatever it had been, it could not have been rain, because the streets of Keel Watch Harbor stayed dry.

With the exception of the mystery sound, the day passed without consequence and with no word from Galahad. I dared to stay up later than I should have, but by the time ten o'clock came, I figured I was going to pass another night unbothered by Skalterra, and crawled into my covers.

I fell into a dream that felt real enough. I stared at my hands and was trying to determine if they'd always had six fingers each, when a voice cut into the scene.

"Let's see if it works this time. Wren Warrender?"

I looked up from my hands at the fuzzy darkness that opened before me.

"Galahad?" I asked.

"There she is," Galahad's gruff voice responded. "Already asleep, are you?"

The darkness shifted, closing in on me until I was under a low ceiling lit by glowing yellow orbs resting on sconces. The floor was uneven beneath my leather boots, and warped wood creaked as I stumbled backwards to catch my footing.

"See? That salesman didn't rip you off." A familiar hand pressed against my back to steady me. Ferrin's facial hair had become rugged and unkempt in the days we'd been apart. "Welcome back, Just-Wren. Miss us?"

"What happened?" My stomach felt sluggish, and my limbs buzzed with an uncomfortable energy. Something invisible pressed on my chest, and breathing was difficult. My veins burned with a dull heat, like my blood was attacking me from the inside. "I feel like garbage."

"Maybe the salesman did rip you off after all," Ferrin mused. "The Skal was probably diluted with something."

"She'll be fine," Galahad grunted. "Lots of Nightmares get made out of diluted Skal for cheap labor."

"I hate it." I thought I'd be more relieved at seeing they were okay, though maybe "okay" was a bit of a stretch. As my eyes adjusted to the dim light, I could tell they were both dirty, and their clothes were torn. Galahad had a black eye that looked several days old.

"Just-Wren is back?" A door to our right slammed open, and Orla tore from the room to wrap me in an embrace. "Thank the Three Magicians, we thought you might be dead!"

"Dead?" I pushed her off of me. Her short brown hair stuck out in every direction, and one of her goggle lenses was cracked.

"The rotsbane! It had you. We thought Galahad might've been too late in releasing you," she gushed. "And then the rotsbane ate all the Skal on the steamcart, so we couldn't call you back. And the city sent a rescue cart, but one of the diners figured out you had been a lucid Nightmare, which is illegal, so we had to run into the woods, and then it took us two days to walk here without any Skal."

"Oh." I looked between the three of them, relieved I'd missed spending time in the woods. "But no Grimguard?"

"Not yet." Either the yellow light of the wall sconces made Galahad's wrinkles look deeper than usual, or the forested trek to wherever we were now had been harrowing enough to age him several years. "But we can't be too careful. He's had plenty of time to catch up. He could be here in the city for all we know."

"The city?" I looked around the dingy hall.

"Vanderfall, the capital of the Grand Barony!" Orla said. "You'll love it. It's the biggest city in Skalterra."

"Yeah, so far it's beautiful." Something lurched inside me, and I leaned against the wall of unfinished wood. Whatever Skal Galahad had made me out of was definitely not sitting well.

"Galahad and I are going to request an audience with the Baron." Ferrin shifted his weight from foot to foot, and looked sideways at Galahad. His hair had lost some of its usual height and now drooped to the side. "We're hoping to secure passage as far north as Riverstead, and maybe secure some better quality Skal, but the Baron isn't exactly known for being generous. We need you to watch the inn with Orla and Tiernan while we're out."

If this was an inn, then the rows of doors on either side of the hall made sense. I glanced down the line of them, noticing Tiernan for the first time where he sat on the floor with his back against what was probably Fana's door.

"We've paid for the entire floor," Galahad explained, "so if anyone who isn't a Riftkeeper comes up here, get rid of them."

Orla nodded importantly, and her cracked goggles slid from their perch on her head to hang around her neck. Ferrin pulled her in to press his forehead against hers.

"We won't be long," he assured her in a hushed tone.

"But the Baron—" Orla protested.

"Doesn't scare me, and shouldn't scare you either. You know I've handled worse."

She nodded against his head, and Galahad grumbled for Ferrin to hurry. He pulled away from his niece and gave me a tiny salute as he followed Galahad over the uneven floors to the stairwell.

"Orla, rest up," he called back. "Wren's the only one of you with Skal. She'll keep watch."

Ferrin and Galahad's boots echoed down the stairwell, and Orla watched the empty hallway with apprehension.

"They'll be fine," she said, more to herself than to me. "The Baron is a bit intense, but— well, you heard Ferrin. He's faced worse." She gave me a brave smile. "I knew you were still alive. Tiernan said you were probably reduced to Skal particles swirling inside the rotsbane, but Galahad would never let that happen."

"Right." I snorted. "Couldn't let his favorite weapon go to waste."

I glared at Tiernan's bowed head down the hall as Orla led me through the open door of her room. The space was small and sported a dusty wardrobe and thin bed with a lumpy mattress that smelled like damp straw. Bright lights pushed against the moth-eaten curtains that obscured the window, fighting back against the otherwise drab atmosphere.

"Galahad only pretends to be terrible." Orla fell backwards to sit on her mattress and tried to smooth down the brown sheets where they wrinkled around her. "He does it because he's afraid we'll all figure out he's secretly a softie."

I gravitated towards the window but hesitated with the curtains in my hand.

"A softie?" I repeated through a laugh.

"It means kindhearted and gentle," Orla explained. "Sorry, it's easy to forget you aren't familiar with all our phrases."

"I know what it means. We have that word too, and it's not one I'd use to describe Galahad." I pulled the curtains back to reveal a view of the river below. Water flowed parallel to the street below us, and while our side of the river was barren and quiet, busy shops and restaurants lined the cobbled road across an arched stone bridge. Glowing pipes dipped in and out of walls in a dizzying tangle of steamed Skal. People in robes, cloaks, and leather milled between storefronts despite the late hour, and the Skal-glow that emanated from wrought iron street lamps kept the night sky above obscured.

"Oh," I breathed. Maybe the chainmail and the parapet from my first encounter with Skalterra had thrown me off, but the elaborate network of pipes weaving between bright shops and stone terraces was a shock. There was still something aged and rural compared to the neon cities I was familiar with, but it was more than I had expected. "I didn't think you guys had all this."

"Beautiful, right?" Orla sighed. "This is only my second time here. You should see the Baron's mansion."

"You mean where Ferrin and Galahad are going?" I thought I recognized Galahad's leather duster making its way through the crowd next to Ferrin's coiffed hair. They stepped through rain puddles that reflected the lights of the shops in hues of yellows and oranges.

"Yes." Orla played with the hem of her cloak where she sat on the lumpy bed. "It's a risk leaving us here, especially with no Skal, but it's a greater risk taking Fana. She's valuable, and the Baron likes valuable things."

Ferrin and Galahad turned a corner and disappeared behind a merchant's booth. I pressed my lips together. Galahad's diluted Skal sat heavy in my stomach, uncomfortable and hot.

"If it's such a risk to not have Skal, what if we went and found some?" I asked.

"Skal is expensive. Usually we replenish our store at private springs owned by the Sovereign families or by their Riftkeeper. But on the street? Buying enough Skal would bankrupt us. Ferrin will see what the Baron is willing to give us, and then we'll use that to get to Tulyr and restock there."

I silently watched the Skalterrans across the river for a moment. Despite the variety in clothing styles, almost all of them wore bottles of glowing Skal at their hips.

"This mission benefits all of Skalterra, right?" I asked. "Keeping Fana alive and the Frozen God in his glacier?"

Orla nodded, but her lips drew into a frown.

"Of course. The Four Magicians built Skalterra as a safe place for magick to exist."

"But we can't just ask for Skal, and tell them we're saving Skalterra?" I watched a woman in a bustled dress down a vial of glowing liquid on the cobbled street beneath us.

"Definitely not." Orla laughed. "Some Skalterrans wish we could return to Keldori and view our world as a prison, so they aren't really big fans of the Riftkeepers."

"Okay." I straightened up. "Then we take Skal without asking."

I pushed away from the window, back towards the hall. Orla rushed to follow me.

"I don't know what's normal in Keldori, but here we don't—"

"We are defenseless." The floorboards of the hall creaked beneath my leather boots. "We don't have Skal. I have some inside me, but it feels like poison. If Skal will help us keep Keldori and Skalterra safe, then us taking some will benefit everyone. Think of it like a tax."

Tiernan glared at us as I led the way to the stairwell.

"What are you—" he growled, but I cut him off.

"We'll be back," I assured him. "You don't need us."

I knew his pride wouldn't let him argue the contrary, and he was silent as I led Orla down the twisting steps to the first floor.

"Wren," Orla hissed after me. "We can't steal Skal! We'll get caught!"

Back at home, I'd never do this. But I wasn't at home, and I wasn't really me, either. I wasn't Wren, the waitlisted college hopeful. I was Just-Wren, the warrior weapon with great hair and little-to-no consequences as long as a rotsbane didn't get involved.

The low-ceilinged lobby of the inn was dark despite the light that filtered in through the windows. A grizzled man read a dusty book in the light of an azure skalflame at the front desk. He glanced up as we passed, and Orla shot him a nervous smile.

"Wren," she said again through gritted teeth.

I stepped out onto the street, letting the noise and smells wash over me. Something savory wafted on the wind, mingling with the scent of recent rain. Iron-wrought lamps topped with glowing orbs of Skal lined the riverwalk, and I followed them to an arching bridge of stone.

I paused at the peak of its arch so I could look down into the water. It reflected my blue-haired figure back up at me, and Orla's harried reflection joined mine in the rippling water.

"Let's go back to the inn," she insisted. "Ferrin said I should get some sleep—"

"Do you want to sleep?" I asked her seriously, pushing blue hair back from my face. Her lips twisted, and her eyes darted to the bright storefronts on the other side of the river behind me.

"No, but—"

"You're from the mountains, right? Your uncle showed me a map."

"I grew up in the Second Sentinel."

"How often do you get to leave the mountain?"

She looked back at our reflections in the water.

"This is the first time," she admitted. "But I have a duty to Fana, and it doesn't include stealing Skal."

"It does if it means keeping her alive."

I took Orla's wrist and pulled her after me across the bridge.

The stone buildings rose up around us, boasting open storefronts of trinkets, clothing, and food. Spiraling sets of staircases led up to second and third story terraces that connected to each other via footbridges that arched overhead.

Elaborate networks of pipes and glass carried Skal between the shops and to the streetlights to cast warm yellow glows over the crowds of cloaks and leather.

"You know, if Galahad told me *this* is what Skalterra is like, I probably would've agreed to keep coming back sooner." I craned my head to watch a footbridge as we passed underneath it. Puddle water splashed up my legs, drawing my gaze to my boots. "Did it rain today?"

"It was awful." Orla nodded. "Rained all night and all morning. We were soaked when we finally arrived in the city."

I chewed on the inside of my cheek, thinking about the nonexistent rain I'd heard on the rooftop throughout the morning.

But then, a sweet smell caught my attention, and I whipped my head up to look into the nearest storefront.

"Are those pies?" I faltered at the outskirts of the gathered crowd to stare at a baker preparing a doughy crust behind a counter. A jumble of pipes dipped in and out of the wall behind him.

Orla glanced backwards down the way we came. The dark windows of the inn stared back at us from across the river.

"Yes, but—"

"This way." I tracked the path of the pipes along the wall and rounded a corner. There were more storefronts here, and I resisted the smell of simmering meat to pass under more archways.

Men and women in leather and goggles sipped from glasses where they lounged on large, stone steps around a fountain that sprayed water twenty feet into the air. Pipes hugged the wall behind the water feature, and I followed them around another corner. It was less crowded here, and there were fewer lamps to light the way.

"Getting closer."

"To what?" Orla hissed. "Look, I'm far from being the smartest Riftkeeper, but even I know that this is stupid."

I stopped to look back at her.

"Orla," I said, "you're plenty smart."

She blushed and looked away.

"You weren't there for the rotsbane attack after Galahad released you," she mumbled.

"You all survived. Whatever you did can't have been that bad."

"I lit the steamcart on fire."

I took a moment to gather myself.

"Did anyone get hurt?"

"Well, no—"

"Then it was fine. You aren't stupid." I turned to lead the way down the street.

"But Tiernan—"

"Tiernan?" I spun back to face Orla again. "That guy? Mr. Broods-A-Lot? We care what he thinks?"

"He's only brooding because he's mourning Caitria." She wrapped her long, thin arms around herself. "He's still my friend."

My stomach lurched in a way that had nothing to do with the nasty Skal Galahad had used to form me.

"Friends aren't rude to each other, even when they're sad," I said. "Friends who treat you like garbage are actually just that. Garbage."

"Tiernan—"

"Is garbage," I snarled. "You're worth more than how he treats you."

I whisked into the shadows of an alley before Orla could stop me. She hesitated on the main street, and I tried to quash the rising guilt in my throat. Maybe what I had said was harsh, but if someone had told me that bad friends aren't actually friends, I could've avoided everything Linsey had put me through.

"Do you have bottles?" I tapped on a pipe that jutted out of the stone wall and dove down under the cobbled walkway.

Orla finally followed me into the alley and lifted her cloak to reveal a row of empty bottles swinging from her belt.

"*That*'s where you want to steal Skal from?" Orla blanched.

"Better than picking someone's pocket." I played with my fingernails. The diluted Skal in my veins felt like sludge, but it was still Skal and would do what I needed it to do.

"No, this is a lot worse! That Skal still belongs to someone!" Orla glanced back at the main street, but we were alone. The distant sound of laughter mixed with that of the fountain splashing. "This is the Baron's Skal. The Baron we need to *like* us if we want help getting north."

"No one named 'The Baron' has ever been a good guy." Maybe it was the fact that Skalterra gave me the freedom to be whoever I wanted, or maybe Sarah's comment at the Keel Watch Harbor library about being switched at birth was getting to me, but whatever it was, I liked this new Wren.

The fingernail on my right pointer finger elongated when I willed it to, and then sharpened and hardened into a steel point. I pressed it against the metal pipe and turned my wrist back and forth until I felt a small groove begin to form beneath my nail.

"That's a new trick," Orla mumbled. "I've never seen a Nightmare change themself like that before."

"Yes, you have. You watched me turn my tree trunk into tree legs, remember? It needs to be sharper." The metal of the pipe was thick, but it looked like copper, a relatively soft metal. I willed my steel fingernail to be stronger and sharper, then pressed into it.

The point punched through, and I grinned at Orla.

"Bottle." I held my free hand out to her. She gulped, but unclipped a rounded bottle from her belt. I imagined a small channel running through my fingernail, and the Skal flowed.

It poured out as a glowing pale-blue liquid that was thinner than water but thicker than steam. It fell into the bottle with a soft whisper, filling the glass with both liquid and gas that swirled up towards the bottleneck. Despite the weightless appearance of the Skal, the bottle felt heavier than I would have expected once it was full.

"Next." I passed the bottle and its swirling contents off to Orla. She traded me for an empty bottle.

"Does Ferrin know you can do this?" she asked.

"The fingernail thing?" I frowned at my makeshift siphon. "I'm not sure. Tiernan does, I think. He saw me make bone spikes on my arms when we fought the Grimguard. But if I can imagine it, I can be it. Or, at least, I haven't found the limit yet."

Orla was quiet for a moment.

"You can do all that, and yet you can't make a decent sword," she finally said.

I laughed.

"Forget making flails and swords out Skal," I said. "I can make flails and swords out of my arms!"

She flashed a reluctant smile, and traded me a new bottle for the filled one I now held.

"That would be good for fighting, but probably not much else."

"Good thing fighting is all Galahad needs me for." I grinned at Orla, but her smile had dissolved into a tight frown. She focused on the bottle in my hand.

"You're good for more than just fighting," she said. "You're also a good friend."

"Would you still be my friend if I had flails for arms?"

She smirked.

"Yes, Just–Wren." We traded bottles again. "And you'd still be a better friend than Tiernan. Because you're right. He is garbage."

"He is! Thank you!" The Skal flowing through my steel fingernail was making my hand warm. "Poor Fana, getting stuck with that guy."

"Especially after she had someone as wonderful as Caitria as her primary Riftkeeper. You would've loved Caitria," Orla insisted. "I hope the Grimguard killed her quickly. I hate to think about her in pain."

"I'm sorry." I didn't know what else to say. "I wish I could've known her too. I'm sure she went down a hero."

The face of the dead woman on my first night in Skalterra was still burned into my brain. I'd tried not to think about it since coming to terms with the fact that Skalterra was real.

That had been a real woman lying dead right in front of me.

"What do you think you're doing?" A gruff voice pulled me out of my reverie. A man in a maroon vest with matching goggles stared at us from the mouth of the alley.

"Oh," Orla gasped. "That's bad."

The man charged at us, and I tried to pull my fingernail from the pipe, but the heat of the siphoned Skal must've expanded the steel tip, because it didn't budge.

"By order of the Grand Barony, you're under arrest!"

"Orla!" I hissed. I yanked harder, but I was properly stuck.

"Make it smaller!" Orla yelped.

I tried, but it was hard to focus with the man in maroon bearing down on us. A bright red staff of Skalmagick erupted in his hands.

"Hold on!" Orla pulled her goggles into place and took a hearty swig of Skal. A green blade lengthened in her grip, and she brought it swinging down.

It sliced through my wrist, hot and painful. I cried out, but Orla was already pulling me down the alley as the guard gave chase.

"My hand!" I yowled, looking down at my wrist. Where there should have been blood, flesh flaked away from my arm in streams of ash.

"Grow a new one!" Orla pressed the Skal bottle into my remaining hand, and I took a sloppy sip as we rounded the corner in a sprint. The liquid dissolved the weight in my stomach, and new energy buzzed in my limbs as I pushed through the crowd waiting outside of a noodle house.

"Stop them!" the guard bellowed. Bright lights and new smells assaulted my senses from every angle, but I kept my focus on my wrist. I could grow a hand.

Orla looked back over her shoulder, and the panic in her eyes told me the guard was still tailing us through the thick crowd. We'd be easy to track. As diverse as the wardrobes here were, I was the only one with blue hair.

But as I looked down at my growing fingers, I realized my hair was a fixable problem. In fact, I could fix much more than just my hair.

I focused on one attribute at a time. If I changed too quickly, someone might notice. But if I did my hair first, then my eyes, then my nose, my chin, my clothes...

"Put your hood up." The deep voice that resonated in my throat didn't sound like my own.

"Who—" Orla yelped. She let go of me, and I raised a freshly grown finger to my lips.

"It's me! I changed my face! Go that way!"

We slipped down another alleyway. Orla yanked her hood up over her face just as the guard came around the corner. I met his eye, and gave a half-hearted wave.

He faltered, seemingly taken aback by the man standing before him. He craned his neck to look past us down the empty alley, then continued on through the crowd.

Orla sighed, and shook her hood off.

"That's a neat trick." She gestured towards my face, and I ran a hand down my cheek, feeling the shape of Liam's chin. His face was the first one I'd thought to change into. "What is *that*?"

I looked down at the perfect replica of Liam's Von Leer hoodie that I was now wearing.

"It's, um, a coat. Kind of." I couldn't get used to the sound of Liam's voice coming from my mouth. "I figured that since Galahad forms my clothes when he makes me, I probably have control over what they look like."

"It's hideous."

"I know."

"You're hideous too."

I grinned, and wondered if I had the same stupid smile on my face that Liam had given me so many times.

"Thank you." I pulled my fingers through my hair, imagining my hair lengthening as I did so and procuring a hair-tie to keep it out of my face. It reverted back to blue with no effort, and my face rippled beneath my skin as my preferred bone-structure returned. "Do you still have the Skal?"

Orla flicked her cloak back, revealing the four bottles secured to her belt.

"I still don't approve of your methods, by the way," she said, though she smiled in spite of herself. "Stealing is —"

She cut off, and her eyes flitted to something at the far end of the alley. She snapped her goggles into place, and a green blade fired to life. I whipped around, igniting my silver flail.

A cloaked figure staggered out of the deepest shadows of the alley. His clothes were tattered, and he walked with a heavy limp, but orange irises set against black sclera glowed bright above his dark cowl.

"Blue," the Grimguard croaked. An orange blade erupted in his hand as he took the first running steps towards us.

And then the orange blade turned to steam, and he fell forward, unconscious.

Fourteen

Advance Sports Medicine

Orla and I stood at the ready with our weapons humming in our hands, but the Grimguard remained face down on the dirty cobblestones. This was the first time I'd seen him in semi-decent lighting, but I was sure his cloak had been less tattered and muddy the last time we'd met.

Orla's blade sputtered out, and she pushed her goggles back with a knuckle.

"Is he dead?" she whispered.

"How should I know?" I kept my flail at the ready and tip-toed forward. I nudged the Grimguard's shoulder with the toe of my shoe, which was still modeled off of Liam's sneakers.

The Grimguard remained lifeless, and my flail dissipated with a crackle. I knelt down to roll him onto his back. His head lolled to the side, and his eyes stayed closed.

"Holy crap." I sat back to better survey his condition. Large portions of his leather armor and tunic had burnt away to reveal patches of burned torso. What wasn't crusted over continued to ooze blood and pus. Wounds puckered with inflammation, and the tell-tale signs of infection turned white skin red.

Tiernan's explosive the other night hadn't completely done in the Grimguard, but it had come close.

"Check his pulse," Orla whispered overhead. I pressed a tentative hand against his neck. The faintest of heartbeats pressed back.

"Alive."

Orla sighed and pulled her goggles back into place.

"Alright. Look away if you like. I'll make it quick." Her green blade reignited, and my mouth dropped open.

"Make *what* quick?" I positioned myself between her and the unconscious Grimguard. Her eyebrows drew together above her cracked goggles.

"He wants to kill Fana," she said. "This is what we signed up for as Riftkeepers. To *keep* the *Rift*, which he wants to open! With child murder!"

"That doesn't mean we murder a defenseless man!"

"He would kill us if the roles were reversed," Orla pointed out.

"That's what makes him the villain and us the good guys!"

Orla pressed her lips together.

"My mother was killed by Grimguards." As terrible as the words were, she looked more defeated than angry. "And if we leave him, he'll die anyway. It's kinder to put him out of his misery."

It was a good point. The way his injuries looked, it was a wonder he was still alive. I peeled his cowl away from his face, as if that might help him breathe easier. His pale skin there was unmarred and smooth, though his lips were dry and cracked.

"Orla, he's so young," I said, but it was hard to read Orla with her tinted goggles fixed over her eyes. "I was brought to Skalterra to protect Fana. I won't be a murderer."

What if he had a family somewhere? What if they never found out what happened to him, like with Liam and his parents and cousin? If Skalterra was real, that meant this Grimguard was too, and even if he was evil, I would not let him become someone else's Riley.

"You might not have signed up for this, but I did," Orla insisted.

"You signed up to kill a defenseless kid?"

Orla nodded, but her chin quivered. I set my jaw and rose to my feet.

"Fine," I said. "Do it."

She gulped.

"I will."

I stepped to the side, and Orla took my spot standing over the Grimguard, staring down at his unconscious body. Her knuckles whitened as she tightened her grip on her shaking blade.

She raised it, holding it directly over the Grimguard's head. For a second, I thought I might have misjudged her, but then the blade dissipated, and she staggered backwards, pushing her goggles up her forehead.

"Dammit, Wren." She hid her eyes behind her hand. "Then what do we do?"

I looked back towards the busy street. We hadn't come too far from the inn, and Orla was right when she'd said the Grimguard would die if we left him in the alley.

"Use your cloak to hide his injuries." I focused on the muscles in my arms, willing strength into my Nightmare form, and I managed to get the Grimguard half-way upright. Orla slipped her cloak over his head and adjusted its folds so that they hung over his festering burns.

"Great." She grunted as she slipped under his other arm to help carry him. "Now what?"

"We go to your room." I adjusted my grip on my side of the Grimguard. His dark-haired head lolled between us, and I wrinkled my nose. He smelled like dirt and sweat.

"Excuse you?" Orla leaned forward to glare at me around the Grimguard's chest. "My room?"

"We'll hide him there and treat his injuries as best we can."

"And if he follows us after we leave Vanderfall?"

"I think you might be overestimating our First Aid abilities. He's not following anyone anytime soon."

The streets had thinned out with the late hour, though we still received plenty of side-eyes as we dragged the Grimguard between us.

"Too much to drink." I smiled apologetically at an older man in a duster like Galahad's. He grunted and returned to his own drink at the street-side bar where he sat.

The Grimguard's feet dragged behind us as we walked, the toes of his leather boots bumping over cobblestones. I wasn't sure he would last long enough to make it to Orla's room, but by the time we pulled him into the lobby of the inn, ragged breaths were still forcing their way up from the back of his throat.

I nodded for Orla to lead the way up the stairwell, and again focused on strengthening my muscles under my imitation Von Leer hoodie. I took the bulk of the Grimguard's weight and hoisted him over my shoulder.

"I've got him," I grunted, and followed Orla up the stairs. Each step was a different height than the last, and I staggered up the stairwell with the Grimguard's head pressed against mine. We were almost to our floor when Orla doubled back into the stairwell, nearly knocking both me and Grimguard back down the steps.

"Tiernan," she hissed. "He's still outside of Fana's door!"

"So do something!" I whispered back.

She bit her lip, then nodded.

"Alright, but be quick. I don't know how long I can keep him distracted." Orla whisked back into the corridor and sprinted into the hall. "Tiernan, the Grimguard! He's climbing through Fana's window!"

I waited for the sound of Fana's door banging open before darting into the hall with the Grimguard. Tiernan's shouts mingled with Orla's frazzled warnings and Fana's shrieks of surprise. The Grimguard's boots had just passed the threshold of Orla's door when Fana's door slammed down the corridor.

"Are you trying to wake up the entire inn?" Tiernan's voice growled. "No one was out there!"

"Before he left for the Baron's mansion, Ferrin told me to test you." Orla injected her tone with a fake apology. "Don't worry. I'll tell him you did great. If there *had* been a Grimguard outside Fana's window, he wouldn't have stood a chance against that broom you threw."

I dropped the Grimguard onto Orla's bed, and it depressed under his weight.

"Is he dead yet?" Orla shut the door behind her as she came in.

"It's hard to tell in the dark." I stepped aside so as much light from the window would pour across the Grimguard's chest. "I think he bled on your cloak. I'm sorry."

"It was already dirty." She sipped from one of her glowing Skal bottles before handing it off to me. With a snap of her fingers, the wick of the bedside candle flashed green and then settled into a gentle orange flame.

Meanwhile, I extricated the Grimguard from Orla's cloak and held the bottle of Skal aloft so I could work by the light of its glow. My stomach turned at the sight of the oozing burns.

"How much medicine do you know?" Orla asked in a low tone.

"Not enough." I went to work unbuckling what was left of the Grimguard's armor. It resisted my pull, glued to his body by dried sweat and blood. I exhaled heavily to cover the sound of raw flesh unsticking from leather. "I did Sports Med in high school, but mostly we just shoved tampons up bloody noses."

"Right." Orla nodded importantly. "Then we find a tampon. What is that?"

"It doesn't matter. I don't think they'll help much here. I need fresh water, a towel, bandages, and the strongest alcohol you can find."

"I can get you water and alcohol, but my cloak will have to do for a towel and bandages. I'll be right back." She whisked out of the room, leaving me to extricate strips of the Grimguard's tunic from his wounds. With the leather and cloth pulled away, I could better see the festering wound that splashed across the Grimguard's torso. The gentle rise and fall of his chest made me wince. Even the tiniest movement looked painful.

The tendrils of burns reached towards his neck, and I leaned in closer to try to see where the injury stopped along the line of his collar bone.

His hand shot up from his side, and fingers wrapped around my neck. I froze with my hands hovering over the Grimguard's chest. His grip tightened as I raised my gaze from his collar bones to his face. He looked at me through his dark eyelashes. The whites of his eyes didn't look as black as I remembered them to be, and his irises were more amber than orange and lacked their usual light.

"Are you going to kill me?" His voice was hoarse and hardly louder than a whisper.

"Not if you don't kill me," I choked out against his grip.

His fingers relaxed, and his arm fell back against the moth-eaten sheets of Orla's mattress.

"You blew me up," he croaked.

"That was Tiernan. He blew me up too."

"Good."

He tried to sit, but I pushed him back against the mattress.

"Oh, no," I said. "You can't fight. Not like this. And if you go out into the hall, Tiernan will probably blow you up for good this time. Lucky for you, he doesn't know you're in here. So be good, lie back, and let me help you."

He glared at me but didn't have the energy to argue. His labored breathing worked its way through his nose, and his eyes darted around the room. He was probably looking for an escape, but he wouldn't have been able to fight Jonquil, let alone the Riftkeepers.

"Why?" he finally growled.

"Why am I helping you?" I sat back against the bedside table, taking care to avoid the candle. "Because I'm not a murderer."

"No, you just work for them."

I gave him a cold smile.

"Daithi was a murderer too." I reminded him. The Grimguard turned his head to the side so that he didn't have to look at me. "Do you have a name? And maybe an emergency contact in case you don't make it?"

The silence that passed between us was so prolonged, that I thought he might have fallen unconscious again, but then he spoke.

"Ciarán Grimguard, Servant of the Frozen God. And you, Blue?"

I bit the inside of my cheek.

"Wren Warrender, Prospective Von Leer Viking. Nice to meet you, Ciarán."

Ciarán gave a weak grunt in response and rolled his head back to face me. His black hair hung in his face, clinging to his forehead with sweat, and his black and amber eyes were wide. His chapped lips parted, like he was going to say something, but then the door creaked open, and Orla hurried in.

"I got the things, but—" She paused with her arms full of flasks. "Oh, gross, he woke up."

I took the bottles from her and gave the first one a tentative sniff. Alcohol burned my nostrils, and I gagged.

"You said to make sure it was strong." Orla shrugged.

"Please tell me that's for drinking," Ciarán rasped.

"I really wish I could say it was." I braced myself over his chest. "Try not to scream. If Tiernan hears—"

"I get it."

I handed Orla the Skal bottle to hold aloft for me, and she nodded to signal she was ready.

"Bottoms up," I mumbled.

The wound was the most shallow near his abdomen, and I gently poured the alcohol over the gashes in the skin there. Ciarán gritted his teeth and arched his back in a futile effort to escape the pain.

"Hold him down," I commanded. Orla obeyed, pressing against the Grimguard's shoulders, and I moved to the center of the wound at his chest, figuring it would be doing him a favor to get the most painful part over first.

Tears streamed down Ciarán's face, and he moaned through his clenched jaw. Orla reached for her discarded cloak and held it over his face to stifle his cries.

After a moment, his back relaxed against the mattress, and his arms went limp.

"Did you suffocate him?" I hissed.

Orla lifted her cloak to inspect the Grimguard.

"No, I think he passed out from the pain."

Good. It was probably better this way.

I alternated between water and alcohol, taking my time now that Ciarán was unconscious again. Orla cut her cloak into bandages, but I hesitated before applying them.

"He probably needs an antibiotic."

"I don't know this word." Orla frowned. "Is it like a tampon?"

"Something to fight the infection." I hovered my finger over the lines of red that ran under his unburnt skin. "Even if this heals, the infection could kill him."

Orla shook her head.

"The best we could do is bloodletting, but—"

"Bloodletting?" I repeated, finally tearing my eyes away from the Grimguard to gawk at Orla. "You still do that here?"

"How else are we supposed to fight infection?"

"You guys have magick! Doesn't the Skal do anything?" I asked. She looked away with a tight frown on her face. "I'm sorry. I'm not mad at you. It's not your fault Skalterra hasn't invented penicillin."

"You and your Keldorian words tonight," she sighed.

"Penicillin?" I let out a dry laugh. "It's not that fancy. It's basically mold."

"I'm sure we could find some mold somewhere. Maybe the underside of the mattress? Or in the lavatory down the hall?"

I gave a low chuckle.

"While I'm sure the underside of this mattress is disgusting, it's penicillium mold specifically. And even then, I have no idea how I'd purify it into something that would actually work." I leaned back against the table again, watching the rise and fall of Ciarán's chest. Sports Medicine had prepared me for rolled ankles and bloody noses, not extensive flesh wounds and pioneering antibiotics in a parallel realm. I'd done all I could. If Ciarán died, I would know it wasn't because I didn't try. "It's funny. I actually did my final project on penicillin last year in my biology class."

Orla nodded, but I knew the concepts of final projects and biology classes were probably as foreign to her as tampons.

"You're very smart, Wren Warrender," Orla whispered. The dull light of the bottle in her hands cast gentle shadows up her face to accentuate her cheekbones. "It's very impressive that you are a physician at such a young age. Unless it's just your Nightmare that appears young?"

I laughed absently, still watching the rise and fall of the Grimguard's mottled chest.

"I'm not a physician. Far from it," I said. "But yeah, I'm about as old as I look. I turned eighteen a few months ago."

Orla's face brightened in the Skal-light.

"The same as me! And you may not be a physician, but you sound like you know more than our experts, with your penicillin."

"It would be more useful if I could actually get him some." My eyelids itched, but I resisted the urge to pull at my eyelashes. Even if they'd grow back the next night when Galahad remade me, I didn't want Orla seeing me pluck.

I pulled the sleeves of my Von Leer hoodie down over my hands to help keep my fingers at bay, but then I pushed them back up, all the way to my elbows, so I could stare at my palms and forearms.

I didn't know the chemical composition of steel, but I'd still fashioned my fingernail into a metal siphon strong enough to puncture copper. My anatomy knowledge was rusty at best, but I'd still been able to grow shards of bone from my arms.

Maybe I didn't need to know how to make penicillin. Maybe *wanting* it would be enough.

With the exception of the scar on my palm, my skin was blemish-free.

"I have an idea," I whispered. The Skal I'd drank in the alley swirled inside me, warm and buzzing. I focused on it, still staring at my arms.

The first ring of mold rose from my skin near the inside of my elbow. It had a faint purple hue in the flickering candlelight, and its edges crept outwards until it brushed against the rounded edge of a second mold ring.

"Your arms!" Orla cried, stumbling away. "Are you doing that?"

A smile forced its way across my face.

"Penicillium," I breathed. The mold crawled down my arms, past my wrists and across my palms, itching as it went. "I need it to be potent and transferable."

I said it out loud as if to speak it into existence. I was in control. If I decided antibiotic mold sprouted from my skin, then it *would*, and it would *work.* Normal penicillium mold needed to be purified to create a usable antibiotic, but I wasn't making normal penicillium. I was making something better.

The mold reached my fingertips, and my veins buzzed with burning Skal. I turned my palms towards Ciarán and took a steadying breath. When I'd taken my boots off on the steamcart, they'd turned to dust on the floor. This was different. This was something *living.*

"It will be transferable," I said again, and pressed my hands against the raw, burnt mess of Ciarán's chest.

His wound was sticky and hot, but I ignored the lurch in my stomach to focus on the itching mold in my hands. It *would* work.

"Is anything happening?" Orla asked. I shook my head.

"I don't know. I might not be able to get it to—"

A spot of mold bloomed on an unmarred strip of Ciarán's skin.

"There!" Orla held the Skal bottle closer to the ring, the pale blue light highlighting its edges.

"Antibiotics." I grinned.

"And you're sure your mold is better than bloodletting?" Orla asked.

"Definitely, but bloodletting isn't off the table if he comes after us again."

Mottled, ringed patterns of purple spread between the wounds carved across Ciarán's chest. Normal penicillium mold would probably make him more sick, but I'd built this with the intention to heal, and I had to trust that it would.

"Bandages," I whispered, and Orla reached for the strips of her cloak she had prepared. I tried to ignore how clammy Ciarán's skin felt as I rolled him onto his side while Orla pulled the makeshift bandages tight around his back.

When we'd finally finished and double checked that Ciarán was still alive, we leaned against the window to survey our work. Orla sipped at a flask of leftover water while I rubbed at my arms. The mold had receded now that I didn't need it, but the body alterations had left me feeling dizzy and drained.

"Do you think he'll stop hunting us now that we've helped him?" Orla asked into her water flask.

"You know more about Grimguards than I do." I was glad Ciarán had stayed unconscious, though he was in for a real treat when he eventually woke up covered in mold. "Thank you, Orla. For not killing him. And for helping me, even after what his people did to your mom."

Her shoulder shifted against mine as she sighed.

"It's what she would've done too, to be honest." The candlelight caught the swoop of her nose and sent orange light dancing up her forehead. She smiled at the mention of her mother.

"What the hell is going on here?"

We both jerked our heads up at the voice, and Orla's water flask shattered against the wooden planks of the floor as she dropped it in surprise.

It could've been worse. It could've been Galahad or Tiernan. They would've killed the Grimguard without asking questions, but that didn't mean I was thrilled to see Ferrin standing in the open doorway.

Fifteen
Negotiation Theory

Ferrin's face was unreadable with the light of the corridor sconces at his back. He stood motionless, staring at the unconscious man on the bed.

"That's the Grimguard," he finally said. It wasn't a question, but I answered him anyway.

"Yes."

"He's in Orla's bed."

"He's used it more than I have. I think it might be his bed at this point." Orla watched her uncle with apprehension, her hands poised against the window sill, ready to propel herself into action if the need arose.

Ferrin yanked his goggles down over his eyes and held out a hand.

"I don't know where you got the Skal on your belt, and quite frankly, I don't think I want to, but you are going to hand it to me, and I'm going to end this."

I pushed Orla behind me and strode forward to stand between Ferrin and the bed.

"I didn't carry him all the way up here so he could be murdered."

Ferrin closed the door behind him.

"And we did *not* waste Skal bringing you here so you could save the man who wants to destroy both our realms!" he hissed through gritted teeth. "Why is he up here at all?"

"We found him injured in an alley while we were hiding from a Grand Barony guard." The longer I spoke, the quieter I got.

Ferrin ripped his goggles from his face.

"*What?*"

"They were angry that we stole Skal from the city supply," Orla explained.

Ferrin's gaze raked over Orla, looking again at the bottles of Skal on her belt, and he pressed the heels of his hands against his eyes.

"Galahad and I are securing Skal! From the Baron! Who you stole from and who probably won't give us Skal *or* passage to Riverstead now!" He pulled his hands down his face, and then paused with his fingers in his beard and his eyes trained on my chest. "Where the hell did you get that?"

I tugged at the edges of my Von Leer gear.

"It's called a hoodie. I willed it into existence, I think."

"Ferrin, you should see what Just-Wren can do—" Orla interjected.

"I can tell you what she *can't* do. She sure as hell can't offer an excuse good enough to explain the unconscious Grimguard in my niece's bed!" His eyes widened as his gaze lingered on Ciarán's bandaged chest. "Orla, is that your *cloak?*"

"We didn't have bandages!"

Ferrin's eyebrows had long-since disappeared into the shadows of his cockatoo hair, and his nostrils flared as he exhaled heavily through his nose.

"We're headed *north!*" His words strained with the effort of keeping quiet. "Into the *mountains!* Orla, you'll freeze! And we're supposed to be halfway to the Grand

Baron's mansion by now. We've been granted an audience, but this—"

Silence fell as we waited for Ferrin to find whatever words he was looking for, but they evaded him, and he settled for shaking his head again and pulling on his beard. The candle crackled on the bedside table.

"You can't kill him," I finally said.

"Why not?" Ferrin's eyes glinted.

"You just said we're on our way out of this city. He's in no condition to follow us. Once he's able to so much as sit up, we'll be long gone."

"And if he does follow us somehow—"

"We aren't murderers."

"Wren Warrender, you don't know us." A low growl rattled on the edges of Ferrin's words.

"Mother wouldn't do it." Orla's voice wavered.

Ferrin blinked in the candlelight.

"I knew your mother longer than you—"

"Then you know she'd never kill someone who couldn't defend themself."

"And that got her killed, and nearly me with her."

"She knew what she signed up for. So do I, and I'm *not* here to kill defenseless boys."

Ferrin's eyes darted to the Skal on Orla's belt, and her and I both tensed as we prepared for him to lunge. But then his shoulders fell, and he ran a hand over his tired face.

"I can't fault you for being Bryony's daughter. Grab your pack, Orla. We aren't coming back." He stepped aside to make room for us to pass into the hallway. "The Grimguard is lucky I don't have time to fight you both, but if he pursues us, I'll make him wish he *had* died tonight."

Orla slung her rucksack over her shoulders and filed out past Ferrin, but I stayed put and pointed to the hall.

"After you," I said.

"You may be useful, but you're also a nuisance," Ferrin snapped, but he obeyed and moved towards the door. "And change your clothes. You'll stick out like a ramstag in a skallery if you go out in that."

Ferrin led the way out of the room, and I shook out my shoulders, focusing on shifting my clothes back to the leather armor and cloak Galahad had originally summoned me in.

"A ramstag?" I looked to Orla for explanation.

"Keldori doesn't have ramstags?"

"I don't think so."

I glanced back at the Grimguard as I closed the door behind me. Hopefully he lived, and hopefully I'd never know it since my goal was to never see him again.

"Orla, get the others. Tell them we're leaving." Ferrin had been the nice one. Gentler than Galahad, kinder than Tiernan, but I'd disappointed him. While I stood by my actions, I couldn't help the guilt that rose in my chest.

"I'm—"

"I used to be like you." He didn't sound angry, but I still felt like I was in trouble. "Maybe I still am, since I'm leaving the Grimguard alive when we both know he'd kill us all without hesitation, but if you wrap my niece up in something like this ever again, I'll feed you to a rotsbane."

"She's more capable than any of you give her credit for."

"I love Orla like she's my own daughter, but she wasn't made for Riftkeeping." Ferrin pinched the bridge of his nose. "My sister never wanted this life for her."

"She can make her own decisions," I asserted. "She helped save a life tonight."

"And it remains to be seen if that's a good thing or not." Ferrin turned to watch Orla harass Tiernan outside of Fana's room. "I like you, Just-Wren. So does my niece. Please don't ruin that. I'd hate to have to hurt you."

The cobbled streets of Vanderfall had thinned out, but it was still busy enough that no one looked twice as we moved as a group between lamps and bridges. Most of the shops had closed up, and the remaining crowds congregated around the few taverns and eateries that remained open.

The night air was cool, but the fresh Skal swirling in my belly warmed me from the inside out. We'd disposed of the evidence of our thievery by drinking all the Skal we'd stolen, and while its magick heated my veins, Orla shivered in the nighttime chill without her cloak. Luckily, Tiernan didn't seem to care enough to ask about its whereabouts and walked with a protective arm around Fana's thin shoulders. The hem of her robes had soaked several inches deep after being dragged through puddles.

Ferrin paused ahead of a brightly lit intersection and turned around to face us with a grim expression.

"From here on, I'll do the talking. Stay close to Fana. Touch nothing. And remember, Wren. No one can know you're a lucid Nightmare. If anyone asks, you're a Quillguard like Orla and me. Even if they do find out you're a Nightmare, do not tell anyone your full name."

"My name? Why?"

"Names give control. It's how Galahad is able to drag you back here every night."

"Wouldn't it be safer to send the Nightmare home?" Tiernan asked. "If the Baron finds out she's lucid, we're all dead."

"But who will you blow up if Wren isn't here?" Orla shot back.

"I'll make do." Tiernan's yellow eyes glinted dangerously under his hood.

"The Nightmare stays," Ferrin said. "She'll be useful if things *do* go sideways. Now stay close, and for the love of the Three Magicians, behave."

He strode around the corner, and Tiernan shot me a dirty look as he followed.

My irritation with Tiernan dissipated as we turned. The street was wider here, offering a clear view of the mansion that sat on the hill at the center of the city. The monument looked more like a steam plant than a mansion, and it towered over the surrounding buildings. Pipes and plumes broke up copper walls that reflected the dusky blue glow of cascading Skal. The arching windows of the mansion glowed a burnt red, and the moat that segregated the building from the rest of the city mirrored the color. Steam hissed from pipes and vents, giving the illusion that the Grand Baron's mansion was alive.

"Where'd they get all that Skal?" I hissed, watching the liquid pour from the sides of the edifice.

"There are seven known major Skalsprings across Skalterra," Ferrin explained without looking back. "Each one is owned and protected by one of the Seven Provinces. The locations of six of those springs are kept secret by those who protect them. Only the Grand Barony was bold enough to set their capital building right on top of theirs."

"Why would they do that?"

"Because no one is dumb enough to steal from the Grand Barony," Tiernan grunted. "Except you, apparently."

The stolen Skal churned in my stomach as the mansion loomed overhead, and Ferrin stopped at the edge of the moat. Across the water, a guard in a window nodded, and steam hissed as metal creaked. The mansion wall directly ahead unlatched from the side of the building. Gears cranked, chains clanged, and Skal whistled as the drawbridge lowered to greet us.

The cobblestone underfoot quaked with the weight of the bridge slamming against the road. Ferrin strode forward, and Tiernan rushed to be the first to follow him, still holding Fana at his side. Their footsteps echoed against the metal walkway.

"Come on, Quillguard." Orla winked at me as she used my new alias. "This makes us pretend cousins, doesn't it?"

"Only if you don't announce it to the entire Barony, my niece," Ferrin murmured under his breath before flashing an assured grin at the blank-faced guards who watched us from the overhead walkway.

"Nightmares?" I gave a half-skip to catch up to Ferrin.

"Probably. The Baron's known to employ a mix." He put a reassuring hand between my shoulders and guided me into the entry hall of the Baron's mansion. "And there will be plenty more."

Skal cascaded down the walls on either side of us, sounding more like falling sand than water. The slippery hiss echoed through the high-ceilinged chamber, and gears groaned as the drawbridge returned into its raised position. It grated into place, leaving us in the dim blue light of the falling Skal. The only way was forward, up steep steps of stone that led to open doors.

"Quillguard," I practiced in a whisper. "And I'm from the Second Sentinel."

"Good work," Ferrin said, "but most people don't go around mumbling their titles and hometowns under their breath."

"Most people aren't constructs of dirt and magic." Even if there had been guards in the hall, they would have struggled to hear me over the echo of the waterfalling Skal.

"Everybody ready?" Ferrin stopped at the top step, and Orla and Tiernan snapped into position on either side of Fana. "Guard our backs, Wren."

I fell back past the others. Fana's brown eyes were wide under her hood, and I gave her a reassuring smile. Ferrin surveyed us over his shoulder, gulped, and led the way into the grand chamber.

A single waterfall of Skal rushed down the far wall like a curtain before slipping down the steps of a raised dais in streams and collecting in glowing basins that lined the throne room.

And "throne room" was the best descriptor I could come up with. At the top of the dais, in front of the waterfall, a woman sat in a massive chair made of elaborately twisted metal. Leather trousers hugged every curve of her legs and hips, which were made to look even curvier by the black corset that cinched her waist. She shook back the wide sleeves of her white blouse so she could better pin back her long ringlets of bright red hair.

Her efforts did little to hold the curls, and most of them sprung back into place around the goggles atop her head, but she didn't seem to notice as she stood up from the throne to survey us through the monocle that sat wedged between her brow and cheek.

"I was getting nervous for your friend, Ferrin." Her voice rang out despite the hissing of the falling Skal behind her. "I thought maybe you'd thought better of your efforts here and turned tail."

"I'd never do you the disservice of leaving Galahad in your care." Ferrin may have had his back to me, but I could tell by his tone that he was flashing the woman a grin.

I'd been too busy staring at the woman and her throne room to notice Galahad seated on the bottom step of the dais. A mammoth of a man stood over him, keeping him seated with a large hand planted firmly on top of Galahad's head. The man's muscles strained against leather armor, and dark tattoos stood out down one arm. He ruffled Galahad's silver hair when he caught me staring, and Galahad scowled.

The woman signaled for Ferrin to step aside, and he obeyed with the slightest hint of a hesitation. Fana hunched her shoulders under the woman's ice-blue stare.

"Fana, the Divine Sovereign Fireld," Ferrin said, "meet Tamora Alarbus, Baron of the Grand Barony."

"And she's the last one?" Tamora's lips pulled into a half-smile, and she adjusted her monocle. The high heels of her black leather boots clicked against each slate step of the dais as she descended. Up close, I could see the smattering of freckles that splashed across her flawless porcelain skin.

"The last Sovereign," Ferrin confirmed.

"Who else knows?" Tamora pulled back Fana's hood to beam down at her.

"The Riftkeepers you see in this room, our families, and the few who hunt us."

Tamora drew away.

"You're telling me that the integrity of the Seven Provinces rests on this child and *no one* outside your little cult knows?" She placed a hand on her chest in faux-scandalization. "Ferrin, my pet, you flatter me letting me in on this little secret, but I fail to see why I should part with my hard-earned Skal and resources to help you, especially with rotsbane attacks on the rise. I had four steamcarts worth of export sucked into oblivion just this week alone. I don't have the supply left to be handing out charity."

"Skalterra is on the brink of—"

"Collapse?" Tamora's red curls flew as she twirled to cut Ferrin off. "I don't give a ramstag's hide about Skalterra, Ferrin. I care about Skal, something you are asking me to part from and something that Keldori is teeming with. Why shouldn't I kill the Sovereign and open the door to the other side myself?"

She spun again, this time towards Fana, and pulled her goggles into place over her monocle as she did. A scimitar of red extended from her grip until the tip of it balanced inches from Fana's nose.

A golden rapier erupted from Tiernan's hand, the handle guard wrapping up his wrist and arm. He batted away Tamora's curved blade and stepped between her and Fana.

"You will not threaten the Divine Sovereign," he growled.

"You come here asking for aid and would raise a weapon to me in my own home?" Tamora swung her sword to rest it on her shoulder as she surveyed Tiernan with a tilted head. "You who claimed to have no Skal? What wicked trick is this, Ferrin?"

"It's not a trick." Ferrin put his hands up in surrender. "Please, we are trained to protect the Sovereign, and Tiernan must have some residual Skal left in his system. He's young. You can't—"

"I can't *what?*" Tamora hissed. "Can't expect my guests to treat me with respect in my own home?"

"No, you—"

"Can't demand honesty from those who would ask me to part with my hard-earned resources?"

"No—"

"Can't kill the Sovereign here and now?" Tamora's round face split into a grin. "Release the Frozen God myself and give us all unfettered access to Keldori and its Skal?"

A second scimitar appeared in her free hand, but her smile slipped at the sound of Galahad laughing from where he sat on the dais step. It was a labored chuckle, and I noticed the sheen of sweat on his forehead for the first time.

"The Lyrian thinks something is funny?" Tamora mused. She kept her Skal-swords pointed at Tiernan but turned her goggled gaze to Galahad.

"I thought you'd have the business acumen of your old man, but I guess that didn't pass down quite as easily as his hair color," Galahad rasped. "Or maybe you're still too young?"

Tamora's cheeks tinged red.

"I'm flattered you think me young, though we must all seem like such children to someone old enough to remember Tulyr before its fall. Alas, your seniority does not give you the right to speak to me so callously. Titus, put him with the others."

The gargantuan man dragged Galahad forward, and shoved him towards Tiernan. Tiernan let his sword dissipate before he accidentally skewered Galahad on its point, and Orla helped to steady the old man.

"If you kill the Divine Sovereign, you'll release Saergrim from his prison!" Ferrin shouted. "Not even you are foolish enough to think you would stand a chance against the Frozen God."

"The Frozen God is just a man, despite what his nickname suggests. And I fear no man, Quillguard." Tamora turned away to climb the dais back to her throne. Her swords evaporated as she fell back into the seat of twisted bronze, and she blew a loose curl away from her goggles. "The audacity of you and your cult of Riftkeepers is to be admired. Genuinely, I do mean that. But I'm bored of Skalterra, I'm tired of rotsbane sucking my exports dry, and I'm done with this conversation. This next chapter will be fun. I'm sorry you won't be here to see it."

Tamora raised both hands in front of her, and I automatically looked to the floor. I'd seen enough movies to be wary of secret trapdoors. However, Ferrin's shouted warning brought my attention snapping back upwards.

The waterfall behind Tamora glowed red, and an armored figure stepped out from the cascading liquid. A scimitar like Tamora's lengthened in his hand, and he regarded us with blank eyes as he stepped down the dais towards us.

"Stop playing," Ferrin hissed. "You know a Nightmare isn't going to stop us."

But then another Nightmare stepped from the curtain of Skal on Tamora's other side. And another. The streams that ran along the perimeter of the room glowed too, and Skal ran off the shoulders of Nightmares rising from the basins.

"Kill them all." Tamora settled back into her throne and crossed one leg over the other. "Tonight, Skalterra is freed from the prison the Four Magicians locked us in."

Green flashed in Orla's hands as she procured a sword and shield. Ferrin grimaced and followed suit.

"Where the hell did you all get Skal?" Galahad growled. He leaned heavily on Orla, unable to stand on his own, and I wondered what Tamora had done to him to make him look so ill.

A silver flail formed in my hand, and I forced myself to turn away from Tamora on her throne so I could protect us from the back.

"I found the Skal." I kept my eyes on the Nightmares marching closer.

"I helped," Orla admitted somewhere behind me. If I died here, I would wake up back at home, but there was no telling what sort of new world I would be waking to if Fana died with me, if the monsters of this world could make their way into mine.

"Ah, so *you* were the thieves my guardsman caught siphoning Skal from the city's supply," Tamora sang.

"You *what?*" Galahad fumed.

"I thought he had to have been mistaken when he mentioned blue hair," Tamora said, and I blushed. "But here you are, armed with the very Skal you stole. No matter. Justice will be swift. Nightmares, kill the girls first."

She lowered her hand, and the blank-faced Nightmares descended as one.

Sixteen
Intro to Economics

The worst part about the Nightmares was the silence. There were no battle cries, no grunts, no yelling of commands to their comrades.

Just the slippery hissing of falling Skal behind Tamora's throne as body after body descended on us.

Tiernan cried out behind me, splitting the horrible silence, but I kept my focus on the Nightmares attacking from the back.

They moved as one, rushing at me in tandem with Tamora's scimitars in hand. I had banked on dodging in my fight with Ciarán in the woods. If I did that here, Fana and Galahad would be vulnerable.

I tried forming a shield like Orla's, but ended up with a second flail. I flung it at the nearest Nightmare and willed extra strength into my muscles to brace for the oncoming onslaught. My arms and legs bulged under my tunic and greaves, and Nightmares collapsed into dust clouds beneath my remaining flail only for new Nightmares to quickly replace them.

"Tamora, stop this!" Galahad bellowed. His back jostled against mine, and gold and green flashed in my periphery as Orla and Tiernan fought back against the onslaught. "We aren't the enemy!"

"No, you are just thieves and liars!" Tamora sang.

"You'll ruin the Barony if you free the Frozen God!"

"I will not take advice on how to run a province from a Lyrian of all people!" Tamora called.

A fresh wave of Nightmares fell over me, and pain ripped through my arms as I willed my bones to form the lethal spikes I'd used to fight Ciarán. White spikes tore through muscle, skin, and leather, and I drove them into the nearest Nightmares.

They weren't *real*, I had to remind myself as the Nightmares dissolved into ash. Even if the resistance of flesh against weapon felt real, I wasn't killing anyone. If anything, I was freeing them from a poor night's sleep.

I wondered if I knew any of them. If Linsey or Liam or even Gams might be unwittingly piloting the Nightmares I was skewering. A scimitar cut through my thoughts and my greaves to graze my thigh.

Better armor, I told myself as I ran my bone shards through the Nightmare who'd nicked me. I'd made a Von Leer hoodie. I could make better armor.

Leather turned to kevlar, but why stop there? The Skal in my veins lost its warmth as I burned through it, but I wasn't done. I needed more. I searched for more magick inside me, feeling for its familiar buzz.

I found it in my chest, trickling in from an unseen source. It had the same sludgy feeling as the Skal Galahad had formed me out of at the beginning of the night, but it would have to do. I drew on it, and my skin itched and crawled as it thickened into heavy scales.

Galahad slumped against my back and slid to the floor, though I wasn't sure how he'd been hit. Orla cried out in pain, but I couldn't look away from the descending Nightmares. For each one I destroyed, there was a new one to take its place before the former's ash had even settled.

The gold to my right sputtered out as Tiernan fell. Ferrin shifted, trying to fill the space left open, but there was less and less room to maneuver. Less room to fight.

Tamora had an endless supply of Skal and Nightmares. We couldn't fight them all.

But we *could* fight Tamora.

I threw my flail away into the crowd of Nightmares.

Armor, I told myself. Gray and green scales peeked at me through the tears in my clothes. I pulled on the diluted Skal I could still feel trickling into my system. *Strength. Speed.*

Pain lanced my fingers as each one elongated into a talon, and I tore into the crowd of Nightmares, pushing past Orla and Ferrin. I kept my eyes on Tamora's bright red hair as I ripped a path of Skal and ash through their ranks. Titus, the large man who'd held Galahad, stood between me and the throne, but he stumbled back at the sight of my bone spikes, dyed red by my own blood.

To her credit, Tamora sat unfazed as I pressed a spike against her throat. She rolled her eyes behind the monocle and raised a lazy hand.

The room stilled behind me, but I kept my boot on the lip of the throne and my spike at the ready.

"Now, aren't you disgusting?" Tamora drawled. Her eyes raked over my arm spikes, my kevlar armor, my talons, and the scales that crept up my neck and to my face. "I should've known what you are when you walked in here with blue hair, Nightmare. What's your real name, then?"

"You may call me Blue," I said with a wry smile, remembering Ferrin's warning about sharing my full name.

"Ferrin, you know lucids are illegal." Her voice was light and airy, though she remained tense underneath me.

"What are you going to do about it?" Ferrin grunted. "Kill us harder?"

Tamora's red lips twisted.

"I could feed this one to a rotsbane. We've got one under the mansion. Would you like to see?"

"You're going to give us passage to where we want to go." I pressed the spike tighter against her throat. "And you are going to give us the Skal we need to get there."

"You're formidable, I'll give you that," Tamora conceded. "But you won't last. Your Skal's almost gone. Just look at what you did to your poor nocturmancer. Bled him damn near dry of his Skal. If this temporary threat upon my life is my only reason to help you, then you have nothing."

I glanced back at Galahad where he was collapsed on the floor. Had I done that? I didn't remember hitting him.

"You'll help us because Ferrin is right." I twisted back towards Tamora. I could worry about Galahad later. "If you release the Frozen God, or if we fail to protect Fana, your kingdom is ruined."

"Kingdom?" A red eyebrow arched over Tamora's monocle.

"Barony. You'll ruin your barony."

"Oh? And you know all about keeping a barony running?"

"Not really," I admitted, "but I know enough about supply and demand, and that's what this place is built on, right?"

"Supply and demand?" Tamora mulled over the words for a moment. "Explain."

"You have power because you have Skal and other people need Skal. You have supply. They have demand." I pointed at the waterfall behind her throne. Hunger rumbled in my stomach at the sight of the Skal. I wanted it. I *needed* it. But I forced myself to focus on Tamora. "If Fana dies, and Keldori with all its Skal opens up, you don't have control over supply, and they don't need you anymore."

Tamora scoffed.

"Even if I lose control of the Skal supply, I still own every steamtrail across Skalterra. No one has technology as advanced as ours. We will expand my province into Keldori—”

“Steamtrail? You mean the railroads? I don’t think Keldori will be as impressed with those as you think.”

“Your land doesn’t stand a chance against the technology of the Grand Barony,” Tamora sneered. “The Keldorians will have no choice but to bow to me and—”

I laughed, forcing as much false confidence into the sound as I could. I drew my spikes away from the Baron, and pushed off her throne with my boot. I did not know who this new, threatening, scaly Wren was, but I liked being her, as hungry as she was.

“I’m almost tempted to let you try just to watch.”

Tamora’s gaze flitted away from me, and she locked eyes with Titus. I took the moment to look towards my friends. Tiernan was still on the floor, but he was breathing. Fana hid behind Ferrin, clutching the straps of his leather armor in her fists. Orla’s short hair ran with blood, and she held Galahad in her lap on the floor.

Ferrin stood with his blazing sword ready as he stared up at me with a new apprehension. I gulped and felt my scales sink back into my skin. My burning thirst for Skal dampened just a little as they did.

“Congratulations, Nightmare.” Tamora clapped her hands, and I spun to face her again as she stood. “Very few people are able to convince me to change my mind once it’s made, and you’ve just become one of them. We leave tonight. Let’s take the river to avoid any rotsbane.”

“We?” Ferrin growled.

“Of course. If the future of my barony rests on the survival of this child, then Titus and I will join you to help ensure she, and my province, stay alive.” She strode down her dais, and the legion of Nightmares silently split to let her through. She stopped in front of Ferrin and Fana. “Your Nightmare is fascinating. I look forward to learning more about her. Titus, take them to the docks.”

She stalked past, stepping over Tiernan's splayed legs, and exited through the large doors we'd entered from. Ferrin turned to tend to Tiernan and helped him into a sitting position.

"I told you, didn't I?" Orla sang. "I said you should see the things Just-Wren can do."

"Yes, it was quite something, wasn't it?" Galahad's soft rasp was labored and weak. "How long have you been hiding those tricks?"

I faltered as I walked down the dais towards them.

"You're the Nightmare expert. You didn't know I could do that?" I looked at the passive Nightmares that stood at the ready around us, then at Galahad where he lay in Orla's lap. "What's wrong? Are you hurt?"

"You took too much," Galahad wheezed.

"Too much what?" My talons retracted back into fingernails, but Ferrin kept his sword raised.

"Skal, dammit!" Galahad spat. "You did the same thing the other night in the woods, didn't you? I thought it was the running that was exhausting me, but it was you, bleeding me dry."

I thought back to the magick I'd felt dripping into my chest and how I'd pulled on it. I hadn't realized it had been the magick that flowed between Galahad and me. I hadn't realized I would hurt him.

I put my hands up in surrender.

"I'm sorry, I didn't know."

Galahad and Ferrin shared a look, and when the latter nodded, Galahad turned back towards me while Ferrin watched Titus where he lurked near the throne.

"We can talk about it later," Galahad growled. "For now, it's best you go home. The Baron folded too easy, and I don't like the way she was looking at you."

"Wait, but—"

"Goodnight, Wren. We'll see you on the river."

And the Baron's throne room slipped away.

Seventeen
Anxiety and Stress Disorders

Either I was bad at research, or the internet had an upsetting lack of easy-to-follow resources on using flails in battle. I leaned against the wooden railing of the shop's back deck, enjoying the heat of the summer sun mixed with the cool marina breeze as I spent my lunch break scrolling through videos.

So far, Live-Action Role Players seemed to be the leading experts on how to use a flail, though the ones they swung around in their medieval-styled battles had a lot more cushioning than the one I was trying to get used to in Skalterra.

"Wren Warrender." Galahad's voice, weak and raspy, prodded at the back of my head, and I nearly dropped my phone into the water below in surprise.

"I can't sleep right now," I snapped. "I have work."

"Don't get your leathers twisted," Galahad growled. "I'm here to tell you we won't need you for a few nights."

"What?" I straightened up and looked around. I hated talking to someone I couldn't see. Where was I supposed to glare? "I just saved all our lives! What do you mean you don't need me?"

"You nearly killed me last night."

"You need me." I jammed my phone in my pocket, and then pulled it back out, still unsure where to look.

"Oh, yes. You made it clear you're a valuable weapon, but the Baron is just as interested in that as we are. We don't need her studying you for personal gain, or trying to figure out your name and pulling you under her control."

"That's stupid."

"It's not—"

"Let me talk to Ferrin. He'll listen."

"Ferrin's studies haven't advanced as far as Nocturmancy, so you're stuck with me unfortunately."

I scowled at the harbor, stewing in frustration.

"You need me," I repeated. It was the only argument I had.

"Wren Warrender, here I thought you wanted nothing to do with Skalterra." I hated the smug lilt in his gravelly voice, but not as much as I hated that I wanted to go back.

"Don't flatter yourself," I spat. "Keldori gets boring when you can't turn into a scaly lizard lady."

"You turning into a scaly lizard lady nearly killed me. Even if I wanted to, I don't have the magick left to bring you here. For now, enjoy your nights off."

I mumbled a colorful goodbye that I wasn't sure Galahad was still around to hear. The shop door creaked open behind me, and I made room for Liam at the railing.

"Were you yelling at someone out here?" he asked.

"It was a video," I lied and half-heartedly waved my phone at him.

"Larping?" He grinned at my screen. "We've got a club at Von Leer, and I know the guy in charge. Do you want his number?"

I jammed my phone into my pocket before Liam could snoop any further. A few days ago, I might've replied with some irritated quip, but I didn't have the energy to snap at Liam anymore.

"I don't do clubs," I said. "If you're out here, is my break over?"

I whisked towards the back door.

"My uncle found Riley's truck."

I froze.

"Oh." I turned back to look at him, but he kept his back to me as he leaned against the deck railing. "Is that good or bad?"

"Neither. It was on Von Leer's campus, which was where he was seen last, so it doesn't really offer any new information. Teddy drove it back yesterday, so some of us were going to take it to the cove tonight and have a bonfire for Riley."

"But isn't it evidence?" I asked. "Shouldn't the police look it over?"

"Maybe, but there's no official investigation. My aunt and uncle don't want one."

"Why not?"

He shrugged, and when he finally turned to look at me, he forced a smile.

"Wish I knew. Anyways. Tonight, the cove. Did you want to come? I know you don't know Riley, but you've been so helpful in the search. His friends might want to meet you."

The guilt and shame that crept in my stomach felt like Galahad's diluted Skal from the night before.

"I haven't been that helpful."

Liam took my half-confession as humility and laughed.

"Sabrina is coming here after work. If you promise not to fall asleep at the beach, you can go with us."

"I'm not going to fall asleep." I glowered at him.

"Okay, fine. If you really *must*, you can fall asleep. Lucky for you, I'm pretty good at getting you up those stairs." He beamed at me and flexed his arm in jest.

"Oh, my god," I growled and made to exit back into the shop again. "I'm not going to fall asleep, and if I do, leave me on the beach!"

The sound of his laughter followed me all the way to the register.

Gams was so thrilled that I'd agreed to go to the bonfire that she called Mom to let her know I was officially "making friends". Her voice echoed from the stairwell behind me, loud enough to be heard all the way across the shop at the ice-cream stand, and I avoided Liam's gaze.

"Shut up," I growled at him when we finally made our exit to the street.

"I didn't say anything!"

"You were about to."

"Never. I don't tease my friends."

I swatted at him with the hoodie I had draped over my arm, and he danced out of the way, cackling.

Sabrina leaned against the hood of an old gray pick-up truck. It was smaller than I expected, with a rusted dent in the front bumper and enough stickers in the back window to make me question just how much window could be obscured and still be considered road-legal. Two stand-up paddleboards stuck out of the truck bed.

"Got the boards in the back already!" Sabrina sang. "Xander and Molly are already there, I think, and Pax, Fiona, and Luke are on their way!"

I faltered on the sidewalk as Liam got into the driver's seat.

"That's a lot of people." I tried to sound casual. It wasn't too late. I could still cancel, but Sabrina shrugged me off.

"They're nice. You'll like them."

I shuffled into the middle seat of the truck cab, and Liam apologized as he reached into my space to grab the stick shift. Sabrina slid in on my other side, and I pressed my knees together, trying to be smaller. I cast one last, wistful glance at the shop. Jonquil watched us from the other side of the glass window, her tail flicking as we pulled away from the curb.

Sabrina and Liam passed the drive with idle small talk. They seemed to be avoiding the topic of Riley, though I caught Sabrina gently patting the dashboard several times, as if doing so somehow brought her closer to the missing man.

Liam, meanwhile, kept his trademark grin in place, but his brow remained knotted as he watched the road. When the conversation lulled, the silence fell heavy until Sabrina would inevitably break it.

We pulled off the main highway and onto backroads. Flashes of sparkling blue winked at us through the trees that lined the drive, but the ocean didn't seem to be getting any nearer. When Liam pulled into a wooded, gravel parking lot, I recoiled in my seat.

"Where's the beach?" I demanded. The cramped truck cab was suddenly stifling.

Sabrina swung her legs out of the cab and dropped to the gravel.

"The beach is down there." She jerked her head in the direction of the forest and went to tend to the paddleboards.

Liam exited on my other side, going to help Sabrina lift the first board from the truck bed. Misplaced panic, warm and unwelcome, welled in my chest as I eyed the dark trees. They swayed in the sea breeze, moving in a way that made them look like a single organism.

"But the boards—" I tried to say through a tightening throat.

"They're light, don't worry!" Liam called from the back. His voice sounded distant and muted, hard to hear over the roaring of blood in my ears.

A red SUV was parked a few spots away. Whoever had driven it might already be in the woods.

No.

That was silly.

No one was waiting for us in the woods.

The woods were safe.

Liam and Sabrina were—

Metal rang out behind me as Sabrina accidentally swung a paddle into the side of the truck. She shouted an apology, but the sound had brought my thundering heart into my throat.

I was not afraid of the woods. I was Just-Wren. Nightmare. The one who had brought the Grand Baron to her knees.

But the woods didn't know that.

And this... This was a trick. It had to be. It had been last time.

No.

I forced myself out of the truck cab. It was in my head. Liam was my friend. Gams had said so to Mom on the phone.

But Linsey had also been my friend, and for so much longer. And I had been nothing but rude to Liam since I'd met him.

A door slammed shut, and Liam came around the front of the truck with a board under his arm.

"Inflatable, see?" He gave the board a shrug to show off its light weight. "We'll be fine. If you could grab the paddles, though—"

"No." I spat the word. I hadn't meant for it to be an attack, but I couldn't take it back now.

"Then take a board, and let's get moving." Sabrina came up behind me with the second board under her arm. "Molly and Xander are waiting."

Waiting. In the woods?

No, the woods were safe. Safe. It was daytime. I'd fought the Grimguard in the woods and at night.

But as real as Skalterra was, that had still, in a way, been a dream. And this felt too real.

This felt too much like graduation night.

I stared at the board under Sabrina's arm, and then at the paddles on the ground.

I wanted to go to the beach with them. I wanted to meet Riley's friends. I wanted to have one night where I could relax and feel normal and maybe forget about Grimguards, barons, and rotsbane.

But I could not go through those woods.

More importantly, I couldn't let Liam and Sabrina know why. I couldn't let them see the mess of a human that I was hiding.

"I said no." It was more of a snarl this time, and Sabrina's eyebrows jumped up into her strawberry curls. "I changed my mind. I don't want to go."

"Wren—" Liam started, but I whirled around to face him and cut him off.

"You didn't say there'd be so many people," I accused. "Or that we'd have to walk there."

"It's really not that far," Sabrina said.

"That's not the point!" My voice rose, but it was as if someone else was talking. It wasn't me yelling at Liam and Sabrina. I'd never yell at them, not over something so trivial. "You both lied! And the road was windy, and I don't feel good, and after we get down there, we're going to have to walk back up when we're done!"

Liam and Sabrina exchanged a look. Liam's raised eyebrows told me he was taken aback, but the wrinkle of Sabrina's nose indicated something closer to disgust.

"So wait here. See you in a few hours." Sabrina maneuvered one of the paddles into her free arm and turned towards the wooded path. "Come on, Liam. If she changes her mind, she can find us."

I leaned against the truck, relieved to have temporarily won, but burning with panic and embarrassment. I'd have to call Gams to come get me. She'd understand.

I waited for Liam to follow Sabrina, but he came back to the truck and heaved his board back into the bed.

"What're you doing?" I snapped.

"Liam?" Sabrina called from the pathway.

"I'll meet you there!" He waved at Sabrina and went to tighten the straps that held the paddleboard in place. "I'll take Wren back to Ethel's."

Sabrina blew a curly lock of hair from her face and rolled her eyes as she turned away. Liam smiled at me over the truck bed. I glowered back.

"Grab that paddle for me?" he asked.

I stooped to grab the paddle from the ground and place it next to the board. The panic was gone. I was safe. I would not be going into the forest. Instead, shame burned at my every fiber.

I was silent as I slid into the passenger seat, and I stared straight ahead as Liam backed us out of the parking spot.

We went back up the windy road, and were several miles down the highway before I couldn't stand the silence any longer.

"I'm sorry."

I said it loud enough, I was sure of it, but for several moments, Liam didn't say anything back. When he did, he said the worst thing possible.

"It's okay."

Something hot burned at the edges of my vision, and I blinked back whatever traitorous tears were threatening to spill over. I didn't want his pity or his understanding. I wanted him to be angry. He deserved to be angry.

"It's not."

"I get it." He was trying to sound gentle, but his tone was tight and careful. "You don't like meeting new people."

"I don't like the trees," I blurted.

"Oh." I could see him looking at me in my peripheral vision, but I continued to stare forward at the road. "I didn't know that."

"I mean, I don't really like people either. But it's mostly the woods."

"I know."

"I shouldn't have yelled."

"Probably not, but it's okay. Wren?" He reached across the center seat to put a hand on my shoulder. "You're okay."

I pressed my hands against my eyes. I wanted to undo the last thirty minutes. I wanted to go back in time and decide to stay home, lonely but safe.

Liam took an exit off the highway, though I was sure we were still several miles out from Keel Watch Harbor.

"What're you doing?" I demanded, finally turning to look at him. He had that stupid grin on his face again.

"Don't worry. We aren't going into the woods."

"But where are we going?"

"The beach."

Grassy marshes extended on either side of the road here, and in the distance, the ocean shimmered.

"Your friends are waiting for you."

"They're Riley's friends, first of all." He pulled on the window crank to let salty air into the truck cab. "Second, there's more than one way to get to the cove. You don't mind the water, do you?"

We pulled into a new gravel parking lot. This one overlooked a sandy beach where families played. The waves that lapped at the shore hardly reached a foot in height, and a dog chased after his owner in the gentle surf.

Liam got out first, returning to the truck bed to pull out the paddleboard.

"You'll have to sit still," he instructed as I got out on the passenger side. "It's hard with two people, but doable if your sense of balance isn't trash."

"We're going to paddle to your friends?"

"Riley's friends," he reminded me. "It's less than a mile to the cove from here. It'll be easy. You'll want to leave your shoes in the truck, though."

I threw my shoes in the truck bed, exchanging them for the paddle, and chased Liam to the sandy beach. He waded out past the white foam wash of the tide and set the board down in the gentle surf.

"Riley and I used to do this all the time to get to the cove. You'll like it. At least, I think you will." He held the board steady, and his dark blond curls caught the sun. "It'll be fun."

I slid onto the front of the board, tucking my feet under myself to sit crisscross. Liam dragged us out into deeper water, soaking his trunks and the hem of his t-shirt. The board lurched when he pulled himself up behind me.

"Careful!" I hissed as Liam stood up.

"Don't worry, you'll only fall in if I want you to fall in."

"So reassuring."

The flat of the paddle reached forward and dipped into the water beside me as Liam propelled us forward. We glided over kelp, rocks, and sand, and I tried to keep my balance centered while craning my neck to look into the water below us.

"Starfish!" Liam said. "To your right!"

"Technically, they're called sea stars," I mumbled. "They aren't fish."

"Starfish," Liam repeated, louder and slower.

A purple sea star splayed out across the rocks beneath us, and we wobbled as I strained for a better look. I wondered if Skalterra had sea stars too, or if it was another word that would baffle Orla.

"So, do I get to know why you don't like the woods?" Liam asked.

"Nope." I settled back, leaning on my hands now that I was more comfortable on the board. The sea breeze ruffled my hair as we glided forward in the direction of a rocky outcropping that cut into the water a couple hundred yards ahead of us. Trees clung to the cliffside as if spilling over from the forest that sat atop the bluffs.

"What about the scar on your palm? Do I get to know about that?"

I curled my fingers in on themselves, wondering when Liam had noticed Galahad's mark.

"Definitely not."

"Okay. Then why Von Leer?"

"What?" I whipped my head around to look up at Liam, and the board lurched with the movement. Liam kept his eyes on the rocks ahead but smirked as he dipped the paddle back into the water.

"You want to go to Von Leer. Why?"

"Why do you care?"

"I don't, but your Von Leer admissions officer will. Have you been practicing interview questions?"

"No, but—"

"So why Von Leer?"

I scowled and turned back to face forward.

"They have a good biochemistry program."

"Great. Why biochemistry?"

We weren't too far from the shore yet. I could probably abandon ship and swim back still.

"It's interesting, and I like it."

"Sorry, your admission to Von Leer University has not been accepted. Try again."

"But that's the truth!"

"It's not good enough."

"Okay, fine. It's a challenging field, and I like challenges."

"Miss Warrender," Liam said with an air of fake austerity, "how dare you waste the time of an institution as prestigious as ours."

I shifted my weight to one side, and Liam fell to his knees behind me in an effort to keep the board balanced.

"Watch it," he laughed.

"You watch it!" I flicked water backwards at him, and he rose back to his feet. "I like challenges. Biochemistry is challenging."

"No, there's got to be more to it than that."

"I like the idea of biochemistry because it would impress my mom. Maybe I could be a doctor, or a research scientist—something she could brag to her author friends about. But that's it, so if Von Leer wants something more, I'm screwed."

"Oh." Liam took several pulls on the paddle before speaking again. "But what do you *like*?"

"I like volcanoes." A gull cried out in the silence that followed. When Liam continued to say nothing, I forced myself to keep talking. "Von Leer has one of the best geophysics programs in the country. How could it not with all the nearby mountains? Not only that, they're the school closest to my mom that even *has* a volcanology track. But I'm afraid to tell my mom because my dad is a geophysicist, and they haven't talked since before I was born. I wasn't even allowed to mention him growing up. I'm *still* not."

"Volcanoes, huh?" Liam was gracious enough not to linger on the topic of my estranged father.

"I don't know, I think it's interesting that a good portion of the world is living within the blast zone of giant explosion machines, and there's nothing we can do about it. We can try to predict when they'll blow, but ultimately we're at their mercy. How could I *not* try to understand them? How isn't *everyone* obsessed with them?"

"Welcome to Von Leer, Miss Warrender. Our geophysics program will be thrilled to have someone as enthusiastic about giant explosion machines as you are." Liam pointed the paddle at another purple sea star exploring the rocks below us. "Starfish. That's two-zero."

"I didn't know the sea stars were a competition!" I leaned over the water, scanning for more. "How many points do I get for a crab?"

"Depends. How big is it?"

I watched the orange shell of a Dungeness crab shuffle sideways towards Liam's sea star.

"Pretty big."

"Zero points. It's not a starfish."

I smiled in spite of myself. Liam wasn't such bad company, and I was starting to dread when our paddle would come to an end at the cove. I still didn't understand why he was so nice to me, even now after I'd yelled at him and Sabrina.

Maybe it was because my bad attitude had yet to deter his attempts at friendship, but it had been a long time since anyone had made me feel so comfortable just being myself. Liam had no expectations. He took me as I was, even when I wasn't sure I even liked myself.

"It was graduation night," I said before I knew what I was doing. "About three weeks ago."

"What was?"

"The night in the woods."

"Wren, you don't have to—"

"It's okay," I said through a tightening throat. "I was really rude to you and Sabrina. I don't want to make excuses for myself, but you deserve to at least know why, and maybe I'll feel better if I talk about it. So this is the story about the time I thought I killed Linsey Harper."

Philosophy of Friendship

The paddle dipped into the water beside me, and I took Liam's silence to be an invitation. Now that I'd committed to telling the story, it demanded to be told. It pressed against my chest, weighing on my lungs, heart, and stomach, and I knew if I could just get the words out, the pain would subside.

"I already told you I got my friend Linsey expelled from Von Leer before she'd even started." I stared at the bow of the board

"She got herself expelled by cheating on a test," Liam said.

"But I'm the one who snitched, and everyone knew it. They said I did it because I was mad Linsey got accepted to Von Leer when I was waitlisted."

"You did it to get the grade you deserved."

"I did. But that doesn't mean they were completely wrong either. It felt good to snitch on her. She'd been insufferable ever since getting in, and maybe my physics grade will help me get into Von Leer in a couple weeks, but if not, I got the consolation prize of watching Linsey get humbled."

"And what does this have to do with the woods?"

I scratched listlessly at the paddleboard.

"One of our classmates threw a party at his parents' summer cabin after the graduation ceremony. I don't usually get invited to those sorts of things, but when Linsey said I should come, I figured it was an olive branch. I didn't want to go, but I wanted things to get better between us, so I said sure."

"You didn't," Liam groaned. I hated that he could already see what a terrible idea it had been. I hated that I had no way to go back and tell myself not to go.

The summer cabin in the mountains, Linsey, and all her friends felt so far away as I floated on the ocean with Liam, but the memory of that night churned in my stomach. My heart hammered at the thought of Linsey's friends gathered on the front porch as I pulled up the gravel drive.

"When I showed up, her friends were upset. Linsey had sent them a text about how embarrassed she was about Von Leer, how her life was over, and that she'd gone into the woods to..."

I swallowed the end of the sentence, but Liam could tell where it was headed. I'd already told him, after all, that this was the story of how I thought I'd killed her.

"Did she—"

"It was a trick," I spat, "but obviously I didn't know that. I told her friends to call the police, and then I ran after her. There was an overgrown trail behind the cabin. I didn't know where it went, but I figured it was better than sitting around and waiting for cops and paramedics."

"And she wasn't in there."

"No." A sea star stretched out beneath our board, but neither of us pointed it out. "But there was a mannequin in a tree."

"Wren."

"It wasn't her." I forced levity into my voice. "Of course, I couldn't tell that at first. The sun had set by the time I found it, so it looked like her. They'd put a wig on it and some old clothes. I didn't realize it was fake until I was right under it. They'd painted the word 'snitch' on its chest. I think it was supposed to be me."

"What did you do?"

"I cried," I admitted. Liam had already seen me blow up at him and Sabrina. It wasn't so embarrassing to admit to crying in the woods. "It was out of relief at first. Linsey wasn't dead. Then, I cried out of anger. And then I realized I didn't know the way back to the cabin and that it had gotten very dark very fast."

"But the trail—"

"It was overgrown, it forked a lot, and I hadn't paid attention to the way I'd come. Plus, it all looked different at night. I walked for hours with no cell service and only the flashlight on my phone to light the way. When my phone died, I gave up and curled against a big tree."

"Were you scared?"

"Yeah," I whispered. "I could hear coyotes nearby, and there's cougars and bears in those woods too. I kept waiting for someone to show up. They had to be looking for me. Except that they weren't, so no one ever came."

The paddle dipped back into the water, and Liam sighed as he pulled us forward.

"I hate them," Liam said so matter-of-factly that he might have been pointing out another sea star. "Wren, I hate every single person who was at the party that night."

"Eventually, the sun came up, and I was able to find my way out," I explained. "There were still a few people awake at the cabin. They didn't say anything. They just watched me get in my car and drive away. Linsey was one of them."

A wry smile tugged at my lips. Mom had been up all night too, waiting for me to get back. At first, she'd looked so angry with me, waiting on the porch in her robe, thinking I'd deliberately stayed out so late without texting or calling, but she'd been able to tell something was wrong before I'd even put the car in park. She was there at the door to catch me when I stumbled out from behind the wheel, sobbing and covered in dirt and sticks.

She'd made sure I was okay, then had driven off in her own car, still in her slippers and robes. I still wasn't sure where she'd gone, but she returned a short twenty minutes later, drenched in water and promising Linsey would never bother me again.

The paddleboard lurched, and I stiffened as arms wrapped around my shoulders from behind.

"What are you doing?" I asked Liam as his dark blond curls pressed into my cheek. He smelled like sandalwood deodorant and sea spray.

"I'm hugging you."

"Yeah, I gathered that much. Why?"

"Because you didn't deserve any of that. You deserve someone who would go into the woods for you."

I bit back the impulse to tell him to get off of me. As much as I wanted to snap at him, I didn't *actually* want him to move. I relaxed, one timid muscle at a time, and leaned into the embrace.

"It could've been worse." I reached up to place a hand on his where it rested on my shoulder. "They could've given me a really embarrassing haircut instead."

Liam's hair tickled my face as he laughed.

"Your hair is fine," he promised. "I'm just an idiot with a knack for putting my foot in my mouth."

We sat still for a moment, feeling the board roll with the tide beneath us. A gull cried, waves lapped at the rocky shore, and for the first time since graduation, some hidden knot inside me loosened.

Liam was annoying and perfect, but it was nice to have a friend.

"Also," he whispered, "there was a starfish back there—"

I leaned hard to one side, and the ocean rushed up to swallow us.

My attack did not go without reward, and by the time we finally paddled into the cove, we'd pushed each other into the water a fair number of times. We'd stripped to our swimsuits, and our wet clothes sat in sopping wads at the bow of the board as I paddled us towards the beach.

Riley's friends had already started the bonfire, and my face warmed in embarrassment at the sight of Sabrina watching us get closer. I focused on my grip on the paddle, watching where I dipped it into the water to pull us forward rather than meet her narrowed gaze.

Liam jumped into the water to pull us ashore the rest of the way, and I dropped to my knees to keep from losing my balance.

"I thought you were taking her to Ethel's." Sabrina made no effort to mask her irritation.

"We worked it out," Liam said. Sabrina must've trusted him a great deal, because she fixed a strained smile on her face and waded into the water to offer me a hand off the board.

"I'm sorry," I mumbled. "For earlier."

"Liam seems to have forgotten already," she said, "so I guess I will too. Don't worry about it."

Her shoulders still seemed tense, however, and her smile refused to relax, but she was at least trying.

If she'd mentioned my parking lot blow-up to Riley's friends, they didn't act like it. One of them pulled Liam into a bear hug and they stood in the water, both in their swim trunks.

"He's going to come back," Liam promised. The other young man finally pulled away and pushed curly brown hair back from watering eyes.

"Yeah." He nodded, but the tight press of his lips told me he'd likely already given up on his missing friend. He caught me staring and quickly composed himself. "Sorry, I'm Xander."

Riley's other friends introduced themselves as well, but I forgot their names as quickly as they said them. They knew me, however, as they'd all grown up in Keel Watch Harbor and all knew Gams.

The sun sank, but not before drying mine and Liam's clothes. I huddled in my salt-crusted t-shirt by the bonfire as the others recounted their favorite Riley memories.

He sounded like a good guy, despite a mischievous streak. Sabrina laughed through a story about Riley trying to steal a vat of lemonade from the storeroom of her mother's tavern to take to a child's birthday party down the street. Another friend talked about a time he'd dared Riley to sneak into Gams's workshop after she'd made it clear no one was to ever disturb her there. Riley had been caught, of course, and sentenced to cleaning Jonquil's litter-box for a week. However, after the week of kitty litter finished, he continued to come back to the shop each day for the rest of the summer to clean Jonquil's messes.

I laughed along with the stories, feeling like I'd known Riley. And maybe I had. I had a few fuzzy memories of visiting Gams as a little girl and playing with the Keel Watch Harbor kids, but their faces were blurred, and I couldn't remember their names. I liked the idea that maybe one of them had been Riley. I couldn't bear the thought that maybe it was too late to meet the guy starring in the stories around the bonfire.

Everyone had something to say about Riley except for Liam.

He sat on the same driftwood log as me, staring into the flames of the fire with the smallest crease to his brow. The hard lines of his neat frown would crack the tiniest of smiles when the stories warranted it, but the smiles never quite reached his eyes. The serious set of his jaw reminded me of Tiernan in a way, and Orla's chiding voice echoed in the back of my mind.

He's mourning Caitria.

But where Tiernan's grief had made him rude, Liam's had only made him kind, even when I'd given him no reason to be. Even when I'd been what I would've described to Orla as a "garbage friend".

I thought about him kneeling down on the paddleboard to comfort me.

Not everyone was as unpleasant as Tiernan. Not everyone was as cruel as Linsey.

I slid down the driftwood log. Liam kept his eyes on the fire, but he shifted his leg so that our knees touched. I stared at the fire too, and lifted a careful arm. I hovered it over Liam's shoulders for an awkward moment, and then lowered it to hold him at my side.

He remained silent, but leaned into me, and we stared into the fire together.

When the bonfire fizzled into dying embers and the inky dark of night had fallen overhead, spotted in an array of stars that made me dizzy if I stared upwards too long, Riley's friends and Sabrina grabbed their things.

I stared at the mouth of the wooded path that wound its way back up to the parking lot, and when Xander told us there would be room in his car for us, Sabrina, and the boards if we wanted a ride to Liam's car, I held my breath.

"That's okay," Liam insisted. "You guys head back. Wren and I will go back the way we came."

He waved them away as he dragged our paddleboard back to the water.

"Are you sure?" I whispered. "It's late, and you're tired."

He looked up at me from where he bent over to fasten the velcro leash of the board around his ankle.

"Are you okay with the woods?" he asked seriously. When I couldn't bring myself to answer, he smiled. "The water is beautiful at night. You're going to love it."

And he was right.

Nineteen
Fluid Dynamics

Liam didn't bring up graduation night, Linsey, or forests anymore, and I didn't mention his cousin Riley unless someone else brought him up first. There was a new understanding between us, and I started to look forward to him bringing me my daily bagel sandwich as the start of his shifts.

Gams noticed our growing friendship, and took it upon herself to crawl out of her workshop for forty minutes each day to watch the store so Liam and I could start having our lunch breaks together. Liam came to every lunch prepared with fresh mock-interview questions for me. They ranged from practical to unhinged. I'd be answering a question about my graduate school plans, and then he'd smack me with a question asking me to determine which volcano would win in a Battle Royale style fight.

Meanwhile, it took Galahad three days to summon me back to Skalterra.

He pulled me unceremoniously through whatever veil existed between our two realms as I was brushing my teeth in my room. The taste of mint evaporated from my mouth, and I materialized on a wooden deck.

Wind pulled at my blue hair, and I stumbled to catch my footing as the floor rolled beneath me. Steep cliffs rose up on either side of me, lit by the gentle red glow of the steamed Skal escaping from twin smokestacks that towered overhead.

I was on a steamboat.

"Fascinating." Tamora's cool voice greeted me, and I found the Baron leaning against the bronze railing of the upper deck, looking down at me. Red light from orbs of skalflame that floated around her sent fire-like highlights through her hair. Her red curls hung free, bouncing around shoulders left bare by a blouse that seemed to barely be holding itself up. "So she comes with blue hair every time? That's a bit unusual, isn't it?"

"It's what she likes," Galahad grunted. He stood somewhere behind Tamora, obscured by the lip of the deck. I backpedaled to get a better view of him. His hands were shoved in the pockets of his duster jacket, and a trace of concern marred the irritated look on his face.

"What's happening?" I asked. The river was wide enough to fit another two or three boats across its width, but the cliffs towering on either side of us made me feel claustrophobic and trapped. Twin crescent moons winked down at me from between the dark lines of the cliffs.

"I'm taking you and your friends to Riverstead, as promised." Tamora smiled sweetly. "We've got another few days, of course. Traveling upriver can be a real slog. I thought poor Galahad was going to be laid up the entire trip, but look! He rallied just for us and managed to bring you across the Rift."

"Where's Fana?" I looked at Galahad as I said it. The deck where I stood was barren, lined with a low bronze rail. A set of bronze double doors led into the steamboat's main cabin, and a stairway on either side of me rose to meet the upper deck. "And the others?"

"Fana is safe, don't you worry. You're off-duty tonight. Galahad brought you here for me." Tamora shook her hair out. I didn't like what she was saying, and I definitely didn't like the way she was staring at me, like I was some sort of bug she was about to pin to a board and study. "Lucid Nightmares are exceptionally rare. Those that *do* come through Skalterra usually have enough sense to keep what they are secret. They're illegal across all seven provinces, and the other night, you made it clear why."

"And the others?" I was still looking at Galahad.

"They're resting." Something about his frown told me he didn't want me here, which could only mean Tamora had forced him to summon me. The red of the floating lights made him look all the more serious.

"Tell me, Nightmare," Tamora purred, "what did you say your name was?"

Galahad gave me the tiniest shake of his head, but I didn't need the reminder.

"Blue." I grinned up at Tamora. The insincere expression gave me a small hit of false confidence, and I vaguely wondered if that's why Liam was always smiling despite everything he'd been through.

"Sure." Her smile tightened into an impatient grimace. "Well, *Blue*, this boat ride has been ever so boring. I haven't been properly entertained since you showed off in my court three nights ago. I was wondering if you could give us a demonstration?"

I looked to Galahad again for guidance, but he was passive and unreadable.

"But I hurt Galahad last time."

"He'll be fine. We've got plenty of Skal to keep both him and you fueled and alive," Tamora assured me. "Now, have I introduced you properly to Titus yet?"

Her bodyguard stepped forward. He'd been standing too far back for me to see him, but now I had an unimpeded view of all six and a half feet of him. He stared down at me from over harsh cheekbones, and his muscles rippled beneath tattoos and chest armor as he vaulted over the railing to drop to my deck level.

He landed with a heavy thud that shook the wooden planks beneath me, and I stumbled back.

"Hi, Titus," I gulped.

"Don't worry, Blue," Tamora sang. "It's just a play-match. No Skal-weapons, and while Titus does play rough, if the worst happens, you'll wake up back at home unharmed."

The scars on the palm of my hand itched, and I glared over Titus's shoulder at Galahad. I did *not* want to waste one of my dwindling lives on a demonstration match against the human embodiment of protein shakes and creatine.

Unfortunately, like nearly everything else that had happened in Skalterra, it didn't seem like I was going to be given much of a choice. Titus lurched forward, and I stumbled away.

"But what if I hurt him?" I called up to Tamora, dancing out of the way of Titus's massive fists. He chased after me with lumbering steps.

"This is what I pay him for. He'll be fine. Now show me your tricks, Nightmare! This voyage has been boring. Entertain us!"

Titus already had me cornered against the railing. Water rushed behind me, split by the bow of the steamboat, and my blue hair twisted in the wind as Titus grinned.

He fell forward in a fresh attack with his hands outstretched, and I let my bone shards burst free of my forearms. I gritted my teeth against the hot, slicing pain as sharp bone shot through muscle and skin.

The boney razors glinted red with my own blood as I raised them in defense, and Titus howled as they dug through the meat of his arms.

"Boring!" Tamora called. "You already showed me that one! I want something new!"

Titus grabbed a bone spike in each of his massive hands and snapped them like twigs. I willed more muscle mass into my legs and launched at him, tackling him around his middle.

Heavy, I thought to myself. *Be heavy.*

I found the same warm trickle of Skal in my chest that I'd felt the other night. I drew on it and felt my limbs turn heavy with muscle. I landed with Titus pinned under me, but his arms were free. He reached out to grab at me, so I willed talon-like claws into my hands and forced both of his arms back to the deck.

His hands glowed red, and a javelin spear materialized in his grip, growing outwards with the pointed-tip towards my face.

"You said no weapons!" I yelled at Tamora, rolling off of Titus to dodge his attack.

"Oops," she called back. Titus hurled the javelin, and I ducked to the side. It splintered into shards of light against the cliff face behind me.

Titus procured two new javelins, hurling them one after the other. I dodged the first one, but the second one followed too quickly. Without time to dodge, I pulled more Skal from that trickling stream in my chest and focused on my leather armor, feeling it grow heavier as it hardened into thick kevlar.

The force of the javelin blow sent me stumbling backwards against the rail, and I looked over my shoulder at the dark river water that swirled below.

"Galahad!" I called. "Make her stop this!"

He knew I had limited lives. If he really did need me to protect Fana, then it was in his best interest to make Tamora call off her bodyguard.

There was a heavy thud up above, and I looked up to see Galahad slumped against the upper railing.

"Galahad?"

Titus bore down on me, and I ducked away, leaving him to slam into the railing. He lunged again. I was too slow this time. He caught me around the throat, and I clawed at his calloused hands. His fingers tightened until lights burst in my vision.

"That's enough, Titus," a cool voice warned.

Titus let go, and I dropped to the deck, massaging my neck and forcing air back into my lungs as I gathered my bearings.

The clicking of Tamora's boots descending the staircase brought my attention back upwards. Her red orbs of light followed her through the air, and I braced myself as she approached.

She leaned down to inspect my chest armor in the glow of her Skal-lights.

"The color changed, didn't it?" She tapped on the material, and her eyes narrowed behind her monocle. "And so did your leather. Galahad, you noticed that the other night, didn't you? She can change her clothes as well as her anatomy!"

I glanced up at Galahad. He sat on his knees, gripping the bronze railing with both hands and surveying me with the same careful regard he'd held the night in Vanderfall.

Tamora moved to inspect a spike of bloody bone that protruded from my arm. I flinched away, but held my arm steady. Tamora brushed a finger along the edge of the blade, and then turned her hand so I could see the droplet of blood that clung to the cut the shard had left there.

"Very sharp. Does it hurt you as well?"

"No," I lied. The twist in her smile told me she didn't believe me.

"Give me your chest plate."

"Excuse me?" I recoiled.

"Your armor. I want to try something."

The spikes protruding from my arms made unbuckling the kevlar tricky, but I managed to retract them halfway back into my body, hiding my face behind blue hair as I did so Tamora couldn't see me gritting my teeth in pain.

The kevlar fell away, leaving me shivering on the deck in a sweat-drenched tunic. Titus stood over me with his arms crossed and a triumphant smirk on his lips.

"Fascinating." Tamora turned the armor over in her hands. "This material, is it Keldorian? I've never—"

It disintegrated in her hands, and she staggered backwards as black grains of ash slipped between her fingers and disappeared on the river wind.

"Fascinating," she murmured again, though there was something darker there. "I never considered a Nightmare's apparel to be an extension of their form, but I suppose it makes sense. Galahad, are you seeing this?"

Galahad hobbled down the steps behind her. His face was unreadable under his grizzled gray mane of hair, and he sipped on a bottle of glowing Skal.

"Yes, Baron, it is truly spectacular. Would you please let my Nightmare and, by extension, me, have a rest now?" He glowered as if I were in trouble, though I wasn't sure what I had done to offend him. If anyone should be angry, it should be me. I was the one who'd been dragged here just to play the role of a lab rat for Tamora.

Tamora rubbed her fingers together, inspecting what little remained of my chest armor.

"Of course, Galahad." She brushed her hands off and straightened up. "This exercise has left me with plenty to ponder until the next one."

"Next one?" I blanched. Tamora winked at me behind her monocle.

"Come, Titus. Let's let them rest."

Titus followed Tamora into the double doors that led into the cabin of the steamboat, and I waited until the doors had swung shut before laying into Galahad.

"Are you trying to keep me from making it to the Second Sentinel?" I staggered to my feet so I could shove my palm in his face. "I've only got three lives left! I'm more than a Nightmare, okay? I have a life back in Keldori! And friends and family, and you're trying to kill me!"

"Oh, *I'm* trying to kill *you?*" His bushy eyebrows jumped upwards towards his goggles. "You nearly killed me in the Baron's mansion the other night. Where do you think your magick comes from? Who do you think pays the price when you use so much of it?"

"How was I supposed to know it was coming from you?"

"All your magick comes from me, girl." He gestured with the half-drank Skal bottle in his hands. "And to use those tricks in front of the Baron, no less—"

"The lady who was trying to murder us and dissolve the barrier between our realities?" I snapped. "Yes, so sorry for saving us all."

A ghastly, rattling howl that sucked what little warmth the Skalterran night had to offer interrupted our argument. Galahad shoved me behind him, and we both scanned the clifftops. A dark shadow glided along the lip of the cliff, its black edges illuminated by the dual moons. It rushed back and forth, as if frustrated, then howled again.

"It's a rotsbane," I breathed.

"It can't reach you here," Galahad said, but I didn't like the waver in his voice. "They don't do well with water."

"Very reassuring. Thank you," I snarled. "Can I go home now?"

Galahad looked back up at the rotsbane as another shadow joined its side. They sniffed at the red steam that wafted from our smokestacks and howled in tandem, sucking as much of the glowing air into their open mouths as they could.

"No." Galahad frowned behind his messy beard. "You'll be fine."

"But—"

"You are not leaving until you learn to feel and stem the flow of magick that you draw from me. I will not be killed because you don't know how to pace your appetite for Skal."

My face burned at his words.

"Sure, you won't be killed, but who gives a crap if some kid from Keldori dies?"

"If you die, it will be in service to the Riftkeepers, and you will be remembered with honor and prestige for your sacrifice."

"I don't want honor and prestige, I want to go to college!" I forced my fingers back into talons, and Galahad grimaced.

"Careful," he warned in a low growl.

"If you don't want me taking your magick, then don't let me take it!" Hard scales worked their way up my arms, and Galahad faltered as I drew more of his magick in.

The tiny Skalspring in my chest, it was a tether. Magick ran along its length, connecting me to Galahad and the Skal he'd just drank. My bone shards grew to their full length, and I worked to mentally adjust my tunic as my muscles swelled and my legs lengthened.

Talons forced their way through my fingertips, and muscle rippled under my tunic until I loomed over Galahad. I had no idea what I looked like in this form, I could tell by the way his jaw gaped and his eyes widened that I must be horrifying. He fell to his knees, and I could feel it—the flow of buzzing magick leaving him and filling my every molecule.

I was powerful. I was unstoppable. I was hungry.

I wanted more.

I *needed* more, and I wondered if I ripped Galahad apart with my talons, if I'd find more Skal inside him.

And then, like a dog finding the limits of its leash at the end of sprint, something yanked me back and choked me. I tried to strike out at Galahad with a muscle-swollen, serrated arm, but some invisible force held me at bay.

Magick receded, and I thrashed against Galahad's influence.

He was taking the magick back.

"Galahad," I choked. I withered as Skal vacated me, and I collapsed in a huddled, weak mess on the deck of the boat. Post-adrenaline fatigue was nothing compared to this post-Skal rush, and I lay shaking in nothing more than a white tunic and brown trousers. My armor and boots faded to ash along with my bone spines. Scales and talons reverted to skin and fingers, and I shuddered, hugging myself with weak, useless arms.

Galahad stood over me, triumphant.

"Did you forget which of us is in charge?" he growled. "I'll admit, I forgot too, for a moment. But you're right. The magick between us *does* flow both ways, and only one of us is an actual Magician."

The door to the main cabin creaked open, and Ferrin's voice, though groggy with sleep, set my racing heart at ease just slightly. He wouldn't let Galahad hurt me.

"Galahad, what's happening? What's wrong with Wren?"

"She's fine," Galahad thundered.

"I want to go home." I curled in on myself, and my hair fell over my face. I hid there, not wanting to look at Galahad or the rotsbane howling on the cliffs. Their song sounded like someone screaming inwards, violently inhaling over strained vocal cords.

"You will. When you finish what I called you here to do. Fana is inside. She needs guarding." Galahad's stomping boots echoed against the wooden planks as he retreated. "I'll be in my room. Have Orla bring me a tea, would you? I'm parched."

Careful hands pulled me into a sitting position, but I kept my head bowed so that I could continue to hide behind a curtain of blue hair.

"Wren, what happened?" Ferrin asked. "Are you alright?"

I was still shaking from the aftereffects of so much magick deserting me so quickly. My pride smarted, and my anger flared. But there was something else there too.

Fear.

Not towards Galahad, nor towards the rotsbane that still sang their ghastly songs overhead.

But towards myself, the monster I'd so quickly devolved into, and the insatiable hunger that the monster had brought with it.

Twenty

Maritime Trade and Management

My fight against Galahad followed me into Keel Watch Harbor, leaving me winded and fatigued as I went about my usual shop duties. Liam had brought me an iced coffee with my bagel, but the caffeine mostly made my heart race. The cool touch of the plastic cup at least soothed the scars in the palm of my hand. They'd been burning all morning, and I wondered if Galahad was making them sting on purpose as a reminder that he was the one in charge.

To add injury to insult, Galahad gave little-to-no warning when he called me to Skalterra the next few nights, each time earlier than the evening before. I was never ready, and woke up to new bruises each morning after hitting furniture on my way to the floor of my bedroom.

Tamora continued her experiments, but Galahad was getting better at stemming the flow of Skal between us. After the third night of giving her nothing more than my usual arm spikes, Tamora grew bored of my fights with Titus. Instead, Galahad put me to work sitting outside Fana's cabin while she slept. Those nights, long and boring as they were sitting on the wooden floor all alone, were almost worse than being pitted against Titus.

A week into this routine, I was left to close shop alone after Gams left for a game night with her friends at the library. Jonquil meowed for dinner up the apartment stairs as I locked the shop door.

"I get it," I called up at her, taking the steps two at a time. "You don't need to yell at me. There's no way your food is *that* good."

"It's time, Nightmare," a voice growled at me from the shadows at the back of my head, and I froze on the darkened staircase. Galahad was summoning me.

"Not yet, I'm not—"

The wooden steps underfoot rushed upwards to welcome me to Skalterra.

I fell upright, landing again on the deck of Tamora's boat. The water was wide and slow here, looking more like a lake than a river, and the sun, hanging low over forested hills, lit it in hues of orange and red. The steam pouring from boat's smokestacks bled with the sunset and filled the air with a smell akin to that of warm dirt after a sudden rain.

I leaned against the railing of the deck, trying to orient myself in the late-day warmth. A village lay ahead, floating atop the river as a network of boardwalks and wooden cabanas.

Whatever relief I might've felt at finally seeing civilization after a week of dark landscapes was eclipsed by the fury that rose in my chest.

"Galahad!" I yelled for the old man and spun around, still leaning against the railing for support.

"Calm yourself, Nightmare," Galahad said. He stood with the others, all laden with packs, Skal bottles, and travel cloaks.

"You couldn't give me one more minute to get into bed?" I snarled.

"I told you to be ready." Galahad adjusted Fana's pack, refusing to look at me. I pulled on the well of Skal that connected us to get his attention, drawing his magick into myself before he pulled back. He glared at me from over his grizzled beard.

"I was on the stairs!" I shouted. "My grandmother is going to come home from Game Night and call an ambulance when she finds me!"

"Ambulance," Orla repeated in a whisper. She stood without a cloak, rubbing her arms to stave off the cool breeze that rolled over the river and cut the summer warmth.

"We're disembarking," Ferrin explained in an even tone. "I'm sorry you were in an inconvenient place, but—"

"Inconvenient?" I seethed. "My bedroom floor is inconvenient. The *staircase* is dangerous. What if I fell? What if my neck is broken?"

"Then I suppose it's a good thing your grandmother will find you." Ferrin bit back a smile, but his sense of humor was less than appreciated.

"I'm going to wake up in a hospital."

Ferrin shrugged at Galahad. "Could you send her back really quick? Just long enough to let her get to bed?"

"And waste all the Skal I just used to bring her here?" Galahad stalked to the bow of the boat to watch our approach towards the village docks. "She'll be fine on the stairs."

I whirled to face Ferrin, but all he could offer me was a sympathetic hand on my shoulder.

"We do need you," he insisted. "This next part of our journey will be tricky."

He held my gaze, but ginger curls flying in the breeze caught my eye over his shoulder. Tamora watched us from the upper deck, leaning against the railing as her Nightmare deckhands hurried around her to prepare for docking.

"I can't sleep on the stairs," I said through gritted teeth. Ferrin nodded with his hand still on my shoulder.

"I'm sorry. I'll make sure it doesn't happen again, but you'll have to worry about it in the morning."

"Why? *Her?*" I pointed at Tamora, and she smiled down at me. "I thought she was letting us go when we got to Riverstead."

Ferrin leaned in close to hiss in my ear.

"The Baron doesn't let anyone go." He patted my shoulder and went to meet Galahad at the bow of the boat.

I rubbed at my neck, knowing I was going to wake up with my worst knot yet. Maybe stretching the joint here would make my real body back in Keldori a little more limber and comfortable on the staircase.

"I'm sorry about the stairs," Orla said. "And the ambulance. Whatever an ambulance is."

Tiernan snorted next to her, and Fana pushed back her hood to look up at him.

"What?" she asked.

He shook his head, and the gold beads in his twisted locks clicked together as he did.

"Nothing."

"Don't mind him," I snapped. "He's suffering from indigestion because he doesn't know if he should be angry I'm here or happy my real body's neck might be broken."

Tiernan shrugged back at Fana.

"I guess the Nightmare isn't a complete idiot after all." His gold-flecked eyes flitted to meet mine, and his scowl deepened.

Orla hooked my elbow in hers and dragged me away from Tiernan before I could take my frustration out on him. Tamora's Nightmares had descended on our deck, and now they ran between us in leather trousers and tunics, carrying ropes.

"I'm sorry Galahad pulled you over too quickly," Orla said, "but I'm glad you're here. I feel like I've hardly seen you all week."

"Yeah, it's hard to catch up with each other when Tamora insists on using me as her bodyguard's punching bag."

Orla frowned and cast a backwards glance at the Baron.

"Speaking of catching up, the Grimguard couldn't have followed us here, right? Do you think we're in the clear?"

"I'd be surprised if he's even conscious yet. And honestly, I'm a little jealous. I could go for a good coma. I'm starting to forget what sleeping feels like."

"Don't worry," Orla assured me, "once we make it to the Second Sentinel, you'll get to relax! We both will, and I'll get to show you my home."

"Will you?" As much as I hated being linked to Galahad and getting left unconscious on the stairs, the thought of saying goodbye to Orla and the rest of Skalterra made me pause. "Galahad won't need me anymore."

"But you're still our friend." Orla frowned at the Nightmares lowering a gangplank to the dock. Dockworkers yelled to each other below, running lines and rope along the planks. "Galahad would bring you back if you wanted to return."

"Orla, I'm *your* friend, not Galahad's. It costs him magick to bring me here."

Orla forced a grin and hitched her knapsack up higher on her shoulder.

"Then I'll have him teach me how to bring you here myself, Just-Wren. It's an advanced skill, but I'd figure it out to see you again."

"Let's focus on getting home first." Ferrin came up behind her and brushed dust off his vest. "Welcome to Riverstead, the southernmost port of the Breachriver Prefecture."

"Officially putting you and your friends outside of my jurisdiction." Tamora's voice rang out over the deck as she approached. Tiernan drew Fana closer to his side as she passed, but the Baron didn't seem to notice. Instead, she grinned at me and held a slender hand out to mine. "I hope you enjoyed your escort. I know I did."

Ferrin gave me an encouraging nod, and I accepted her handshake. Her monocle made me feel like she could see straight through my skin and to the Skal that swirled inside me.

"I wish I could say it was a pleasure, Baron," Galahad grunted, already mounting the gangplank to disembark. "But alas. It wasn't."

"Careful," Tamora sang. "We may be outside of the Grand Barony, but you're still on my boat, Lyrian."

Galahad made a show of shuffling down the gangplank and landing heavy on the dock.

"Tiernan and Fana, you next." Ferrin beckoned them forward. "Forgive Galahad, Baron. He's difficult to impress. We thank you for your generosity."

Tamora shook her curls back over her shoulders.

"I prefer his honesty to whatever this awkward groveling is. Take care of pretty little Blue here. It'd be a shame for such a strange Nightmare to go to waste." She winked at me, turned around, and stalked back towards the cabin.

Ferrin mumbled something under his breath and shepherded Orla and me towards the gangplank with a protective arm around our shoulders.

Lamps of swirling white Skal cast the wooden sides of docks and cabanas in shifting, dull light that fought to stave off the rapidly falling night. The entire town of Riverstead sat atop the water, comprised of wooden huts and stalls built into a messy network of docks. The evening was still young, and fishermen and dockworkers bustled around us, carrying cages of crawdads, fishing equipment, and nets of river fish.

I held a hand over my nose as a woman carrying a basket full of trout passed by, bringing with her a cloud of nauseating fish smell.

"The Baron gave us enough Skal to last a few days if we don't run into any trouble," Ferrin said, gathering us under the swirling light of a lamp. "We'll still need to refill in Tulyr, and there are a few more supplies we need to stock up on before we leave Riverstead. Orla, you'll come with me to find a new cloak. Tiernan, go with Galahad to find food. Just-Wren, you're in charge of Fana. I want her as far from the Baron as quickly as possible, so get her to the forest beyond the riverbank, and wait for us there."

"The forest?" I chewed on my lip.

"But I'm Fana's Riftkeeper," Tiernan protested. "She should stay with me."

"She'll be plenty safe with Wren." Ferrin watched the Baron's boat over our shoulders. Tamora's Nightmares passed back and forth over the gangplank, restocking the boat for the return journey to Vanderfall, but the boat's continued presence darkened Ferrin's brow under his coiffed hair. "Orla, let's move quickly."

Orla waved goodbye to me, and Tiernan glowered as Galahad led him towards bright storefronts that sent light spilling across the river's surface.

"Alrighty!" I slapped my hands together and spun to face Fana. Despite having been dragged back to Skalterra night after night to keep the kid safe, my interactions with the Divine Sovereign had been few and far between. "Fana."

She blinked up at me with round brown eyes. "Yes?"

"Oh. Nothing." Forget Divine Sovereigns, I hadn't much interacted with children in general. I didn't know what they liked in my own realm, let alone Skalterra. "I was just saying your name."

"Alrighty." Her lips twitched into a smile under her yellow hood as she repeated the word. "Just-Wren."

I pulled my own woolen hood up to hide my blue hair and put a tentative arm around her thin shoulders to guide her forward. The last remnants of day still hung in the sky.

The setting sun outlined the distant mountains in hues of red, and rolling hills to the west peeked out at us from between the roofs of cabanas. Cicadas chirped at each other in the forest, loud enough that we could hear them all the way out on the water.

Fana's hood swiveled back and forth as she watched children running barefoot down the planks and leaping over the gaps between walkways. A couple of women pulling cages from the depths of the river chided them as they harvested their crawdads.

"Can we do that?" Fana asked. One of the children landed on the edge of a walkway, teetered for a moment, and then fell backwards into the water to the laughter and cheers of his friends.

"Ferrin said to get to the forest as quickly as possible," I said, though I would've loved the excuse to avoid the woods. "It won't take long for the others to finish their errands, and if we aren't at the riverbank—"

Fana's shoulders fell, and she turned away from the kids to stomp ahead of me.

"I don't know why I thought you'd be more fun than Tiernan."

"I'm way more fun than Tiernan!" I quickened my step to catch up to her, and she looked up to raise a dubious eyebrow.

"Your hair color is more exciting, but that's about it. Tiernan says 'fun' is a luxury."

"And when's the last time he let you have fun?"

She thought for a moment.

"It was fun in the steamcart when you shocked his nose with your little lightning."

"So I *am* more fun than Tiernan."

I studied the serious set of Fana's brow below the hem of her hood and wondered what sort of upbringing she must've had. She was the last Divine Sovereign, so her entire family was dead. Even if she'd had a happy childhood, no amount of fun could heal losing so much.

Fana's eyes darted to a pastry stand manned by an old woman, and her steps faltered.

"Did you want something, lovely?" the old woman sang, and Fana turned to me with big, begging eyes.

"I don't have money," I hissed back at her.

She shoved her hands into the pockets of her cloak and pulled out a few silver coins.

"Tiernan does." She smirked.

"That's Tiernan's money?"

"Yes."

I held her gaze for a moment, knowing Ferrin wouldn't want us to stop, but feeling bad for the kid in front of me. Her and I were the only two in the group who hadn't volunteered for any of this.

"Fine. And since Tiernan's paying, I want something too."

Fana's face split into a grin, and her robes billowed around her as she skipped towards the pastry woman. She pulled her hood back to better survey the selection of sweets at the woman's counter, and I watched, satisfied at having secured my place as more fun than Tiernan.

"Do you know you're being followed?"

That voice, smug and with the slightest, lilting rasp, made the Skal in my veins feel like ice. I spun around, looking for the man I knew it belonged to, but Ciarán stayed hidden.

"Fana!" I warned. Fana looked up from the counter, a pastry already in her mouth.

"None of that, Blue. You don't need to worry about me." Ciarán's dark laugh sounded from every direction, and I put a hand against my head. Fana returned her attention to the sweets, and I stumbled back until I found the edge of the dock. "I'm far, far away, though I do have questions for you. Namely, what the hell is growing on my chest? It looks like mold."

"You're in my head," I hissed, horrible realization dawning over me. Ciarán, the Grimguard hunting us, had somehow gained access to my consciousness. "How?"

"How?" Ciarán repeated. "Have your friends not warned you? Never tell your full name to a nocturmancer if you don't want to give them access to your mind."

Dread churned my stomach. They *had* warned me, but not until after I'd given the Grimguard my name as he lay injured on Orla's bed.

"So, Wren Warrender, prospective Von Leer Viking, back to my question," Ciarán continued. "Do you know you're being followed?"

Twenty-One
Sports Design and Innovation

The laughter of the village children sounded far away, the docks turned cold, and the light of the steam-lamps seemed to dull. Skalterra was collapsing in around me, and my breathing hitched.

I'd given Ciarán my name. Now he held power over me.

"Get out," I hissed, my eyes trained on the back of Fana's hood. "Or I'll tell Galahad—"

"Now don't do *that*," Ciarán chided. His voice was so clear, so loud in my head, that it took everything in me not to search the boardwalk for him. "You know what Galahad will do if you tell him, don't you?"

"He'll tell me how to get rid of you."

"Oh, Blue, there's no getting rid of me. Not now that I know your name. We're *tethered*, the same way you're tethered to that old man. But don't worry. I promise not to get too jealous."

I ripped my eyes away from Fana to glance up and down the walk, searching for Galahad and Tiernan at the neighboring shops.

"Galahad will fix this," I asserted, both to myself and Ciarán.

"He will," Ciarán conceded. "By killing you."

I froze with my hands balled into fists at my side.

"He wouldn't," I said, but the scars on my hand said otherwise.

"You're a liability," Ciarán sang. "You can't get rid of me, but *he* can get rid of you. You think he'll let you tag along if I'm in your head? You think he'll let you go back home knowing I might call you to my side and make you *my* weapon?"

Fana giggled at something the pastry woman said, and I shook my head, trying to clear it, trying to dislodge Ciarán's voice from the ridges of my brain.

Would Galahad kill me if he knew I was compromised like this? The fact that I even had to ask the question was a bad sign.

"I saved your life." My voice trembled. "I *helped* you."

"Did you? I still have questions about that, but they'll have to wait. Because, again, you're being followed."

"By you."

"No. Well, *yes*, but like I said, I'm still far enough that you don't have to worry." His laughter sent a shiver down my spine. "No, Blue. I'm talking about the brute with the tattoos hiding behind those crates three huts over."

"Tattoos?" I spun, and my foot slipped on the edge of the walkway. I managed to catch myself before I fell into the river, but Fana turned back to look at me, her arms laden with fresh pastries. "Fana, we're going."

Fana pushed Tiernan's money across the counter to the woman, and skipped to reclaim her spot at my side. I put a protective arm around her and tried to pull the hem of my hood lower over my face.

Titus was supposed to be preparing for his trip back to Vanderfall with Tamora, not following us through Riverstead. I couldn't imagine the Baron letting her bodyguard go too far without a good reason. Maybe he was helping to restock the boat? But that didn't explain why he'd hidden from sight.

"Taking my warning seriously, then?" Ciarán crooned. "Good. I was afraid it might take extra convincing."

Not only was he in my head, but he could see what I saw. He'd be able to track us all the way to the Second Sentinel through me.

Galahad would absolutely kill me if he found out.

I glanced back as I led Fana down the busy walkway, but it was hard to see through the fishermen and stacks of crab cages.

"He's still there, to the left," Ciarán said, and I saw a flash of tattooed arm disappear into a cabana.

Tamora had only helped us after seeing what I could do as a lucid Nightmare. She's spent the voyage up the river testing me and my limits, studying me.

Now that study was over. She'd gotten what she wanted out of us. She could revert back to her original goal.

She wanted Fana.

The shifting light of the steam-lamps brightened as night fell heavier. The patterns of white light cast across the boardwalk and up the walls of cabanas reminded me of sunlight refracting through water, and I felt like I was drowning.

Titus was following us.

Ciarán was in my head.

Galahad would kill me.

"What's wrong?" Fana asked through a mouthful of pastry. Bits of jelly and crumbs stuck to the corners of her mouth.

I chanced another backwards glance. Children played with orbs of Skal, and a teal ball of skalfire escaped their game. It rolled through the air, dissipating as it went, but not before its green-blue hues illuminated the side of a hulking man hiding in the shadows of towering crab cages.

I recognized the edges of Titus's face just as the fizzling light returned him to the dark.

"This way!" I tightened my grip on Fana's arm and took a hard turn to the left.

"What is it?" she whispered, fear creeping into her voice.

"Nothing."

"Wren?" Fana stopped next to a barrel that reeked of fish and algae to stare up at me over her pastries.

I took a steadying breath. I didn't want her to panic, and I didn't want Titus to realize I knew he was behind us.

"You said you wanted to play." I forced levity into my tone. "So come on. You better run fast if you want to make it across."

"Across?"

I took off at a sprint, and Fana laughed as she chased after me. The edge of the walkway approached quickly, and I slowed down just enough to let Fana jump first. Her hood flew backwards, her robes billowed out, and her laughter, trilling and infectious, echoed across the boardwalk. A bit of pastry fell from her arms and into the river as she leapt, but she didn't seem to notice.

She spun to face me after landing across the gap, and I sped up to leap after her.

"See?" She bounced up and down. "That was *fun*!"

"Great!" I prodded her forward. "Then don't stop now!"

A group of fishermen stepped aside as we sped past. An old man grumbled at us, but we were running too fast to make out what it was he said.

"Clever," Ciarán said. "Make it a game. I like that."

"Shut up," I growled.

"I especially like playing games with *you*, Blue."

"I'm going to kill you."

"Are you? My wounds that you so lovingly cleaned for me say otherwise."

"What did you say?" Fana slowed to look up at me.

"Just talking to myself. Keep going, we're almost at the next jump!"

She grinned and sped up to hurdle over the next stretch of river. A group of nearby children cheered for her, and I hurried to catch up.

The steam-lamps became farther apart the closer we got to shore, but swirling lights spilled out from the windows of cabanas and the cabins of small, moored boats. The people were more sparse here as well, which only made our sprint easier.

My footsteps must've been echoing, because as we hurried forward, I could've sworn I heard an extra set of foot falls, but every time I glanced behind us, it was to an empty boardwalk.

"Stop looking," Ciarán said. "He's still there. Keep going."

The rolling hills of the riverbank loomed ahead. We were almost there, but we hadn't lost Titus yet.

"Faster!" I said when Fana's running strides faltered at the sight of the next gap in the boardwalk.

"It's too wide!" she protested. "I can't jump that far!"

"I can!"

Stronger, I willed my muscles. Galahad would have to understand. *Stronger. Faster.*

I scooped Fana into my arms without breaking pace as I sprinted towards the dark water at the end of the boardwalk. The walkway that ran parallel to this one *was* a bit farther than our last jumps had been. I'd never make it in my real body.

I willed my legs one last time as I hurled us out over the water. Once in the air, there was nothing I could do but hope I'd managed to inject enough strength into my Nightmare form to get us across.

My boots slammed into the wooden planks of the parallel dock, and Fana shrieked in delight.

"Well done, Nightmare," Ciarán chuckled. "I thought you might be taking us for a swim there."

I dropped Fana in a mess of cloaks, and she staggered back into a run beside me, laughing.

"What's so funny?" I wheezed.

"You're right. You are more fun than Tiernan!"

We seemed to have lost Titus after that final leap, and I pulled our hoods up to better blend in with the dwindling crowds. Campfires dotted the riverbank, and townspeople gathered around them to sing and roast fish on spits together. The river city glowed on the water behind us, and I glared at the trees that loomed ahead.

Ferrin had said to wait in the forest, and while the trees weren't nearly as tall as the ones in the mountains back at home, the way they swayed in the dark still made me nervous.

"He's not following you anymore," Ciarán said in my head. "No need to get your heart racing. Unless it's because you're thinking about me, of course."

I exhaled heavily through my nose as I led Fana towards the dark of the tree line. Not only could Ciarán see and hear everything I could, but he somehow knew my heart was thundering too quickly in my chest.

Could he hear my thoughts too?

I waited for confirmation, but my mind stayed quiet.

Good.

It was a small relief, though. Galahad would absolutely kill me if he found out. And then he'd kill me again, and again, until I'd used up my limited lives.

Fana finished off her pastries as we waited in the shadows of a birch grove, watching the main gate of Riverstead. I pulled at my eyelashes in the privacy of the dark. We were barely ten feet into the woods, but it was still nearly too much to handle. When Ferrin and the others finally came ashore together, carrying knapsacks full of fresh supplies, I breathed a sigh of relief and flagged them over with a tiny silver flame.

Galahad jogged ahead of the others with ruddy cheeks that puffed out with the exertion of running up the embankment.

"Watch out, Blue," Ciarán chuckled in my mind, and I realized too late that Galahad was beelining towards me.

He balled my cloaks in his fist, and pulled me off balance.

"What did I tell you about taking my magick, Keldorian?"

"Stop!" Fana pushed Galahad away, and while I knew the tiny girl couldn't be the stronger of the two, Galahad fell back. He flexed his gnarled fingers, and I wondered if he was imagining them around my throat. "We were just playing!"

"Playing?" Tiernan screwed up his face as he, Ferrin, and Orla caught up with Galahad.

"Yes. Just-Wren and I made a game." Fana crossed her arms and stood between me and the men.

"You wasted my magick on a *game*?" Galahad snarled.

"Titus was following us," I admitted. "I invented a game to get us away without him knowing we knew he was there and to keep Fana calm."

Tiernan grabbed Fana so he could scour her for any trace of injury. Galahad, meanwhile, held his breath. I knew he still wanted to be mad at me, but Ferrin pushed past him to put a reassuring hand on my shoulder.

"That was very clever, Wren. Good work."

"But why would Titus follow them?" Orla asked from under her new cloak. "The Baron doesn't still want Fana, does she?"

Galahad finally deflated and turned to look back at the river town. The smokestacks of Tamora's boat were visible over the roofs of the cabanas, still spitting red steam into the night sky.

"What does Tamora love more than anything?" he growled.

"Power?" I guessed.

"Skal." His head swiveled towards the dark woods that lay ahead. "And she knows I'm from Tulyr. She's probably guessed that's our next stop, and she's going to follow us all the way there."

"Okay," I said slowly. "If she wants to go to Tulyr so badly, doesn't she have a map?"

"Tulyr is hidden," Galahad explained. "Most people don't care to find it because they believe the Skalsprings there dried up fifty years ago when the city fell. Old, dry ruins aren't worth the risk of the surrounding terrain and rotsbane, but Tamora knows better. She's always looking for ways to expand the Barony, and if there's any chance she'll find Skal in Tulyr, then she'll want it."

Ferrin exhaled heavily.

"Then we better move fast. No magick, and cover your Skal. If they do manage to follow us, we'll lose them at the Umberdust Plains," Ferrin said, readjusting his belt so his travel cloak blocked out the glowing light of his Skal bottles.

The birch trees rustled overhead, and I suppressed a chill. I did not want to go farther into this forest without a light.

"Ferrin and Orla, take point. Tiernan and Fana, with me. And Nightmare," Galahad turned towards me, "you'll follow alone. If you sense someone following you, divert your path away from ours. Lead them off course."

I gulped and nodded.

Alone. In the woods. Without a light.

The scars on my palm itched.

"Is that panic I feel?" Ciarán's voice asked. "Afraid of the dark, are we?"

Orla tried to say goodbye, but her words sounded far away and garbled. I managed to nod in response, unsure of what she said, and I focused on my breathing as the others left one by one.

I stood swaying in the grove. I could stay put. Galahad wouldn't know, would he?

But I didn't want any harm to come to Fana, and if that meant venturing into the forest, then dammit, I guess I was venturing into the forest.

"Tulyr, huh?" Ciarán sighed, and I punched a birch tree in frustration.

"That doesn't help you. You don't know where Tulyr is," I snarled. "No one does. Galahad just said so."

"No, but that only makes this more fun for me."

"I'm so glad one of us gets to have fun."

Low bushes crowded the forest floor, and I pushed my way through, trying to focus on the leaves of the undergrowth rather than the tree trunks that towered overhead.

"So. The dark." The way he said it, I knew he was smiling.

"I don't care about the dark." I pushed through another thicket. Some creature howled in the distance. It sounded more like a coyote than a rotsbane, but my heart jumped into my throat.

"The woods? You did so well in them last week! What happened?"

Last week, when I'd fought Ciarán in the forest, I'd thought Skalterra was a dream. It hadn't been real.

Now, the trees that threatened to swallow me felt all too vivid, and even though I knew if I let myself look up, I'd only see branches and trunks, another part of me feared I'd see my effigy swinging by its neck from the canopies, put there by Linsey and her friends.

I didn't want to see any more bodies in trees, real or not.

The coyote howled again, and I stopped to hide against the paper-like bark of a birch.

"Blue?" Ciarán's voice prodded.

"I'm fine," I spat.

"I can help you."

My fingernails scraped against bark as I curled my hands into fists against the tree.

"How?"

"Galahad's grip on your consciousness is strong, I'll give him that. I can't take you away from him without your permission. But if you yield to me, if you take my magick, I can take control and reform you at my side."

"What?" I looked up, half-expecting to see his orange eyes glowing at me from the shadows.

"You'll be out of the woods, because you'll be with me as *my* Nightmare."

"Screw you."

I marched deeper into the trees.

"It was just an offer, Blue."

"It's a trick."

"I don't want you to suffer."

I laughed at the trees, but the sound was humorless and scared. My heart thundered, and I couldn't breathe deep enough.

I was in danger.

No, no I wasn't. Not immediately. And even if there was something hiding in the shadows to hurt me, I had three lives left in Skalterra.

But I hadn't died in the forest behind that mountain cabin, either, and I still couldn't shake that night.

"Breathe, Wren." Ciarán's voice turned uncharacteristically gentle. "You're okay. Keep moving."

I struggled through another patch of bushes, and thorns pulled at my arms. Droplets of blood formed on my skin, then turned to ash that clung to my arm hairs.

"I don't need help," I lied.

"I know you don't. You've faced worse than anything in this forest."

Worse like him. He'd already killed me once.

"Why are you being so nice?"

"Because you're useful. Now breathe," he said again. I forced air into my lungs to take several deep breaths.

"That's right. Just like that. I don't like feeling your panic any more than you do."

"Then leave."

"If I stop talking, you'll be alone in the dark. Do you really want that?"

"Yes." Except that wasn't true. He was infuriating and unwelcome, and if Galahad somehow figured out he was in my mind, I was dead. But I did not want to be alone. I wanted even less for Ciarán to know that. "Get out."

"Very well. See you in Tulyr, Blue."

I paused with a hand braced against a tree, waiting and listening.

"Ciarán?" I hissed into the shadows. The coyote yipped again, and it sounded like it was laughing at me.

The dark pressed in, and I screwed my eyes shut and sank to the dirt, unable to bring myself to keep walking, even if it meant helping Fana.

I curled up beneath a tree and waited for Galahad to release me.

The hours passed dark and slow, but when the first hint of daylight dusted the edges of the canopy overhead and the birds started to sing, Skalterra dissolved around me, and the forest ebbed away.

It was the most comfortable position I'd woken up in all week, with a soft pillow under my head and blankets pulled up to my chest. I was sure that Gams had to have called an ambulance, and I had to be in a hospital bed. However, the smell of the quilt that weighed me down was too familiar, and someone nearby was purring.

"Jonquil?" I mumbled. She was curled in the crook of my neck. "Are you trying to smother me?"

I sat up, taking stock of my bedroom. I was on top of my bed sheets, but under the quilt from Gams's couch. A glass of water sat on my bedside table, and my stomach churned at the sight of the note that lay next to it.

"I told Jonquil to keep the nightmares away, but here's some water just in case. –L"

My cheeks burned with embarrassment at the thought of Liam having to carry me to bed a second time, but at least I was safe. I was out of the woods. I wasn't in a stairwell or a hospital bed.

But my mind wasn't my own anymore, and now my consciousness belonged to more than just Galahad.

"Ciarán?" I whispered at my room, wondering if the Grimguard could hear me.

However, the only sound to reply in my head was the buzzing of my own thoughts. If Ciarán could hear me from across the Rift, he wasn't about to let me know.

Twenty-Two
Basics of Barbering

Liam's bedside note and glass of water had been a sweet gesture, but his darkened brow and matching scowl when he arrived for work told me he wasn't exactly happy at having to carry me to bed again. He hunted me down where I was restocking the canned goods shelves near the back of the store.

"Have you talked to a doctor?" he demanded.

"Good morning to you too." I glared up at him from where I crouched on the floor, pushing around chili cans to make room for pinto beans. "Where's breakfast?"

He scowled, then jammed his hand into a paper bag to procure an avocado and bacon sandwich on an asiago bagel.

"I found you on the stairs."

"Is the bacon crispy this time?" I ignored him as I bit into my sandwich.

"Wren."

I stalked back towards the register.

"Liam." I mimicked his tone back at him.

"I'm serious. I've got half a mind to tell Ethel—"

I spun around, and he bumped to a stop when I jammed a threatening finger into his chest.

"Don't you dare."

"Do you know what's wrong?" he asked. I rolled my eyes and slipped behind the register counter. "I thought it had to be narcolepsy, but I was searching some things on the internet. Have you heard of POTS? I can't remember what it stands for, but—"

"I don't have POTS," I said through a mouthful of bagel, "but I'm wondering what the diagnosis code is for overly-involved friend."

"Friend?" he repeated with a coy smile.

"Don't push your luck," I warned. "I'll revoke my friendship faster than I can fall asleep."

"That's not funny."

I leaned against the back wall and raised an eyebrow at him.

"It's kind of funny."

"You were sleeping on the stairs, Wren! And you bruised your cheek!"

I rubbed the sore spot below my right eye. I'd spent a good portion of the morning covering the fresh bruise there with make-up.

"I'm fine," I insisted again. "Really. I'm just tired and stressed out with all the Von Leer things."

Liam sighed heavily and ran his hands through his curls.

"When's the phone interview?" he asked, finally giving in on the issue of my apparent fainting spells.

"Next week. Wednesday morning."

"So I have to open all by myself?" He retreated back to the ice-cream station to grab his apron.

"Not if you'd rather do the phone interview for me. Can you do a girl voice?"

He cleared his throat and flashed me his favorite jaunty smile.

"Hello, Von Leer," he said in an over-the-top falsetto, "I'm Wren, and my favorite things include volcanoes, extreme sleeping, and scaring the crap out of my friends by pretending to be dead in the stairwell."

I fought against the laugh that worked its way up my chest, but was unsuccessful.

"Then yes, you're opening the shop all by yourself on Wednesday."

The day saw a steady stream of customers that kept Liam from lurking by the register too much. He still found reasons to come over to my side of the shop between ice-cream cones, and judging by the way he continuously surveyed my face, he was waiting for me to pass out again.

"I'm fine," I hissed at him a little bit after lunch when he reached for my forehead with the back of his hand.

"What?" He blushed. "You've got hair in your face. I'm helping."

"You're checking my temperature!"

"Am not." He batted my hands away and pushed my flyaways back from my forehead. "See? That's better."

I ducked away again, and strands of loose hair fell back into my face.

"Liam, you've got a line."

We both jumped as Gams came out of the stairwell door behind me. Liam spun around to look at the two teenaged girls looking over their ice-cream options.

"Sorry, Ethel." Liam hurried back to his station, and I smiled at my grandmother.

"Don't let Gladys and Sarah see you two being so chummy with each other." Gams smirked at me. Jonquil leapt up to the countertop and bumped against Gams's hand in search of scratches. "You'll be the talk of the town if you aren't careful."

"You told me to be nice to him, so that's what I'm doing."

"Be nice, yes." She scooped Jonquil into her arms. "Be a friend when he needs one. But that's it."

She tickled Jonquil's chin to avoid looking me in the eye.

"You know he isn't like my high school friends. He won't hurt me."

"That's not what I'm worried about."

Gams turned to make her way back to her workshop.

"You think *I'll* hurt *him*?" I whispered after her.

"I think you're on different trajectories," she said matter-of-factly. "You're going to do great things some day, Wren, just like your mother. This town is too small for you the same way it was too small for her. But Liam's a good boy, and he belongs in Keel Watch."

"Gams!" I hissed after her as she and Jonquil headed towards the workshop door.

"Restock the chips when you have a moment, would you?" she called back. "They're looking a bit picked over."

She closed the workshop door behind her.

I blew a flyaway hair from my face, and when it fluttered back into place, I ripped my hair tie out and let my pathetic ponytail collapse. I flinched as I pulled a strand of hair from the nape of my neck where my undercut was becoming unruly.

Gams had told me to be nice to Liam. She's been so happy about me making friends, but now I was supposed to reel that in? I scowled at Liam, but he was too busy scooping ice-cream to notice me.

What did Gams know about what I was going to do with my life? What did she know about *Liam*? What if he wanted to leave Keel Watch after he graduated? What if *I* wanted to stay? The town was on a tectonic fault line after all. If I did become a geophysicist, it might not be a bad place to live.

Liam looked up from the cake cone he was fussing over and met my eyes.

I pulled another hair.

The girls took their ice-cream to the chicken shelf, and I marched out from behind the register to grab more chips from the storage closet, still fuming over Gams's words.

It was just like the Riley thing all over again. Help put up posters, but also don't. Be Liam's friend, but don't be too friendly.

The storage room smelled like old cardboard and dust, and I shoved bread loaves and cereal boxes out of the way to scoop chip bags indiscriminately into my arms.

The air-conditioned air of Gams's workshop blew out from under her door to chill my ankles as I stomped past, hopefully loud enough for her to hear in her basement.

I dropped the chips to the floor before kneeling down and shoving them into their respective spaces on the shelf. I probably should have checked which brands and flavors actually needed restocking before grabbing random bags, but I was too annoyed to go back and trade out my picks.

"That was definitely him right?" a hushed voice asked one aisle over.

"For sure. He looks just like the kid in the picture."

"Let me see it again." Paper rustled in the silence that followed, and then, "Okay, they're absolutely related. Look at the noses!"

I tip-toed out from the chip aisle. The faint reflection of two girls huddled together was difficult to make out in the giant back windows, but I could tell their backs would be to me when I came around the corner. They were still holding their ice-cream cones, but were crouched so the tops of their heads weren't visible over the aisle shelves. In-between them, they held a familiar, crumpled flyer.

"I dare you ask him if he did it," one of them giggled.

"I don't know, he was nice. And cute. Maybe he didn't kill his cousin."

"The cute ones usually end up homicidal. His parents are dead too, remember?"

"Maybe it was the missing kid's dad. He works at a shop down the street. Let's go there next—"

"Actually, I think you're leaving."

The girls jumped so hard at the sound of my voice that the one with beachy blonde curls dropped her ice-cream. Her dark-haired friend fixed a defiant scowl across her angular face.

"We're not done shopping," she said.

"You paid for your ice-cream. Now get out."

The girl looked ready to argue, but then Liam came around the corner, wiping his hands off on his apron.

"Wren? Is everything okay?"

The two girls spun to face him, and the blonde crumpled the Riley poster in her hands.

"Come on." The dark-haired girl grabbed her friend's bicep and dragged her towards the door, causing her to drop the crumbled flyer. She paused to look back at me at the end of the aisle, smirked, and let her ice-cream fall to the floor.

"Hey—" Liam started, but I cut him off.

"Let them leave."

He stayed silent as the bell over the door signaled the girls' exit. Liam's gaze dropped to the discarded flyer, and he bent down to pick it up. He smoothed out the wrinkles and gave his cousin's picture a careful frown.

"What were they saying?" he asked quietly.

"Nothing."

"Wren." He raised pleading brown eyes to meet mine. "Come on."

I sighed, glanced at Gams's closed door, and then squared my shoulders.

"They think you murdered Riley. That or maybe your uncle did it. You should probably call the bagel shop and warn him. They were talking about going there next."

I expected anger, but instead he shrugged and shoved the flyer into the back pocket of his jeans.

"At least word is getting out. We'll find him faster this way." He forced a smile. "You take care of the register. I'll clean up the ice-cream."

I wanted to say more, but he was already headed to the supply closet. I didn't understand how he could be so calm in the face of it all. Losing his parents, losing his cousin, being blamed for their apparent deaths—but he carried on, shrugging it off and mopping ice-cream.

It was infuriating. If he wasn't going to be mad at those girls, who'd only come here because I'd disobeyed Gams and reposted the Riley posters, then what was I supposed to do with *my* anger?

I hurried back to the register, eager to be out of the aisle when Liam returned with a mop.

By the time Gams came up to take the closing shift, I'd dusted the register counter with a smattering of hair pulled from the back of my neck. I brushed it away before she could notice, and disappeared into the stairwell up to the apartment.

My looming Von Leer interview, thoughts of Skalterra, and the quiet sadness that Liam carried the rest of the day had caused enough turmoil for me to seek comfort in pulling at my lengthening undercut. I'd done enough damage that my fingertips could feel where my hairline at the nape of my neck had been made uneven.

Jonquil wove between my ankles in the tiny bathroom across the hall from my bedroom while I dug in a small black tote for my electric razor. It was near the bottom of the bag, hiding beneath a bottle of aloe vera.

It hummed in my hand when I pressed the power button to test its charge, and I pursed my lips. Mom had shaved down the undercut for me, but she was probably in Spain by now.

Jonquil jumped onto the counter, knocking the black tote of razor guards to the floor.

"Be my eyes for me, will you, Jonky?" I pulled up on my ponytail with one hand, and held the buzzing razor to the nape of my neck with the other.

I froze, concentrating on my reflection, wishing I had a way to see the back of my head and wishing I didn't have to shave down my hair in the first place. Why did the Nightmare version of me have beautiful, long hair? And a slender neck and graceful chin?

She wasn't afraid of breaking the rules, of monsters, or of people.

That was who I should be, not the scared kid in the mirror with no way to give herself a decent undercut, so screw it, here goes nothing.

"What are you doing in here?"

I jumped as Liam appeared behind me in the mirror. I slammed the razor to the counter and spun around.

"I'm trying to cut my hair. What are *you* doing in here?"

He lifted a plastic bag.

"I brought you a burger. I thought we could practice more interview questions, and I was looking up iron deficiency—"

"I'm not iron deficient." I cut him off and looked at the steaming bag. It smelled too good for me to be angry at him. "But yes. Burgers would be nice. I'll meet you on the back deck."

He set the bag down and squeezed into the tiny bathroom beside me. He gave Jonquil a head scratch, then picked up the razor.

"Just a clean up, right?" He positioned himself behind me, but I kept a hand over my neck.

"I don't need help." I would rather have the world's most uneven undercut than let Liam Glass see the patchwork mess my hair pulling habit had made of the back of my head.

"Are you sure?" His reflection stared back at me, and I tapped my fingers against the counter where I leaned. I needed help. He wanted to help. Why was this so difficult?

I gave a heavy sigh, trying to force out whatever stubborn pride I was holding onto.

"Just be quick, okay?"

I held my hair out of the way and closed my eyes with my head bowed over the sink. Liam's fingers brushed against my shoulder as he held me steady with one hand and used the other to lift the razor to my neck.

The razor tickled against my skin as Liam ran it up the base of my head. He let go of my shoulder to brush bits of hair into the sink.

"Where's Sabrina?" I asked as he put the razor back to my hair.

"Working. Who do you think made the burgers?"

I frowned at the brown hairs gathering in the white sink basin. I wasn't sure I'd won my way back into her good graces after my blow-up at the beach parking lot.

"Did she know who they were for?"

Liam laughed and brushed at my neck again.

"Don't worry, she wouldn't poison your food if there was any chance I might eat it on accident."

I jolted my head up to look at him through the mirror, and he laughed.

"I knew it. She doesn't like me."

"Sabrina doesn't like most people. Once you've made an impression, it's hard to change her mind about you."

"Oh." I looked back down as Liam lifted the razor again. Jonquil bumped against my arm from her perch on the counter, but I suspected she was searching for Liam's attention rather than mine.

"But it's not impossible to win Sabrina over," he assured me.

I wouldn't get my hopes up, not when I was the one who had originally taken down Riley's posters and had only replaced a fraction of them. If she ever did find out it had been me, she was sure to tell Liam. He was kinder than Sabrina, but he would never forgive me.

He gave my neck a final brush and turned off the razor.

"If architecture doesn't work out, maybe I'll be a barber." He grinned at me in the mirror. I ran my fingers over the shortened hair at the back of my head. Even if I couldn't see the haircut, it at least felt the same as when Mom would shear it down.

"I'll have to take your word for it." As genuine as my next words were, they still took an embarrassing amount of effort to summon forth. "Thank you, Liam."

Liam backed out of the bathroom and scooped the plastic bag up from the floor. Jonquil bounded off the counter to give chase, chirping as she landed on the tiled floor.

"What do you say?" He shook the bag at me, and Jonquil wove between his ankles. "Dinner on the back deck?"

Gams's warning from earlier in the day echoed at the back of my head. She'd been right. A friendship with Liam wasn't sustainable, and he deserved better.

But the burgers did smell good, and he was kind, and as terrible as taking Riley's posters down had been, I felt like I deserved at least a little bit of kindness.

The sun sinking over the harbor was still warm. We sat at the edge of the shop's back deck with our legs through the railing to dangle over the high tide. Liam was back in his Von Leer hoodie, and I watched him eat his burger, thinking of the way I'd stolen his face and clothes in Skalterra to escape arrest with Orla.

Orla had called his face and clothes hideous, and while I disagreed, the memory of it made me smile.

"What?" Liam asked through a mouth full of burger.

"Nothing." I ran my fingers over the fresh undercut again. "Sabrina did a good job on the burgers."

"You think so?" Liam surveyed his half-eaten burger. "Riley always liked them too. Siobhan's going to cater his memorial free of charge."

"Memorial?" My appetite ebbed, and I lowered my burger. "Did they find something?"

Liam sighed, and set his burger aside on the to-go container between us.

"No, but he's probably not coming back." He kept his eyes on the water beneath us. "Everyone knows it."

"Nobody knows anything," I said, too aggressively.

"It's not the first time this has happened, you know."

My stomach churned, and I set my burger down next to his.

"I know. I heard about your parents. Liam, I—"

"I told my aunt and uncle about those girls today," he said. "They were going to keep looking for Riley, but after that... They want it over."

I dug at my undercut, wishing there was still something there for me to pull on. None of this was normal. It didn't make sense, and maybe it wasn't my mystery to unravel, but I hated the look on Liam's face.

"People don't just disappear," I said. "They have to go somewhere, even if they're dead. Why does it keep happening here?"

"It happens everywhere, Wren. All the time."

He rested his chin against the bars of the railing and reached his hand to rest on top of mine. "But thank you. It's nice that someone else believes he might still be alive. It's exhausting keeping up hope."

"I won't give up. Even if you do, I'll believe he's still alive for the both of us," I promised him. His fingertips curled around my palm. "And I'm sorry about your parents."

"Did Ethel tell you?"

"Gladys and Sarah."

"That makes more sense." He chuckled softly, and a tiny smile finally cracked the grief that weighed on his face. "It made for a good sob story for Von Leer at least. I was waitlisted, just like you, so I played up the dead parents thing in my in-person interview."

"That works?" I cocked an eyebrow at him and leaned against the wooden bar of the railing.

"You should've seen the poor admissions officer." Liam whistled. "Nearly had him in tears. If you get the same guy, you should try it."

"My mom's not dead," I reminded him. "She's just in Europe."

"And your dad?"

"I already used the absentee father thing in my admissions essay."

The setting sun turned the harbor orange, reminding me of Ciarán, and I pulled my hand out from under Liam's.

"Then use Riley." He pulled apart a bit of hamburger bun to drop to a couple of bufflehead ducks floating on the water below. "He'll think it's funny."

"I don't know enough about Riley to make that convincing."

"You heard all about him at the beach the other night." He looked up from the ducks to meet my eye.

"I heard his friends talk about him, sure, but you didn't say much."

He picked at the railing, the setting sun turning his hair a bright honey color.

"Riley would do anything for anyone. He'd drop whatever he was doing if someone asked for help, and after my parents disappeared, I needed a lot of help."

The furrow between his eyebrows returned, and the smile the ducks had brought to his face slipped away.

"I didn't mean that you have to talk about him now," I backtracked. "It's okay. Tell me about architecture class. What's that like?"

Liam sighed and shook his head.

"He sold a ton of his things to make room for me when I moved in, and then used the money to buy me a new mattress. When he left for school, he came back every weekend to see me, until Uncle Teddy made him stop because his grades were slipping. And then Riley started buying me train tickets to visit him whenever he could afford it." His eyes turned glassy. "When Mom and Dad died, he was all I had left. I mean, yeah, I had Uncle Teddy and Aunt Olive and Ethel and Sabrina, but Riley was different. He was home."

He cleared his throat and brushed a hand across his cheek.

"He sounds amazing," I said. "If he was even half as kind as you—"

"I just wish I knew what happened." He struck out against the railing, and the salt-weathered wood cracked beneath the hit. "I just want to know where he went! Where Mom and Dad went. And why. Why does everyone have to leave me?"

He buried his face in his arms, disappearing behind the blue sleeves of his hoodie. His shoulders shuddered, then stilled, and a tentative quiet fell over our deck.

I wish I knew how to help. I wish I knew how to find Riley for him, or at least make him feel better. But I was useless.

"I'm not leaving you," I whispered. "I know I'm not Riley, but I'm here."

He raised red-rimmed eyes out from behind his arms, and his throat bobbed as he swallowed hard.

"You keep passing out, and you don't even care."

I shifted closer until our shoulders touched.

"Please don't worry about me," I said. He put an arm around me, and we leaned into each other the same way we had at the bonfire.

"Promise me you'll see a doctor," Liam pleaded, the side of his head leaning against mine.

"I already have." The lie was effortless. I knew there was nothing wrong with me, but how was I supposed to explain to Liam that I kept passing out because my consciousness was being dragged to a separate reality to pilot a much more attractive version of myself? "It's fine. I promise. I'm not going to disappear."

His shoulder relaxed against mine as we both settled into each other.

"Thank you," he murmured. "And I'm sorry."

"For what?" I laughed. "Getting upset? You've seen me do much worse over much less."

"You're okay. You're a good friend. Riley's going to love you once he comes home, you know."

The sun bumped up against the horizon ahead of us. Galahad would be calling any minute, but I couldn't bring myself to break the moment. Sitting here, leaned up against each other, we were both sad, but at least we were sad together.

"Liam?" I whispered.

"Yes?"

I balled my hands in my lap.

"If I fall asleep here, will you carry me upstairs again?"

His arm tightened around my shoulders.

"Of course, Wren."

I wasn't sure how much time passed before Galahad's voice growled at the back of my head, but I wanted those quiet moments of dying daylight to stretch on forever, sitting in both sadness and comfort, side by side with Liam.

Twenty-Three

Intro to Agriculture

In that horrible half-second of darkness between realms, I wasn't sure who would be waiting for me when I opened my eyes. Galahad's voice had been the one to call me across the Rift, but what if Ciarán managed to intercept my consciousness and pull me to his side?

"Welcome to the Wisting Wilds, Wren Warrender."

Galahad's exhausted face materialized in front of me, and Liam's warmth sapped away from my side, replaced by the nighttime chill that rolled over the bluffs where I stood. A calm sea lay before us with wind currents sending ripples across its dark surface. It stretched on for what looked like miles before blending into a darkening mess of hills and cliffs on its opposite shore. Beyond that, jagged, rough-edged mountains cut into the night sky. Three peaks stood higher than the rest.

"Are we taking another boat?" My relief at waking up with my usual friends instead of Ciarán was short lived. Fana was curled up between Orla and Tiernan in the shadows that sat heavy along the edge of the birch forest, and all three were haggard and dirty. I wondered if they'd had any rest since I'd last seen them.

"Boat?" Ferrin paced in front of a crudely-drawn map in the dirt, and looked up to give me an amused smile. "Miss Just-Wren, look again."

I spun back towards the sea, my blue ponytail catching on the wind. The dark water continued to ripple, but the longer I stared, the more it looked like wind blowing over grass than it did an ocean breeze stirring water. It wasn't a sea at all, but a massive field. Tall, grassy fronds bowed and bent in unison, sending streams of glowing blue pollen into the air like embers from a fire.

"The Umberdust Plains," I said, finally understanding. "Like you mentioned last night."

"Tiernan saw Titus following us just a few hours ago," Galahad explained, coming up next to me on the bluff. "The grass of the plains is tall enough to make it nearly impossible to follow anyone through, but the Skal in the pollen will make it easy to track our progress from up here."

"The wind and the migrating ramstag herds will disrupt the pollen enough to hide our path," Ferrin assured me, "but we are going to split up to better our chances. We'll reconvene on the other side, which we should reach by morning."

"Right." I watched the plumes of glowing spores disappear into the star-studded sky. "And ramstags are...?"

"More afraid of you than you are of them," Galahad grunted. "You're the only Nightmare I'm making tonight, so should the need arise to draw from my powers, there will be magick there for you to take. But *don't* take too much again, understand?"

He poked my leather-armored chest with a gnarled finger, and I nodded.

A burst of wind sent me staggering back from the bluff's edge, and Orla steadied me by my shoulders. Her new cloak fluttered behind her in the gale.

"I'll miss you tonight, Just-Wren!" she said. "Travel fast, and I'll see you on the other side!"

"I'm not going with you?" I asked as Orla lowered herself over the lip of the bluff to climb down.

"You'll be with the Sovereign and Tiernan," Ferrin said. "Orla, Galahad, and I will go our own ways to confuse Tamora's trackers as much as possible. Keep Skal use to a minimum to avoid being seen."

I watched Tiernan from the corner of my eye, and I got the sense that he was doing the same to me as he fretted over Fana's cloak. He added her pack to his and turned to Galahad.

"Use the Nightmare as bait," Tiernan said. "I don't need its help."

"Fana needs extra protection," Galahad explained while he watched Orla climb down the cliffside. I leaned over to track her progress with him. A small plume of blue pollen floated upwards where she disappeared into the tall grasses.

I pulled backwards to watch the glowing particles drift up past our vantage point on the cliff to join the stars. A metallic click brought my gaze down to my waist where Ferrin was fastening a lead to my belt.

"This will keep you from getting separated in the plains," he explained, linking Fana's belt to the other end of my lead. She was already connected to Tiernan on her other side.

"Galahad," Tiernan growled, "as the only Riftkeeper to a living Sovereign—"

"You don't outrank me, boy. The Nightmare goes with you," Galahad asserted. "Now move. Remember the rendezvous and protect the Sovereign. And Wren Warrender? Control yourself. Take too much magick from me, and I'll make sure it hurts."

Ferrin and Galahad watched us clamber down the bluff. I took solace in the fact that as long as I was attached to Fana by the lead, Tiernan wouldn't try to knock me off the cliffside. Unfortunately, it meant I couldn't do the same to him, though I let myself fantasize about it as we descended.

Fana proved a skilled climber, and my Nightmare body made the task easier than I would've thought. Wind pressed us against the rock face, and the unpredictable gales pulled on my cloak and hair.

I wondered if Liam was back at home keeping his promise to carry me upstairs as I maneuvered down the cliff face in Skalterra. Maybe someday, if I knew he'd believe me, I would tell him about Skalterra and the tiny role he'd played in saving both realities by taking me to my bed each night.

The grasses had tall, broad stems that fanned out in tufts of fluff that reminded me of dandelions at their heads. I bumped against the tufts as I descended past the tops of the grass, and bits of fluff broke off to rise overhead, glowing blue.

Tiernan reached the ground first and helped Fana down after him. I took stock of our surroundings as I followed and quickly understood why Ferrin had linked us together with leads.

The grass wasn't just tall, towering twice my height, but it was also dense. Tiernan craned his head back far enough for his hood to slip from his dark locks, and I followed his gaze to the two silhouettes that looked down at us from the lip of the bluff.

"Keep up, Nightmare," Tiernan growled. "I'm not waiting for you if you get lost in the grass."

"I'm pretty sure Ferrin made that impossible to happen." I tugged on the lead, and Fana giggled between us. Tiernan yanked on his end, and Fana stumbled after him.

A haunted, bugling cry sounded in the distance to our right, and I froze.

"What was that?" I asked.

"A ramstag?" Tiernan looked back to glare at me. "Don't you have those?"

"I'm pretty sure we don't."

Tiernan tried to scowl at me, but a sneeze racked his body, and he sniffed loudly.

"Allergies?" I asked, looking up at the blue spores.

"I'm fine," he said through a stuffy nose, and then turned to forge forward, pushing grass out of his way. Our leads and the density of the grass stalks made it difficult to move too quickly, and more than once Tiernan would bat a stalk out of his way just for it to spring back and smack Fana or me.

The poor girl stumbled between us, struggling to keep her footing on the uneven ground. A bit of pollen fluff had drifted down to stick itself in her hair, and it glowed blue in her curls. Tiernan sneezed again.

"We made it to the Umberdust Plains, I see."

I tripped at the sound of Ciarán's voice in my head, and Fana and Tiernan both looked back.

"Sorry," I mumbled.

"I told you to keep up." Tiernan continued the path forward, and I held back a sharp quip. It wouldn't be fair to Fana if I picked a fight with Tiernan while she was between us.

Besides, his battle with pollen allergies kept his attention off me as we made our way through the plains. He was forced to resort to using the hem of his cloak as a tissue and couldn't go farther than a few yards without sneezing.

Ciarán stayed quiet in my head, but I knew he was there, watching. I kept my eyes on the ground, afraid he might be able to track us better if I gave him a glimpse of the stars.

"How much farther?" Fana asked after what felt like hours of fighting our way through stalks.

Tiernan slowed to a stop, took a few heavy breaths through his mouth, and uncorked a bottle of Skal. He swirled the liquid inside, and then sipped at it in silence.

"Tiernan?" Fana asked. "Are you okay?"

"Watch out, Blue." Ciarán's voice seeped back into my head.

"Watch out?" I repeated. Fana gave me a questioning look, but Tiernan pulled her attention back.

"We should be far enough away now," Tiernan murmured. "Stay out of the way, Fana."

Gold light erupted in Tiernan's hands, and red burns split the stalks around him in a glowing arc.

"Ferrin said no Skal—" I started, but then Tiernan turned and launched at me with his glowing sword raised.

Instinct brought a silver flail to my hand, and I swung it to wrap the chain around Tiernan's blade and force it to the side.

"Nice block," Ciarán chuckled.

"What are you doing?" I hissed at Tiernan.

"I'm lightening our load!" He kicked me in the stomach, but when I stumbled backwards, my lead brought Fana after me. Tiernan lurched, knocked off balance by the tug on his own tether.

"Stop it!" Fana cried, putting her hands between Tiernan and me. "Ferrin said—"

"Ferrin got Caitria killed" Snot oozed down Tiernan's face, and he tried to wipe it away with his leather bracer. It smeared across his face instead, and the golden light of his blade highlighted red-rimmed eyes. "And if this Nightmare hadn't been so *useless* that night, maybe we could've saved her."

He swung the blade down, and I rolled on top of Fana, turning the leather of my armor to kevlar and thickening the skin of my back into heavy scales that Tiernan couldn't cut through.

The blunt force of the strike knocked the air from my lungs, and I spun away from Fana, arcing my flail with the movement. Tiernan leaped out of its reach, and Fana cried out as his lead pulled her after him.

"You're hurting her!" I yelled.

Stalks of tall grass slapped across my face as I lunged at Tiernan, pushing him into the dirt. He bucked beneath me and rolled us so he came out on top. Clouds of glowing spores silhouetted his dark twists of hair against the starry sky.

"Galahad thinks I need your help, but I don't." He pressed his hand against my throat. Fana clawed at his arm.

"If you yield to me, Blue, I can get you out of there," Ciarán purred in my head. "Just say the word, and you're mine."

"Go to hell," I choked out at both Tiernan and Ciarán.

"Tiernan, please," Fana begged. "Get off her! She didn't do anything!"

Tiernan pressed harder against my trachea. Galahad had given me permission to use his magick tonight. Did that count if it was against Tiernan?

"My sister is dead because of her." Tears that had nothing to do with allergies streamed down Tiernan's face, and I went limp under him.

"Sister?" I gasped beneath his chokehold.

"If Orla hadn't stopped to help you the night the Grimguards attacked Cape Fireld, she would've gotten downstairs earlier. We would've caught up with Ferrin and Caitria, and Caitria—"

I was so stupid. Orla and Ferrin had explained that Riftkeeping ran in families. If Caitria and Tiernan both worked for Fana's family, then of course they were related.

Ciarán laughed darkly in my head, and the Skal in my blood boiled at the sound.

"She was my only family." Tiernan's fingers tightened. "You'll get us all killed in the end."

I could've fought back. I could've drawn from Galahad's power and made bone spikes, or replaced my hands with eagle talons. But as tears and snot dripped off Tiernan's face and onto my chest, I could only think of Liam and his grief for Riley and his parents.

Tiernan's fist glowed gold, and he drew it back, preparing to strike me in the face, but Fana fell on top of me.

"Stop it!" Her curls pressed against me as she turned to look up at Tiernan.

"Caitria is dead because of her!" Tiernan cried. "And Galahad expects me to forget that?"

"Caitria is dead because of *me!*" Fana said.

"No, she died *for* you, it's different." He tried to pull Fana away, but she wrapped her arms tighter around my neck.

"It doesn't feel different," Fana whispered. "I don't want anyone else to die."

Tiernan's shoulders heaved, and his throat bobbed as he swallowed hard.

"Is that an order, my Lady?"

"Yes." She mustered as much authority as she could into the single syllable. Tiernan took a heavy breath, and then gave in to the girl's command. He stood up and glared down at me, still wiping snot from his face.

"I hope to the Three Magicians that the road to the Second Sentinel is short, Nightmare, so I can bury my memory of you, which is more than I was able to do for Caitria."

Another cry split the night, but unlike the bugling call of the ramstag, this one was a haunted howl that sounded like it was choking on its own scream. My veins turned to ice, and I froze where I lay on the ground, unable to so much as think through the panic the sound filled me with.

"A rotsbane." Tiernan extinguished his gold light.

"What do we do?" Fana whispered.

"I— I don't know."

"Wren," Ciarán's voice was sharp now, "Wren, you have to yield to me. A rotsbane will kill you."

I shook my head, trying to breathe. I would not yield. I would let Tiernan kill me before the rotsbane could devour my consciousness. I still had three lives left. I could spare one.

The ground trembled beneath my back, and a distant roar grew louder as the trembling turned into a violent quake.

"Get down!" Tiernan pushed Fana to the ground next to me, shielding her body with his.

A beast with antlers that spiraled out in dizzying patterns broke through the wall of grassy stalks, and I rolled over to join Tiernan on top of Fana as a barrage of hooves rained down around us. I dared to lift my head just a little to watch the stampeding ramstags pass around us.

If they were running away, we needed to run too, but it was impossible to move with so many massive animals speeding past. Fana shook beneath me, and I focused on Tiernan's haggard assurances to her that it would be okay.

"Come on, Blue," Ciarán growled. "You'll be safer with me."

When the dirt finally stilled and the last bleating ramstag galloped after its herd, we pried ourselves off of Fana. The ramstags had flattened the tall grasses around us, blazing a trail away from the direction of the rotsbane.

Blue pollen hung in the air around us, illuminating the crouched form some twenty yards away.

I put a warning hand on Tiernan's shoulder and silently pointed. He followed my finger as the figure slowly stood up.

Titus, Tamora's mountain of a bodyguard, stretched out his arms as he straightened. We had indeed been followed into the plains.

"So much for using the others as distractions," Tiernan growled.

"You made it too easy." Titus's grin glowed blue in the light of the spores. "Ramstags don't sneeze."

Tiernan's golden blade reappeared in his hand, and he charged.

The lead that connected him to Fana and me yanked him backwards, and Titus turned to run back into the safety of the tall grasses.

"Don't lose him in the plains!" Ciarán commanded. "Otherwise he'll keep following you!"

I echoed the words out loud for Tiernan, and pulled him to his feet to sprint after Titus.

Tiernan, with his bearings gathered, summoned a golden javelin and hurled it at Titus. The tip of the weapon pierced through his shoulder and knocked him face-first into the ground with a muffled cry.

We charged forward with Fana between us, but Titus remained immobile on the flattened grass as if pinned there by Tiernan's upright javelin.

"Is he dead?" Fana whispered. I knelt down next to Titus as Tiernan's javelin dissolved. Maybe the blue spore light was making the wound look strange, but there was something familiar about the way his blood gathered and clumped where the javelin had pierced his shoulder.

"Careful, Nightmare," Tiernan said, sniffing loudly.

I ran my hand over the shoulder wound. What should have been warm with blood was buzzing with used Skal, and my fingers came away with a coating of thick, ash-like dust.

"It's dirt," I murmured, and realization dawned on me too slow.

The behemoth of a man rolled over, eyes flashing red over an open-mouthed grin. His hand shot out from under him, and I pushed Fana out of the way. Fingers morphed into claws, and Titus's tattooed hand transformed into a massive talon that gripped me around my chest, and dug into my armor.

I cried out, grabbing at the wolf and scimitar tattoo on his forearm to keep myself steady. I swung my arm upwards as my favorite bone spikes shot from beneath my skin. They sliced through Titus's talons. Dust poured from the appendage until he stemmed it with a new lethal claw.

Fana, Tiernan, and I staggered backwards as one.

"He's a Nightmare," I breathed.

"No shit," Tiernan spat. Twin swords appeared in his hands.

"It was nice of you to teach me those pretty tricks of yours back on the Baron's boat." Titus flexed the sharpened points of his regrown talons. "I never would've known this was possible without your help."

Wings sporting brown plumage expanded behind him, and he beat at the air. The force of the wind knocked us backwards in a tangle of limbs and rope.

From the air, Titus would be able to track our progress across the plains. He and Tamora would follow us all the way to Galahad's old home.

I ripped the rope of my lead with my bone spike, freeing me from the others, and I ran after Titus. I willed all the strength I could muster into my legs and sprang after him, digging claws of my own into his thighs.

"Wren!" Fana cried after me.

"Go!" I pulled on Galahad's magick to make myself heavier and dragged Titus back to the ground. "I'll make sure he doesn't follow you!"

Fana hesitated, but Tiernan pulled her towards the cover of the grass. The rotsbane howled again, closer this time, and Tiernan stopped his and Fana's retreat to look back at me with wide eyes.

"I'm fine!" I shouted. "Get Fana out!"

Titus beat his wings harder, but I was too heavy. He landed on top of me in a mess of wings, and Ciarán crooned in my head.

"Birds have hollow bones, Blue. Break him."

"I know how birds work!" I turned my fist to steel as I brought it swinging into his side. His ribs snapped in my wake.

He screamed in pain, and the sound blended with that of the howling rotsbane. I ignored the approaching monster and managed to pin Titus beneath me.

Bits of blue hair had escaped my ponytail to hang in his face. He blew them away as he glared up at me.

"How long have you been Tamora's pet then?" I asked.

"I'm not her *pet*, I'm her partner!" Titus erupted in porcupine-like quills, and I was forced to leap off him. He made another break for the grasses. I lunged at his unprotected legs and slashed my bone spikes into his ankles. He collapsed as his tendons severed.

"Titus is a fake name, right? To keep you safe from other nocturmancers?" I stood over him so he could watch his blood turn to dust on my spikes. "I've met dogs named Titus. They're always lap dogs for some reason."

"I'm not a pet."

"Then who are you? How are you lucid?"

He grinned.

"No clue, but here's a word of advice. Don't question it. You can be anyone you want here, so enjoy it as long as they let you."

"Does the name Maxwell Brenton mean anything to you?" My estranged father was still my number one theory on how I was lucid.

"Is this really the time for an interrogation, Blue?" Ciarán asked. "The rotsbane is getting closer."

Titus's face screwed up.

"Never heard of him," he spat.

"Where do you live?" I ran through Ferrin's other theories on lucid Nightmares in my head.

"I live here, at Tamora's side," he asserted. "Whatever life I have in Keldori is only so I can keep living this one."

"Then why are you working against us?" I asked. "We're trying to save both Keldori *and* Skalterra. If you ruin that—"

"I'm not going to hurt the girl." Titus pushed up onto his hands. "Tamora only wants the Skal from the old man's hometown. How does that put your mission at risk?"

Admittedly, it didn't, but I didn't need to know much about the Baron or Skalterran politics to know she didn't need any more Skal than she already had.

"You'll leave us alone," I said.

"I'll do whatever Tamora tells me to do so I can keep coming back here every night."

"He's about to attack," Ciarán warned.

Sure enough, a red knife appeared in Titus's hand, and he threw it at my head. Ciarán's warning gave me the time I needed to duck out of its trajectory. I procured a silver flail, ready to retaliate, but the weapon dissolved before I had the chance to so much as swing it.

"What—" I looked at my empty hand, trying to figure out where my flail had gone, but then a screeching howl ripped the night.

A rotsbane towering as tall as the waving grass, all shadow, bone, and claws, broke through the foliage and charged into our clearing. Titus leapt to his feet and threw another knife, but the rotsbane sucked it into the black hole of its mouth.

I turned and ran. I couldn't fight a rotsbane. I didn't want to die.

"You can't outrun it, Blue!" If I didn't know any better, I would've thought Ciarán sounded worried. "Yield to me! Let me save you!"

A strangled scream brought me to a stumbling halt at the edge of the clearing, and I turned around in time to see Titus trying to take to the sky with regrown wings.

However, four sets of dark claws clamped around his torso and dragged him back down.

"Tamora!" he wailed, struggling in the rotsbane's grip. "Tamora, please!"

But Tamora was too far to hear Titus.

The rotsbane unhinged its jaw and screeched its unearthly wail, preparing to devour Titus, consciousness and all.

"No," I breathed, taking the first shaking step back towards Titus.

"He's already dead, Blue! Now yield so you aren't next!" Ciarán demanded.

I ignored the splitting pain as I snapped a bone spike off my arm. I forced strength and power into my legs, ignoring Galahad's warning tug on his end of our connection.

"Dammit, Blue," Ciarán growled, "at least aim for its mouth if you're going to be this stupid!"

Fallen stalks of grass slipped beneath my boots as I ran, then leapt, at Titus and the rotsbane.

The rotsbane's howl turned my insides to lead, but I mustered up every bit of strength I had left into my arms as I drove the end of my spike through the back of Titus's head and into the rotsbane's gaping maw.

Titus gave a gargling gasp and turned to ash beneath me. I fell to the trodden grass, and the rotsbane collapsed over me, squealing a sustained note that sounded like a screaming tea kettle. Its horrible, shadowy limbs twitched like a dying spider, and the pinpricks of lavender light in its deepset eyes dimmed as it choked on my bone spear.

I dragged myself out from under cold, twitching limbs, and it continued to watch me, reaching out with its claws to scrape at the dirt between us. Its boney blackened jaw opened and shut over my spear, gasping for air and Skal. The rotsbane gave a final gurgling wheeze, and its shadowy form dissipated, evaporating upwards in a cloud of dull, multicolored dust that mingled with the glowing pollen that still hung in the air.

The clearing stilled, and I sat staring at the pile of dust that had been Titus, hoping I'd been fast enough to send him safely back to bed in Keldori.

I staggered to my feet, and gut-wrenching pain ripped me open. I hadn't noticed the rotsbane carve its claws through my chest and abdomen, but dark dust spilled from the gashes in my armor. I fell back to my knees, gasping through the pain.

"Ciarán?" His name was a weak rasp on my lips.

Ciarán sighed in my head.

"I'm here, Blue, but I think this might be goodnight."

I grasped at Galahad's magick, but it was too late. The wounds across my torso hemorrhaged Skal faster than I could draw it in. I rolled onto my back and watched blue pollen stream across the star-studded sky until the image faded to the darkened ceiling of my bedroom.

Something sharp cut across the palm of my hand.

I was down to two lives left in Skalterra.

Twenty-Four
Public Relations 101

The silver ridges of my scars caught the morning sunlight, and I studied the new line of puckered skin that cut across Galahad's "T". With two lives left in Skalterra, maybe I should've been more concerned as I walked down Keel Watch Harbor's empty Main Street. I was two dream-deaths away from dying for real.

Instead, I marveled at how the new line of scar looked just as old as the ones it had joined in the night, as if it had been there on my hand for years rather than hours. The gashes the rotsbane had carved into my stomach were also looking older than they actually were. They'd bled a bit when I first woke up, but the broken skin had already fused back together, leaving me sore and bruised, but in one piece.

I curled my fingers over the scars of my hand and shoved my fist into the pocket of my open zip-up hoodie. My one-size-too-big flip-flops smacked the pavement of the empty sidewalk. Monday morning had brought a lull in visitors, so Gams had given Liam the day off to help his aunt and uncle plan for Riley's memorial.

This, of course, meant someone had to go retrieve Gams's morning bagel sandwich.

Teddy's bagel shop was situated at the end of the street, right where the road veered away from the water and up the windy hill to the library. The yeasty smell of fresh-baked bagels wafted out onto the sidewalk, and my growling stomach quickened my pace into the shop.

It was dark and cozy inside after the bright, morning sun of the street, and Teddy waved at me from behind a display counter full of different types of bagels. Ceramic chickens of every color decorated the register, and I recognized Gams's craftsmanship in their patterns and shapes.

"Wren! There you are! I've got your food right here!" Teddy called out. Liam's blond curls bounced around his forehead as he looked up from the binder he was bent over in one of the shop's vinyl-seated booths.

He raised a hand in greeting, and my cheeks warmed. He had carried me to bed again last night. That was three times now. I tried to smile back.

"Let me help you with that." A woman with graying brown hair braided over her shoulder got up from Liam's booth to retrieve a brown bag from behind the counter. She smiled at me as she handed me the bag, but her eyes were rimmed red and heavy. "It's nice to see you again, Wren. When was the last time you were in Keel Watch?"

"I don't know, middle school maybe?" I ran through the faces in my memories of visits to Gams growing up, but I couldn't place the woman. "I'm sorry, I don't think I remember you."

"Olive." She offered a slim, long-fingered hand. "Riley's mother, and Liam's aunt."

She winked at Liam and went to join her husband at the register.

"Sleep okay last night?" Liam asked behind me.

I spun around, ready to defend myself after falling asleep in yet another inappropriate location.

"Look, I—" I looked at the open binder in front of him. Its pages boasted images of floral arrangements. He, or maybe his aunt, had circled a few of the options. All sense of fight fled me, and I deflated. "Yes. Thank you, Liam."

He smiled and shifted over in the booth, patting the striped vinyl next to him.

"No nightmares?" he asked. I had to work hard to keep the pain off my face as I took the seat he'd offered. The rotsbane's claw marks were healed, sure, but the muscles there were sore and tender.

"Eh." I dug inside the brown bag until I found my usual avocado and bacon breakfast sandwich. "More of the same. You?"

"Weirdly enough, I slept great." He frowned at the binder, then pushed it towards me. "What do you think? I don't really like the lilies. They feel too... I don't know. Final?"

"Lilies are funeral flowers." I nodded in agreement. "Is this for the memorial?"

"Yeah. Aunt Olive is Team Lilies, but I like the more leafy ones. I guess Riley's her son though, so she should get final say." Despite insisting he'd slept well, his eyes were heavy and his hair messy. "She picked out lilies for my parents too. She is— well, *was* my mom's sister."

I looked back at Olive. The librarian, Mr. Lane, had come down the hill to get breakfast, and she laughed with him at the counter while Teddy made Mr. Lane's order.

"Which ones would Riley like?" I asked.

"None." Liam flipped the binder shut. "He'd call it a waste of money because he isn't dead."

My phone buzzed on the table and the screen lit up. I thought maybe Gams was getting impatient for her bagel, but the name on the screen sent my heart plummeting.

Why the hell was Linsey Harper texting me?

Adrenaline buzzed in my extremities like fresh Skalmagick, and I fought the instinct to throw my phone across the bagel shop. Instead, I took it in my hands and opened the message.

"What is it?" Liam asked. I shook my head, and tilted my phone towards him so he could see.

A web link glowed under Linsey's name, and while the thumbnail was pixelated and blurry, I recognized the woman in the image.

I tapped it, and Liam shifted closer to watch the video load.

The video title loaded first, in all caps, at the base of the screen: "ROMANCE AUTHOR GOES ON RAMPAGE".

"No," I whispered. Mom appeared onscreen, wearing her favorite green robe with her hair disheveled, and standing on Linsey Harper's front porch. The angle of the video suggested the footage was taken from a security camera, and I held my breath as Mom hammered on Linsey's front door.

"Is that your mom?" Liam hissed. I shushed him, but he continued. "Wow, she looks *just* like Ethel."

"You better get your ass outside in the next three seconds, Teresa, or I'm breaking your goddamn windows and coming in there myself!" Mom screamed in the video. She kicked over a potted plant with a slippered foot before rapping on the door again.

"Get off my porch before I call the police, Eliza." I recognized Mrs. Harper's voice speaking over the camera's intercom.

"Oh, *please* call them so I can tell them what your cheat daughter did to Wren!"

"This is on the internet," I said blankly. Mom lifted the upturned plant pot and smashed it against the concrete porch.

Liam patted my shoulder and leaned in closer to better watch.

"Linsey hasn't been home all night," Mrs. Harper chided. "And *your* daughter got mine kicked out of school, so—"

Mom launched into a tirade that drowned out Mrs. Harper's words, and I cut the volume on the phone. Mom ripped the welcome mat from the ground and frisbee-threw it into the front yard, still yelling.

"It could be worse," Liam said, watching Mom destroy the Harpers' porch decorations.

"How, Liam? How could this be worse?"

"It's not like you're ever going to see anyone from high school again," Liam said. "And no one would be dumb enough to give you crap about it because your mom might come murder their lawn flamingos."

Mom punted a garden gnome across the screen.

We watched in horrified silence as Mrs. Harper turned on her garden sprinklers, forcing Mom to abandon the porch as water blasted her from all angles. She lost her slippers on the lawn in her hurry to escape, but still found time to turn back and flip the Harpers' house the double bird before retreating to her car and peeling away from the sidewalk.

The video ended, and the screen turned black to reflect our stark faces back at us.

"I have to go." I sprung away from the booth, grabbing the brown bag with Gams's breakfast. I left my half-eaten bagel on the table. I didn't have much of an appetite anymore.

"Wren—" Liam reached for my hand, but I drew away. Blood pounded in my ears, and the shop, so dark and cozy before, now seemed too bright.

The bell over the door rang out as I ran onto the street, and my flip-flops slapped with every running step back towards Gams's store.

I knew Mom had been angry the morning I'd stumbled out of my car covered in sticks and dirt, and yes, she'd driven off in a hurry, but she'd seemed so calm after coming home, if a bit wetter than before.

Sabrina raised a hand in greeting as I passed her on the sidewalk, but I ignored it, surely setting our flimsy friendship back even further. However, there was no time for Sabrina right now, because Linsey Harper had put my mother's tantrum on the internet.

When I pushed into the air-conditioned interior of Gams's shop, I thought she'd already seen the video. She waited for me, leaning against the counter with her arms crossed and her eyes narrowed behind her round glasses.

But then I saw the wrinkled missing flyer in her hand, stained with bits of day-old melted ice-cream.

"I found this in the trash can." Riley's black-and-white face smiled back at me. "What's extra weird is that it has the Port Fletcherton Community Board approval stamp. How did this get to the Port Fletcherton Community Board, Wren? And then all the way back here?"

I held up my phone.

"Mom's on the internet."

"Well, I should hope so! Her books are very popular in certain circles, but—"

"It's a video."

Gams stared at me for a moment, her lips twisting as she breathed heavily through her nose.

"Fine," she snapped, and slammed Riley's poster onto the counter. "What's this video?"

I silently held my phone out to her and let the video play. I didn't have the heart to watch it again. Gams's eyebrows shot up her forehead, and she nodded along as she watched in awed silence.

"I would've chosen different words than 'cheat daughter' for that Linsey girl, but still. Very impressive. Is that it?"

"Is that it?" I repeated. "Gams! Everyone can see this!"

"So delete it!"

I pulled at my hair, feeling my ponytail come undone beneath my fingers.

"That's not how the internet works!"

"Von Leer isn't going to care. It's okay—"

"I don't care about Von Leer! I care about Mom! I care about her book tour!" I yelled. Yes, there had been a time where this video would've mortified me in a different way. I would've been embarrassed to have my mother freaking out and getting sprinklered online on my behalf, but Liam was right. I wasn't going to see anyone from high school ever again, and I'd already solidified their opinions of me when I got Linsey expelled from Von Leer.

And Von Leer? They already knew my mother. She'd been their student. She'd done more speaking engagements there for her romance novels than anywhere else. Her books were in the student store, despite their filthy content.

No, this wasn't about me. This was about how I'd been dumb enough to get stuck in the woods and set Mom off like this. This was, just like most things, my fault.

Gams threw her head back and laughed, and the sound brought embarrassed warmth to my cheeks.

"Eliza is a grown woman, and she was perfectly within her rights to dropkick those ugly lawn gnomes. Maybe not legally speaking, of course, but any good mother would've done *at least* that."

"But—"

She held up her hand to cut me off and pulled her own phone out of her pocket.

Mom answered on the first ring.

"Mom? What's going on? Is it Wren?" Mom's voice was tight with worry.

"There's a video of you on the internet." Gams cut straight to the chase.

"Whoops." Mom's laugh echoed over the speaker. "Is it from the tour? The other day in Nice, things got a little out of hand. In a fun way, of course."

"It's from Linsey Harper's front porch." Gams smirked at me.

"Linsey's— *oh.*"

"Yeah."

"Has Wren seen it?"

"She's standing right here. Say hi, Wren."

"Hi, Mom," I mumbled.

"Oh, god. Wren, look. I'm sorry," Mom gushed. "I flew off the handle a little bit, I'll admit, but I never meant to embarrass you."

"I'm not embarrassed." I crossed my arms and stared at Gams. "I don't care what Linsey thinks about us. I care about your books."

Mom laughed again, and Jonquil jumped up onto the counter to bat at the phone.

"I promise the sort of readers checking out my books do not care about me breaking a couple of tacky flamingos. This is free marketing. It actually explains the bump in sales I've had today."

"You got sprinklered," I said. "Because of me."

"I got sprinklered because Linsey's mother is a nasty, old bat and her daughter is no better. They're lucky I don't write them into my next book just to kill them off."

"But—"

"Check the comments, Wren." Mom sounded exasperated. "I promise, I'll be okay."

I hesitated, still staring at Gams. She nodded at the phone in my hand, and I scowled as I reopened Linsey's video.

"TurtleLauncher47 says it's a publicity stunt," I said, scrolling through the comments. "And some guy named Cliff doesn't like your robe."

"Cliff is jealous," Mom sniffed. "What else?"

Each rude comment made my heart sink lower, calling Mom all sorts of nasty names, but Mom was right. Most of the commenters seemed to be on her side, or, like TurtleLauncher47, thought it was fake.

"This one says she knows a momma bear when she sees one and that you should've broken the ugly fountain next to the porch too." I frowned. "I hate that phrase. 'Momma bear'."

"I had my eye on that fountain," Mom admitted. "I thought about going back for it until I was halfway home."

"I don't want you risking your career for me!" I asserted. "Or getting arrested!"

"Teresa wouldn't dare call the cops," Mom snorted. "Not when she knows her own kid is guilty of worse. Call it an unspoken agreement. You don't press charges against Linsey, they don't press charges against me, and none of us have to ever see each other again."

I leaned against the shelf full of blue chickens, and ran my hand over my eyes.

"Yeah. Fine, Mom." Europe had never felt so far away. I needed her here to tell me it was okay. I needed to see her face to know she wasn't lying.

"I have to go get ready for my next event, but I don't want you thinking about that video anymore. And block Linsey Harper's number. I don't know why you still have it," she said. "I love you, Wren."

"Love you too."

Gams ended the call and gave me a smug look.

"Your mother can take care of herself." She stepped forward to wrap me in her arms. I set my chin on top of her white-haired head and tried to still my hammering heart. "And don't think I've forgotten about those posters."

I pushed away and shook my head.

"I was trying to help," I said.

"How many did you put back up?" Gams scowled.

"Just a few in Port Fletcherton, but obviously it was enough." I marched past Gams to snatch the flyer from the counter and crumble it into a ball. "You were right. A couple girls came by yesterday to gawk at Liam, and now his family is going forward with Riley's memorial when he could still be out there."

The search for Riley getting cut short was another thing I could take the blame for, as roundabout as it was. The space behind my eyes stung, but I took a steadying breath. I'd killed a rotsbane last night. This was nothing to cry over.

Gams frowned and retreated behind the counter to grab her purse and keys.

"Where are you going?"

"To take down the rest of the flyers. I promised I wouldn't make you do my dirty work anymore. The store is closed today. Go upstairs. Take a shower. You need a break."

She came around towards the door, but I stared out the far windows rather than meet her eye. I was messing everything up for everyone. No matter what I did, it was wrong.

"You're doing amazing, Wren," Gams insisted. "I'm sorry I put you in this position to begin with. Please be kinder to yourself. This isn't the end of the world, and even if it was, it's not your fault."

She stood on her tiptoes to peck my cheek before bustling out the front door, but I could've done without the reminder that the world ending was another thing resting on my shoulders.

Twenty-Five

Recreational Climbing

Mom's video had over two hundred thousand views by the time I trudged to my room for an early bedtime. Against my better judgement, I continued to read the comments as they rolled in. Many of them remained firmly on Mom's side, gleaning what they could from her angry rant, but there were still plenty of strangers online who didn't hold back.

"Trashy writer, trashy woman" was among the kindest of these responses. The rest had me grateful that Gams didn't know how to look up the video and read the comments for herself.

Rather than wallow in guilt and shame, I crawled into bed while the sun was still setting, eager to fall asleep and wake up in a world where Riley's memorial, my upcoming Von Leer phone interview, and Linsey Harper didn't exist, even if it meant facing more rotsbane.

The others waited in a half-circle when I came to in Skalterra. We were back under tree cover, but these trees were unlike any I'd ever seen back home. Massive, grooved trunks reached high into the sky where their shallow canopies spread out like the underside side of mushroom caps so that I felt more like I was in the belly of a grand cathedral rather than another forest. Stars twinkled in the spaces between foliage, and I caught a glimpse of the twin moons.

"What happened?" Galahad was the first to get in my face, and after a full day of reading nasty comments about my mother online, it took me a moment to remember the fight against Titus the night before.

"Oh." I ran my hand through my blue hair to pull it back into a ponytail. "You mean Tamora's dog?"

"Tiernan said he's a lucid Nightmare." Ferrin frowned. His goggles were in place over his eyes, and he focused on the glowing green knives he was creating in his hands. "Is he the one that ashed you? Is there any chance he followed us?"

"Ashed?" I repeated. "You mean killed?"

"Yes, girl!" Galahad shook me by my shoulders. "I felt you go halfway through the night! Did you or did you not at least manage to keep Titus off our tail?"

I flipped my blue ponytail over my shoulder and smirked.

"Don't worry. I killed Titus. Or ashed him. Whatever the word is. There's no way he followed you."

"Then who killed *you*?" Galahad demanded.

"A rotsbane."

The color drained from Galahad's face, leaving him pallid in the light of Ferrin's knife.

"No." Orla stumbled forward to take my hands in hers, and she searched my face for signs of lingering injury. "But then, you should be dead-dead! If it killed you —"

"It didn't eat me." I made a stabbing motion at my stomach. "It was its claws. And for what it's worth, it died first."

"Died?" Tiernan's eyebrows raised in something other than disgust for once.

"Yeah, I killed it." I took a special delight in their blank stares. They didn't need to know Ciarán had tipped me off about a rotsbane's mouth being its weak point.

"You..." Ferrin's mouth cocked in a disbelieving half-smile. "You killed a rotsbane?"

"That's why I'm here, isn't it?" I pointed out. "I'm supposed to be the perfect weapon."

"Sure, but rotsbane are incredibly difficult to kill." Ferrin twirled one of his knives.

"And dangerous!" Orla interjected.

"Obviously." I gestured at my abdomen again. "I died. Anyway, where are we now?"

Moonlight cast lines of silver across the barren forest floor, and I craned my head back to look up at the patchwork of leaves and branches overhead. An owl hooted in the distance.

"We're properly in the Wisting Wilds now." Ferrin stepped back and spread his arms wide to welcome me to the forest. "Four hundred years ago, when every Magician was forced into Skalterra, this is where they appeared. Now, it's all but abandoned and near impossible to navigate."

"*Near* impossible," Galahad grunted. He turned his back to me and pointed deeper into the forest. "You're on point, Ferrin. Orla, with Tiernan and Fana. Miss Warrender, you'll be with me tonight."

"Really?" Orla groaned. "I thought it was my turn to be with Wren again."

"With Tiernan and Fana, Orla," Galahad growled. Orla cast me a forlorn look and stretched her fingers out towards me in farewell.

"Tomorrow night, then," she promised. "I want to hear more about the fight with the rotsbane."

The trees were sparse, standing straight and stoic like lonely giants. Aside from a few ferns and the occasional glowing mushroom, the forest floor was free of undergrowth. Even split up, the others were clearly visible walking ahead of us.

Galahad limped alongside me with the aid of a silver walking stick made of Skal.

"How many lives left is that then?" he asked between heavy breaths exhaled through his nose.

I unfurled my fingers in front of me to show off the gray lines of scar.

"Two," I admitted. He gave a grunting laugh, and I scowled. "One of them was Tiernan's fault."

"Then you best hope Tiernan doesn't blow you up anymore."

I stopped in a shaft of moonlight that cut to the forest floor, but Galahad continued his forward shuffle.

"You can take it away, you know. I don't need..." I wrestled with my pride as it stood in the way of the words I was looking for. "I don't need the extra motivation. I don't want Fana to die. Or any of you. I'll help. Just, take it away, alright?"

I held my palm out for Galahad, and he staggered to a halt. He turned back to glare at the scars he'd left on my hand.

"No." He continued his forward march.

"No?" I repeated and rushed to catch up to him. "I'm telling you I want to help! You don't have to put my life on the line to keep me here anymore. I'm here because I want to be."

"You're here because I brought you here, Wren Warrender." He kept his goggled eyes trained on Fana's back up ahead.

"Right! So take away the limit on how many times I can die so you can *keep* bringing me here!"

"Don't tell me you've grown attached to Skalterra. Is Keldori really so miserable that you'd rather have us, with our rotsbane, barons, and cruel old men?" He turned his eyes on me, and even though it was impossible to see through the opaque glass of his goggles, I knew he was glaring.

"I don't want to die," I said.

"Then do your job."

"That's gotten me killed three times already!"

"So do your job better!" He batted at my head with his walking stick. I smacked it away.

"I'm doing my best," I grumbled.

"Then may the Three Magicians save us all."

I balled my hands into fists as he continued ahead of me. I glared at the back of his leather duster and wrestled with my pride. There was one more thing weighing on my shoulders, but of all the people in either of my lives, Galahad was near the bottom of the list of who I wanted to dissect it with. However, as sullen and cruel as Galahad could be, he was my anchor in Skalterra. It was his magick that formed this version of me every night.

"It's not about Keldori or Skalterra," I admitted.

"Oh, Miss Warrender, I already know you aren't here to be a hero. Every Nightmare is an idealized version of themselves. I imagine it's addicting, getting to exist as something better than yourself. But this isn't *you*." He paused and pushed his goggles up to stare at me with fierce gray eyes that caught the silver light of his staff. "Skalterra isn't your home. The Wren Warrender asleep in Keldori is who you are. You are here to help because I've called you here, and after we reach the Second Sentinel, you won't be coming back."

"This Wren kills rotsbane!" I smacked my chest armor as I said it. "This Wren doesn't mess everything up."

"Then you better not die anymore so you can enjoy your last two weeks of being 'This Wren'."

"Why not remove the curse?" I held my hand at the wrist, as if to offer the scars up to Galahad. His bushy eyebrows softened. "I'm not going to run anymore."

"Maybe it would be a mercy for you to die in Skalterra rather than never return to this version of yourself. Perhaps I simply don't like you much. Or, Wren Warrender, it isn't a curse that can be reversed, and if I could I would, but I can't."

"You..." I trailed off, letting the weight of Galahad's words settle in my gut. "You can't."

"Two weeks, Wren Warrender," he said again. "It's funny. If you hadn't proven yourself so useful, I might've stopped calling you back before now."

A low laugh in the back of my head made my cheeks burn. This was not a conversation I wanted Ciarán to overhear, but it was far too late for that.

I closed my fingers over the scars on my hand and bit my tongue. Whatever sharp words I wanted to throw at the Grimguard for eavesdropping would have to wait. If Galahad knew Ciarán was listening in, he'd be sure to expend my final two lives himself.

Ciarán didn't give any more indication that he was lurking in my mind, and the night's march brought us to smaller trees and heavier undergrowth. As the trees closed in around us, I took comfort in my friends around me. These woods weren't nearly as dense as the birch forest from a few nights prior. I would be okay.

The terrain became steep and rocky to the point of having to climb in some areas. Clusters of tiny white flowers broke through cracks in the rocks. Their delicate petals emitted a soft light, and while I helped the others set up a humble camp before daybreak, Fana played with the glowing flowers and wove them into her curls.

After Galahad released me for the night, I woke up at home well-rested despite all the walking and climbing. Then I remembered that there would surely be more comments on Linsey's video of Mom and my phone interview with Von Leer was in two days, and I wished I could be back in Skalterra.

Liam's return to work only made me feel worse. He did his best to smile, but he looked absolutely miserable scooping ice-cream for the few families that trickled in throughout the day. I wondered vaguely if his aunt and her white lilies had won the battle over memorial flower arrangements but thought better than to ask.

It was a relief when the day finally ended, and I could crawl back to my room after an early dinner with Gams in the kitchen. I breathed a sigh as my bedroom ceiling morphed into a darkening sky over the Wisting Wilds.

The terrain was steep and rocky enough to force us to stay together, and more than once we had to set up a system of ropes to ascend cliff faces. I paused on one of these ascensions, tethered between Ferrin and Orla, to look out over the forest we'd traveled through the night before. I could see the Umberdust Plains beyond the trees, and more forests and rivers beyond that.

"You should see it during the day." Ferrin caught me staring out at the landscape. He clung to the rocks with one hand and used the other to push sweat-soaked hair away from his forehead.

"You should bring me by sometime," I laughed.

"I thought you said you have a life back in Keldori." Ferrin grunted as he hoisted himself farther up the cliff.

"Only most days." I scaled the next few feet. Climbing was easy for me in my Nightmare form, and I had to be careful not to move too quickly for Ferrin and Orla. "If I can convince my grandma to let me sleep all day, I'm yours."

"Tomorrow?" Orla asked hopefully. "Or maybe the next?"

"Not the next." A bit of loose rock crumbled under my hand and fell away. Tiernan yelled something up at me, but I ignored him. "I have a big phone call that day."

"Phone call?" Orla asked through a curious smile. She was handling the climb much better than Ferrin with her long limbs.

"It's like a meeting," I explained. "This one is very important. And it's in the morning, so Galahad better not keep me too long tomorrow night."

"We'll be safe in Tulyr by then," Ferrin said through gritted teeth. The bottles at his belt, which were mostly empty now, grated against the cliff face as he used his legs to propel himself up another two feet. "I'm sure Galahad will agree to let you go a little early, especially since we haven't seen the Grimguard since we left him in Orla's bed."

Ciarán, who had stayed silent until now, gave a low chuckle in my mind, and I pressed my forehead against the rock face.

"Maybe he decided not to hunt us anymore," Orla suggested. "Since we helped him."

"Perhaps." Ferrin's eyes met mine under his lifted arm, and I looked away before he could somehow see that the Grimguard was hiding in my head.

The rest of the night passed with more climbing, one run-in with a mountain lion that Tiernan was able to lead away, and setting up camp in a shallow cave that overlooked the Skalterran landscape. The rising sun had just started to dye the distant hills a dusty orange when Galahad sent me home.

However, when Gams greeted me downstairs with a reminder that my phone interview with Von Leer admissions was the next morning, I wished I was sitting in the Skalterran cave with my friends, even if it meant Ciarán was listening to everything I said.

Liam tried to run through practice questions with me at lunch, but we were both distracted with our own worries, and ended up staring out at the water in silence more than anything. Still, the company was nice, and he was polite enough to not make me talk about my feelings.

Gams mentioned an early bedtime to prepare for my interview in the morning, and I happily took her up on the suggestion. The sooner I could be in Skalterra, the better.

I got comfortable under my covers while Jonquil took her spot on the foot of the bed, and then I waited until my bedroom twisted and fell, leaving me standing atop the bluffs we'd climbed the night before.

"We'll reach Tulyr in a few hours if we hurry," Galahad was explaining to Ferrin nearby. "The plateau is safe. It might be a good place to stay an extra day and let everybody rest up."

"Either you're growing soft or you're tired too," Ferrin laughed back.

"Just-Wren!" Orla appeared at my side, laden with her and Fana's packs. "Are you ready to see Tulyr? Not many people ever get to visit. I'll bet you're the first Keldorian since it fell fifty years ago, though most Skalterrans don't get to see it either since it's a dead city."

"A dead city?" a voice called out. We whipped around to look up at a young woman standing on a ledge fifteen feet overhead. Her long silver hair caught on the wind, and she glared down at us through icy gray eyes set against smooth tanned skin. Her silver-plated armor made it hard to notice that one of her legs wasn't a leg at all, but a prosthesis built of glowing silver Skal. "Is that what Galahad told you?"

Tiernan loosed a golden javelin at the woman, but she raised a hand, and the weapon shattered in a burst of light when it met her palm. Tiernan staggered backwards in shock.

"Don't waste your magick. She's a Skalbreaker," Galahad growled. He hobbled forward to stand between us and the woman. "I wondered when you'd be out to meet us, Iseult. It's been a while. Your mother's armor fits you well."

"Don't flatter me, Grandfather. You know it won't gain you entry to Tulyr. Turn back now, and I won't kill you where you stand."

Twenty-Six
Medieval Architecture

I seult stepped from the ledge and dropped into the middle of our camp. Her leg of Skalmagick took the brunt of her landing, and her armor clinked as she straightened up to look around at us.

Tiernan procured a golden sword and leveled it at her throat, but Iseult grabbed the blade with her hand, and the weapon dissolved.

"Stop wasting Skal, Tiernan. I told you, she's a Skalbreaker. She'll destroy anything you make." Galahad pushed Tiernan back and approached his granddaughter. "I'm here with the Divine Sovereign, Iseult. You need to give us passage."

"The law is the law," Iseult said. "Anyone who leaves Tulyr isn't welcome back. That includes you, Grandfather."

"A Grimguard is after us. Let us refuel at the Sanctum and—"

"You led the Grimguards here?" The light of the rising moons bounced off the curve of her armor and caught in her silver hair. She seemed young, but she radiated ethereal power. Even Ferrin looked intimidated by her, keeping an arm out to shield Fana.

"We think we lost him, but—"

"Then the Grimguard *isn't* after you?" Iseult lunged towards me, and I tried to stumble away, but she caught me by my wrist. The Skal-made blood in my veins buzzed at her touch. "Which is it, Grandfather? Tell me before I break your pretty Nightmare."

I fought to break free from her grip, trying to channel power into my muscles, but it was as if her touch had formed an invisible barrier around me, making it impossible to pull any extra magick away from Galahad. The air crackled with electricity that hummed through my every particle, and while it wasn't painful, I could feel it pressing against me in every direction, ready to ignite.

"Galahad?" I asked, frozen to the spot. If Iseult made me burst into a million, glowing bits like she had Tiernan's weapons, would it count as another death in Skalterra?

"Leave her be," Galahad said. Iseult's eyes raked over my palm, and she yanked on my arm to show it off to the others.

"You gave her the curse?" she asked.

"Curse?" Ferrin's eyes narrowed at Galahad. "What curse?"

"The Curse of Tulyr." Iseult's lips twisted. "To help preserve Tulyr's location, our nocturmancers would put the curse on their Nightmares. If they die in Skalterra, they die in Keldori, and our secrets die with them."

"What?" Orla pushed forward and pried my hand away from Iseult's. The buzzing in my blood quieted, and the pressure that had pushed down on me a moment ago let up. Orla ran her fingers over the scars on my skin. "It can't be true. Just-Wren has already died. There can't be a curse."

I pulled my hand away, rubbing my wrist. Orla stared at me with wide green eyes, silently begging me to tell her I was okay.

"She kept ashing herself when we first brought her here." Galahad shrugged. "So I set a limit on how many times she can die, and here she is, better behaved than ever."

"You should have told us," Ferrin growled. "She's just a kid, Galahad!"

"As is the Sovereign." Galahad pointed at Fana.

Tiernan caught my eye from behind Galahad. His glowering expression was difficult to read, and his hands clenched into fists at his sides.

"How many lives does she have left?" he asked, still looking at me.

I held up my hand for the rest to see the scars.

"Two more," I said. "I started with five."

Iseult inhaled sharply and reached for my hand again. I drew it away before she could touch me, and she frowned at her grandfather.

"She's lucid," she said.

"Well, yes," Galahad grunted. "I wasn't going to curse a mindless drone."

"Grandfather, that's dangerous! You know I can't let her in. You all need to leave."

"It's not like last time," Galahad insisted.

"Last time?" I asked, but they both ignored me.

"The others won't allow it." Iseult shook her head.

"I'm sorry to put you in this position," Galahad said, "but we really are just passing through for Skal. Once we have what we need, I promise, you'll never see us again."

"Tulyr's laws—" Iseult started.

"Is your allegiance to a dead city really going to stop you from helping us protect the Divine Sovereign?" Galahad cut her off. "In another life, you would've been a Riftkeeper too."

"The others—"

"They will listen to you." Galahad stepped forward and set a gnarled hand on Iseult's metal shoulder plate. "Let us in, Iseult."

"But the Nightmare—" She glanced at me, and I didn't understand the fear that flitted across her tan features.

"She's safe. More importantly, she's useful. She killed a rotsbane."

Iseult's chest plate clinked as she heaved a mighty sigh.

"In and out. Get your Skal, and then you're leaving."

"Of course." Galahad patted her shoulder again, then motioned for the rest of us to get ready to go. He threw his pack over his shoulder and smirked. "Wouldn't want you to have to kill us."

Iseult blushed in the rising moonlight, but kept her gaze down as the others hurried to grab their packs.

Iseult led the way, easy to follow with her illuminated leg. Its soft light rebounded off her metal armor, and I felt like I was following a star to the top of the plateau. Rugged terrain, dotted with short, gnarled trees and clusters of glowing white flowers, gave way to even ground and tiered inclines.

"It's paved," I realized, looking at the cobblestone path hiding beneath the vines growing over the ground. Another cliff loomed ahead, but its face was split by a set of stairs carved into the stone. "Is that a staircase?"

Orla walked beside me. She held my scarred hand in hers, running her fingers absentmindedly over the marks left by Galahad.

"I don't get why he didn't tell us about the curse," she mumbled.

"Something about being afraid you'd put your own life at risk if you knew mine was in danger." I shrugged. "Which is fair. We both know you would."

"But if we knew, Tiernan might not have blown you up," she said.

I stared at the space between Tiernan's shoulders where he sauntered ahead of us. His cloak had become so dirty in the last weeks that it looked closer to brown than yellow.

"We both know he would have," I said.

Orla pressed her lips together. She kept her eyes forward but seemed to be looking at someone other than Tiernan. I followed her gaze to Iseult where she ascended the stairs set in the cliff.

"Orla?" I asked. Orla dropped my hand to run her fingers through her short hair. "What is it?"

"Galahad's granddaughter." She shook her head. "I don't know if I want to *be* her or *kiss* her, you know?"

"I *don't* know." I laughed. "She wanted to kill us. She's also one quarter Galahad, so that puts me off from wanting either of those things."

"That's a good point. She might end up looking like him when she's old." Orla screwed her face up. We took the first few steps of the carved stairs together. A tree grew out of the rock ahead, its twisted trunk arching over the steps, and vines and moss cascaded down the cliffside in an overgrown mess. "In Keldori, is that even a thing? Girls kissing girls?"

"Definitely." I nodded sagely.

"You?"

"I don't do much kissing of anyone."

"Me neither." Orla frowned. Up ahead, Tiernan's head turned to the side, and I wondered if he could hear our conversation. "Not a lot of time lately. Or options. No offense."

"You're not my type either." I smiled to myself. "Besides, I'm gone after we make it to the Second Sentinel."

"Don't say that." Orla sighed and buried her fingers in her short hair. "I told you, I'll learn Nocturmancy. If Galahad won't bring you back, I will."

She tripped when a stone step crumbled beneath her boots, and I caught her by the arm. Orla was wonderful and kind, but if Nocturmancy was as difficult a skill as Galahad described it to be, I didn't dare count on her bringing me back to Skalterra anytime soon.

"What about Iseult's Skalbreaking trick?" I asked. "How hard is that to learn?"

"Impossible," Orla said. "You have to be born with the ability. It's pretty rare too. I had no idea Galahad was related to one of them."

I nodded, relieved that it wasn't a common ability.

The final steps of the stairway felt like ascending into heaven as the cliffside slipped away to make room for the expansive starlit sky above. Orla craned her neck back to look at the wash of stars, and I guided her up the last few steps to keep her from accidentally stepping over the edge.

"I don't get it," I said, looking over the empty plateau. "I thought there was supposed to be a city here."

The others stood in a line, silhouetted against the stars and the distant mountain range under a crumbling stone arch. Orla and I hurried to join them, and Orla sighed at the sight ahead of us of the grand stairway descending into a crater that stretched clear to the other end of the plateau.

Starlight lit the edges of stone ruins that sat nestled in the protection of the crater. Some of the buildings had been reduced to nothing more than crumbling walls overgrown with grass and vines. Others stood taller, and one near the center still had twin spires that stood as high as the lip of the crater. Flying buttresses arched off the exterior of the edifice, but many of them were crumbling or missing, giving the impression of a broken rib cage sitting at the city's heart.

The light of Iseult's leg caught the grooves of Galahad's scowl.

"The once great city of Tulyr," he said. "Skalterra's birthplace and where the first family of Divine Sovereigns died."

"Welcome home." Iseult stepped forward first, but Galahad shoved past his granddaughter to take the lead down into the crater.

"Stay close," Ferrin warned me. "There aren't many people left in Tulyr, but they don't like strangers and they especially don't like Nightmares."

"Really? But Iseult seemed so friendly and welcoming." I bit at the inside of my cheek.

"I'm serious, Wren. It's an honor to get to see Tulyr, but a dangerous one." He frowned at me in a way that I didn't quite understand. He'd given Orla the same worried look before, but I wasn't sure why he'd waste it on me. "You should have told me."

"I thought you knew." I rubbed at the cursed scars on my palm. "I figured Galahad would've told at least you."

"You don't really think so poorly of me that you thought that was something I'd be okay with, do you?"

My cheeks burned with shame, and I looked down at the fallen city in an effort to avoid Ferrin. I tensed when he surprised me by putting an arm around my shoulders.

"You're our friend, Just-Wren, and it isn't fair that you are in this position. I promise not to let Galahad off easy for this."

"His granddaughter hates him and tried to turn him away," Tiernan said behind us. "He's having a rough night already."

I turned back to glare at him where he marched somberly at Fana's side.

"Oh, would you look who suddenly grew compassion," I snipped.

"After the Grimguards killed Fana's family, Galahad rushed to Cape Fireld to offer his services in keeping her safe." Tiernan's eyes flitted to meet mine. "He knew he wouldn't be allowed back, and he still left to fulfill his duty as a Riftkeeper. Take it from me, there is nothing easy about leaving home."

As admonishing as his words were, they didn't hold any of his usual vitriol. Ferrin must've been able to sense my embarrassment, because he patted my shoulder where his hand rested.

"It's alright," he murmured. "Galahad's not had it easy, it's true, but that doesn't excuse him sentencing you to possible death."

"If Tulyr is isolated, how did he hear about Fana's family?" I stared at the dirty back of Galahad's duster ahead of us. He and Iseult kept a cold distance between them, despite being family.

"He said it was raiders," Ferrin said darkly. "Criminals emboldened by the death of a Divine family. They searched out Tulyr, looking for the Skalspring. The attack was brutal and unexpected. Galahad's only child died, and his only grandchild lost her leg as well as both her parents."

I was suddenly overcome with the need to give Gams a giant hug.

"Oh," I said simply, suppressing a chill.

"Galahad questioned the surviving raiders for information on what was happening outside of Tulyr. When he heard about the Firelds, he left the next day."

"After Iseult had just lost her whole family?" I ducked out from under Ferrin's comforting arm. "Knowing he wouldn't be allowed back?"

"Galahad is Galahad. He loves his family, but nothing is more important to him than keeping the Rift." Ferrin shrugged.

"And Iseult let him leave?" I asked. If it had been Gams, I would've chased after her in a heartbeat. "She didn't go with him?"

"She'd just lost her leg. That sort of injury takes a long time to heal," Ferrin said. "And Galahad didn't want to wait."

I suddenly didn't blame Iseult for threatening to kill us when she'd first found our camp. She'd been abandoned.

The farther down the stairs we got, the higher the ruins rose around us. A flash of light greeted us on the bottom step, and a man in metal armor, wielding a sword of silver, stepped out from behind a crumbling wall.

"Lady Iseult, what—" His sword dissipated, and he pushed a metal visor up his helmet to stare at us with wide eyes over a neat beard.

"They're with the Divine Sovereign, Urian. Cape Fireld has officially fallen." Iseult stepped ahead of Galahad to greet the knight. "They're here for Skal, and then they're leaving. That's it."

"If they were followed—"

"We weren't." Galahad shoved passed the knight, who blinked after him.

"You weren't supposed to come back."

"I'm not back, just passing through." Galahad stopped to look at us where we still stood at the base of the grand stairway. "The Sanctum is this way. You want Skal or not?"

He continued to hobble forward, paying the knight's protests no mind.

"Should I wake the others?" Urian asked. Iseult shook her head, sending waves down her silver hair.

"They'll be gone soon. Help me take them to the Sanctum."

Urian nodded, but the tight, worried frown he gave us said he wasn't fully sure about this plan.

"It's just, if the others find out—"

"Then they'll answer to *me*, Urian."

"Yes, Lady Iseult."

Galahad, usually the slowest of the group, limped ahead. His silver head was bowed, and his duster billowed out behind him. He was purposefully keeping his head down, as if to avoid looking at the ruins around him.

"How long has it been since he's been here?" I kept my voice low so he wouldn't hear.

"Four years." Iseult's face was stony, but the facade cracked just a little bit as her mouth turned down in a frown. "Does he talk about me?"

"Oh, well—" Ferrin searched for words, but the panic in his eyes told me Iseult didn't come up much between the two men. "He isn't really—"

"Yes," Fana said. "All the time."

Tiernan and Ferrin both looked at Fana in surprise, but she looked back at Iseult.

"My grandfather talked about me to the Divine Sovereign?" Iseult frowned at Fana.

"I watched my family die." Fana sounded too matter-of-fact for a ten-year-old child. "It was hard to sleep, so he told me about his granddaughter who also watched her family die."

"That's sweet," Iseult said, though her tone implied otherwise. "He was all I had, and he left me and turned me into a bedtime story."

"You were all he had too." Fana shrugged. Iseult stopped in her tracks, but Fana looked to Ferrin. "I'm hungry. Is there anything to eat here?"

Ferrin found some dried meat in his pack for Fana, and we continued our march through the ghost city in silence. The same glowing flowers that had dotted the mountainside peeked through cracks in old buildings and the walkway. I counted them as we went.

Near the middle of the crater, Iseult stopped. Galahad continued to forge ahead, but she held out a hand to the rest of us.

"We're nearing the Sanctum," she said. "Urian, stay here and watch the Sovereign and her guards."

"We don't get to see the Sanctum?" Orla's disappointment was apparent in her tone.

"Lyrians only." Iseult's grunted response reminded me too much of Galahad. "And the Nightmare. You don't leave my sight."

I gave Ferrin a panicked look, but he nodded.

"You'll be okay. Go help Galahad."

Urian gave his new wards a nervous look, but he stood aside to let Iseult guide me after Galahad through the maze of ruins. The spired building loomed up ahead. The towers were dark against the stars, and ivy climbed up the front face of the edifice. It looked like it could've been a forgotten cathedral in Europe, and I wondered if Mom had seen similar buildings on her tour. Hopefully those cathedrals had been in better shape, but there was something hauntingly beautiful about this corpse of a basilica.

Galahad hobbled up the front steps of the Sanctum and pushed hanging lichen out of the way to step through the wide doorway.

I held back a gasp. I'd expected something more typical of a cathedral. Namely, a floor.

A ravine stretched from the entrance of the Sanctum all the way to the far wall. Skal pooled in its depths, sending soft blue light up the pillars and buttresses that supported the moss-laden walls of the canyon. Above us, stars twinkled down from where a ceiling should've been.

"Stairs are this way." Galahad limped around the Sanctum's perimeter. He passed through shafts of moonlight that poured in through circular holes in the stone walls where I was sure there had once been stained glass.

Blue light lit the stairwell through crumbling spaces in the rock wall, and I caught peeks of the Skalspring through the stones as we descended.

The piles of rubble did little to detract from the beauty of the space. The light of the Skal lit the farthest recesses of the alcoves that surrounded the pool, and the moss and lichen that grew across the walls, pillars, and floor all emitted their own soft glow.

A stone statue in knight's armor had been carved from the rock bed that stood at the head of the spring. Her palms were turned out, and Skal poured from both her hands to add to the glowing basin with a slippery hiss.

"Congrats," Galahad growled, and it took me a moment to realize he was talking to me. "You're the first Nightmare in over fifty years to enter the Sanctum of Tulyr."

He limped to the pool's edge and then stepped out onto the flat rocks that spotted the Skal like stepping stones. Iseult paced along the chamber's edge, watching her grandfather navigate the stones until he'd reached the one nearest the statue of the woman.

"Is the Skal better over there?" I asked.

"Lyrians believe that the Skal collected nearest Lyria is more potent." Iseult looked up at the statue of the woman.

"Is she one of the Three Magicians?"

"Yes. The Tulyrs descended from her. They were the most powerful of the Divine families. The other families, the Quills and the Firelds, both sought shelter in the mountains or on the coast, but the Tulyrs? They stayed right here at Skalterra's birthplace."

"It's beautiful."

"It's not what it used to be," Iseult said, "but it's the best I've ever seen it."

She leaned against a pillar with her arms crossed to watch Galahad fill his bottles. A tiny frown pulled at her face, and silver hair fell over her shoulder.

"What did it used to look like?" I asked.

"Not like a pile of rubble." She snorted and looked up at the stars through the missing ceiling. "My mother told me this entire chamber used to be full of Skal, but she wouldn't know either. It was sucked dry before she was born."

"Sucked dry?" I repeated. There was more Skal in the chamber than I could imagine being used in a lifetime. If there had been even more, I wasn't sure what could've used up all that magick.

"At the Fall of Tulyr." Iseult looked at me with a cocked eyebrow. "Did Grandfather not tell you?"

"Galahad doesn't tell me much. I'm more of a tool than a teammate to him."

Iseult sighed and pushed away from her pillar.

"That sounds like Grandfather. He's always been practical. Maybe he has to be, though, to make up for what happened at the Fall." She strode along the pathway along the perimeter of the chamber, and I followed. "Do you know why the Seven Provinces outlawed lucid Nightmares?"

I wasn't expecting the question and fumbled for an answer.

"We're dangerous," I said. "We can do things normal Nightmares can't, and we're harder to control."

"And you know too much."

"About Skalterra." I nodded in confirmation.

"No." Iseult stopped, and her gray eyes bore into me. "About Keldori."

I stared at Iseult, unsure of what she meant, but feeling dread creep up my chest all the same.

"I don't understand," I admitted.

"Have you told them about your home?" She shifted her gaze to Galahad. He paused between filling each bottle to fold his hands together and bow his head to the statue.

"No," I said automatically, but that wasn't entirely true. "I mean, a little, but not too much."

"You shouldn't tell them anything. A lot of Skalterrans assume Keldori hasn't progressed since losing all its Magicians, but based off the rumors I've heard,

Keldori has far exceeded Skalterra in terms of technology. It sounds comfortable."

"I guess, but—"

"You shouldn't tell me about Keldori either, Nightmare. Your home is a tempting prize. It was for Balin, at least."

"Balin?" I asked.

"Grandfather's brother. They were the Riftkeepers in charge of keeping the Tulyrs alive. Grandfather was happy protecting the Divine Sovereigns, and so was Balin for a time, until his favorite lucid Nightmare told him all about Keldori. Balin became bitter, and he sought to free the Frozen God, subdue him, and take both Skalterra and Keldori for himself."

"The Baron thought she could do the same." I rolled my eyes.

"The Baron is an idiot. The Frozen God is trapped in a glacier that separates Keldori from Skalterra, and it took three of the most powerful Magicians to imprison him there. If freed, there are very few who could overpower him, but Balin? He might've stood a chance."

"But he failed, obviously," I said. "Otherwise, I wouldn't be here."

"Balin was a skilled nocturmancer. One night, he raised an army of Nightmares and took control of the city centrum. But Grandfather was powerful too. He made his own Nightmares, and the ensuing battle ended with the Tulyrs dead and half the city destroyed."

"And the other half?" I asked.

Iseult responded with a wry smile.

"Balin figured if he had a never-ending supply of Skal, he could channel it into his Nightmares, and they'd become unstoppable. So he came here."

I looked around the chamber, trying to imagine it without the lichen that hung from the rafters, or the pillars and walls that had collapsed into the glowing pool.

"Then what stopped him?" I asked. "He killed the Tulyrs, but he didn't go on to free the Frozen God. What went wrong?"

"Nightmares are powerful." Iseult surveyed me with steely gray eyes. "You know that. But feed a Nightmare too much, and it'll only become hungrier. Give it too much Skal, and no amount of Skal will ever be enough."

I thought back to my exercise with Galahad on Tamora's boat deck. I remembered channeling his magick away from him, and I remembered the elated hunger that had felt like I was being turned inside-out before Galahad had brought me to heel.

I wasn't sure I wanted to know what would've happened if he hadn't.

"And Balin's Nightmares?" I asked.

"You've seen them. They grew in size until their skin stretched and ripped, revealing the monster underneath."

"They— what?" My skin itched, as if there was a monster inside me too, begging to be let out. I grabbed my arms, trying to hold my pieces together, to keep the beast caged.

"That was the night Balin brought rotsbane to Skalterra."

The chamber, so peaceful and beautiful a moment ago, now felt cursed. Blood screamed in my ears, or maybe it was the sound of a monster hiding inside my bones, screaming to be fed. To be let out.

"Rotsbane can't be people," I stammered. "Because I killed a rotsbane and I didn't— I don't want that. I can't —"

"Don't feel bad." Iseult was watching Galahad again. "The human it used to be died fifty years ago. What you did was a mercy, and it had probably eaten Nightmares just like you."

"Galahad's Nightmares, the night Tulyr fell..." I trailed off.

"Devoured," Iseult confirmed. "Consciousnesses and all."

"No." I looked at Galahad. He'd had no way to know he'd consigned all those people to death when he'd brought them to Skalterra to fight for him. I wanted to believe he felt bad about it, but if he did, would he have continued to bring Nightmares to Skalterra? Would he have consigned me to fight and possibly die for him?

"The Nightmares weren't enough to sate the rotsbane," Iseult said. "Nothing ever is. They tore the city apart looking for more Skal, eventually coming here."

Iseult ran a hand over a stone pillar. Her fingers caught on gouge marks that marred its otherwise smooth surface.

I glanced around the chamber again. The lichen, moss, and years of wear worked to cover the scars left by the rotsbane half a century ago, but the marks were hard to miss now that I knew they were there. They were scratched into the walls and the floor, and I tried to imagine the space full of enough rotsbane to deal that sort of damage.

"What about Balin?" I asked. "Galahad's brother. He was here, wasn't he?"

"He was right there." Galahad's gravelly voice sounded behind us, and I spun around to see him pointing at the rock he'd perched on to fill his bottles. My cheeks heated in embarrassment at having been caught talking about him, but he kept his eyes on the stone.

"Galahad, I'm sorry, I—"

"My brother forsook his duty to protect the Tulyr family and brought destruction and death to the greatest city in Skalterra. A cathedral full of rotsbane, and he was still the biggest monster here that night. I tried to save him, but they got to him first."

His gray eyes flickered to me, and I felt like he was staring through my exterior to the beast he knew waited beneath my skin.

This Wren, this blue-haired thing, was supposed to be the better version of me. So why did I suddenly want to crawl out of myself?

Galahad turned away, and the fresh bottles of Skal on his belt clinked together as he did.

"Lady Iseult!" A wail echoed through the Sanctum, and I jerked my head up to see an outline silhouetted against the night sky. Urian, the knight from before, leaned over the ravine. "On the southern cliffs, there's—"

He cut off in a cry of pain as orange light burst behind him.

Twenty-Seven
Combat Theory

Urian clung to the lip of the edge, and more orange lights flashed above him. Dread sat heavy in my stomach, rooting me to the spot.

Ciarán had caught up. He had found us.

And it was my fault.

"You told me you weren't followed!" Iseult yelled at Galahad, already running for the stairs.

"We weren't!" Galahad pulled his goggles into place and downed one of his fresh bottles of Skal. I hesitated, unsure if I should stay with him or follow Iseult, but he wiped his mouth with the sleeve of his duster and pointed at the stairs. "What are you doing, Nightmare? Go!"

I raced after Iseult just as an armor-clad figure leapt from the stairwell. His eyes were passive and his face blank, but he held an orange scythe ahead of him.

He swung the glowing blade at Iseult. She caught it like she had when Tiernan had attacked her, and the weapon burst into bits of glowing dust. Iseult thrust her hand through the debris to grab the Nightmare by his face, and he collapsed in a pile of ash.

"So much for you being the only Nightmare down here in fifty years," she growled at me.

I looked back at Galahad where he stood at the edge of the pool.

"I said go!" he grunted.

I took the steps two at a time, racing after Iseult.

"Ciarán?" I dared to ask the stairwell. I waited for his voice in my head, but the only sounds were the yells and blasts echoing outside of the Sanctum. On the off chance he *was* there, lurking in the corners of my mind, I growled a warning. "This better not be you, asshole."

A dark chuckle vibrated at the back of my mind.

"Or *what*, Blue?"

Ciarán's rasping purr sent a chill down my spine, and turned my muscles heavy with anger and fear.

I reached the top of the stairs in time to see another two Nightmares crumble under Iseult's touch. She fell next to the edge of the open floor. Urian's hands gripped the stone as Iseult tried to pull him up by his wrists.

"Your armor," she gasped. "It's too heavy!"

Another wave of Nightmares came up the Sanctum steps, and Iseult abandoned Urian to defend the doors. She pivoted on her real leg to bring her Skal prosthesis swinging into the first two Nightmares as she grabbed another two and turned them to dust.

"I've got you!" I took her spot over Urian and strength flowed through my muscles, aided by Galahad's fresh Skal. I grabbed Urian's arms and heaved. His metal armor grated over stone, and I dropped him at Iseult's feet.

I paused to stare down at Galahad where he still stood by the pool below us. He held a bottle aloft, as if toasting to me, and then drank up. I bit my lip, the story of Balin and his doomed Nightmares still fresh on my mind, and a fresh wave of power rolled through my limbs.

"There's more!" Urian pushed himself up onto his hands to point through the open door at the small horde of Nightmares running down the street towards the Sanctum.

"How many Nightmares did this guy make?" Iseult hissed.

"I made enough," Ciarán sang in my head. "I can make them go away, Blue. All you have to do is yield, and I'll leave Tulyr alone."

"He has to run out of Skal eventually," I said, ignoring Ciarán.

Leather and skin tore open along my arms as I armed myself with my favorite spikes of bone.

"Very well." Ciarán's voice turned poisonous. "We'll do this the hard way."

Orange lights burst in the sky over the southern lip of the crater, and I felt like I was back on the parapet under siege my first night in Skalterra. Screams echoed over the ruins as orange flames lit the grand staircase that led in and out of the city.

"Urian, where is the Sovereign?" Iseult's wide eyes reflected the distant orange light.

"I sent them to—"

"Don't!" I pressed my hands against my ears, not wanting to give Ciarán any more information than I already had. Iseult and Urian stared at me, but the new wave of Nightmares had reached the Sanctum steps, sparing me from an awkward explanation.

Urian slapped his helmet visor into place, and Iseult led the charge down the stone stairs. The first few Nightmares collapsed at her touch, and she slammed her silver leg into the Nightmares that rose to take their place.

I followed the Lyrians into the fray, wielding my bone shards ahead of me like pikes. I focused on the thought of the Nightmares waking up in their beds back at home, safe and warm, rather than linger on the way their bodies resisted my serrated bones. For being made of dust and magick, they felt horribly real.

Galahad's magick surged through me again, and I directed it to the muscles in my legs, forcing myself deeper into the tangle of Nightmares.

They were armored in leather and each Nightmare carried a different weapon, but they lacked the wits to move quickly or react to our attacks. What they lacked in formidability, however, they made up for in numbers.

An armored Nightmare grabbed me from behind to tackle me to the ground. My arm spikes snapped off against the stone steps, and the Nightmare's blank stare reflected the orange light of the dagger in her hands.

She brought the dagger swinging down, but I caught her by the wrist and tried to force her hands away. She was stronger than I anticipated, but another wave of Skalmagick rolled down the bond between me and Galahad.

"Yield, Blue, and this will all be over," Ciarán hissed in my head.

I threw the Nightmare off with renewed strength, and she crashed into the Nightmares behind her. A flail fizzled into shape in my hand, brighter than I remembered it being the last time I'd summoned one, and I swung it into her skull.

The Nightmare crumbled to dust under my attack.

"A bit brutal, don't you think?" Iseult asked, dissolving another pair of Nightmares.

"Brutal?" I swung the flail into another attacker, trying to remember the LARPing videos I'd studied. "It's quick. Besides, Galahad says they can't feel anything."

"Do *you* feel it?" Iseult's shoulder pressed against me as we fought Nightmares side by side. "When you get hurt here?"

"It's different," I grunted. "I'm lucid. They're not. It's just a bad dream to them."

"Is this not just a bad dream to you too?"

"Not if there's a chance Galahad accidentally turns me into a rotsbane tonight."

"Then it's more than a bad dream to them too. If you turn into a rotsbane, you'll devour their consciousnesses."

"I don't need you to lecture me about Nightmares." I sliced through three of them at once as Iseult protected me from a swinging sword. "I know firsthand how crappy it is to be one of us, and at least *they* get the luxury of not remembering any of this."

"I'm not lecturing anyone. I only commented on the brutality of your choice of weapon."

My leather armor hardened into kevlar at my bidding. New bone shards grew through the gashes the old ones had left in my arms, and I worked Galahad's magick into my hands to create talons.

"Is this better?" I asked.

"I don't know," she admitted. "I think we'd all be better off without Nightmares."

"Lady Iseult!" Urian's cry came from behind us, and we both turned to see him grappling with a Nightmare on the top stop while another three ran past him into the Sanctum.

"Protect Lady Lyria!" Iseult abandoned the steps to chase after the Nightmares who'd made it past us. More Nightmares surged up the steps, and the force of a blow to my back knocked me to my knees.

I sliced through limb and tendon to force my way back up. Galahad's magick roiled inside me, and a distant, familiar hunger burned in my veins.

A swarm of Nightmares intercepted Iseult and pinned her against the Sanctum wall. They brought their weapons arcing downwards, but every blade dissipated into nothingness as it made contact with her skin.

"Iseult!" I reached through bodies with lethal talons and dared to pull more of Galahad's magick. My skin hardened with scales like an alligator's, and orange weapons deflected off of me as renewed strength propelled me forward.

"Don't!" Iseult yelled in warning. The Nightmare pinning her on her right side brushed against her face, and then crumbled into dust. He was quickly replaced. "If you touch me right now—"

I would die. Her Skalbreaking ability would not discern between me and the other Nightmares. Frustration mounted inside me, bringing with it more strength from Galahad. I tried to cut down the Nightmares that surrounded Iseult, but there were too many.

More power from Galahad. More strength. A swelling hunger that drove my arm spikes into another wave of Nightmares.

And then, the sizzle of Skal against Skal.

Nightmares wielding weapons of silver light rushed from the Sanctum to push against the tide of Ciarán's army.

Galahad had sent reinforcements.

Painful, acidic greed tore at my insides. Something metallic and delicious wafted on the air, and I breathed the scent in.

Skal.

I could smell it, swirling below us in Lyria's pool.

I *needed* it.

"Careful, Blue." Ciarán's voice was back in my head. "The old man is overfeeding you."

Silver sparks flew into the air as I tried to get rid of the Skal in my veins. I would not let the hunger win.

"Iseult!" I caught my breath on the steps, watching Galahad's Nightmares fight against Ciarán's. "Get your grandpa. Take him to the others. I'll make sure no one follows you."

Skal sent a shudder through my body, but I had the hunger under control. For now.

"I'm right here, Nightmare," Galahad boomed behind me. He stood in the doorway to the Sanctum, lit by the several belts-worth of Skal bottles he wore at his waist.

"Urian, where did you send the Riftkeepers?" Iseult hurried to her grandfather's side, and he leaned against her. Exhaustion weighed on his face, and I wondered what sort of toll making so many Nightmares had taken on him.

"The boathouse, Lady Iseult." Urian staggered to his feet. Blood ran from beneath his helmet, but he otherwise seemed unharmed.

Iseult stepped away from Galahad to take Urian's armored hand in hers.

"I think I will miss you the most, my friend." She bent to kiss his hand, and he recoiled.

"You aren't leaving." He pushed his visor up to better see. "Lady Iseult—"

"I failed Tulyr tonight." She pushed silver hair back from her face to look at me with hard gray eyes. "And my grandfather may have abandoned me four years ago, but I won't abandon *him*. He's my only family. I will make sure he and the Divine Sovereign find safety. Tell the others—"

"Don't," Urian begged. "Please."

"Lyrguards have only ever brought sorrow upon our home. I was no different. Tell the others I'm sorry."

"Iseult—" Galahad started.

"No," she cut him off as she slipped back under his arm to support him. "I couldn't follow you the last time you left Tulyr. This time, I can."

Galahad sighed in defeat and looked to me.

"How many lives do you have left?" he asked.

"Two."

He nodded, as if satisfied by my answer.

"Then I'll see you tomorrow night, Nightmare."

More of Ciarán's army charged through the street, mowing down Galahad's Nightmares.

"We'll lead them away." Urian slapped his visor back into place. "Lady Iseult, it's been an honor."

I turned away from Iseult and Galahad before I saw which direction they went. I didn't like that Galahad asked how many lives I had left. If he kept drinking the Skal at his belts, I could survive the night.

"This way, Nightmare!" Urian ran with a limping gait, holding his longsword high to light our path. I looked back to make sure Ciarán's Nightmares that had broken past Galahad's ranks were following us, but a cry brought my attention back forward.

Nightmares charged from around a corner ahead of us, turning the street orange with the glow of their weapons. Urian crumpled under them, and I charged, channeling the Skal I had left back into talons, claws, and swollen muscles.

The Nightmares collapsed under my attack, and I stood over Urian as I continued to hold them off.

"How are there so many?" he croaked in the dirt. A swipe of my talons sliced through three Nightmares at once, and I shook my head.

No matter how many of Ciarán's Nightmares I destroyed, there were always more to take their place.

A blow to my back knocked me away from Urian, and I caught myself in the dirt. I drove my arm blades through the Nightmares that fell over me. They rushed at us from every direction, and I burned through the Skal in my veins faster than I could keep up.

Then, as one, the Nightmares stopped their advance. They stood around me, blank faced and waiting, though I didn't know what for. I could've cut them down where they stood, but even though I knew they would wake up safe in their beds, I couldn't bring myself to attack an enemy that wasn't fighting back.

"Tired yet?" Ciarán's voice sounded as clear as if he were standing beside me.

"Where are you?"

"Somewhere you can't fight me with those nasty spikes of yours." His low chuckle reverberated in the back of my head.

"I saved your life," I snarled, "and you *used* me!"

"That's funny, I remember helping you. Same way I'm going to help you now. Let's have a rest, Blue. You've earned it."

"Go to hell." I spun around, searching for him even though I knew he wouldn't be there.

"I won't let any harm come to you. It'll be okay."

"Or you can come out and fight me yourself, coward." I tried to draw more of Galahad's power into my limbs as I prepared to go down fighting. I still had two lives left. Even if I died tonight, I'd be okay. And if I *did* lose a life tonight, it would be worth it if it meant making Ciarán regret using me.

I would make him wish he'd died in that Vanderfall alley.

However, the waves of power from Galahad were dwindling, and when I pulled on the magick between us, I was met with dregs of energy that fizzled and died in my fingertips.

He'd made his escape. He didn't need to keep feeding me Skal. I'd stayed behind to help them get away, and he'd abandoned me knowing I would still have one life to spare.

I didn't know why I was surprised.

"Wren Warrender, Prospective Von Leer Viking." Ciarán's voice cut the silence that had fallen over the broken city. "Yield, or watch the Lyrian die and what's left of Tulyr burn."

Urian looked up at me from where Ciarán's Nightmares held him against cracked cobblestones. For all his armor and pretty silver weapons, he'd been hiding in Tulyr for decades, just like every other Lyrian. He was likely the best warrior Tulyr's ruins had to offer, but he was not a fighter.

"Don't hurt him," I said.

"That's up to you, Blue."

"Who are you talking to?" Urian grunted into the dirt. I ignored him.

"How do I know you won't hurt him after I yield?" I asked. Ciarán didn't know I was out of Skal. If he did, he might burn down the whole place anyway. "How do I know Tulyr is safe?"

"You don't."

I tried to count the Nightmares. There were definitely too many for me to fight off without more magick.

But if Ciarán brought me to his side, even if it was as his pet, I could fight *him.*

A Nightmare raised an orange scythe over Urian's neck, and the knight screwed his eyes shut.

"Fine!" I shouted at the night. "I yield."

"Excellent choice."

The Nightmares that pinned Urian against the ivy-laden street dissolved first, and then the rest followed, falling in a wave of dust. Urian blinked up at me as he pushed himself up out of their ashes.

The night stilled, and for a moment, I thought maybe Ciarán wasn't going to take me after all. Or maybe he'd overestimated his Nocturmancy skills, and he wasn't able to pull me away even after I'd yielded to him.

But then some unseen force pulled at the Skalmagick buzzing through my being, gently at first, as if testing its strength. Something heaved inside me, flipping my stomach and catching my breath.

The invisible tether between me and Galahad snapped, and darkness rushed over me.

When my eyes fluttered open, I was met with bright orange irises set against black sclera.

"There she is," Ciarán said under his black cowl. "Welcome back, Blue. Did you miss me?"

Twenty-Eight
Advanced Interview and Interrogation

After hearing his voice in my head night after night, I was finally face-to-face with Ciarán Grimguard, Servant of the Frozen God, again.

And I was going to kill him.

I lunged forward, and his orange eyes widened in surprise.

Something hot seared into my wrists, and the muscles in my shoulders strained as my hands yanked me back. I fell against a stone column, landing on my backside.

My wrists were bound behind me, shackling my arms around the width of a pillar. Loose blue hair fell into my face when I fought against the bonds. My armor was gone, leaving me in a plain tunic and trousers, as if Ciarán hadn't wanted to waste Skal on anything he didn't deem necessary.

That was fine. I didn't need armor to take down Ciarán, which was exactly what I was going to do as soon as I figured out how to break free.

"Is that a yes, then?" Ciarán crooned. "You *did* miss me?"

"What is this?" I kicked out wildly and strained against the hot bonds that held me captive. I couldn't see them, but the way they sizzled and burned told me the rope wrapped around my wrists was made of Skal.

"You were in my way." Ciarán stood over me. Soft blue light seeped through the holes in his dark cloak and threw shadows across his patchwork leather armor. He'd done a crude job in trying to repair the pieces that Tiernan's explosive had ripped to shreds.

Bits of night sky shined through the dilapidated roof above him, ringing his inky curls in a halo of stars that made the blacks of his eyes seem all the more dark.

"We're still in Tulyr?" I demanded, looking around the stone room. The flooring was made of cracked cobblestone, and parts of the walls were falling down and replaced by curtains of lichen.

"Near it." The bottom half of Ciarán's face was covered in his black cowl, but the set of his eyebrows held a smirk. I flexed my fingers and tried to imagine them elongating in claws, but they stayed frustratingly human. "An old, forgotten outpost by the looks of things. It's a bit drafty, but it suits my needs."

He stepped aside so I could see the trickle of Skal leaking from a crack in the wall and pooling in a small basin. A bottle sat in the pool, collecting Skal as it streamed down the wall. A line of bottles stood beside the basin, half of them already full of the glowing liquid.

"A Skalspring?" It was tiny compared to the one in Tamora's throne room and Tulyr's Sanctum.

"Oh, yes. I could've made Nightmares for you to fight all night long, Blue."

"You used me to follow us."

"I could've stayed silent." Ciarán knelt down so that his strange orange and black eyes were even with mine. He reached up to pull his cowl down away from his face. The blue light of the Skalspring turned his skin a sickly color, but he still looked a lot better than he had when I'd left him in Orla's bed. "I didn't have to speak to you to know what you were feeling and seeing. I could've gotten what I needed from you without you ever knowing I was there."

"So?" I strained against the bonds again.

"I didn't have to let you know Tamora's brute was following you in Riverstead. I didn't have to help you fight him in the Umberdust Plains. And I certainly didn't have to tell you how to kill the rotsbane."

"You helped me to help yourself. You wanted Titus and Tamora out of your way, and if the rotsbane had devoured me, you would've had no way to track the others."

His mouth quirked, and he straightened up to stretch.

"You saved my life in Vanderfall, Blue. That's no one's mistake but your own. You better get comfortable. As long as you're with me, the Lyrian can't call you back to his side."

He stalked to the doorway and leaned against the crumbling wall to stare out at the ruins and cliffs around us with his back to me.

"What do you mean?" I shifted around the stone column to keep him in view. "As long as I'm with you? You can't keep me here!"

"Except that I can. I'm the stronger nocturmancer, and while it was tricky getting you to yield to me, there's no way I'll let you go now that I have you here, even if the old man tries to pull you back."

"I have a job back at home," I said. "If I don't wake up, there are people who will worry. They'll—"

My stomach dropped in painful realization, and I looked to the horizon glowing in the distance, trying to gauge how long I had until morning. How long I had until my phone rang with a Von Leer admissions officer waiting on the other end.

"Your friends in Keldori won't let any harm come to you." He moved away from the doorway to crouch in the middle of the room. "Your body is safe."

"I don't give a crap about my body! It's my interview I'm worried about!"

Ciarán smiled as he piled dry twigs on the stone floor.

"An interview?" He snapped his fingers over the twigs, and a flame flickered to life.

"Someone asks me questions, I answer them, and they decide if they let me into their stupid school or not. And if I miss it, they definitely won't let me in."

"I know what an interview is." He pulled a metal container from a nearby pack and nestled it into his fire.

"Then why are you laughing at me?" I yanked on the bonds again. They stung against the skin of my wrists and were frustratingly sturdy.

Ciarán ignored me, pouring water from a skein into his metal cup and then adding chunks of something from inside his pack.

"You're making soup?" I seethed.

"I'm hungry."

"You don't need me!" The bonds burned against my wrists, but I strained against them anyway. "Let me go back to Keldori, at least! I'll be out of your way!"

"And tomorrow night?" Ciarán stirred his soup lazily. "Galahad will call you back, and you'll be in my way again. I saw how you cut down my Nightmares. You aren't the same useless girl I killed in the woods outside Cape Fireld anymore, and I can't summon a horde of warriors every night to steal you away from Galahad."

"Then call me first." The idea was repulsive, but not nearly as repulsive as the thought of missing my phone call. Ciarán frowned at his soup. "Unless you can't."

His continued silence was confirmation enough, and I forced a laugh just to get under his skin.

"And you say *you're* the stronger nocturmancer?" I jeered. "You can only steal me away when I'm already in Skalterra and if I yield to you, otherwise you would've called me sooner."

Metal grated against stone as Ciarán used a stick to push his soup out of the fire.

"I don't know why I can't reach you from across the Rift and Galahad can. I've tried nearly every night." His admission threw me off guard. He had no good reason to tell me the limits of his skills. "So now that I have you, you'll have to stay here. Otherwise, you'll continue to get in my way. They'll be easy enough to track now that I've caught up. They escaped on the river that flows down the mountain. It shouldn't be too hard to follow them."

"How long do I have to stay here?"

"Long enough to miss your interview."

"How long?"

His eyes flitted up from his cooling soup to meet my gaze.

"As long as my powers allow, Blue. So, like I said, get comfortable."

My insides chilled at the thought of being leashed in this run-down house for nights on end. My shoulders were already going numb from the angle my arms were tied at.

"You're going to leave me here?"

"I'll send you enough Skal down our bond to keep you alive, but yes. Until I have the Divine Sovereign, that spot on the floor is your new home."

"I saved your life, and Galahad will kill me." As I said it, my Von Leer interview still felt like the more pressing issue, but the Galahad thing at least offered something else to worry about. "You said it yourself. If he realizes I gave my name to you—"

"He doesn't know you're here." Ciarán closed his eyes as he sipped his soup. "With so many Nightmares to cater to tonight, he has no way to know I've stolen you from his ranks. He'll assume you fell in battle."

"And then he'll try to call me back, at which point he'll realize he can't!"

"The man is ancient." Ciarán's low chuckle set my teeth on edge, and he opened his eyes to survey me with his horrible orange irises. Strands of hair fell from his bun to hang in his face. "He'll be quicker to blame his dwindling ability than a second nocturmancer."

"I should have told him about you." The words were more for myself than for Ciarán.

"If you'd rather be dead than trapped here with me, then yes, you should have. Though I fail to see how being dead would help you with your interview problem."

I shifted against the stone pillar at my back. Ciarán was focused on his soup again, and I tested the bond between us, trying to draw magick away from him to form my arm spikes.

I might as well have been playing tug-of-war with a brick wall because the invisible channel of Skalmagick that kept me linked to the Grimguard gave me nothing. Ciarán must've felt my attempt, however, because he looked up at me through thick eyelashes. His mouth curled into a half smile.

He stood up, his soup in hand and his tattered cloak trailing behind him, and he crossed the dirt-laden floor to crouch eye-to-eye with me.

"Does that work on Galahad?" He set his soup down to better survey my face. His glowing orange eyes bore into mine, and I didn't like feeling like he could see straight through to my mind. "He lets you steal his magick?"

I settled against the column at my back with my head held high, and then struck out with my foot to kick his soup over. The steaming contents splashed across cracked cobblestone, and Ciarán frowned.

"That was my dinner," he said simply.

"Then you better lick it up quick if you're hungry." A tuft of blue hair fell into my face.

Ciarán sat back and drew his knees up to rest his elbows on. His head lolled to the side as he continued to study me, and I stuck my chin out at him.

I braced for the interrogation that I knew was coming. He would ask where we were taking Fana. I didn't even have any fake answers I could feed him. The only place I knew the name of was where we *were* taking her.

He narrowed his eyes, and I held his gaze. I was ready. I wouldn't break, no matter what he did.

"Tell me, Blue," he said, "do you have friends in Keldori?"

The question caught me off guard and quite frankly stung more than whatever torture technique I assumed he'd use to get information out of me.

"Yes," I snapped. It wasn't a lie. Liam was a coworker, but he was more tolerable than he had been at the start of summer. Plus, Jonquil and I were getting along better. Kind of. "What kind of question is that?"

"You don't seem very likable, so I was curious."

Heat rose in my face, but I refused to let him know he was getting under my skin.

"What about you?" I blew a bit of hair away from my face. "Lots of friends in the Grimguard business?"

"Not really." He pulled something that looked like beef jerky out from the folds of his cloak and took a bite. "*Your* friends keep killing them."

"Daithi killed—"

"Caitria." Ciarán nodded solemnly. "I know. You want some?"

He held his jerky out to me, and I recoiled, pressing my head into the column behind me.

"Hard pass."

"It's ramstag. Caught it and smoked it myself just a couple of days ago." He shrugged and took another bite. "Is your hair blue in Keldori?"

"No." This interrogation wasn't going the way I thought it would. Not that I had been in many interrogations, but I was pretty sure this was less than conventional. "When are you going to ask me your real questions?"

"Are these not real questions?" The tiny smile that pulled on his lips told me he knew what I meant.

"You want to know what I know about the Riftkeepers," I said.

"And would you tell me if I asked?"

"No."

"Then what's the use in asking?"

"I figured you'd used some sort of magick to torture the answer out of me," I admitted.

"I don't want to hurt you, Blue." His heavy eyebrows furrowed over his eyes.

"No, you just want to ruin my life by keeping me here."

Ciarán smirked and stood as he raised his hands out to his sides.

"Guilty." He stalked over the Skalspring to replace the bottle he'd left under the steady trickle of pale blue liquid with an empty container. "You should consider yourself lucky. There are worse places to be held captive."

"Oh, yes. I'm overflowing with gratitude to be trapped in a leaky, old outpost," I snarled.

"This leaky, old outpost is one of the oldest buildings in all of Skalterra." He sat down next to the Skal pool to organize his bottles. "The style comes straight from Keldori itself. I think they called it Romanesque. Does it remind you of home?"

I exhaled heavily through my nose, searching for patience I knew wasn't there. Iseult's warning to not tell anyone in Skalterra about Keldori was fresh on my mind.

"Definitely. Nothing says 'home sweet home' like a dilapidated stone shed."

"Perfect. Then you should be plenty comfortable." He settled into the floor by his line of bottles and pulled his pack closer to use as a pillow.

"What are you doing?" I demanded, once again struggling against the Skal that kept my wrists bound together. "You can't go to sleep!"

"You keep telling me what I can't do," he rolled over so his back was to me, "but I'm not the one tied to a post. Making all those Nightmares wasn't easy, and your friends won't make it far. They'll be easy to track, so I might as well take a nap."

"But my interview—"

"Is not my priority, Blue."

Outside the door to my right, I could see the lightening horizon. The stars that shined through the holes in the roof seemed dimmer than before. Dawn was coming. My interview was in a few hours.

Ratting out Linsey to get a better grade point average would be for nothing. Spending a night alone in the woods would be for nothing. Mom going viral on the internet for punting Mrs. Harper's lawn ornaments into oblivion would be for nothing.

Everything would be for nothing.

I had to get into Von Leer.

"I've worked too hard for this!" I tried to kick a bit of potato from his spilt soup at him. It rolled a pitiful few feet before becoming lodged in a bit of moss.

"I've worked hard for this too," Ciarán said, his back still to me. "I just happened to be the one who landed on top."

I wanted to scream and thrash against the Skal that held my wrists together behind the column at my back. I wanted to kick my boot across the room and watch it smack Ciarán in the back of his head. I wanted to pull this stupid Romanesque outpost down stone by stone and take us both down with it.

But instead, I settled against my column and shook out my elbows to keep circulation moving through my shoulders. The sun wasn't completely up yet. I wasn't sure how daylight here correlated with daylight at home, but I had to have at least a few hours before Von Leer would call me. Screaming and melting down wouldn't help me. It would only give Ciarán something to laugh at.

I tested the Skal around my wrists again, but it continued to hold strong even as its creator drifted to sleep across the room from me. It burned against my skin just enough to hurt, but not enough to cut into me, otherwise I happily would've sacrificed a severed hand to escape.

The column at my back felt sturdy too. I pushed against it, hoping it might crumble, but it stayed frustratingly upright.

My fingernails dug into the skin of my palms. Maybe being patient wasn't the answer. Maybe I *should* scream until the Grimguard became so annoyed that he released me.

His shoulders rose and fell in time with his steady breathing. He'd fallen asleep quickly. Maybe creating all those Nightmares had taken more out of him than I'd realized. I chewed on the inside of my cheek.

He might not feel me try to draw his Skalmagick away when he was asleep.

I took a steadying breath and straightened up against my column. I siphoned away as little as possible, drawing it down our bond and feeling it tickle my fingertips. It felt different from Galahad's magick. Even though I'd only taken a little bit, there was something electric about it that made my extremities feel lighter.

I waited and watched Ciarán for any signs that he had noticed. His breathing went uninterrupted. I looked back at the horizon over the tops of trees that swayed in a nighttime breeze. The sky was still dark except for the bright line where land met sky in the far distance. I had time. The birds weren't even awake yet.

I bowed my head so that more blue hair fell in my face, as if it might better hide me from Ciarán. The next bit of magick slid down the bond too fast, and Ciarán's deep breaths hitched.

I held my own breath, feeling the next tiny bit of magick bounce along my nerves as I waited for Ciarán's breathing to resettle. I would have to take even smaller amounts, and maybe not so close together.

I forced myself to wait and counted to one hundred in my head before taking the next bit of Skal. And then I did it again, and again, and again, all while watching the lightening horizon.

When the first birds started to sing, I got nervous, and took more than I should have. Ciarán rolled over so that he was facing me, and I shrank against my column, but his eyes stayed closed.

I counted to five hundred before I dared to take more. The magick was tangible in my fingers, buzzing with electricity that wanted to be let out, but I wasn't sure if it was enough to modify my body or break the Skal around my wrists.

If I tried and failed, it might wake up Ciarán, and then he'd make sure I missed my interview.

The birds outside became louder, and the horizon wasn't just getting brighter, but I could now see the hazy shape of the sun taking form to dye the tops of trees in hues of red.

I siphoned more magick than I should have again. Ciarán, with his eyes still closed, screwed his face up. I counted even longer than before, losing track of my numbers somewhere in the seven hundred range.

The sun was rapidly chasing away night. Von Leer would be calling any moment. I shook hair out of my face. I hadn't managed to steal as much as I would've liked. It definitely wasn't enough to give me my favorite bone spikes, or even to form a weapon.

But I could tell by the way the Skal that bound my wrists buzzed and snapped that it was *almost* enough to overpower the magick there.

Almost.

I shimmied my way up the column until I was standing. I would have one shot, but the sun was nearly fully risen, and it was now or never.

I gave the invisible bond that bound me to Ciarán's service a final, mighty pull and magick poured into me. Ciarán's eyes snapped open, and the flow of magick stopped so suddenly that it flipped my stomach.

I pushed every bit of magick I'd stolen from him into my wrists before he could pull it back, and orange sparks flew as I broke free of the tie.

"Dammit!" Ciarán scrambled to his feet, but I was already sprinting out the doorway towards the rising sun. "Blue!"

Low, crumbling walls covered in moss streaked past me, and birds took flight as I charged through the outpost. A fine, morning mist hung over the ruins, and droplets of dew clung to my bare arms as I hurtled through it.

"Wren Warrender," Ciarán thundered behind me, "I command you—"

I reached the lip of the cliff and launched myself into open air. I twisted to catch a final glimpse of Ciarán standing on the cliff edge, his hand outstretched in a last ditch attempt to stop me and his tattered cloak billowing in the wind.

And maybe I was my mother's daughter after all, because as I plummeted into the bright golden air of dawn, I lifted both hands and flipped him the double bird.

The stone below rose to greet me, and darkness swallowed the red-gold sky overhead.

Twenty-Nine
Communications

Those few moments where I was falling in the sunrise were the closest I'd come to knowing peace for the rest of the day. Consciousness slammed into me, and I threw my quilt across the room before my eyes were fully open. Jonquil squealed in anger and bolted under my dresser as I fought to orient myself.

"Phone!" I leapt out of bed to turn wildly in the center of my room. "Where's—"

It was, of course, right where I'd left it the night before, sitting on my bedside table. I lunged for it, ignoring the pain in my knees as they collided with the table.

A missed call notification lit up on my screen.

"No!"

Jonquil hissed back at me from under my dresser.

I jabbed at the screen with shaking fingers. I'd missed it by two minutes.

Two. Measly. Minutes.

I ignored the voicemail notification glaring at me from the corner of the screen, and I hit the callback button.

My bare feet padded across the wooden floorboards as I paced, waiting for someone to answer. It wasn't supposed to go like this. I was going to practice in the mirror beforehand. I was going to put on a blazer and do my hair to feel more prepared. I was—

"Von Leer University Admissions Office, this is—"

"I missed your call!" I interrupted the woman. "I'm sorry, it was—"

I cut off and looked around my room for a lie. Any lie. Jonquil glared at me from her hiding spot beneath the dresser.

"My grandma's cat. She was choking. She always eats too fast and- and you know. She's a Persian, so she's already pretty bad at breathing."

What the *hell* was I saying?

To my relief, the woman on the other line laughed.

"I'll be sure to put 'cat rescue' down in my notes," she said. "This is Wren Warrender I take it?"

"Yes!" I said. Was I talking too loud? "Sorry. I was, you know, with the cat."

I was going to *kill* Ciarán.

"Don't worry about it." She sounded genuine, but I was still worried. "This is Dr. Woodway with Von Leer University Admissions, but you can call me Carly."

"Carly." I repeated. "Nice to meet you."

My heart was in my throat. I held the phone away from my face so she wouldn't hear my heavy breathing.

I needed to calm down. I slapped a hand to my face, my fingers itching to pull at whatever eyelash or eyebrow they could find first, but I stopped when I saw the new mark slashed across the palm of my hand.

I'd lost another life, even though I hadn't been under Galahad's command when I'd jumped. Next time I died, I wouldn't wake up.

"Wren?" Carly asked, and my stomach dropped when I realized she'd been speaking. "Did you catch that?"

"Sorry, the cat—" I could've sworn Jonquil narrowed her eyes at me. "My phone cut out. Could you repeat that really quick?"

If I didn't calm the hell down in the next thirty seconds, I was going to completely botch this.

I fled to the hall, caught a glimpse of my tousled hair and oversized band t-shirt over pajama shorts in the bathroom mirror, silently mourned the interview outfit I never got to wear, and then continued to the kitchen.

"I was hoping you could tell me a bit about yourself." How many horrible interviews had Carly suffered through to sound as casual as she did now?

"Right. Well..." I ripped the refrigerator door open and shoved my head inside. Mom had taught me this trick. The cold air helped. Kind of. It at least seemed easier to breathe with a container of half-eaten cottage cheese inches from my nose. "Both my parents are Von Leer alumni."

"Okay, but what about you?"

"I'm not an alumnus, no." I would've facepalmed myself if I wasn't so deep in the fridge.

Luckily, Carly laughed.

"I imagine if you were, we wouldn't be on the phone," she said.

"Right, but don't most legacy students get in?" I didn't know where the words had come from, but now that they were out, I couldn't hold them back. Maybe part of me had already given up—on passing the interview, on getting into Von Leer, on surviving Skalterra. "Both my parents went there, but I didn't make it in. That's not normal."

"Oh, well—" Carly stammered.

"I'm not saying you should let me in because of my parents! It's dumb that legacy admissions happen at all at any school," I said quickly. "Actually, I think it's because of my dad. He's never met me. I wrote my essay about him and how much he sucks, but the university likes him, so now I think I might be the only legacy to never get admission on the first try."

It was like I was still falling off that cliff. I couldn't stop the words as they tumbled from my mouth.

"So what *have* you done?" Carly asked.

I'd practiced this question with Liam, but suddenly, every club and after-school activity I'd ever been a part of evaporated from my head. The obvious answer was that I'd spent nearly every night of the summer so far in a parallel world trying to keep save two different realities and fighting monsters.

Carly probably didn't want that answer.

"I haven't done anything yet."

Carly probably didn't want that answer either, because she fell silent. Jonquil bumped against my ankles, but I suspected she was hoping I would drop a bit of leftover chicken from the fridge shelf.

"I mean, I *have*," I clarified. "I did clubs and stuff, but that was all listed in my application, so you already know that. I haven't done anything I care about yet. Nothing that wasn't to pad a college application. None of that matters. What matters is what I'm *going* to do."

"Oh?" Carly sounded pleasantly surprised. I dared to come out of the fridge. I leaned against the door and played with the hem of my shirt. "Then what is it you hope to do?"

"I'm going to become the best geophysicist to ever come out of Von Leer University. Not because of my deadbeat, world-renowned geophysicist father, but because volcanoes are cool and over a billion people, including us, are living somewhere that a volcano might wipe them off the face of the planet, and someone needs to monitor them."

"Good news for you, then," Carly said. I looked down at Jonquil, and she stared back expectantly. "We have one of the top volcanology tracks in the country, though it sounds like you know that."

"I do," I said quietly. I'd practiced so hard with Liam. He would be so disappointed.

"In that case, Miss Warrender, would you be free for an in-person interview?" Carly asked. I stood straight up, nearly kicking Jonquil.

"In-person?" I demanded. I spun around to face Gams's magnetic calendar she kept on the fridge. "Yes! I mean, yes. Definitely. I could do that."

"The school year starts in a few months, so earlier is better. How's—"

"The fifteenth." I jammed my finger against the calendar. Gams had penciled in the day I was visiting campus with Liam. Maxwell Brenton's talk was on the evening of the fourteenth. "I can do the morning of the fifteenth. It's a Friday. I'm going to be over there anyways."

"The fifteenth it is! How does ten—"

"It works perfect," I cut her off. "Sorry. And don't worry. My grandma's cat is staying home, so I won't be delayed by any food-related Persian incidents."

Carly's laugh was forced, but I didn't care.

I'd moved on to the next interview. It would've been better if she'd told me I'd gotten in then and there, but I couldn't blame her. After the night I'd had and the interview I'd given, this was absolutely the best I could've hoped for.

She hung up, and I fell back against the fridge, running my hands through my tangled hair.

I could breathe again. It had worked out. It had cost me a life in Skalterra, but I'd managed to escape Ciarán, and I'd somewhat passed my interview despite being two minutes late and accusing the school of nepotism.

I unfurled my fingers to look at the new scar on my hand.

It had been worth it. Maybe. I still had one life left, and according to Galahad, we were getting close to the Second Sentinel.

I would survive both Skalterra and my next interview.

I would make sure of it.

Jonquil wove between my feet on the stairs to the shop. I danced around her, and she beat me to the bottom step. She pawed at the door with her tail held high.

"Stop pretending you're excited for me," I sighed at her. "You just want my grandmother."

I opened the door, and Jonquil chirped as she ran out. Gams looked up from where she was sweeping a spotless floor that I was sure she'd been stress-cleaning all morning.

"Well?" She threw the broom across the empty shop in her enthusiasm, and Liam ducked to avoid it at the ice-cream station.

"I got an in—"

"You got in?" Gams squealed.

"I got an in-person interview," I corrected her. Her cheeks turned ruddy, and her eyes narrowed behind her glasses.

"What's that mean?" she asked. "They're going to make you do another dance for them before they accept you?"

I shrugged and looked to Liam. Unlike Gams, he beamed.

"They did that with me too, when I was trying to get off the waitlist."

"When?" Gams spun to face him as he came out from behind the ice-cream stand to return her broom. "I don't remember that!"

"You gave me extra time off last summer for it," he laughed. "Riley drove me."

Liam's words were a little reassuring. So it wasn't a second interview because my first one had gone so awkwardly. It was normal.

"I set it for the weekend we're already going to be there," I said. "It's in the morning."

Gams pressed her lips together and held her head high.

"Then I suppose this is good news. I'll call Siobhan."

She marched to her workshop door with Jonquil on her heels.

"Siobhan?" Dread gnawed at my stomach. "No, we don't need another party."

"Can't hear you, dear!" Gams called as she closed her workshop door behind her. "Too busy calling my friends to brag about my granddaughter!"

I curled my fingers into fists at my sides as I stared at the workshop door.

"I really don't want a party," I said. Liam laughed and grabbed my wrist to pull me in. It was our first hug since the awkward one we'd shared on the paddleboard, but after carrying me upstairs so many times now, it probably felt normal to him to be so close.

I froze for a moment, and then let myself sink into his chest, but kept my arms at my side. His apron smelt like waffle cones, and I rolled my head to the side so I could hear his heartbeat through his sternum.

"We can leave after we get our burgers," he promised. "I know a place that has pretty good ice-cream if you want to go for dessert together."

I craned my head back to smirk at him.

"Yeah, I know the place you're talking about. I heard the guy that scoops the ice-cream is a tool."

"A tool?" He laughed again, and I let my head drop back against his chest. "I'm delightful."

I heaved a sigh, breathing in the scent of fresh waffle cones and men's deodorant.

"Was that true?" I asked. "Did your phone interview result in an in-person interview?"

"Yes, Wren." He adjusted his arms to give me a reassuring squeeze. "You did great. I don't remember there being a fitness test, though. What was all that slamming upstairs?"

My cheeks grew hot, and I pushed away.

"I was frazzled. It worked out."

A customer came in through the front door, and Liam grinned at me as he retreated to the ice-cream station.

"What?" I glowered, but my annoyance was mostly fake. The way his grin widened told me he knew that.

"Nothing," he said. "I'm just proud of you is all."

Liam kept his promise to sneak away from Siobhan's Tavern with me that evening. While we hadn't let Gams in on the plan, she caught on quick and made a show of standing up and asking me to go check on Jonquil. I stooped down so she could kiss my cheek on our way out.

Liam and I finished our burgers, as well as a couple of ice-cream cones from the shop, on Gams's sagging couch. He pet Jonquil where she curled between our laps as he told me about Von Leer, which architecture classes he'd be taking in the fall, and how he and his aunt had finally come to an agreement on what flower arrangements to order for Riley's memorial.

"It doesn't really matter, though." He shrugged. "He's coming back, and he's going to be mortified his parents wasted money on plants because they thought he was dead."

I rolled a fraying bit of blanket between my fingers as I thought.

"It doesn't have to be a waste," I said. "Are there any hospitals nearby? We could donate the flowers after the memorial is over. Do you think Riley would like that?"

Liam ran a hand through his dark blond curls.

"I think he'd love that," he said. "He'll still hate that the memorial happened at all, but this will help."

I stood up and stretched. It wasn't that late, but Galahad would be calling soon.

"Headed to bed?" Liam straightened up on the couch.

"Figured I should, just in case."

"Just in case you fall asleep?" he clarified. "You promise you have that under control? I know you said you were seeing a doctor, but—"

"I'm fine." I gave him a smile, but his tiny frown stayed in place. "But, you know what? I think I'd feel better if you slept here. Gams is always out late playing cards with her friends."

Liam had slept on Gams's couch before. I knew he didn't like being at home without Riley, and he settled back into the cushions.

"You sure?" he asked, but Jonquil was already making herself comfortable in his lap. "I don't want to intrude."

"Keep the nightmares away, would you?" I asked.

"Of course." He grinned. "See you in the morning."

"See you in the morning," I repeated.

The scars on my palm itched as I exited down the hall to my room.

He'd lost his mom, dad, and cousin.

And I was only one death away from him losing me too.

Thirty

Thermal Analysis

errin had been lecturing Galahad for several minutes in the bow of our longboat while Orla held my hand in her lap to inspect my scars by the light of her Skal bottles. The vessel rocked with the gentle river rapids, and Tiernan and Iseult held us steady with oars where they sat on either side of Fana.

"She's just a kid!" Ferrin gesticulated in my direction. "She will die!"

"This boat is full of children, and any one of them might die," Galahad growled. "The Nightmare isn't special. We do what we have to do to protect the Sovereign."

Fana stared at me from her bench with saucer-like eyes.

"I don't want anyone to die," she whispered.

"No one is going to die," Orla assured her.

"Don't coddle her." Tiernan sat on the bench next to Fana with his eyes trained on the dark waters ahead. He dipped his oar into the rapids to pull us to the right.

My stomach churned with the movement, but hopefully the fast river would help speed us away from Ciarán. I dropped my eyes to the wooden hull at my feet.

He was probably still in my head. Watching. Listening. Using me to get close.

"You never should have put the curse on her to begin with!" Ferrin seethed, still arguing with Galahad.

"I made her manageable, and she's helped get us this far."

I looked up to see Galahad glaring at me from the bow of the boat. He would absolutely kill me if he knew Ciarán could see inside my head. I dropped my eyes back to my feet. If Ciarán *was* in my head tonight, he'd kept quiet so far.

"How did you die last night, then?" Orla asked, finally relinquishing my hand back to me.

"There were too many Nightmares," I lied. "I'm not sure which of them got me. When it happened, it happened quick."

I dared to raise my eyes back to Galahad. Ciarán had insisted Galahad wouldn't have been able to tell I'd been stolen by a rival nocturmancer, but Galahad's narrowed eyes and tight scowl did little to reassure me.

"I should've stayed back so I could fight alongside you." Orla squeezed my hand. "Wren, I'm sorry."

"You only have one life as well, my niece," Ferrin sighed. The boat wobbled as he fell heavy into the bench at the bow. "You at least volunteered for this. Just—Wren was forced here. By us."

"It's a bit late for that," Galahad grunted. "Miss Warrender has made it this far. She need only survive a little longer."

Ciarán stayed silent in my head as we traveled. I tried to keep my eyes down, vaguely registering trees and cliffs on either bank, but doing my best not to focus on any landmarks that might offer hints to Ciarán. When we finally pulled ashore on a rocky bank, I was able to catch a moment alone as I walked into waist high grasses under the guise of keeping guard while the others set up camp.

"I don't know if you're there," I said into the darkness, "but if you are, I want you to know, the next time I see you, I will kill you."

For a moment, the only response was the wind whispering through the grass, but then a silky purr rasped at the back of my head.

"Is that a promise, Blue?"

I closed my eyes. I wouldn't let him see where we were.

"Yes."

"Is that what the funny hand gesture meant? The one you made after you jumped."

I opened my eyes to glare at the toes of my boots.

"The middle finger? Yes. It was absolutely a promise to kill you."

"I see. I thought it might have been some sort of Keldorian curse you put on me, but this is considerably more manageable and less frightening. I'll see you soon, Blue."

His voice melted into the sound of whispering grasses, and I stood a moment alone in the dark before Orla called my name and I retreated back to camp.

The next few days passed in a blur of more interview prep, selling ceramic chickens, and magical nighttime landscapes that I did my best to not look at. We continued to travel by boat for the next two nights, and the first waterside village marked our passage from the Wisting Wilds into the Royal Shogunate.

The buildings were reminiscent of those I'd seen in the Japan travel guide Mom had bought a few years prior before canceling a trip she was supposed to take with writer friends. She'd told me she was worried about the flight, but I'd always suspected she'd been more worried about leaving me behind.

Most of the homes along the river were simple lodgings, made of wood and tatami and illuminated by stone lanterns that lit the underside of red maple leaves. The fancier buildings sported multiple floors with pointed rooftops and sloping eaves.

On the third night of traveling by river, Ferrin sold the boat to a fisherman, and we continued farther north on foot. The passing evenings remained peaceful and unhindered by Grimguards. The mountains ahead loomed higher with every mile, and the scars on my hand stopped worrying me.

Ciarán stayed silent in my head, even when I addressed him directly. I would've liked to think something had happened to him, but I could still feel the magick tether between us, even if I refused to draw any Skal from it.

In Keel Watch Harbor, meanwhile, Liam seemed to grow more agitated the closer we crept towards Riley's memorial. His usual smile became more strained everyday. Gams gave him several days off, but he still brought us bagels every morning and would return to spend my lunch break answering my questions about Von Leer and helping me prepare for my next interview.

He at least laughed when I finally told him how horribly the first one had gone. I'd started to miss the sound of that laugh, so I took to looking for other things that made him smile.

The biggest guffaw came when I stuck a paper mustache and monocle to Jonquil one morning to surprise Liam when he brought breakfast. I thought the cat looked too much like Tamora with the monocle on, but Liam was so delighted that he picked up an extra shift right there, even if it was just to take pictures of Jonquil on his phone between customers.

He stuck around for dinner with me and Gams, but didn't say much. Luckily, Gams had plenty to say about how she was certain Sarah had been cheating at their game nights but had no way to prove it. When Gams left for another night of trying to catch Sarah hiding cards up her sleeves, Liam made himself comfy on the couch.

"I'm headed to bed," I said. "Are you okay?"

He stood up and pulled me into his chest. I hugged him back, since this embrace was more for his benefit than mine, and his fingers contracted against the folds of my shirt.

"He was supposed to be back by now," he whispered into my hair.

"I know."

"He's gonna lose it when he sees Jonquil in a monocle."

"He will."

I waited for him to be the first to let go before I slid away, but he slipped my hands into his when I did. He forced a smile.

"Don't do that," I said.

"Do what?"

"Pretend that you're happy. It's okay to be sad."

His smile faltered.

"But being sad is admitting he's gone."

"He is gone. For now. Even if it's temporary, you're allowed to be sad until he's back."

He let the smile fall.

"Thanks." He gave my hand a squeeze, his fingers brushing against the scars on my palm, and he fell back onto the couch. "I'm happy you're my friend."

"I'm happy I'm your friend too. Keep the nightmares away again?"

"Of course, Wren." This new smile was small and sad, but despite the weight it carried, it at least looked genuine.

Steam swirled past my head, giving me a disorienting welcome back to Skalterra. I stumbled on a water-slicked stone floor that shined in the dull light of paper lanterns. Crickets chirped somewhere out of sight, hiding in the maple trees and shrubs that lined the courtyard where I stood.

The wooden building behind me emitted a cozy orange and red glow from behind papered windows, and wooden posts supported the slanted roof of an eave.

"Galahad?" I spun around, looking for Galahad, Ferrin, and the others.

"Down here, Nightmare."

I stepped back, and the swirling steam cleared enough for me to see the two pools of water that spanned the small courtyard. Orla, Iseult, and Fana sat in the water to my left while Ferrin, Galahad, and Tiernan soaked on my right. Despite the cloudy appearance of the water, I could tell instantly that something was missing from each of my friends.

"Oh my god!" I slapped my hand over my eyes. "Are none of you wearing clothes?"

"Do you bathe in your clothes in Keldori?" Orla asked. I peeked at her through my fingers. Her short hair stuck to her forehead, so she must've dunked her head under the steaming water.

"No?"

"Then why would we be wearing clothes?"

I pressed my lips together and looked up at the night sky.

"We don't do group bath time, either," I said. "At least, not where I'm from."

"Then don't look." A splash to my right accompanied Tiernan's voice, and heat burned in my cheeks. I raised a hand to protect my peripheral vision as I listened to Tiernan's wet feet slap against stone floor.

"Done already?" Ferrin asked.

"I relaxed. I washed. I need to be prepared just in case," Tiernan said.

"That's what Just-Wren's for," Fana giggled up at me. Her curly hair had frizzed considerably in the steam, and her slim shoulders peeked out at me just above the water level.

Tiernan grunted, and the sound of a sliding door behind me told me it was safe to lower my hand.

"We're in the foothills of the mountains, so we'll be passing into the Skalterran Highlands soon." Ferrin raised his arms out of the water to set his hands behind his head, and he settled back into the stone wall of the water basin. "It won't be long until we reach the Second Sentinel."

"And you got Galahad to agree to a spa day?" I asked.

"There's a blizzard in our way." Galahad's silver hair was gathered into a bun at the top of his head, but his braided beard floated on the water in front of him. "We'll wait for it to pass and continue tomorrow."

"A blizzard this time of year?"

"The closer we get to the Frozen God's glacier, the colder it's going to get," Ferrin explained.

The door behind me opened again, and a fully-clothed Tiernan took up post next to me.

"You can watch them." I pointed at the men and shifted closer to the pool with Orla, Iseult, and Fana. "I'll stand over here."

"Now that Tiernan is on guard, you should join us!" Orla shifted over in her pool to make room between her and Iseult. The water may have been foggy and opaque, but I averted my gaze anyway.

"No," Galahad growled. "The Nightmare is working."

"By the Three Magicians, Galahad," Orla groaned. "Have you ever lightened up even once or would it actually kill you?"

"It's okay," I insisted. "I don't really do the naked-with-friends thing."

Orla glared at Galahad through the steam.

"What about just your feet?" she asked.

Galahad didn't protest, so I wiggled out of leather boots and wool socks that dissolved into dust as soon as I took them off. I sank to the stone floor to dip my feet into the water, and a shudder ran down my spine at the water's warm touch.

Orla dipped her mouth beneath the water to blow bubbles at a giggling Fana, but Iseult, with her long silver hair pulled into a floppy bun, frowned at the swirling bath with a blank stare.

"Iseult?" I asked in a low voice.

She shook her head and ran her fingertips along the top of the water.

"Sorry," she whispered. "I'm not used to all this yet."

She swallowed hard and looked around the courtyard.

"Right," I sighed. Her decision to leave her home had been so abrupt. I wondered if she was already regretting it. "This is the first time you've been outside of Tulyr."

"First and only, since there's no going back." She let her hand sink back under the water. "It's beautiful, but all I can think about is home and if it's even still there."

As strange and ethereal as Iseult was, she was suddenly the most relatable member of the group. Skalterra was new to her too.

"I think Tulyr will be okay." Ciarán had called off his Nightmares as soon as I'd yielded to him, but I couldn't tell her that without also explaining how I'd *actually* died that night. "By the time I went down, your friends nearly had it under control."

She raised her gray eyes from the water to me, and gave a soft smile. I tried to return it but was sure it looked more like a grimace.

"Thank you, Wren," she said. "You are kind. I didn't know Nightmares could be that way."

"Probably because Nightmares aren't supposed to be kind." I extended my leg so that my toes stuck out of the water. This conversation was nice, but I'd prefer it if all parties were clothed. "We're supposed to be whatever our handler wants us to be."

"That's funny," Galahad interjected behind us. "I don't recall ever wanting you to be a nuisance."

"If I'm such a nuisance, why do you keep bringing me back here?"

Galahad's responding grunt was accompanied by splashing. I fixed my eyes on my toes where they stuck out of the water. I didn't want to see any of my Skalterran counterparts naked, but Galahad was at the bottom of the list.

"Leaving home is hard," Orla said on my other side. She peered around my knees to get a better look at Galahad's granddaughter. "I'd never done it either until a couple years ago when my uncle and I left to join the other Riftkeepers in Cape Fireld."

"But you get to return." Iseult sighed and slipped under the steaming water so that her face was submerged up to her nose.

"I don't." Fana stopped paddling her tiny laps between the walls of the bath to look at Iseult. "And my whole family is dead. But Orla says there are other kids at the Second Sentinel, and even though I miss home, there weren't other kids there. Plus, Ferrin says I'll be safe and won't have to run anymore. So sometimes it's a good thing to leave home."

Iseult straightened up, letting her face come out of the water.

"You're very wise for someone so young," she conceded. "Thank you, Divine Sovereign."

"It's Fana." Fana took in a mouthful of bath water and then sprayed it up into the air. She smacked her lips and wrinkled her nose. "That was disgusting."

"Maybe it's time to get out of the water," Orla laughed. "How about we catch crickets before bed? Just— Wren, could you grab our towels?"

"And my crutch," Iseult added.

I pulled my legs out of the water. The heat had tinged the skin of my shins a deep pink, and the air, though warm with steam, felt cool against my legs. Galahad had disappeared into the inn, but I still kept my eyes down as I collected the folded towels and wooden crutch from the deck that led into the building.

Orla and Fana, wrapped in their towels, hurried into the inn while I gave Iseult a hand out of the bath. Tiernan, standing watch on the deck, politely lowered his gaze as I handed Iseult her crutch and held the towel up to give her privacy.

"Thank you." She wrapped herself in the towel and leaned into her crutch. It was weird to see her without her leg of silver Skal, but it made sense she would be preserving the magick, even if we were so close to the Second Sentinel. "For being kind, even though I wasn't when we first met."

"Don't worry about it. Tiernan blew me up when *he* first met me." I said it loud enough for Tiernan to hear, and he rolled his eyes.

"I wouldn't have if I knew Galahad had cursed you, and that's not my fault," he said. Fana and Orla came back out of the inn with bare feet and borrowed silk robes. They ran to the far end of the courtyard to begin their search for crickets. "And it worked for the most part. It injured the Grimguard enough to keep him off our heels until Tulyr."

I caught Ferrin's eye. He was the only one still bathing, and he rested with his chest against the edge of the pool and his arms folded on the tile of the courtyard.

He'd so far kept our secret misadventure with the Grimguard in Vanderfall a secret.

Iseult passed into the inn, and Tiernan watched her go before turning back to glance at Fana and Orla where they played. The skin beneath his eyes was dark with fatigue, and he leaned against a wooden post that supported the deck eave.

"Go sleep if you like," I offered. "I can watch them. I killed a rotsbane, remember? Fana is safe."

Tiernan clenched his jaw, still watching his ward.

"She's definitely safe." Ferrin splashed in the bath behind me, and I closed my eyes at the sound of his approaching feet on the wet tile.

"I would've grabbed your towel," I mumbled. After a moment, I dared to open my eyes. Tiernan was gone, having taken me up on my offer, and Ferrin had pulled trousers on.

He messed with a tunic and its inside-out sleeves, leaving his torso bare. Water from the bath rolled over deep ridges of scar tissue that spiraled out from what must have been a years-old injury on his abdomen. The muscles there were contorted and misplaced, as if whatever blade had caused the damage had been twisted, torquing the viscera of Ferrin's flank into a gruesome spiral.

I looked away too late. Ferrin must've seen the subtle drop of my jaw and the widening of my eyes, because he sighed and rubbed at the back of his neck.

"It's an old keepsake from a Grimguard," he explained.

"Daithi?" I asked, remembering Ferrin's unconscious body slumped against the wall when we'd encountered Daithi on my first night in Skalterra.

"No." He leaned against the wooden post and watched the steam from the baths curl up into the sky. "It was the night of my biggest failure as a Riftkeeper. The night the House of Quill fell, and the night my sister died."

"Orla's mother?"

Orla stood with Fana on the opposite side of the baths. They crouched in their borrowed silk robes to peer into the bushes. Orla pulled back from the foliage with her hands cupped over something. Fana squealed in delight when a cricket leapt from between Orla's fingers and disappeared back into the plants.

"Her name was Bryony, and she looked just like my niece." Ferrin watched Orla now too, with a hand over the deformed skin of his abdomen. "She was a Riftkeeper like me, and after we got word that Fana's family had been murdered, Bryony took the final Quill, a man named Oren, to a secret outpost. She was worried that whoever had killed the Firelds would come after him next."

"And she was right?"

Ferrin pulled his tunic over his head and took a moment to smooth out the wrinkles where they fell over his scar. His hair, normally so coiffed, now drooped in the steam over a furrowed brow.

"I caught word that Grimguards were seen in the area, and I rushed to warn my sister and Oren. The Grimguards arrived just before I did." He took a steadying breath. "It at least looked like Bryony died quickly. Oren was still fighting. I tried to save him, but a Grimguard skewered me clean through and left me to bleed out while they killed Oren next."

"Ferrin," I sighed. I knew Grimguards had killed Orla's mother, but I had no idea the story was so awful. "I'm sorry."

"The pain was excruciating, but do you know what haunts me more?" Ferrin's green eyes met mine in the light of the lantern at our free, and the look on his face made me unsure that I wanted the answer. "The sound of Oren gagging on his own blood while he, a grown man, cried out for his dead mother to save him."

Orla and Fana laughed across the courtyard as they stumbled after another cricket together. The clenched muscle in Ferrin's jaw relaxed, and a soft smile crept across his face as he watched his niece.

"Then why did you leave the Grimguard alive in Vanderfall after you found him in Orla's room? After everything his people had done?"

The smile faltered, but he kept his eyes on Orla.

"Several reasons, Just-Wren, the simplest of which is that you would not have allowed it, and I wish it could be just that simple." Something darker replaced Ferrin's smile, something I hadn't seen him wear before. "The Grimguards thought they'd killed me. But they hadn't, and despite my injuries, I was able to catch them off guard and gain the upper hand. I killed them slowly and deliberately for what they'd done. As horrible as the sound of Oren's dying breaths had been, I relished the Grimguards' screams. I made them beg for mercy, then I made them beg to be put to death. I made them watch each other die. But as much joy as I took in their suffering and as much joy as I continue to take in the memory of it, I don't like who I became that night. When I saw the young Grimguard helpless in Orla's bed, I wanted to become that person again, but I do not want my niece to see me like that."

I stood rooted to the spot, unable to look away from Ferrin and unable to come up with a suitable response. He finally turned away from Orla to give me another sad smile.

"Don't let them stay up too late, alright? We're leaving as soon as that blizzard has worn itself out, and they'll need their rest for the final bit of the journey."

I nodded wordlessly, and Ferrin disappeared through the sliding door into the tatami-floored room.

The crickets chirped in their bushes, and Fana and Orla's feet slapped against wet stone as they chased them, but there was another sound there too.

Heavy, choking breaths shuddered in the dark, and I had to force the muscles in my throat to loosen before I whispered into the shadows.

"Ciarán? Are you there?"

But the continued breathing in the back of my head, panicked and short, was the only response.

Thirty-One

Event Management and Design

Riley did not like the color black.

At least, that's what the text Liam had sent me the night before claimed. I searched through my clothes, trying to find something that wasn't too dark but still memorial-appropriate.

The harbor outside my window was busy with townsfolk in their own memorial attire, though none of them seemed to have received Liam's memo about Riley's apparent distaste for black. They bustled about the docks in dark button-ups and dresses as they prepared the marina for the vigil. I recognized Liam's Aunt Olive near the end of the dock where she messed with an arrangement of lilies. Gams shuffled down the wooden planks towards her.

I threw on a green dress and enough make-up to camouflage my patchy eyelashes before hurrying downstairs to help however I could.

The shop was closed, and July sunshine streamed through the large back windows to light the empty aisles as I slipped between them. Gams's air conditioning sent goosebumps erupting up and down my bare arms, and I

340

pushed through the back door, eager for the morning heat that the sun was sure to provide.

The bay, blue and calm, melded into the sky through the bit of horizon peeking through two emerald spits of land that cut into the water to form our bay. Gulls cried on the sea breeze, and the bell of a buoy tolled out across the water.

It would've been a beautiful day if not for the solemn faces that carried fold-out chairs, floral arrangements, and a blown-up poster of Riley out into the marina.

That, and the cold of the shop seemed to cling to me. I was unable to shake it as I hurried down wooden steps to the harbor.

"Morning, Wren." Siobhan nodded as I passed her. "Have you seen Liam this morning?"

"Not yet, but he texted me last night. Why?" I tried to rub warmth back into my arms. Siobhan didn't have sleeves either, and the wind ruffled her graying ginger hair, but she didn't seem nearly as bothered by the cold as I felt.

Siobhan frowned in response, and continued her trek to a trailer loaded with folded chairs.

My sandals echoed on the wooden planks of the marina, and Gams looked up as I approached the end of the docks. Olive sat on the planks, messing with her lily-laden flower arrangement.

"Wren, have you heard from Liam?" Gams asked. Olive looked up with red-rimmed eyes. Her pink lipstick was already smudged.

"I have a text from him." I pulled my phone from my dress pocket.

"What's it say?" Olive asked.

"Just that Riley doesn't like the color black."

Olive sighed and returned to her flowers while Gams gave my green dress a glance.

"Why are you shivering?" Gams held a wrinkled hand to my forehead. "Are you sick?"

"No, it's just freezing out here." I clenched my jaw to keep my teeth from chattering.

"I thought it felt nice." Gams furrowed her brow at me. "If you aren't feeling well, maybe you should wait inside until the memorial starts."

I stepped aside as one of Riley's friends from the cove hurried by with the poster of Riley and an easel to rest it on. He wiped sweat from his brow, nodded hello, and then went back the way he came to continue helping set up.

"I'm fine," I insisted. "I want to help."

Olive stood up and brushed off the skirt of her dress.

"Would you try calling Liam?" she asked. "He won't answer me. I know how he feels about the memorial, but Riley would want him here."

"Of course." I nodded. "But if his phone is off—"

Olive pulled keys from her purse and pressed them into my hand.

"Check at home. Riley's truck was still there this morning, so if he went somewhere, he didn't go far and might be back by now."

Gams took my arm to walk with me back down the dock.

"If you can't find him, that's okay," she said once Olive was out of earshot. "The memorial will help Riley's parents, but skipping it might be what Liam needs."

"I don't think he'd skip it." Gams knew Liam far better than I did, but I couldn't imagine Liam, so selfless and so kind, missing Riley's memorial and upsetting his aunt and uncle.

"Are you talking about the Glass boy?" Sarah sat on a bench with Gladys, both too old to help carry chairs but obviously wanting to be in the center of the action anyway. "Is he missing now too?"

"Hush, you," Gams snapped and tried to pull me past the old women.

"People disappear in Keel Watch Harbor," Sarah called after us. "It might save time and effort if we printed out his pretty picture really quick and stuck it next to Riley's."

"He's been gone one morning. That's hardly missing." Gladys pulled her black shawl tight around her shoulders. "Don't listen to Sarah, Wren. She's miserable."

"What you call miserable, I call practical," Sarah sniffed.

"Liam's okay," I said. "He's just running late."

"Riley was running late too," Sarah sang.

"Sarah, if I didn't think it would poison the fish, I'd shove you in the harbor. Come on, Wren." Gams tugged on my arm to keep me walking. "You *are* freezing. Have you felt your arms?"

"Maybe if you didn't constantly run the AC, I wouldn't get so cold," I suggested.

"Nonsense. Jonquil is all fluff. She'd overheat."

"I promise you, the cat is fine." I suppressed another shiver. "Sarah has to be wrong, right? Because Liam—"

"Sarah is jealous *she* hasn't disappeared yet. She'd love to be the talk of the town." Gams scowled. We'd come to the end of the dock, and she reached up to feel my forehead again. "You don't feel feverish."

"I told you. I'm fine. Turn the heat up in the shop, and I'll be okay."

She studied me, and I watched her eyes go back and forth as she scanned my face for other signs of malady.

"You've been pulling at your eyelashes again."

I rolled my eyes and looked away.

"I have to go find Liam."

Gams hummed in disapproval.

"Fine. But if he doesn't want to come to the memorial, don't force him, and don't make him feel bad. He needs to grieve in his own way."

"It's not grieving if Riley—"

"Wren." Gams frowned, a deep sadness pulling on the wrinkles of her face. "It's okay. Find Liam."

She stood on tip-toes to peck my cheek and then hurried back down the dock.

I stopped upstairs in the apartment to grab a jacket before I headed in the direction of the bagel shop. When Liam didn't answer his phone, I quickened my pace and tried to push Sarah's words away.

Liam was fine. He had to be. He was *Liam*.

The bagel shop's windows were dark, and I skirted around the building to find the door to the second-floor apartment. Even though Olive had given me a key to their home, I felt like I was trespassing as I fumbled with the doorknob.

The stairwell on the other side of the door was lined with family photos. Most of them showed Riley with his parents, or Riley in children's sports uniforms. He got older as I climbed, and near the top of the stairs, Liam joined the family portraits.

"Liam?" The living room window overlooked the street. Townspeople walked past on the sidewalk below, dressed in their most solemn blacks. Light from the window lit the living room and kitchen. It looked recently renovated, with white marble countertops and tile flooring instead of linoleum, but the apartment had the same salty, musty smell as Gams's.

The hallway beyond the kitchen sported more family pictures. These ones included images of Liam when he was younger, as well as two other adults. The woman looked just like Olive, if Olive had darker hair, and I figured she must be Liam's mother.

"You better not jump out at me if you're in here." I shivered and tried to pull my jacket tighter, still unable to shake the cold. Maybe Gams was right about me being sick. "I'm serious, Liam. If you scare me, I might punch you in the throat, and it won't be my fault."

I pushed a bedroom door open. Light filtered in through slatted curtains, sending striated shadows across the two twin beds that pressed against opposite walls. Neither looked slept in. Liam had spent so many nights on Gams's couch recently.

A phone sat on one of the bedside tables, and I crossed the room to poke at it. Several missed calls and texts populated the lock screen. The most recent notification was from "Wren Coworker".

"Shut up, you know my last name, idiot." Despite my irritation, my stomach clenched with nerves. Liam clearly wasn't home, but he'd left his phone by his bed.

"Wren Warrender!"

I yelped and spun around at the thundering voice, but I was alone. Galahad was back in my head.

"It's the middle of the morning!" I spat. "I'm busy!"

"I'm sorry. If I could spare you, I would."

"Spare me?"

"Wren Warrender, I command you to return to Skalterra!"

I opened my mouth to protest, but a flurry of snow blew in my face. I coughed and stumbled backwards. The frame of Liam's bed smacked against the back of my knees, and I fell, landing in a field of white stained with blood.

Galahad lay on his side, bleeding into the snow.

"Galahad!" I crawled to his side, fighting through the sideways flurry to press my hands against the wound in his flank. "The others, where—"

"Behind you!" Galahad shoved me off him and pointed into the white gloom. A figure glowed orange in its depths, and I could feel Ciarán's rage needling at the back of my mind. A smaller figure struggled in his arms, and my stomach dropped.

He had Fana.

Ballroom Dance III

Snow blew sideways on the bitter wind that rolled over the field, but I charged through the gale. Galahad's power roiled through me, and I made myself faster, stronger, denser to launch at Ciarán.

Fana shrieked in his arms, and I reached out to grab Ciarán by his face and forced him to the ground beneath me. A burst of green signaled Ferrin's arrival at my side, and he pulled Fana out from between me and the Grimguard. Orange and black eyes glowed up at me from between my fingers, full of loathing.

"They ambushed us halfway across the lake." Ferrin threw Fana onto his back. Snow dusted his hair, and a light ice had frozen his coiffed hair in place.

"They?" I repeated. Blue hair whipped around me in the wind, and Ciarán's muffled scream of frustration reverberated against the palm of my hand. "Another Grimguard?"

"Don't make the same mistake I made in Vanderfall. Kill the Grimguards. And don't you die too."

He took off in a sprint, and Fana gave me a final panicked glance.

Ciarán bucked, and I pressed harder into his face. Cracks radiated out from under his body, and I realized we were on ice. Ciarán's chest, which I had tried so hard to heal a few short weeks ago, heaved with labored breaths beneath me.

"What are you waiting for, Nightmare?" Galahad's voice, haggard and hoarse, carried on the wind. "Kill the Grimguard!"

Orange eyes widened between my fingers. Ciarán stopped struggling, but he shook his head against my hand.

He'd had Fana in his clutches. He'd been so close to taking her.

And he'd continue to try until either he or she were dead.

A single blade of bone pushed through the meat of my arm, and I held it over Ciarán. He choked on my name, his voice muffled through his cowl and my hand.

"Do it, Nightmare!" Galahad bellowed.

Ciarán shook his head again, and I hesitated.

If I killed him, he would become someone's Riley.

He wanted to hurt my friends. He'd killed me. He'd almost ruined my interview with Von Leer.

And I couldn't bring myself to murder him. Not when he looked so young. Not when there might be someone out there hoping he came home safe.

Pain lanced my side, and I cried out as blinding orange light forced me sideways off of Ciarán. Electricity and heat spasmed through my body. I curled in on the gaping wound in my abdomen, my face pressed against ice and snow.

I choked on my breaths as a figure sprinted towards me over the ice.

"Orla?" I croaked, still trying to stem the blood and ash that spilled from my stomach.

The woman raised her arm towards me, aiming a crossbow that was built into her arm bracers.

A glowing arrow formed in her other hand, and she pulled it against a buzzing bowstring of neon Skal.

"Go to hell, Nightmare!" She loosed the arrow.

I had half a second to pull Skal from Galahad to harden my armor and seal the wound in my abdomen. The arrow glanced off my kevlar, but the force of the hit knocked the wind from me a second time.

"Aim for the old man!" Ciarán shouted from where he tried to catch his breath on the ice.

The woman Grimguard formed a new arrow, and I struggled to my feet too late. She leveled her bow arm at Galahad.

"No!" My scream caught on the wind and did little to stop the arrow of Skal hissing through the air.

Orange sparks burst as the arrow collided with Iseult's outstretched hand where she stood over Galahad's injured form. The woman Grimguard slid to a halt.

Her next arrow extended into a pike, and she jammed its pointed end into the ice. Orange light shot through the cracks that spread beneath her, and the lake groaned.

I scrambled on all fours towards Iseult where she tried to drag Galahad away from the breaking ice. A red stain smeared across the snow behind him.

"Grandfather, please!" Iseult begged. "We have to move!"

I helped her pull Galahad to his feet, but his toes dragged in the snow between us.

"Leave me." His breaths were ragged. "You have to stop the—"

"Watch out!"

Tiernan's cry cut through the wind, and I dropped Galahad to spin and face Ciarán as he bore down on us. Behind him, Tiernan charged to our aid through snow flurries while Orla fought the woman Grimguard on collapsing, cracking ice.

I pulled a silver flail from the air and ran to meet Ciarán. He blocked my flail with an orange staff, but

Tiernan attacked him from behind, forcing him to procure a second weapon to block Tiernan's golden sword.

"Help Iseult get Galahad out of here!" I formed a second flail in my left hand. Ciarán's Skal spread into a shield, but the force of my attack knocked him backwards towards Tiernan.

"I will not leave the Sovereign!" Tiernan protested. Ciarán blocked his next attack with ease, still holding me at bay with his shield.

"Great, because she left you! Ferrin escaped with her already. Take Galahad. I'll keep the Grimguards busy." Serrated bones pushed their way through muscle, skin, and leather to erupt from my forearms. Tiernan kicked Ciarán back my way, and Ciarán lifted his shield to ward off the spikes I brought swinging down.

Skal sizzled, and the smell of burning bone stung my sinuses, but my strength swelled as I pulled more magick from Galahad. His injured state made it too easy to control the tide of Skal between us, and I let the magick swell and roll through me. I pressed harder into the shield, forcing Ciarán onto one knee.

"I've got this!" I shouted at Tiernan. "Go!"

He hesitated, but a blast of green and orange from Orla's fight with the woman spurred him towards Iseult and Galahad.

"Running won't save the old man," Ciarán growled at me through his shield. "You're only delaying the inevitable!"

"The inevitable being you?" I turned my foot into steel and brought it smashing down into the ice. The ground cracked beneath us, forcing Ciarán to scramble away.

His shield evaporated with his broken focus, and I swung my fist into his jaw. He staggered back and pulled his cowl down from his face.

"Yes!" He spit blood into the snow. "Me!"

His orange eyes focused on the receding shapes of Iseult and Tiernan with Galahad between them. He lunged, taking off across the ice in a sprint, but I was faster.

I tackled him around his middle, and we collapsed against the frozen lake in a tangle of cloaks, limbs, and blue hair.

I wouldn't hesitate this time. He had to die. He would kill me. He would kill my friends.

"I'm sorry," I said, and leveled my bone spike with Ciarán's pale neck.

"You aren't going to kill me, Blue."

I shook my head at him.

"Just because you've been in my head the last two weeks doesn't mean you know me."

"Then why aren't I dead yet?" His chapped lips pulled into an arrogant smile.

I withdrew my bone spike and forced Skal into my hand to form a lethal claw.

"Careful, Nightmare," Galahad's growl in the back of my head caught me off guard, and I faltered before I could bring my talons swinging down. "Don't take too much Skal too fast."

He pulled back on the magick I'd siphoned away from him, and my strength evaporated.

Ciarán sensed my moment of weakness and swept his leg up and into my torso.

I slammed into the snow, and Ciarán rolled on top of me, pinning my hands above my head.

"Having problems with your handler?" he goaded.

"Screw you." I struggled under his weight and tried to draw on the magick tether between me and Galahad, but Galahad pushed back.

Ciarán froze on top of me, staring at my hands where he had them pinned.

"Your hand." Ciarán's orange eyes widened as he took in the scars on my palm. "Blue, you let the old man curse you?"

"Get off me!"

"How many lives did he give you?" His initial shock at the discovery ebbed away to be quickly replaced by morbid curiosity. "How many have you got left before he lets you die for him?"

"Enough to last long enough to kill you."

His smile quirked, and his eyes softened.

"Ah, Blue. You've had plenty of opportunities to do that, and we both know you won't." He leaned in close so that his nose was inches from mine, and his warm breath washed over my cheeks. "But don't you worry. I'll make sure the old man pays for what he did to you."

"I won't let you kill my friends!"

His taunting smile dissolved into a snarl, and his fingernails dug into the skin of my wrists.

"Killers get killed. Call it an occupational hazard."

"You're the killer!"

"You really think so?" His voice turned as frigid as the ice that pressed against my back. "Even after Ferrin told you how he butchered the other Grimguards? After you watched him kill Daithi?"

"Occupational hazard," I spat.

Ciarán's eyes narrowed.

"I like you, Blue. It was fun being in your head, and you proved very useful. I hope for both our sakes you've got more than one life left, because you keep getting in the way, and you refuse to yield. Unfortunately, that leaves me with so few options."

He closed the few inches between the tip of my nose and his lips. The tiny kiss was cold against my skin. He used one hand to hold my wrists overhead, and an orange knife sparked in his free fist.

"Galahad!" I screamed, twisting beneath Ciarán, trying to get away. I didn't want to die for him.

"Don't tell me." Ciarán flashed a haughty smile and played with the knife in his hand. "This *is* your last life, isn't it?"

"Galahad, help!" I clawed at the invisible tether between Galahad and me. I needed his Skal. He *owed* me his Skal.

"You were always expendable to him, Blue. He doesn't need you anymore, so he's taken his Skal and left you to die."

"No." Galahad didn't like me, sure, but he wouldn't let me die. Not like this.

"You could still save yourself." His grin showed off his canines. "You could always yield to me."

"I'd rather die." I pressed into the ice, but there was no escape.

"I don't believe that. Not when you're on your last life." He held the glowing blade to my neck so I could feel its heat. "Yield, Blue. Become my Nightmare, and we'll work together to bring those killers to heel."

"Go to—"

"Go to hell, yes. I know." He drew back his knife, preparing to bring it down across my neck.

If Galahad wouldn't let me have his magick, I'd force him to give it to me. I gave a final, mighty heave on the tether.

Magick sparked in my fingertips and rushed through my veins, filling me with sudden power and strength.

"Nightmare!" Galahad's voice was a warning bark, but another wave of magick ran through me, and my fingers elongated into claws. Ciarán's eyes widened, and he realized too late that my strength had returned.

I used the same leg sweep he'd used on me, but he managed to scramble away, slipping on the ice.

"You're done hunting us." My bone spikes were back, even though I hadn't felt them come in. My leather boots strained and popped as my feet grew into hind claws. Skin thickened into scales, and Ciarán staggered back, brandishing a staff of glowing orange.

Galahad was full of fresh Skal, and now that I'd broken the dam he built to keep it from me, he couldn't control its flow anymore.

He couldn't control *me.*

"Look what they've turned you into, Blue," Ciarán growled. Bits of black hair hung loose from his collapsing bun, and his lips pressed together. He was putting on a brave face, but his orange eyes widened, and the sharp stench of fear that rolled off him was nauseatingly satisfying.

"I'm stronger than I've ever been!" I lunged at him, and he tried to parry with his staff, but I batted it away with a kevlar-armored arm.

"They've made you into a weapon." He danced out of reach of my outstretched claws. "If you could see yourself —"

Something hot broke across my back, and I spun around to find the woman Grimguard. Her eyes glowed a more neon orange than Ciarán's, but she had the same dark sclera. Curly hair hung down from under her fur-lined hood, and the cowl that covered the bottom half of her face only did so much to hide the freckles that covered her cheeks.

An orange bludgeon formed in her hands, but I drew more Skal from Galahad's stores and caught the weapon in my claws. It burned against my palms, but I reinforced the skin of my hands and squeezed.

The weapon exploded in a burst of sparks, and I reached through shattered light to grab the woman by her face and throw her backwards.

"Wren!" Orla staggered over broken ice, trying to get closer. "Wren, be careful!"

"Get out of here!" I yelled back, but there was something new and harsh in my voice. "I've got it handled!"

"No, you don't!"

The fear on the Grimguards' faces had fueled me, but the stricken look on Orla's made me falter. Her jaw dropped, and she shook her head, but I turned back to Ciarán to launch at him yet again.

My claws left shimmering gashes in the orange shield he held between us, but I couldn't reach him. I pulled more magick from Galahad.

It was intoxicating, and I needed more.

"Wren Warrender," Galahad gasped in my mind, "would you really kill me?"

I wasn't *killing* him. I was just taking his magick to hold off the Grimguards.

"To save both our realms?" I snarled back, parroting what he had said to me my first day in Skalterra. "Gladly."

The woman attacked again, having regained her bearings, this time with a broadsword. It was just as easy to stop as her bludgeon, and it hurt less this time. The sword evaporated into neon steam in my hands, and I breathed deep, inhaling the remnant of the Skal that had formed it.

I needed more.

Panic nudged at the back of my head, but it was dulled by the hunger that roiled in my gut.

"Wren!" Orla shrieked. She sounded far away, and I tried to find her, but the snow flurried harder around me. Silver sparks illuminated my claws, and my stomach churned at the sight of dead gray skin creeping up my fingers.

"Orla?" I called back. Ciarán and his friend were gone, lost in the storm of snow and Skal, but Orla was in danger. My panic screamed now, but the hunger was still louder. "Orla, run! I can't—"

I cut off in a guttural cry as more Skal ricocheted through my body. I was splitting apart. The Skal was stripping me away, but I couldn't stop myself from siphoning more.

Galahad was supposed to stop me.

Why wasn't he stopping me?

I pulled at the connection, and Galahad pulled back, trying to stopper the flow of magick, but it was too late. I'd overpowered him. His Skal was mine, and it was burning me up.

I needed more.

I would become a rotsbane, but I needed more. I would die if I didn't get more, and every bit of Skal filled me with terrible elation and insatiable hunger.

"Blue!" Ciarán's voice split the storm of ice and Skal. "Wren Warrender!"

Tattered cloaks and shoulder-length dark hair whipped around him as he fought his way into my vortex. I should kill him. I was supposed to kill him. But I was fraying. Every molecule inside me was unraveling. If I moved, I was sure to fall apart.

"Wren, you need to stop!" Ciarán called.

"I can't!" I couldn't tell if the outlines of my arms were blurred by the snow or if they were dissolving into something amorphous and shadowy.

I was collapsing in on myself, but exploding outwards all at once.

And I was so hungry.

"Then let me stop you!" Ciarán held his hands up in a show of good faith, and dared to step closer. He had bottles of Skal on his belt, and I salivated at the thought of downing them, glass and all.

It wouldn't be enough, but it was a start.

"You can't stop me," I said through gritted teeth. Galahad had more Skal. I could feel it floating on the ether between us. I reached for it. If I didn't, I was sure whatever beast that was clawing at my insides would break free.

But the Skal made the beast wilder, and I cried out.

I wanted Skal. I did not want to be a rotsbane.

I didn't know which of the two would win out over the other.

I couldn't help myself. I pulled more Skal from Galahad. He would dry up soon. He was saying so in my head, but his voice was muted and faraway.

He would die.

I would kill him.

It would be worth it.

"I can take it away!" Ciarán said. "But you have to yield to me!"

"You'll kill me," I sobbed.

"No," he promised. "I told you. Killers get killed, and you're not a killer, and you're not going to be a rotsbane either. You just have to yield."

"You were going to! Just now!"

"I was messing with you! Wren Warrender, I command you to yield!" His voice reverberated as he spoke aloud as well as directly into my head through our connection.

"Get out!"

Gams would find me dead on the floor of Liam's bedroom, and it might be worth it if it meant sating the hunger that gnashed inside me.

"I see them in your head." Ciarán inched closer, fighting to stay upright in the swirling sparks and snow. "All the people you love. They won't see you again if you give in to the rotsbane! Give in to me instead!"

"No!"

"You have a mother, and a grandmother!" Ciarán continued. He took my hands. My fingers with their dark talons and deadened knuckles looked so monstrous wrapped in his, and I tried to pull away, but his grip tightened. "And you have friends!"

"I don't," I whimpered. Everything hurt. Skal would make it better. Only more Skal could help me.

"I can see him right now inside your mind, Blue, and I see how much you care about him and your mother and your grandmother."

"Just kill her!" the woman Grimguard yelled. Another arrow of orange flew through the flurry, but it dissolved into delicious smoke before it could split me open. I inhaled, savoring the way the Skal filled my sinuses and lungs.

I. Needed. More.

I needed to die.

"I'm not going to kill you. Not if you yield." Ciarán's bright orange and black eyes filled my vision. "But you have to give me control."

The hunger tore me from the inside out, and the scream that issued from my throat didn't sound human. I'd never wanted something more in my entire life.

Not Von Leer. Not a friend. Not a father who gave a damn.

Just Skal.

"Wren Warrender, yield!"

"You just want to use me!"

"So? Is that worth turning into a rotsbane over?"

"Yes!"

He clawed his way up my arms to wrap himself around me. He held me in one piece, pressed into me with his cheek against mine.

"You are not a killer." His breath was warm in my ear. "You are not a monster, and I will not let the real monsters turn you into one."

"Ciarán," I gasped. Hot tears streamed down my cheeks. "Ciarán, help me."

"Yield."

"I—"

I didn't want to yield. I wanted Skal. I wanted to devour every last drop, and rip apart anything and anyone that stood in my way. I wanted to burn all of Skalterra and Keldori to the ground in search of it. I wanted—

"Wren. Please." The voice in my ear was Ciarán's, but the voice in my head was someone else's. The sound of

Liam begging pulled me back to my senses just long enough for me to gasp out two syllables.

"I yield."

The words were barely audible, but Ciarán's arms tightened around me as my stomach flipped. Every bit of magick that threatened to tear me apart fled down the channel that opened between us. My body snapped back into place, and my legs gave out.

He lowered me to the snow. The chill of the ice bit against the exposed skin of my feet, arms, and face. Shivers that had nothing to do with the cold wracked my body.

"You tricked me," I choked. He'd imitated Liam in my head to snap me out of my hunger, but I hated the thought of Liam's voice in Ciarán's throat.

"I saved you." The orange in Ciarán's eyes shined brighter than before, and sparks blew off his back in the wind. His hand buzzed with electricity where it cupped my cheek. He was teeming with the Skal he'd stolen from me.

The Skal I'd given him.

And now I was at his mercy with no magick left.

"You saved yourself," I whispered.

"Don't touch her!" Orla shriek echoed over the ice. "Wren, watch out!"

She hurled a javelin of emerald green towards Ciarán, and he fell away from me to avoid getting caught in its trajectory.

"I told you to run!" I shouted at Orla as she sprinted towards me. It wasn't safe here, especially now that I belonged to the Grimguards. She needed to get to the others. She needed to get away from *me.* "Orla, *go!*"

But she continued her charge, sliding to a stop in front of me with her arms outstretched. The hiss of Skal zipping through the air was cut by a soft thunk, and I stared in horror at the luminescent arrow that protruded from her back.

"Orla—" She fell to her knees. I scrambled through the snow to catch her. "Orla!"

The arrow in her chest dissipated, and blood dripped from the gaping wound it left behind, staining the snow. She gasped for air through shuddering, gulping breaths, and I rallied the last dregs of strength I had left to hold her up.

"What've you done?" I cried.

"You only have one life left," she mumbled. "She was going to take it."

The woman Grimguard was already nocking another arrow, and I tried to pull Orla to her feet.

"We can't stay here!"

She leaned heavily on me, but green fire sparked in her hand.

"I will not let you die in a fight you didn't sign up for, Just-Wren," she grunted. "They killed my mother. Let them kill me too. Promise me you'll run."

"No!"

She shoved me off her, and I collapsed on the ice. I begged my limbs to move, but I was too weak to give chase. I screamed at Orla's back as she staggered forward to face the Grimguards.

Ciarán and the woman converged on her, weapons of orange blazing against the white of the frozen lake.

"Orla!"

Orla lifted her green flame. It expanded until she was a dark silhouette against a backdrop of emerald. I screamed her name again.

Purple light flickered at the core of her flame and then expanded outwards to swallow the lake in a mosaic of amethyst fire and ice.

Thirty-Three
Genetics

right purple light seared across my vision, and hundreds of tiny ice shards bit into the skin of my face and arms. I hid against the ground, still screaming Orla's name, as heat licked at my back and the ice rolled beneath me.

The blast settled, but the lake continued to groan, and I looked up through snow-dusted locks of blue hair. Snow and Orla's lilac sparks hung in the air, and I fought to see through the haze.

A body lay on the ice several yards ahead me, horribly still and lifeless.

"Orla!"

I scrambled through the ice debris, ignoring the cracking of the ground beneath my bare feet. I rolled her onto her back, and my heart plummeted.

The wound in her chest had partially cauterized, but blood still seeped from the edges of the gash, staining her tunic and armor. Her goggles had completely shattered, and her eyelids fluttered over ruddy, chapped cheeks.

The woman Grimguard screamed Ciarán's name somewhere behind me, and when I prodded at the tether between us, it felt weak and brittle.

If he was injured, he wouldn't be able to follow us, but a distant worry for his wellbeing nagged at the corners of my mind.

Orla shuddered, and I wadded her cloak against her chest in an effort to stem the bleeding.

"Orla, can you hear me?" I pulled her broken goggles off her face, and her head lolled back in my hands. "Orla, please!"

She groaned softly, her eyes still closed, and my heart hitched.

"Come on, we can't stay here." When I tried to lift her, however, my legs gave out, and we collapsed back on the ice together.

I needed Skal.

I pushed through Orla's cloak in search of the bottles at her belt. Two bottles were shattered, one was empty, but the fourth glowed with Skal.

The bottle was warm in my hand, and the Skal inside swirled blithely. I needed it to save us both, but I hesitated with my fingers on the stopper.

What if the hunger came back? Judging by the sound of the woman still yelling his name behind me, I didn't think Ciarán was in any condition to stop me if I veered back towards rotsbane territory.

Orla's breathing was shallow and rapid. She didn't have long.

I uncorked the bottle and took a swig of the glowing liquid.

It heated me from the inside, electrifying every nerve. Strength returned to my arms and legs, and while I craved more, it wasn't the same unbearable hunger as before. I formed a new pair of boots over my bare feet as I lifted Orla onto my back.

Her head slumped against mine, and she groaned again.

"Nightmare!" the woman screamed behind me, and I twisted around to face her.

Orla's blast had left a massive hole in the ice, and the Grimguard knelt on the opposite side of it. Her hood had fallen away, and wild hair twisted in the wind. Ciarán lay next to her, unmoving, and I tested our connection again just to make sure he was alive.

The woman raised her bow arm towards me and nocked an orange arrow in place.

We stared at each other, the wind howling between us. Her orange eyes glowed in the snowy gloom, and I held her gaze in a silent dare to fire.

But then she lowered her arm and bent over Ciarán's body. I watched for a moment to make sure she wouldn't change her mind about shooting us, then turned and ran.

"You should've run when I told you too," I muttered to the snow. "And where the hell did you get purple magick?"

Hopefully the others weren't too far ahead. Hopefully there was some kind of shelter at the lake's edge where I could help Orla.

Her chest heaved against my back with ragged breaths, and each one accompanied a weak, raspy exhale in my ear.

"Where do I go?" I whispered. I wasn't even sure this was the right direction. "Dammit, Orla, I don't know what I'm doing!"

"Wren Warrender, do you know you nearly killed me?"

I'd never been so relieved to hear Galahad's voice in my head.

"Galahad, help." I must've slipped back under his jurisdiction when Orla's attack had injured Ciarán. I clawed at the strengthening tether between us, though I was careful not to take any more Skal. "I have Orla, but I don't know where to go. She's– she's not okay."

"But she's alive?"

"For now," I panted, still fighting through the wind in a full sprint.

"And you promise you aren't a rotsbane?"

I blinked away tears, afraid they might freeze my eyes shut if I let them fall.

"I'm not a rotsbane."

"You should be. I felt how much magick you took from me."

"I know. I'm sorry. Yell at me later. I need to know where to take Orla."

"I left you a trail. You'll be able to see it as long as we're connected. Find the silver wisps. They'll bring you here."

I slid to a stop to search the gloom for any glowing wisps, whatever a wisp might look like.

"Sure, no problem," I sighed. "Should be easy to find something silver when literally everything else is gray and white."

"And once again I'm struck by the fact that I ended up with the daftest Nightmare to ever be unlucky enough to travel Skalterra. Don't search with your eyes, girl."

I shrugged off Galahad's comments. I didn't have time to be offended, and I *had* nearly killed him.

I focused on the Skal coursing through my veins, not entirely sure how to find Galahad's trail but figuring it would probably work along the same lines as the magick bond between us. A tugging pulled me to the left, and I trusted the feeling and chased after it. A bit of light glimmered in the gloom, shining like a silver ghost that fluttered in the wind.

"I found it!" I said.

"Hurry, Nightmare. I quite like the Quillguard in your care. I'd hate for her to die so close to home."

"Galahad." I stopped to inspect the glowing silver orb that he'd called a wisp. It was roughly the size of a softball, and a gentle heat radiated off its surface. Another one floated twenty or so yards ahead. "Something weird happened with Orla."

"Weird how?"

"Is it normal for a Magician's Skal to change color?"

Galahad was quiet in my head, and I trudged onwards to the next wisp of silver Skal.

"Wren Warrender," he finally said, "don't you tell me that girl's Skal turned purple."

A dread I couldn't explain crept in my chest.

"How did you know it was purple?"

"Keep that girl alive." Galahad's voice turned hard and brittle. "She is your new priority. Keep her alive, Wren Warrender, or die trying."

I adjusted my grip on Orla and took my sprint back up. Galahad's trail was easy to follow now that I knew how to feel for the Skal he'd left burning in the air for me to find. The rocky side of a mountain loomed ahead, and I forced even more magick into my legs.

When we finally reached the frozen shore of the lake, I laid Orla down on the rocks to take another sip of Skal. Gray, snow-laden crags rose overhead, and the lakeshore stretched into gloom in either direction.

I knelt next to Orla, checking that she was still breathing. Snow clung to her eyelashes, and the tips of her short hair had frozen, but tiny puffs of foggy breath escaped her mouth and nose. She was still alive.

I fashioned one of her broken Skal bottles into a makeshift knife, and cut the hem of her new cloak into strips to use as a bandage. She bled from her back as well as her chest, and I did my best to press the fabric into both wounds, securing it in place with the help of her leather armor.

"Sorry, Orla," I grunted as I lifted her again. Frozen rocks cracked and slipped under my boots, and I twisted around, searching for Galahad's next wisp.

Skal tugged me towards the cliff face where a wisp floated over a line of large boulders.

"Why?" I groaned, and maneuvered Orla up onto the rocks. She was all limb, and I did what I could to not aggravate the injuries I'd just tended.

The next wisp was a few feet below us, floating in the shelter of a crack in the cliff that had been invisible from the beach. It looked like a dead-end, but I had to trust the trail Galahad had left. I slid off the rock first, then lowered Orla after me.

"Galahad?" I leaned forward to slump Orla over my back, ducking extra low to crawl between the slabs of rock.

Wind whistled outside, but we were protected from the snow here. Silver glowed around a corner up ahead, and another wisp tugged at the Skal that linked me to Galahad.

"How far ahead did they get?" I hissed to Orla's unconscious body and trudged forward on legs I refused to let fatigue.

The tunnel widened around the next corner, and the cave walls smoothed. More silver light beckoned me around another corner, and I gasped as we turned into a wide cave with an arched ceiling that stretched deeper into the mountain.

"It's a pyroduct," I breathed. "Orla, we're in a lava tube. Are we near a volcano?"

The silver wisps stretched forward with the lava tube, and I chased after them. They tapered away into nothingness as I approached, and I counted the steps between them. Each wisp brought me closer to the others. I would make sure Orla found help.

However, the silver light of wisps grew dimmer and dimmer, until I caught up with the final orb. It winked away, and the tunnel turned dark.

"Galahad?" I called. My voice echoed through the cave, as if taunting me.

I wiggled an arm out from under Orla, and lit a silver flame in my palm. The cave continued onward for who knew how far, but the wisps had ended right here. I scanned the floors, the ceiling, the walls, until I noticed the low, hand-carved archway to my left.

A steep, stone stairway continued past the arch, but my flame only lit the first few steps because the stairs spiraled out of sight beyond a corner.

"We're in the Second Sentinel, aren't we?" I murmured to Orla. "We just have to go up, right? And you'll be home."

The stairway was narrow, and the steps were uneven, but I climbed their spiraling pathway as best I could with Orla slumped on my back, chasing after the shadows cast by my fire.

The air was thick and stale in my lungs, and I struggled to breathe, but I forged forward. I lost count of the steps, and even with my Skal-enhanced strength and endurance, I worried the stairs would never end.

It was impossible to tell how far we'd traveled when I finally leaned Orla against the curved wall of the stairwell to drink the last of her Skal. I held a hand up to her face, and tiny, warm breaths broke over my fingertips.

Still alive.

"That would be just like you," I grunted as I continued up the stairs with replenished strength. "Save my life and turn your Skal purple, and then immediately die. I would never forgive you."

A breath of fresh, frigid air wafted over my cheeks, and a bit of dying sunlight played with the silver shadows of my skalfire. For a moment, I thought we'd made it to wherever the stairs led, but the next bend in the stairs revealed a slot-like window, nearly two feet deep, carved into the wall. The setting sun turned the mist outside a dusky orange.

"It's almost night." Hopefully the window was a sign that we were at least getting close, and I hurried upwards with renewed energy. "I've been asleep all day back at home. I wonder if anyone's found me."

It would probably be best to not speak out loud and conserve energy that way, but talking to Orla felt good.

Maybe she could hear me. Maybe my voice would keep her here.

"I passed out in my friend's bedroom when Galahad called me," I explained to Orla's unconscious body. "But my friend was missing, so I'm not sure if he's come back yet. It's going to scare the crap out of him when he finds me on his floor. Kind of like how you're scaring the crap out of me right now."

We passed by another window, and I drank in the fresh air.

I would be strong enough to get Orla home. I would have to be.

"Him and you," I sighed. "You're my only two friends, and he might be missing, and you might be dying. Dammit, Orla, Skalterra won't be worth coming back to if you die. You're too wonderful to die, alright?"

The glimpses I caught through the intermittent air vents showed a darker and darker night sky, until my tiny skalflame was once again the only source of light.

My legs grew numb beneath me as I put countless steps behind us. My back ached, but I fixed that by redirecting a small amount of Skal to kill the nerve endings in my muscles. This was a temporary body, anyway. I didn't need pain to remind me to take it easy.

I'd started to think I would be climbing forever, when the stairwell widened. The steps became less steep, and more fresh air than the tiny vents could allow washed over me, extinguishing my flame and leaving me in the dull green glow of some unseen light source.

"Orla," I hissed. "Orla, I think we're there."

She stayed silent on my back.

The stairs opened up to a massive cavern. Lanterns glowing with emerald skalflames lined the space and spat light up columns that looked like ancient lava pillars. A wide opening looked out over the dark landscape below to my right, and the wind that rolled through made the lantern light waver and dance.

"Who's there?" a voice called out, and I twisted to see two guardsmen standing at the feet of a statue tall enough to dwarf Von Leer's main college hall. The face of a stone man stared down at us from the shadows that clung to the cavern ceiling.

I staggered towards the guards. I'd made it. I hoped I wasn't too late.

"I have Orla Quillguard! She needs help!"

"Alert the infirmary!" one of the guardsmen barked to the other before rushing to pull Orla off my back. The green light of the lanterns made her pale skin look all the more sickly in his arms.

"Is- is she dead?" My legs shook beneath me, and I stumbled after the man as he carried Orla to the massive tunnel between the statue's feet.

"I don't know," he admitted. He gave me a sideways glance over Orla's lolled head. "They mentioned you were coming, but they didn't say who you are. How far did you carry her?"

"The whole way up."

"That's over fifteen thousand steps."

"If Galahad could shuffle up this far, then so could I."

"The other Riftkeepers arrived via the lift."

I faltered mid-step.

"There's a *lift?*"

"Of course. You can't expect us to walk fifteen thousand steps every time we want to come and go. Who did you say you are, again?"

"Oh, I'm—"

I cut off as we came out the tunnel's other end. We were in the hollow peak of a mountain. Walkways, railings, and sweeping staircases carved directly out of the mountain's dark stone circled the massive well that sat at the hive's center. Soft blue light filtered upwards, reaching for the hole at the peak of the mountain that offered a glimpse of the stars above.

Rock formations resembling lava pillars cast shadows that were swallowed by dark alcoves and corridors.

"Orla!" A young man ran to meet us. Green cloaks billowed around him, and his hair stuck up like Ferrin's. His nose had the same gentle swoop to it that Orla's had, but his chin was more square. "What happened?"

"Ask the stranger." The guard shouldered past the young man. "Out of my way, Cade. Orla needs the infirmary."

"That's my sister you're holding!" the young man snarled. He shot me a glance, then chased after the guard. Curious faces peeked out at us from the off-shooting corridors and archways, but I ignored them.

"Cade?" I called after the man. My legs were like jelly, and I needed Skal, but I managed to keep up. "You're Orla's brother?"

"I knew this would happen," he muttered more to himself than to me. Orla had never mentioned a brother, and it was difficult to guess which of the two were older. "I told her not to go. Begged her."

"She's not dead yet."

But the ghastly pallor that had taken over Orla's face made me second-guess the words. I'd carried her all this way. She couldn't be dead. Not when I'd tried so hard.

We ducked down a side corridor. Green Skal-light reflected off the polished surface of the floor, and I tried to swallow my heart back down into my chest where it belonged.

However, it continued to beat in my throat as the corridor opened into a long room lined with cots. Moonlight poured in through the open wall opposite the beds, and stars glittered over a carpet of misty clouds that stretched on forever below us. Despite having little more than intermittent columns of rock to block out the elements, the room was warm and windless. White Skal burned in lanterns, and men and women in pale blue tunics hurried to take Orla from the guard.

They lowered her onto a cot and began pulling her armor away. I let myself get shoved to the edge of the fray. Medics called for supplies and for space to work, and one of them pulled Cade back despite his efforts to stay at his sister's side.

I watched them extricate the strips of cloak I'd used as makeshift bandages. They were soaked through with blood.

"Nightmare!" Rough hands grabbed my shoulders to spin me around. Galahad's grizzled face was inches from mine, and I stumbled backwards. His stomach and chest were bandaged under his leather duster, and maybe it was the white light from the lanterns, but he looked paler than usual.

His gray eyes burned with something like fury, and I gulped.

I'd nearly killed him by taking all his Skal.

"I'm sorry," I gushed. "I didn't mean—"

He put his gnarled hands back on my shoulders, and pulled me in for a hug.

I froze in the embrace.

Maybe it wasn't a hug. Maybe it was a very slow tackle.

Galahad gave a shuddering sigh in my arms, and then pulled away with tears in his eyes.

"I thought I'd killed you," he said. "I thought I'd worse than killed you. I was so certain you'd turned rotsbane. I don't know how you didn't."

I shrugged, still taken aback by Galahad's sudden remorse and affection.

"I don't know," I lied. Ciarán's tether was still there, weakly burning in the pit in my stomach. I hoped Galahad couldn't feel it.

He stared over my shoulder at the medics surrounding Orla's cot.

"Who've you told?"

"Told?" I repeated. "You mean the purple—"

He pressed a finger against his lips.

"I'd heard her mother was close with Oren, but..." He trailed off, and I felt as if the infirmary floor had dropped out from under me.

Ferrin had told me about Oren and how Orla's mother had died protecting him.

"Oren Quill?" I asked. "But he was a Divine Sovereign."

Galahad nodded slowly, and I twisted around to try to get a better look at Orla in her bed.

"The Quills were known for their purple Skal," Galahad whispered. "And you're sure it was Orla's Skal you saw burning purple?"

"Positive. But why would they keep that a secret and not tell at least Orla?"

Galahad snorted.

"Riftkeepers are sworn to protect the Divine Sovereigns. Relationships that go beyond that capacity have always been forbidden."

Sweet, kind Orla, descended from the closest thing Skalterra had to a pantheon.

Of course she was. She was, after all, spectacular.

And she might be dying.

"Ferrin is preparing to meet with the Second Sentinel leadership in the Obsidian Hall downstairs," Galahad said. "Tell him what you saw. If Orla's what I think she is... Well. Tell Ferrin first. He knew his sister best."

"Right. And her brother?" I glanced sideways at Cade where he continued to try to push through medics to Orla's side.

Galahad frowned.

"He may be a Sovereign as well, but I'm not sure. Find Ferrin. Tell him to hurry."

"Hurry?" My heart caught. "Orla's fine. She's here now. They're helping her."

"Find Ferrin." Galahad procured a Skal bottle from his belt and sipped at its contents. Energy flowed from him to me and into my back and legs. He beckoned for the guard that had carried Orla to the infirmary. "You there! Take my friend to the Obsidian Hall."

The guard nodded, and I followed him back the way we'd come. I tried to catch a glimpse of Orla as we exited, but there were too many bodies around her.

"Ma'am?" The guard hesitated ahead of me, and I ripped my gaze away from Orla's medical team.

"Sorry. I'm coming."

An entire city hid inside the mountain peak, and I tried to take in as much as I could while the guard led me down stairways that circled the well at the center of the hollow.

The pool of Skal at the bottom was larger than the one that had been in Tulyr. Pale blue light filtered off its surface, illuminating the lava pillars that supported the cavern walls. Dark stalagmites broke the surface of the Skal, and bits of glowing liquid clung to the rocks to make them glitter.

"The Obsidian Hall is through there." The guard pointed to the large, wooden doors that stood across the pool. A stone path cut through the Skal, and I hurried across it to push through the doors.

They creaked on their hinges, and starlight glittered across the polished black floor. Ferrin stood at the end of a long room with a high ceiling, staring out another open window that looked over the same low-hanging clouds I could see from the infirmary.

He turned to look at me in surprise. Dirt and blood smudged his face, and he was in the same tattered clothing he'd been traveling in. He hadn't had the chance to clean up yet.

"Wren?" His brow creased with worry. "You made it. Where's Orla? Is she—"

"She's hurt." I twisted my hands together. "She took an arrow straight through her chest, but she's upstairs, and they're helping her but—"

I broke off, shaking my head.

If Orla died, I would never forgive myself.

Ferrin crossed the polished floor to meet me, concern etched in every line on his face. He put sturdy hands on my shoulders.

"Tell me she's going to be okay."

"I don't know," I admitted. "Galahad told me to tell you to hurry. It's my fault, Ferrin. She did it to save me."

I couldn't help the sting in my eyes, and Ferrin pulled me into a hug.

"It's not your fault," he insisted. "Orla is— well, she's Orla, and she'd do anything for her friends. But we made it. That's all that matters."

I shook in his arms, finally letting myself feel the fear of losing Orla. This might be my last night in Skalterra now that we'd made it to the Second Sentinel, but I wasn't sure how I could go on living in Keldori if I knew Orla was gone.

Both our worlds would be darker without her.

"I'm sorry," I whispered.

"I'm the one who should be sorry. You're both too young for this line of work."

"There's something else." I cleared my throat and pushed away. Ferrin's brow furrowed deeper at the look on my face. "I- I think—"

I cut off, not sure if there was a tactful way to tell Ferrin about his sister's secret, illicit relationship with the man they'd sworn an oath to protect.

"Out with it, Just-Wren." Ferrin laughed, but the sound was shaky and nervous. "What is it?"

"Orla's Skalmagick changed color," I said. "Right after she took the arrow, she made an explosion. Her fire was green at first, but then—"

I gulped as the color drained from Ferrin's face, and his jaw went slack.

"Don't say it," he breathed. "Wren Warrender, don't you dare say it."

"Her magick was purple. Like Oren's."

Ferrin closed his mouth, and his throat bobbed as he swallowed hard. His gaze hardened, and while I'd expected some degree of shock, the cold anger that slipped over his face made me take a step back.

A heavy slam echoed through the room, and I spun around to see a woman standing at the wooden doors she'd just closed. Something about her dark hair, her heart-shaped face, and her warrior-style skirts seemed familiar.

I'd seen her before, I was sure of it. But where?

"Ferrin," she said, and the mental image of a woman dead at the feet of a Grimguard clicked in my head. "If your niece is a Quill, we'll have to kill her too."

I reeled backwards at the woman's words, backpedaling straight into Ferrin. He put his hands on my shoulders, and I looked up at him as he heaved a heavy, resolved sigh.

"So we will, Caitria. So we will."

Thirty-Four
Advanced Combat Strategy

errin's fingers dug into my shoulders, and I froze, watching the woman at the doors. She leaned against the heavy wood and shook dark curls away from her face. Her resemblance to her brother, with the same haughty chin and identical gold and amber eyes, was unmistakable.

"You can't kill Orla." The words felt ridiculous as I said them. Of course they weren't going to kill Orla. This couldn't be real, not if Caitria, who I'd seen dead on the floor, was standing in front of me now.

Caitria's lips twisted, and her eyes narrowed.

"You weren't kidding about the blue hair, Ferrin." She smirked. "But what do we do? We can't kill her. Galahad will bring her back."

"Can I trust you, Wren?" Ferrin's voice was soft in my ear, but his fingernails bit at the skin of my shoulders. Every instinct screamed for me to run, but I was rooted to the spot, choking on a half-formed response.

"One of the sentries reported a rotsbane roaming around the base of the Third Sentinel." Caitria lilted forward, and her dual-slitted skirt billowed with every stride. Her head fell to the side as she surveyed me with cold interest. "I suppose we could feed her to it, but that's half a day's journey away."

I shivered in Ferrin's grip as he reached around me to grab my left hand. His fingers forced mine to unfurl, and his thumb stroked the scars Galahad's curse had left on my palm.

"You wouldn't tell Galahad, would you, little Nightmare?" he whispered, his cheek lightly pressed against mine as he studied my hand.

I did not want to be fed to a rotsbane. I wanted even less to live if it meant Orla would die.

"Wouldn't tell Galahad *what?*" I jerked my hand from his and staggered away. I tried to keep both Ferrin and Caitria in my field of vision. Their reflections in the polished, stone floor swam as my head spun. "Wouldn't tell him that you've been lying this whole time? That you're going to kill Orla?"

"And Fana," Caitria said blithely. Ferrin shot her a look, but she shrugged. "What? We're about to feed her to a rotsbane. It doesn't matter if she knows we're releasing Saergrim."

"The Frozen God?" I looked between the two Riftkeepers, still expecting Ferrin to bust up laughing and tell me it was all a joke.

A terrible, dark joke.

Ferrin's glower, however, remained in place, and my stomach dropped further. I shook my head.

"Fana and Orla should be honored to be so instrumental in ushering in the next great age of Magicians," Ferrin said.

"I thought we were protecting Fana," I croaked.

"Fana was never in any danger." Ferrin said it as if that should be consolation for what he was planning. "I needed her here, closer to the Frozen God, but Galahad is so damn stubborn. So we faked Caitria's death by Grimguard to scare him into letting us move her here."

"But she *is* in danger. From you! And so is Orla. And I helped you bring them here!"

Ferrin sighed and shook his head at his reflection in the floor with his hands on his hips.

"Ah, Wren. I'd hoped if anyone were to understand, it would be you. It's cruel of you to ask me to wet my hands with more blood than need be."

"The rotsbane, then," Caitria said. "It's probably still in the area. If we move quickly—"

"We don't need a rotsbane." Green firelight sparked in Ferrin's hand, reflecting off the black obsidian floor. "Galahad cursed her, and she's on her last life."

"How about that?" Caitria grinned. "The old miser was good for something after all."

Ferrin took a careful step towards me, and I took another back.

"It's alright." Ferrin's frowned in concern, and I hated how sincere the expression looked. "You'll be okay, Wren."

"No." I shook my head as Ferrin pulled his goggles into place.

"It'll be just like all the other times. The only difference is that you won't wake up. Don't worry. I'll make sure you don't feel a thing."

"I thought you were my friend." I hated the crack in my voice. I hated that the look on his face made me feel like I was somehow the one in the wrong.

"Don't do this," he murmured. "Please. I'm prepared to sacrifice my own niece. Do you think killing you will be even a fraction as hard as that?"

"You're supposed to be good. You *were* good!"

"There is nothing more good than what I'm trying to do!" He retreated to the open wall that looked out over the silver-dipped clouds and tried to beckon me to his side. When I remained where I stood, he sighed and rolled his neck. "That out there is the Frozen God's domain. There's a lagoon full of icebergs and glaciers. They call it the Bay of

Teeth because of the way the ice cuts the sky. That's where Saergrim is frozen in the space that divides our worlds. That's where we will free him from his glacier and cross over into Keldori."

"How is that good?" I hissed.

"You have seen Skalterra, Wren. You've seen our monsters, rotsbane and human alike. Don't let our shiny magick romance you. You know your world is more comfortable. You know Keldori is the kinder reality."

"We have monsters too."

"And they will bow to my Skalmagick," Ferrin growled. "Because unlike Skalterra, Keldori is more than monsters and magick. You have electricity and cars and airplanes and infrastructure and medicine that Skalterra could never dream of! I've spent nearly every day of my miserable life in this mountain, keeping guard, making sure the Frozen God doesn't move from where he's spent the last four centuries in the Bay of Teeth, and quite frankly, Wren Warrender, if a better existence than this one is feasible, then why not make that existence mine?"

Iseult's story about Galahad and his brother echoed at the back of my head, along with her warnings to not talk about my home in too much detail. I'd never mentioned half the things Ferrin was talking about, and a cold truth settled in my stomach.

"I'm not the first lucid Nightmare you've met."

Ferrin's lips curled.

"No, Wren. I'm afraid not."

An arm reached around my chest from behind, and dark curls pressed against my cheeks as Caitria held me in a headlock.

"It should be you, Ferrin," she said. "Kill her and get it over with."

Ferrin's eyebrows lifted above his goggles when I couldn't help the smile that slid across my face.

"Get off her!" Ferrin barked, but spikes of sharp, saber-like bone were already bursting from my arms to pierce Caitria's legs.

She howled in pain and let go, but I swung both my arms upwards to rip through as much flesh as I could.

"What you've heard about Keldori doesn't matter!" I lunged at Ferrin, but a shield of green Skal erupted between us. "You can't free the Frozen God, because you can't kill Orla and Fana!"

"How is it fair?" Ferrin demanded through his shield. "How is it *right* that four Magicians decided to cut us all off from our homes, and now Keldori has *everything?* Think of what I could accomplish, with your technology and my power! And you could've helped me!"

I turned my hands to steel and pressed against his shield. It was hot to the touch, but I pushed harder, forcing Ferrin to stagger backwards towards the wide window.

"You told me you didn't want Orla to see you become the person you'd been when you killed the Grimguards," I seethed, "but now you're talking about killing Orla!"

"Then I'll kill her first so she doesn't see what comes next."

The shield burst beneath my hands, and I pushed through the shards as they dissolved into sparks in the air. Ferrin was ready with a sword, but I batted it away with the silver flail that formed in my hand.

"You can't kill Orla! You *love* Orla!" Some part of my mind still rebelled against the idea that this could be Ferrin. Ferrin was kind. Ferrin was *good.*

"And I loved her mother, but I still did what I had to when she got in my way." He held his free hand over the twisted scar I knew was hiding under his tunic. "She almost got me first."

The story he'd told me about his sister's death had been so horrible and so tragic. Somehow, this cruel truth was so much worse.

"The Grimguards don't want the Frozen God freed at all, do they?" Everything had been a lie. But then how had Galahad not known? "They were trying to save Oren, not kill him. And Fana's family—"

Ferrin gave an apologetic shrug.

"The Firelds were miserable hiding in their castle. What we did was a mercy," he assured me.

"You murdered them! And then you blamed the Grimguards!"

"Caitria and I didn't mean to be mistaken for the Frozen God's servants, but those optics worked for us. We left Fana alive, figuring she'd be the easiest to bring to the Bay of Teeth, and I returned home to kill Oren. But while I was gone, Galahad took it upon himself to go to Cape Fireld and take charge over Fana. It took years before the *real* Grimguards showed up, giving us the excuse we needed to move Fana north."

I thought back to every conversation I'd had with Ciarán. He'd never once actually said he was going to kill Fana, just that he was going to get to her.

"Ciarán wasn't hunting us. He was trying to save Fana. From *you*."

"Ciarán?" Ferrin barked a disbelieving laugh that brought the corners of his neat beard upwards. "Are you on a first name basis with the Grimguard, then?"

"You spared him in Vanderfall because you didn't want Orla thinking less of you!" My voice rose, but I couldn't help it. Panic and anger were in control, not me. "What happened to *that* Ferrin? The Ferrin who loves his niece, who has mercy, and is kind?"

"Kindness and mercy had nothing to do with me sparing the Grimguard. How wasn't that your first iota of a hint that maybe there was something else going on? Wren, you're smarter than that. In what reality would I have let the Grimguard live if he was trying to kill us?"

Heat burned in my cheeks, and I hated the shame that rose in my gut at having disappointed Ferrin. I couldn't help it. Part of me was still hoping that as horribly real as everything about Skalterra was, this would be the bit that turned out to be a dream.

"Then why?" My voice shook with rage and disgust.

"I needed a villain," Ferrin said simply. "If the Grimguard died, Galahad would've brought us straight back to Cape Fireld. Not only would that have set back my timeline, but it's unlikely I would've discovered Orla's secret heritage. So thank you, Wren, for keeping precious Ciarán alive. Otherwise, who knows how long it would've taken me to figure out the role Orla is to play."

I pulled at Galahad's reserves of magick. He stoppered our connection nearly immediately, but not before I managed to draw enough Skal to bolster my muscles, turn my spikes to steel, and lunge at Ferrin with outstretched claws.

He tried to fend me off with his sword, but I crushed it in my metal talons and forced him to the floor. We slid across its polished surface, coming to a stop near the low wall that looked out over the cloud-covered domain of the Frozen God.

The heavy steel of my clawed fist reflected the green of Ferrin's fire, and I brought it swinging downwards.

He managed to roll beneath me, and my fist collided with the floor instead of his head. The black stone cracked beneath my hit, and gold light reflected in its broken surface as Caitria attacked me from behind.

At first, I thought she was wielding a flail like mine, but then the rope of the weapon extended, and the dart on the end licked my arm before retracting back towards Caitria on its swinging leash.

Ferrin came at me from the side, swinging dual blades. I tried to pull more Skal from Galahad, but he held firm on his end. I was forced to dance out of the way of Ferrin's blades as Caitria unleashed her rope dart at me again.

I was ready this time, and I ignored the heat that seared against my metal hands as I grabbed the rope of Skal and twisted it around my wrists and fingers. Caitria lurched forward when I pulled, and she let her rope dart dissipate so she could better tackle me against the low wall of the window.

She pressed her forearm against my neck, and the mountainside wind grabbed at my hair through the window. Her free hand grabbed my wrist, and gold sparks flew as a current of electricity wracked my body.

Lights burst in my vision, and the Skal that made up my Nightmare form sizzled against the current of electric magick she sent coursing through me. Every muscle tensed against the shooting pain, and I screamed.

Maybe Galahad would hear me. Maybe help would come.

The electricity passed, leaving me out of breath and weak under Caitria's arms.

"There's a good girl," she growled. "Now sit still. This will be over in a second. Ferrin?"

Ferrin approached with his blades, and I struggled feebly against Caitria's hold.

"It was a pleasure, Miss Warrender," Ferrin said softly. "I wish you could've seen things my way."

He held a blade over my neck, and I mustered enough energy and feeling into my legs to buck under Caitria. It was the same move Ciarán had used on me on the frozen lake, and it proved just as effective now.

Caitria flipped overhead and shrieked as she tumbled out the open window.

Ferrin cried out and brought his swords arcing downwards. I grabbed each one in a clawed fist and forced my way to my feet. His face contorted behind the green glow of his weapons.

"Galahad forced me to work for the Riftkeepers because he knows I'm stronger than you," I snarled. "You can't beat me. That's the entire reason I'm here."

"Nightmares have their limits, Just-Wren." His boot collided with my stomach, and I staggered backwards. "Even you."

Silver sparks flickered and died in my hands when I tried to arm myself. Galahad's magick had dried up, and the connection between us was still stoppered.

Ferrin, meanwhile, geared up for another attack, merging his dual swords into a single massive blade.

I drew magick from the one avenue I had left. The connection was weak, and the stores of Skal there were low, but the magick buzzed like electricity in my fingertips.

Orange fire erupted between us, flaring bright and hot enough to force Ferrin to abandon his attack. He stared at the orange skalflame, his expression unreadable under his goggles.

Then he grinned at me through the neon light of Ciarán's borrowed Skalmagick.

"Wren Warrender, you wonderful idiot. You're bound to the Grimguard?"

The orange fire dissipated as I leapt through it to grab Ferrin by the collar of his vest and pin him to the floor. The spikes of my left arm skewered Ferrin's right, and he grunted in pain.

The heavy doors of the hall slammed open, ripping my attention away from Ferrin. Galahad, leaning heavily on Iseult and with Tiernan as his side, stood in the doorway with the pool of Skal lighting him from behind.

"You want to tell me why you're trying to kill me a second time tonight, Nightmare, pulling my magick away like that?" he demanded.

I had done it. I had won. Help was here. Ferrin would
—

"Help!" Ferrin cried out beneath me. "Galahad, she's trying to kill me!"

"What? No!" I gawked between Ferrin and Galahad.

A golden throwing knife whistled through the air and lodged in my shoulder. I fell off of Ferrin, tearing his arm open as I did. Tiernan's knife felt like fire in my flesh, and I ripped it out.

"He's going to kill Orla and Fana!" I threw the knife at Ferrin, and he backpedaled away from me, clutching his injured arm to his chest. "He's working with Caitria!"

This couldn't be happening. They needed to believe me. They *had* to believe me.

"Caitria is dead, Wren Warrender." Galahad limped forward.

"She's not. She was here!" I looked between Iseult and Tiernan, but they regarded me with the same cold anger as Galahad.

"We have to kill her, Galahad!" Ferrin scrambled across the polished floor to join them. Tiernan helped him to his feet, and Ferrin pointed his uninjured arm at me. "The Grimguard knows her name. She's compromised."

"No." I shook my head at Galahad. "Don't listen to him."

"She found him injured in Vanderfall," Ferrin gushed. His goggles slipped down his face to hang around his neck. "She took him in, treated his wounds, and gave him her name."

"Yes, but—" I pointed a finger at Ferrin, trying to stutter out Ferrin's own involvement in Ciarán's fate that night.

"I suppose that's how he found Tulyr." Ferrin grinned at me now that no one was watching him. "He used her to follow us. She was probably in on it."

"I didn't mean to—"

"So you admit it?" Ferrin demanded, still smiling. Panic swirled in my veins alongside the Skal I'd take from Ciarán.

"No, it's not like that!"

Iseult extracted herself out from under Galahad's arm to take heavy steps forward.

"You put my home in danger on purpose?" she whispered.

"Ciarán was trying to stop *him*!" I pointed at Ferrin, still on my knees. "He killed the Firelds! And Oren and Bryony!"

"How dare you accuse me of murdering my own sister," Ferrin pretended to seethe. "Maybe it's a mercy Orla is incapacitated, so that she doesn't have to witness this betrayal."

"Galahad," I begged. "Galahad, you have to listen. Ferrin is going to release the Frozen God!"

Galahad's face might have been carved from stone beneath his silver beard. His expression hadn't changed since he'd found me with my spike at Ferrin's throat.

The tiniest deepening of his frown was the only warning he gave me before throwing a silver javelin across the room.

I acted instinctively, pulling an orange flail from the air to deflect the attack.

Iseult and Tiernan cried out in tandem and charged as one.

"You *are* with the Grimguard!" Tiernan howled and shoved passed Iseult so he could be the one to do me in. His rapier crackled against my flail, and Iseult shoved passed him with an outstretched hand.

The magick that made up my every molecule buzzed and vibrated as she drew nearer.

A single brush of her hand, and Iseult could unmake me with her Skalbreaking powers. I would be dead.

I pivoted, trying to keep Tiernan between us, but she managed to make contact with our weapons, and they disintegrated into dust on the floor. I brandished my arm spikes at them, but Iseult was undeterred by the threat of something she could easily destroy.

I danced out of her reach. If Tiernan wasn't so hotheaded, he might've had the sense to stand back and let her work. Luckily for me, he insisted on attacking me with a new rapier. I deflected the attack with a bone spike, and shoved Tiernan into Iseult.

They sprawled on the floor together.

"Galahad, make them stop!" I could jump out the window and try to hollow my bones and sprout wings like Titus had when I'd fought him in the Umberdust Plains, but Ciarán's magick was running low and our connection was faltering and weak. There was a good chance I'd plunge to my death if I tried to turn into a bird.

I had my back against the wall, both literally and figuratively. My arm blades dissolved so I could reabsorb what Skal I could from them. I pressed against the smooth wall of the Obsidian Hall and forced the last of my magick into my hands.

I didn't want to hurt my friends, but if they killed me, Ferrin would win.

Iseult was nearly on top of me when I darted out of her reach, spun around, and slammed two metal fists into the perfect surface of the wall. A massive crack ran up to the ceiling. Tiernan managed to avoid the falling obsidian rocks, but Iseult cried out as they rained down on her.

I tried to reach her through the cloud of black dust.

"Iseult!" I hadn't wanted to hurt her. I only wanted to slow her down. I needed her to be okay.

My tunic choked up against my throat before I could reach the rubble, and the room spun as Tiernan threw me to the floor and pinned me under him.

"Is she okay?" I choked as I craned my neck, trying to see Iseult where she lay unmoving under the rocks.

"I can't believe I felt bad for blowing you up." Tiernan's goggles had been knocked askew, and dust and dirt clung to his twisted locks.

"Tiernan." I tried to rally whatever Skal I could find lingering in my veins and along the weak bond between me and Ciarán, but there was nothing left. My strength was gone. My hands had reverted back to human flesh. I had no magick. "Your sister. Caitria…"

"You dare say her name when you've been working to undo everything she died for?" He pulled on my collar so he could slam me back into the hard floor. Pain shot through my skull, and black spots dotted my vision.

"She isn't dead."

"Don't—"

"She's going to kill Fana."

Gold flashed in Tiernan's hand, and he held a knife pointed between my eyes.

"I said don't."

"She killed the Firelds. Ferrin helped. Tiernan, you have to believe me. If you don't, Fana will die."

"Then where is she? Where's my sister if she isn't dead?"

I gulped.

"I threw her out the window."

Tiernan's amber eyes widened, and his nostrils flared. Maybe chucking the only proof that Ferrin was lying off the mountainside had been a tactical error.

"She might still be out there." I stared up at him, fixing him with a look of defiance, daring him not to believe me and reap the consequences. "Hanging to the side of the mountain, trying to climb back up."

"Stop it," Tiernan hissed.

"She's your sister, and she might need your help."

The golden knife in his hand shook, then dissolved.

"Dammit, Wren, if you're lying, I'll throw *you* out the window." He hesitated a half-second longer, and then leapt away to run to the room's ledge.

I rolled to my side and pushed up to my knees as Galahad limped forward. I had no Skal left to fight with, but I wouldn't give up. I would make sure Galahad saw the truth, even if it meant he killed me.

I had trusted them. Even Tiernan. They were my friends. We'd traveled and fought together for weeks.

I thought we'd been a team.

They'd turned on me so quickly.

"What did the Grimguard say to you that would have you sell out both our worlds, Nightmare?" Gray eyes bore into me. "What could he have possibly promised?"

"Ferrin is going to kill Orla and Fana. Galahad, you have to listen."

"How dare you suggest I would kill my own niece," Ferrin growled behind Galahad. "We cared for you, Wren. We *loved* you! Just for you to betray us!"

"I have no reason not to trust Ferrin. He swore an oath to protect the Rift," Galahad said evenly.

"So did your brother."

The color drained from Galahad's rugged face, and he leveled a silver sword with my neck.

"Bold of you to speak to me of Balin," he hissed, "after *you* brought the Grimguard to my home."

"The home Balin destroyed." I leaned forward so that my throat pressed against the tip of Galahad's sword. "If you're going to kill me, then kill me. I did my job. I warned you about Ferrin. Now it's your job to make sure he doesn't murder Orla and Fana."

Galahad hesitated, his gray eyes searching mine.

I needed him to see the truth. He and the others could hate me all they wanted, but I *needed* him to save Orla and Fana.

"Get it over with, Galahad," Ferrin pressed. "I need to check on my niece, and I'm sick of looking at this traitor."

"I'm not going to fight anymore," I said. "Orla nearly died to save me. If I have to die to save her, if that's what it takes to get you to listen, then fine. I die."

Galahad remained frozen with his sword against my throat.

"Galahad!" Tiernan's cry echoed through the chamber, and I dared to twist around so I could see Tiernan helping to hoist Caitria into the room. Her hair was tussled, and scrapes covered her arms, but she was alive and standing. "Caitria!"

Tiernan threw himself at her, sobbing and wrapping her in an embrace that she didn't return. Instead, she cast Ferrin a wild look of panic through her mess of hair. She brought a careful hand to the back of Tiernan's neck.

"Shhh," she crooned. "It's alright. I'm here."

Golden electricity sparked between her fingers. Tiernan cried out, convulsed, and fell, landing with a thud at Caitria's feet, either unconscious or dead. It was impossible to tell which.

"Tiernan!" I tried to get up to rush to help him, but a soft gasp rattled behind me.

When I turned back to Galahad, he had an emerald blade sticking out of his chest.

"Then I suppose that's that." Ferrin pulled his sword back out through Galahad's back and let it dissipate.

"No!"

"Wren Warrender. I—" Galahad's voice grated over my name. Blood bubbled between his lips, spilling into his silver beard, and his eyes turned glassy. He reached out for me with a gnarled hand, and then lurched forward.

I tried to catch him.

If I could catch him, I could undo this. I could stop Ferrin. I could keep Galahad alive.

But Galahad's body fell through mine as I collapsed into dust and darkness.

Thirty-Five
Structural Fundamentals

I fell through the darkness, searching for the tether that had existed between me and Galahad just a moment before. The tether that had dragged me back to Skalterra night after night. The tether that had frayed and burst when Ferrin's sword had run Galahad through.

A different bond reached out towards my collapsing consciousness, and I reached back. Ciarán's presence buzzed weakly in my periphery. I tried to yell his name, but I didn't have a mouth. I was a collection of dust swirling in the ether, but Ciarán's magick, as weakened as it was, surged through my particles, and my form snapped back into place.

A dull glow cut the darkness, and I sprung upright.

"Galahad!" I didn't know where I'd landed, but I couldn't be dead. I had a body, shaky and sweaty, but alive. I stared at my hands in the dark, trying to see the scars Galahad had left on my palm.

They were there. I couldn't see them but *they were there*. They had to be. I refused to believe they weren't.

Because if they were gone, then so was Galahad. And if Galahad was gone, Ferrin would kill Orla and Fana, which was terrible in and of itself, but it also meant Ferrin would come bursting through the barrier between our worlds and continue to hurt the people I loved.

So the scars had to be there, as smooth and unscarred as my hand looked. Maybe they were hiding beneath my skin.

I clawed at my palm, ignoring the bite of my nails, unable to see through the haze of hot tears that spilled down my cheeks.

"Galahad, *please!*" I was alive, but the world was collapsing around me. I'd fought so hard. I'd made it across Skalterra, I'd fought Grimguards and rotsbane, I'd carried Orla up the inside of a mountain.

And I'd lost.

Blood and skin gathered under my fingernails, but I kept digging at my hand. I needed to find the scars. I needed to prove to myself that Galahad was alive. Everything was okay.

"Wren!" Hands, strong and gentle, tried to stop my frantic clawing. I shoved them off, screaming in protest. "Wren, it's okay!"

Liam's face took shape in the dark, catching the dull green glow of a digital clock. He had my wrists in his hands and perched in front of me. The mattress beneath us sank under our combined weight, and the unfamiliar corners and lines of the dark room started to take shape around me.

I was still in Liam's bedroom, on his bed, tangled in his comforter.

"We're in danger," I cried. "My friends, they're going to die. Orla—"

"It was just a dream." It was hard to see him through the film of tears. "You're okay, alright?"

I choked on a sob and fell into his arms.

I'd failed.

I'd failed.

I'd failed.

And who would believe me if I tried to explain?

Liam's arms tightened around me, and his fingertips brushed the buzzed hair at the nape of my neck.

"I've got you," he promised. "Just breathe."

I shuddered in his arms, trying to feel for both Galahad and Ciarán. Both connections were dead. I had no way back to Skalterra.

I balled my fists against Liam's back.

With no way back, I'd just have to be ready to face Ferrin when he reached this side of the Rift.

Ferrin who had been kind and helpful and fatherly, though that last one was embarrassing to admit even to myself.

I didn't care what he and Ciarán said about me not being a killer. If he hurt Orla, I'd make sure Ferrin choked to death on his own blood and bile.

"You've been asleep all day," Liam murmured. "I found you on the floor, but you were covered in goosebumps, so I put you in bed. Sorry, I promise I just washed the sheets."

I pried myself away from Liam's embrace.

"I was looking for you. You were late for Riley's memorial, and I thought maybe..." I trailed off. That morning felt like a lifetime away.

"I skipped it," Liam admitted softly. "The reception is still going on at Siobhan's, but I didn't want to leave you."

"I'm sorry."

"Don't be," Liam insisted. Fresh tears welled in my eyes, and I tried to wipe them away, but the wound I'd gouged into my own hand stung. "Do you want me to call Ethel?"

I froze. Gams would only worry. She'd call Mom. She'd be angry I let myself pass out in Liam's room and had kept him away from Riley's reception.

"Yes, please."

He gave me a smile and took his phone into the hall. I gathered Liam's blankets around me, trying to stifle the shivers that continued to wrack my body, trying to get that final image of Galahad out of my head. But it was there, imprinted on my mind so vividly that I could smell and taste the iron of the blood that trickled from between his lips and ran into his silver beard.

"Ethel, it's about Wren." Liam's muted voice echoed from the hallway. "Yeah, she's here, but she seems a bit shaken..."

I pressed my fingers against my ears, shame and panic both fighting for my attention.

Orla and Fana were going to die, and I had no way to stop it.

"Here." Liam reappeared at my side with a glass of water. He clicked the bedside lamp on, and I turned away so he wouldn't see my red eyes and the tears I'd smeared across my face. "Can I see your hand?"

He sat back down on the bed and placed gauze and bandages on the blanket between us. I hesitated with my fingers curled inwards to hide my palm, but then relinquished my hand to Liam.

In the light of the lamp, I could see how much damage I'd managed to deal to my palm, but through the angry, bleeding marks, there was no sign of Galahad's cursed scars.

"You weren't kidding when you said your nightmares are bad." Liam swabbed an antiseptic over the wound, and I hissed at its sting.

"I don't think I have to worry about nightmares anymore."

Liam gave me a wry smile as he pressed a square of gauze over my hand.

"And why's that?"

"Just a feeling." I watched him fasten the gauze in place with a bandage that he wrapped carefully around the back of my hand. His fingers were warm against mine. "Why did you skip Riley's memorial?"

"Because he isn't dead."

I nodded. I figured he'd say as much.

"Do you think your aunt and uncle wanted you there?"

He kept his eyes on my bandages as he folded his fingers over them, holding my hand in his.

"Probably." His thumb brushed against mine. "They'll come around, though, once he comes back."

"Right." My friends were in the same limbo Riley existed in. I didn't know if they were alive, or for how long they'd remain that way, and I had no way to check.

Galahad was dead. Of that much I was certain. I'd felt his life snuff out as clearly as if it had been my own. I wasn't sure I would still be alive myself if not for Ciarán's connection, however weak it had been.

"You scared me today," Liam said, still looking at my hand in his. "But I guess I'm getting used to that."

"I'm sorry."

"Don't be." He raised his eyes to mine and gave an apologetic smile in the low light. "It's selfish, but it was a nice distraction, watching over you."

A door creaked somewhere outside, and heavy steps echoed on a wooden staircase.

"Liam?" Gams's sharp bark preceded her footsteps hurrying down the hall. "Wren? Where is she?"

The bedroom door burst open, and there was Gams in a glaze-stained Keel Watch Harbor t-shirt.

"Gams?" I didn't want her to worry, but every emotional wound I'd been trying to run triage on since waking up reopened, and tears sprung to my eyes.

Gams shoved Liam out of her way to throw her arms around me, only to immediately let go so she could cup my face in her hands.

"Liam said you're sick. Is that why you felt so cold this morning? I knew it. Do you have enough blankets?"

She bunched Liam's comforter in my lap, and then tried to feel my forehead, but I took her hand in mine to lower it.

"I'm okay now." I managed to hold the tears back. Hopefully Gams couldn't see them swimming in my eyes. She'd left her glasses at home.

"What's wrong?" she whispered. "Is that video online again? Did someone write a mean comment about your mother? Whatever it is, I promise I've said worse to her. She'll be okay."

I choked on a watery laugh. If Ferrin made it through the Rift, I didn't know what his plans were. He'd have all the Skal he'd ever need. He would be able to use magick freely. Maybe that would be enough to satisfy him, and he'd choose to live a quiet life.

But I couldn't trust Ferrin, and whatever hole he tore in the fabric between Skalterra and Keldori would be open for anyone and anything to come through.

I'd been halfway to becoming a rotsbane. I had felt their hunger. I'd almost been destroyed by it. I knew they would stop at nothing to devour as much Skal as they could. They would wreak chaos and destruction and death, even if Ferrin decided to keep his head down in Keldori after murdering Fana and Orla.

"Wren?" Gams squinted to see me better in the light of the bedside lamp, and the dam broke. Hot tears cascaded down my cheeks, and I sobbed ugly, desperate sobs.

Galahad was dead. My friends would soon follow. And if Ciarán tried to stop Ferrin, as he was sure to, he'd probably die as well.

Gams pulled me in, and I cried into her messy hair.

"What is it?" she murmured.

"Everything."

"Linsey?" she asked.

I didn't reply. There was nothing I *could* say. No one would believe me.

"Whatever it is," Gams said, "whether it's Linsey, your interview, all this Riley nonsense, or even a small summer sickness, you are your mother's daughter, and she is mine. And I know you are just as capable at kicking lawn gnomes as she is. You are strong. You will be okay."

The tears fell harder. She didn't know how wrong she was, and yet I wrapped her words around me like a shield. I didn't feel capable of kicking anything, let alone lawn gnomes, but if Ferrin came to my world, I would make sure he lived to regret it.

"Would you like me to call your mom?" Gams asked softly. "She's probably awake by now because of the time zones."

I shook my head.

"No," I croaked. "This is good."

And I let my grandmother hold me there on Liam's bed.

Liam walked us home to Gams's apartment and fell asleep on the couch for the night. I paced the confines of my room. There had to be a way back to Skalterra. There *had* to be.

"Ciarán?" I hissed into the dark. He'd said he'd been unable to pull me to Skalterra before, but maybe without Galahad, he'd be able to do it. "Ciarán, please!"

There was no response, and I lay back on my bed and stared at the ceiling until the sky outside lightened and filtered in through my curtains.

I could at least take comfort in the fact that Ciarán knew Ferrin's end goal. He didn't need my warning to do whatever he needed to do to stop the Frozen God from being released. Besides, he'd probably lord it over me that he'd been the good guy this entire time.

I held my pillow over my face.

It didn't matter that Ciarán was an ass. He'd been right and good, and I wanted to be there to help him stop Ferrin.

And I would make sure I found a way.

I'd slept nearly the entire day before, but standing behind the register a few short hours later in Gams's shop, I felt dead on my feet. While my body had slept, I hadn't had real rest in over twenty-four hours.

Liam's haggard expression reflected mine from across the store. Guilt forced me to look away. He'd been too busy fussing over my unconscious body to sleep much the evening before, and I'd taken up his bed space. Of course, he probably wouldn't have slept anyway with Riley's memorial so fresh.

The bell over the shop door rang out, and I jumped to attention with my heart beating in my throat. Every sudden sound and every sudden movement convinced me that this was it. This was the moment Ferrin came barreling through the Rift.

However, it was only Stanley, the banker from the next town over, surveying the chicken options to add to his ever-growing collection.

"Still all blue, then." He frowned.

"All the best artists go through phases." I rubbed at my eyes with the heel of my hand as I leaned against the bulletin board behind me. Usually I'd worry about smudging my make-up, but I hadn't felt like putting any on after looking in the mirror and noticing there were hardly any eyelashes left for me to slather with mascara.

"Can't say I've been too fond of this color lately." Stanley picked up a chicken to turn in his hands.

"They're Von Leer colors. Gams thinks if she paints every chicken blue, the university will have to take me off the waitlist."

Stanley gave me a sympathetic smile.

"In that case, I'll happily make an exception for the color blue today." He chose three chickens off the shelf and carried them to the register. "Could you wrap them for me?"

I bent down to grab the tissue paper from the shelf beneath the register, and straightened up to survey the chickens Stanley had selected this time.

One was a solid blue with a bit of white swirled through the glaze like hazy clouds. Another was several shades of blue painstakingly painted into a plaid pattern, and the third—

I froze with my eyes on Stanley's hands. He held them at the lip of the counter, tapping out a listless beat while he waited.

It was a particularly hot morning, and while he usually wore the sleeves of his button-up down to his wrists, today he'd rolled them to his elbows.

For a banker, he had a lot of tattoos. Roses, a wolf, a band of pine trees that circled his forearm just beneath his elbow. The way they sat on his arms felt familiar, and I could've sworn I'd seen them before despite having never seen Stanley's bare arms before today.

The familiar scimitar that ran from his elbow to his wrist was what made it finally click. I *had* seen these tattoos before, and I knew Tamora's weapon of choice well.

Galahad had told me over and over that Nightmare's were their idealized version of themselves, but the juxtaposition of the mousey banker in front of me and the broad warrior that Tamora kept as a lapdog didn't make sense in my head.

"Titus," I hissed.

Stanley stared at me for a moment with his mouth slightly open and his head cocked. Then his eyes widened, and he took a half-step backward.

He tried to form words, opening and closing his mouth, before giving up and bolting for the door.

Thirty-Six
Principles of Banking

Jonquil yowled when I stepped on her tail in my hurry to chase after Stanley. Liam shouted my name behind me as I tore through the front door, but I ignored him.

Stanley had a good head start, and after running through Skalterra with an Olympian-Class body all month, I didn't love how stiff and awkward my real legs felt beneath me. However, I wasn't the only one trapped in their actual form. As strong, fast, and formidable as "Titus" was, Stanley was less of an athlete than even me.

He'd barely made it to the corner of Gams's building by the time I caught him by the back of his button-up.

I spun him around and slammed him into the side of the shop, barring my arm across his chest. I had at least three inches on him. His hair was thinning and his features weren't as defined as Titus's were, but there was a definite resemblance there.

"Wren! What the hell?" Liam stood in the open door of the shop, gawking at us.

"It's fine!" I pressed harder against Stanley's chest. "Go watch the register. And if you tell my grandmother, it'll be *your* missing posters that we put up next."

I kept my eyes fixed on Stanley's sweating face and waited until I saw Liam disappear back into the shop after a moment's hesitation.

"How?" I demanded. Lucid Nightmares were supposed to be rare, but here we were. Two of us living in nearby towns.

"You know I don't know." He growled the words, but they weren't nearly as intimidating as I was sure he would've liked.

"Why'd you run?"

"Because you killed me last time I saw you."

"Right. My bad. I promise to let the rotsbane devour your consciousness next time." I half-expected Stanley to disappear beneath me. "Where's Tamora? Did she go back to Vanderfall yet?"

"Why? So you can set your merry band of thieves on us?"

"Tell Tamora to get over it. We only took two bottles!"

"The guard said he saw you with four."

I rolled my eyes so hard that Stanley almost wiggled free, but I pushed him against the wall again.

"Fine. I don't care where Tamora is. How quickly can she get to the Bay of Teeth?"

Stanley wrinkled his nose at me.

"She doesn't care about the Frozen God anymore."

"How many days? She owns all the railroads, doesn't she? How many days for her to get to the Frozen God?"

"They're called steamtrails," he sniffed.

"They're railroads and trains, Stanley," I said through gritted teeth. "And Tamora needs—"

"Tamora needs to be left alone." Stanley relaxed into the wooden siding of the Gams's shop. "So tell your pals Ferris and Galavant—"

"Galahad. His name was Galahad." My eyes stung with unbidden tears, and I slammed my bandaged hand against the wall next to Stanley's head. "And he's dead. Because Ferrin killed him."

Stanley's eyes widened.

"Galahad was your nocturmancer. You can't go back."

"Ferrin is going to release the Frozen God," I said. "He's going to kill my friends to do it. Please. You have to tell Tamora. She has to stop him."

Stanley shook his head.

"I know you don't know Tamora well, but she doesn't *do* things for others."

"The Barony will collapse. She won't control the Skal supply anymore. Ferrin will."

"She's clever. She'll adapt."

I released Stanley and stepped back. Part of me felt bad for him. The difference between his real appearance and his Nightmare form was horribly telling. Every differing detail signaled what he disliked the most about himself, and there were a lot of differing details.

"You didn't run from me because I killed you," I said. "You ran because you're embarrassed."

"Embarrassed?" He tried to sneer, but his sallow cheeks turned red, and sweat beaded on his scalp, visible through his thinning hair.

"You don't like yourself."

"Says the girl who obviously doesn't have blue hair in real life."

"If Ferrin frees the Frozen God and bridges the Rift, what happens to the Nightmares?" I asked.

Stanley's cheeks turned brighter still.

"There will still be Nightmares."

"Will there?" I crossed my arms and flashed him a dubious smirk. "And if there are, will Tamora still *need* a Nightmare bodyguard? She'll have so much Skal. How do you know you won't become redundant? And then you'll be stuck like *this*. Forever."

"There's nothing wrong with how I am!" He raised his voice.

"I didn't say there was. You did." I stood my ground, daring him to tell me I was wrong. Maybe it was cruel to use a man's insecurities against him this way, but Tamora was my best bet to stop Ferrin, and if psychologically torturing a sad banker was my ticket to saving Fana and Orla, then dammit, I would just have to psychologically torture the sad banker. "You love Skalterra, but you love being Titus more. So stop Ferrin. Save Titus."

He sulked, holding himself around his elbows and frowning.

"I'll see what I can do, but Tamora is stubborn. If she decides not to face Ferrin—"

"Then tell her my name, let her summon me, and *I'll* convince her. And then I'll help her kill Ferrin myself."

Stanley's sullen face broke, and he had the audacity to laugh. Not just a chuckle, either, but a full-blown, head-back guffaw, and it was my turn to blush.

"Sure. After everything you just said about me becoming redundant? Why not?"

"I'm trying to help you!"

"You're trying to help yourself!" A cruel grin twisted the kind features I'd come to associate with Stanley, and suddenly the resemblance between him and his Nightmare form was much more striking. "You don't look much like yourself either. Say what you want about saving your friends, but you want the same thing as me. Now your nocturmancer is dead, and you want mine so you can live out your blue-haired, warrior princess fantasies."

"No." I jammed a finger into his chest. "Unlike you, I'm happy to admit I hate myself. Unlike *you*, I know blue hair doesn't change me, and I will happily die over and over and over again if it means saving the people I *do* like. My name is Wren Warrender. Tell Tamora. Tell her I can help."

Stanley pushed my hand away.

"Or what? You'll grow spikes out of your arms and stab me?"

"Tell Tamora. Ferrin will ruin our world if he gets through."

"Then I guess it's a good thing I don't care much for it to begin with. Now if you'll excuse me, I have to get to work."

I stood defeated as he stepped around me and walked to an old sedan parked outside Gams's front door. His key fob beeped, and I kept my eyes forward on the peeling, wooden siding of the shop.

"I saved you," I reminded him. "I could've let you die in that rotsbane's mouth."

"Then maybe you were never cut out for Skalterra to begin with." His car door slammed behind me, and he peeled out of the parking spot and up the hill towards the highway.

Liam didn't try too hard to interrogate me on my interaction with Stanley. Either he knew me well enough by now to know I wouldn't tell him or he was harboring hurt feelings over my missing posters remark. And yes, I did feel bad about that particular jab, but not enough to distract me from my simmering anger.

Because discovering Titus in my grandmother's general store was the doomsday-flavored cherry on top of what had already been a terrible twenty-four hours.

Galahad was dead, Orla and Fana would soon follow, the world was about to be overrun with power-hungry Magicians, and there was a chance to stop it if it weren't for the fragile ego of one mediocre man.

Despite my crappy mood, Liam pulled fresh bandages out of his bag at lunch and silently changed the gauze on my hand as we sat on the back deck, each stewing in our own thoughts and worries. There was an odd comfort to the silence, like neither of us expected the other to break it, and that was okay.

After we closed shop for the day, Liam hung around long enough for dinner. I scrubbed at dirty dishes in the sink while he stood over Gams's shoulder at the dining table, helping her navigate the internet as she fretted over our train tickets and hotel rooms.

My interview with Von Leer felt so pointless now. By the time Fall Semester started, there might not be a college there anymore thanks to Ferrin. However, the thought of the weekend trip made my heart race for a different reason.

At the end of this week, if all went according to plan, I would be meeting my birth father.

Yes, my plans to figure out what he knew about Skalterra were the priority and more important than ever, but after spending eighteen years secretly searching his name online, I harbored a selfish anxiety at the thought of meeting him at long last.

"I think that one's clean, dear," Gams murmured behind me. I hadn't realized I'd been violently scrubbing at a single plate. "How's this room look, Liam?"

"There's only one bed," Liam said. I whipped around to glare at them, but both their backs were to me as they surveyed hotel rooms on Gams's computer. "Though it looks like the couch might be a pull-out."

"I'm not putting Wren on a pull-out."

"I'm not either. That's where I would sleep." Liam laughed softly and looked over his shoulder at me. I turned back to the sink, scrubbing harder than before. "What about that one? It's got two queens."

"Sure, sure. Where'd my wallet go?"

Liam came up behind me and took my sponge and plate away.

"Let me," he said.

"I'm fine," I protested, but shifted over to give him room at the sink.

"I don't want you getting your bandages wet, though they probably need changing anyway."

I balled my hand into a fist, closing my fingers over the gauze and bandages.

"It's okay. I can change them," I said.

Liam's eyes softened, and he chewed on the inside of his cheek. He glanced back at Gams, and then swallowed whatever words he'd been holding back.

"We're going to have fun this weekend," he said instead. I nodded with a tight-lipped smile, knowing neither of us would be in the mood to have fun.

I passed the next few days on edge. Every ring of the bell above the shop door made me jump. I watched the windows, waiting for Stanley or even Ferrin to pass by. My phone battery puttered out before lunch every day after I subjected my browser to constant refreshes. I wasn't sure how obvious Ferrin's arrival in Keldori would be, but there were sure to be signs in the news.

It was hard to know what to look for, however, and more often than not, I ended up back on the video Linsey had posted of Mom. It had surpassed a couple million views, and now that my initial mortification had subsided, there was a strange comfort in watching Mom shatter potted plants.

Apparently book sales had never been better in the wake of the video, and while I wished that meant she could come home from Europe early, I figured this was her summer to make up for all the vacations and opportunities she'd canceled so she could stay home with me.

Still, though. The world had never felt so impossibly big as it did when I wanted nothing more than a hug from my mom.

Not to mention, I was about to betray her. As far as she was concerned, I didn't have a biological father. I'd simply sprung into existence. Maxwell Brenton was a taboo name under our roof. He had given us nothing, so we would give him nothing, not even a passing thought, in return.

However, Thursday morning, I carried my overnight bag down to the curbside, fully intending to finally meet my father later that day.

It was hard to know which was twisting my gut more —the thought of being face-to-face with the man who had become a sort of forbidden mythology, or that my admissions fate with Von Leer sat with an interview the next morning.

Liam waved at me from Gams's sedan where he was loading his backpack in the backseat. It was another beautiful summer morning in Keel Watch Harbor. The heat of the sun was cut but the sea breeze, and the smell of fresh bagels wafted down the street from Teddy's shop. The library glinted on the hill like a bit of glass nestled among the trees and bushes, and children's feet thundered across the wooden boards of the decks behind the shops.

It was almost a shame to leave it behind.

"Alright, let's get on with it! I open in thirty minutes." Gams bustled out of the shop behind me and shooed us into the car.

"We could walk to the station if you're worried about opening in time," Liam offered, sliding into the passenger seat behind me.

"Up that hill?" She took the driver's seat and jammed her hand into the bag of bagels Liam had left on the center console. "You can if you like, but I have a perfectly capable car."

I clutched my backpack against my chest and leaned my head against the window as we drove up the hill. Leaving Keel Watch Harbor felt a little bit like leaving my shelter. Nothing changed here, save the occasional disappearance. Every day was like the one before. It was simple and predictable, and the trip to the train station felt like inviting danger.

The train station was across the street from the library, and even though she was just dropping us off at the curb, Gams jumped out of the car and let it idle. She came around the car's front as I closed the passenger door, and she extended her hands to reveal a blue chicken in each one.

She gave Liam his chicken first before wrapping him in a hug, and then she turned to me.

"For luck," she said, pressing the other chicken into my hands. "I look forward to using a new paint color next week."

She pulled me in and held me there. I was always so struck by how someone her age could hug so tightly.

"Wren Warrender," she pulled away to cup my face in her hands, "whatever ever happens tomorrow morning, I am so very proud of you."

"I know." I nodded into her hands, and her wrinkled face melted into a soft smile.

"And remember," she said coyly, "the best revenge is to live your best life. Now go make Linsey weep."

Thirty-Seven
Locomotive Operations

If I closed my eyes, it was like being back in Skalterra. The train shook the same way the steamcart had, and I pretended the soft murmur of voices of the other passengers were those of Orla, Fana, and Tiernan.

Maybe if I imagined it vividly enough, I'd be able to pass through the Rift myself and find my friends. If Liam weren't sitting next to me, I might've whispered Ciarán's name, just to see if he could hear me.

"Falling asleep?"

I pried my eyes open to deadpan at the seat back in front of me.

"Not if you wake me up."

"You weren't asleep yet. Trust me. When it comes to you, I'm an expert in the subject."

I rolled my head to the side to look at him. He sat with one leg stretched out into the aisle, and his smile fought against the bags that weighed heavy under his eyes. Guilt nagged me at the periphery of my worries.

"Have *you* been sleeping?" I asked.

"Not well," he admitted, and the smile slipped. "Any advice?"

I shook my head and settled back to face forward again. Blue sky and ocean blurred with the green of passing forests outside my window as we hurtled along the coast.

"Not really. I haven't been sleeping well either."

"Nightmares again?" The sudden edge in his voice made me turn my palm downwards. The scratches I'd put there had fused back together, and I no longer needed bandages, but the angry red marks were still sore.

"I haven't really been sleeping enough to have nightmares at all." I spent most nights whispering for Ciarán in the dark, begging him to pull me back to Skalterra. He never responded, and I wasn't sure he could hear me, but I refused to stop. Until I could talk to my father and figure out what he knew, it was my only way to try to get back. "But my narcolepsy issue, it's all better."

"Really?"

"Yeah. I told you, I was seeing a doctor, and they fixed it." I turned back to him and forced a smile through the lie. "No more carrying me up staircases."

"Oh, good. I was about to add a dumbwaiter to the shop. I could shove your body inside, and use a pulley to hoist you up to Ethel's apartment."

"Putting that architecture degree to good use, then."

He chuckled softly and let his shoulders relax.

"Yeah. I'm glad you're okay, though. I was worried."

"I'm the last person you should worry about."

"But you make it so easy."

I slumped in my seat, sliding my shoulders down the vinyl.

"Tell the truth, are you on the clock right now? Is Gams paying you to escort me to Von Leer?"

"Only if you consider train tickets and hotel rooms to be legal tender."

"I'm sorry." What was supposed to be sarcastic came out more genuine than I wanted, but Liam replied with a crooked smile and an awkward shrug.

"I like hanging out with you, especially now that I know I won't have to catch or carry you." He slouched down in his seat to be at eye level with me. His smile softened. "You should try to sleep though. It's a long ride to Von Leer, and you look like crap."

I smacked his shoulder, but grinned.

"Sure. This train is freezing, and I have the most important interview of my life tomorrow morning. Sleep should be easy."

"Sleep, Wren. You'll want to be rested for that lecture you're going to tonight."

I jolted upright, and Liam laughed.

"How did you find out about that?" If he told Gams, she would tell Mom, and Mom would be furious.

"Von Leer posted about it yesterday. You were planning on going, right? You're into all that rock stuff."

"Geology is rock stuff. Rocks are only part of geophysics." I relaxed back into my seat. Liam didn't know the speaker was my biological father. "The lecture is about paleomagnetism, which isn't quite what I want to go into, but I'll still have to know it."

"Right. Which is why you should sleep. I'll need you awake enough to explain everything in the lecture to me." Something warm and soft settled across my chest, accompanied by the smell of sandalwood deodorant and waffle cones.

"I don't need your hoodie," I murmured, but the thrum and rattle of the train were already lulling me to sleep.

It wasn't a good sleep by any means. I spent a lot of it in a timeless fog somewhere between waking and unconsciousness. Sometimes I was aware of Liam sitting next to me, but his presence became all too acute when I realized I was using his shoulder as a pillow.

I sat up in a half-asleep stupor, mumbled something that was sure to have been devastatingly quick-witted and sharp-tongued if it had been at all intelligible, and then tried to lean against the train window instead. The vibrations of the rattling window shooting through my skull forced me to resort to slumping forward on the seat back tray in front of me for the next hour.

However, the moments of sleep that snuck in were better than nothing, and by the time we were halfway through the mountains, thundering past valleys of pine trees and cliff faces streaked with waterfalls, I felt more rested than I had all week.

Liam let me watch the mountains blur past in silence. Maybe he knew I was stewing in thoughts of how this could become a familiar train ride for me if my interview went well. Maybe he was lost in his own thoughts about returning to campus without his cousin.

By the time we rolled into the Bergdale train station, the mountains had reduced to foothills, and it was hard to see much through the forests that cradled the sleepy college town.

My nerves crescendoed, knotting my stomach and tightening my throat. When the train bumped to a stop, I briefly considered staying put. There were a lot of unknowns waiting outside the comfort of the carriage. If I stayed seated, if I let the train carry me to wherever its end destination was, I wouldn't have to face those unknowns.

But Liam extended a hand to me, already standing in the aisle.

"This is us." He shouldered his backpack. "Want to see where you're going to live for the next four years?"

I held his hoodie against my chest as I took his hand and followed him onto the platform.

It was a sunny day in Bergdale, and the historic downtown district bustled with summer vacationers in shorts and hiking boots. We wove between them on the boardwalk style pathway that connected storefronts and shops. The smell of freshly-baked waffle cones made me breathe deep, and I looked around for the source.

Liam caught me staring at the ice-cream and laughed.

"I hope you aren't thinking about cheating on your favorite ice-cream scooper."

"Gams only stocks three flavors. It's not personal."

"Excuse you, it's four flavors."

"If you say so." I stood on my tip-toes to better survey the surrounding street. The buildings were rugged and wooden, as if to emulate an old mining town. A river gushed somewhere out of sight, the gurgling of the water intermixing with the rush of wind through the trees. "Where's campus?"

"Through those trees there." Liam nodded at the forest, and I whipped around to stare at him with blood pounding in my ears. "Don't worry, we won't go through the woods. We'll go around."

A bell tower in the distance tolled out two o'clock, and I bounced on the balls of my feet.

In five hours, I would be sitting in a lecture hall listening to my biological father speak.

As we walked, the historic district turned into something a bit more modern, with bars and hotels, but we veered left before we strayed too deep into the busy streets.

We passed over a footbridge towards athletic fields that were busy with some sort of soccer camp. The forest stayed to our left as we wrapped around it. Trailheads hinted at quicker paths between campus and the train station, but Liam had been courteous enough not offer them up as a possibility.

Buildings rose around us in a mishmash of old and new architecture that told the story of an expanding campus. I wondered which buildings had been here when Mom had been a student, and which had been added since then. Oak trees growing between buildings and green lawns gave the campus a cozy, park-like vibe, and a fountain spitting water to our right reminded me of the city fountains in Vanderfall.

"What do you think?" Liam asked.

I stared at the glittering windows, the gardens, the lawns, and the clock tower that rose from the stone building at the center of campus.

"It's okay."

"I know. It's stupid how nice it is, right?"

The knot in my stomach loosened as I sighed.

"Yeah. I hate it."

I needed to get in. I wanted to make this my school. I wanted to spend late nights holed up in the window-laden library typing up reports on tectonic shift. I wanted to complain about how the school put too much money into making the student center look nice, and not enough into making the cafeteria food taste good. I wanted to spend warm afternoons after class playing frisbee on the quad, and I didn't even *like* frisbee.

The trashcan to our left rustled, and the largest squirrel I'd ever seen bolted from inside, carrying a banana peel.

"Holy crap!" I jumped into Liam, grabbing his arm, and he laughed.

"You'll get used to the squirrels."

"*Was* that a squirrel? Or a small raccoon?"

"If you thought that was wild, wait until you see the one with two tails." He led the way deeper into campus. "Rumor has it that the science majors are conducting experiments on them, but not everyone believes that theory when it comes to old Two-Tails."

The back of his hand brushed against mine as we walked in the shade provided by a row of oak trees.

"And what do *you* believe about Two-Tails?" I grinned. The shifting light that spilled through the tree canopy caught the edges of Liam's curls as he smiled back.

"He obviously stole the tail from another squirrel, who is now running around campus tailless."

"I'm sure someone would've noticed a tailless squirrel."

"Not if he's hiding among the marmots by the river."

He stopped to point at a building made of sand-colored stone. It stood three stories high, and its roof was adorned with chimney-like vents and a greenhouse. "That's the Life Science building."

"Where they experiment on squirrels." I nodded. "Allegedly."

"Allegedly," he repeated, and then quickened his step to hasten us around the corner. A second building connected to the Life Science building by a skybridge, but boasted walls of brick and glass instead of sandy stone. "And that is where you'll be, in the Earth Sciences center."

I tried to imagine what it would look like in the fall, when campus was full of students, and maybe I'd be one of them.

I wanted it so badly that it hurt, burning an aching hole in the pit of my stomach.

"Where do the architecture students go?" I asked.

"With the engineers. But this—"

"It's a very nice building," I insisted, "but imagine if you took me to that ice-cream shop in town, let me see all the amazing flavors that Gams would never stock in a million years, and then told me I couldn't have any. If tomorrow morning goes well, we can come back before our train leaves."

His face relaxed into a smile.

"Of course. But there's no turning back now. You've officially committed to a full, in-depth tour of the engineering building." Liam continued down the path, beckoning me after him. "If we see Two-Tails, you have to buy dinner."

"How's that fair?" I chased after him, indignant, smiling, and wishing campus could always belong to just the two of us.

Liam's tour was extensive and thorough, covering nearly every building on campus. While there were plenty of squirrels, they all had just one tail, so Liam paid for dinner. If he hadn't, I probably would've thrown my food away. It tasted fine, but the closer we got to the lecture, the more my stomach clenched with nerves.

"Is your eye okay? You've been messing with it," Liam noted as we walked back across campus towards the main school hall. I snapped my hand back to my side, embarrassed to have been caught pulling at my eyelashes.

"Yeah, sorry. Big lecture. Big school." I gestured vaguely at the surrounding campus. Sprinklers chittered as they watered the quad, and I thought back to Mom getting doused on Linsey's front lawn. I pressed a knuckle against my temple.

She'd be so angry with me if she knew where I was headed.

"You must really love geophysics if you're this nervous about a lecture. You know there's no test at the end, right? Just enjoy all the rock jargon and volcano talk."

"It's paleomagnetism, not volcanos," I reminded him. "And you don't actually know there won't be a test."

There was already a line of people waiting outside the amphitheater doors, and I shivered even though the evening was warm.

"Is this guy a big deal?" Liam hissed. "It's packed!"

"He's a moderately-sized deal." I wasn't sure why I hadn't told Liam my connection to the speaker yet. Maybe because I knew he'd say it was a bad idea. He might tell Gams, who would tell Mom. I could hardly stand the thought of telling them I wanted to study geophysics. I didn't want to know what they'd say if they could see me standing in line to hear Maxwell Brenton, PhD, speak.

Or maybe I was afraid Liam would make this too much about me when really it was about finding out if my father knew anything about Skalterra, and why I might be lucid when called there as a Nightmare. It had been one of Ferrin's theories, after all, that I was somehow connected to Skalterra through family.

The line shifted forward, and Liam murmured something about them opening the doors.

I wondered if Maxwell Brenton would be on stage already when we filed in. Or maybe he'd be sitting down near the front. An usher handed me a program as we walked through the front doors and through the lobby. My father stared sternly up at me from the front page.

"Paleomagnetism," Liam mumbled next to me, reading off his own program. "What does that mean?"

"The study of how Earth's magnetism has changed over time. Kind of. That's a watered down explanation, but I'm not exactly a student yet."

We passed into the amphitheater, and I pressed into Liam's shoulder. The other attendees ranged in age. Some of them didn't look any older than undergraduate students, while others sported grizzled gray and white beards that would've put Galahad's to shame.

Liam found us a spot near the middle of the room.

"Wren?" Liam asked again. I slapped my hand away from the back of my neck and into my lap.

"Hmm?" I forced an ambivalent smile.

"You don't need to be nervous."

"I'm not." I flipped through the program until I found my father's biography. It listed all of his accolades, degrees, awards, and accomplishments, and even though I'd read it all before online, it still stung that nowhere did it list he had a daughter.

Mom had said he knew I existed, but what if that had been a lie? What if he had no idea he had a daughter at all?

I screwed my eyes shut. I wasn't here to connect with my estranged father. I was here for answers about Skalterra, to help save Orla, Fana, and the world as we knew it.

I opened my eyes to polite applause that echoed through the theatre. The lights dimmed, and the opening slide of a presentation took up the large white screen that hung over the stage.

A woman in a pantsuit introduced herself to the audience as the dean of the Von Leer School of Geophysics, but she sounded muted, like she was underwater.

A dull buzzing had taken over my brain. There, in the front row, a brunet head bobbed along with the woman's introduction, until she called his name and stepped aside to make room for him at the lectern.

He stood up and waved off the ensuing applause. He shook the woman's hand before she exited the stage, and then he pivoted to look out over the crowd.

Maxwell Brenton, PhD, looked just like his pictures.

My fingers balled into fists, my nails digging into my palms.

For the first time in over eighteen years, I was looking at my father.

Thirty-Eight
Paleomagnetism

My father was tall, like I had figured he would be. Gams and Mom both fit neatly beneath my chin, so I knew I hadn't inherited my height from them. Maxwell Brenton, meanwhile, was willowy and lean with a mousey hair color that matched mine perfectly.

He was already talking, but I had no idea what he was saying. My brain only registered the sound of his voice, low and even, but with a jovial lilt. The crowd laughed at something he said.

"I don't get the joke," Liam whispered next to me. I hushed him rather than admit I had missed the joke entirely.

Slides about seafloor expansion took up the screen, and I tried to absorb as much information as my poor, overwhelmed brain would allow.

"If you look right here at the center of the screen—" Maxwell Brenton used a laser pointer to circle a cluster of symbols on his map of the Pacific Ocean, "—you'll see the magnetic anomalies that our research focused on. The location being so close to the Cascadia Subduction Zone was a *Hugo benefit* of what we were trying to do, because —"

He cut off as laughter rippled through the amphitheater, including that of my own.

"Someone better tell him not to quit geology, because his jokes suck," Liam whispered. "I didn't get that one either."

"It's geophysics, not geology," I corrected under my breath. "And the joke is Hugo Benioff. He studied the Ring of Fire. It's a volcano thing. Now shush."

"It's even less funny now that I have context." Liam's white smile glinted at me in the low light, and I elbowed him into silence.

The lecture was dense, combining theories of ocean floor spread and continental drift, but Maxwell Brenton, PhD, was fun to listen to. He cracked jokes, he let a scientist in the third row heckle him about polar wander in an exchange that left the auditorium wheezing with laughter, and the more he spoke, the more I needed him to like me. Not as a daughter necessarily, but as a prospective scientist.

Every laugh he elicited from the crowd made me glow with misplaced pride, and I hung on his every word, even if I didn't quite understand them all. I'd thought he'd be austere and stern, like he always had been in my imagination. However, he was charming and funny, and suddenly I was feeling very guilty about my admissions essay focusing on what a crappy person he was.

Through the jokes and the tangents, at the core of the lecture, he was painting a picture of how Earth as we knew it was formed by the physical laws that governed our world. Those physical laws had to govern Skalterra as well. They had to have played a role when the Four Magicians shaped the mountains, plains, canyons, and rivers of Skalterra.

The more my father spoke, the more he explained how continents moved and formed, the more certain I became.

He had all the answers to what had formed Keldori. *Of course* he had to know about Skalterra too. Maybe those anomalies he'd labeled on his screen were relevant somehow. Maybe that was where Ferrin would break through the Rift.

Applause broke through my thoughts, and the lights came up in the auditorium.

"Is it done?" Liam straightened up and rubbed the sleep from his eyes.

"I think so. Was that already an entire hour?"

"God, it felt longer than that." Liam groaned.

The people around us started to file out, but I stayed seated, watching my father where he stood on the stage answering the questions of a couple scientists in the front row.

"Can you wait for me outside?" I asked, still looking at Dr. Brenton.

"Are you going to talk to him?" Liam gave me a double take, and I scowled.

"What, are you surprised?"

"A little. You don't really talk to people."

"Most people aren't famous geophysicists."

Liam stood up and stretched.

"Thank god for that." He rubbed his neck. "Take all the time you need. I'll go find us a snack."

"We just had dinner two hours ago!" I called after him as he joined the exodus towards the doors.

"I'm hungry again!"

I sat back in my seat and tried to calm my breathing. What was I even supposed to say? I rehearsed several greetings in my head while I waited for the students and scientists who surrounded him up front to slowly disperse.

I forced myself to stand when they'd almost all left and the ushers were making their passes through the aisles, looking for discarded programs and other garbage.

My legs were led beneath me, but I forced them to keep walking down the steps of the auditorium towards the stage.

Dr. Brenton was even taller up close.

He'd abandoned us. He wasn't even on my birth certificate. Mom had never said a single good thing about him, and I had hated him all my life. So now that I was standing in front of him after eighteen years of cursing the name Maxwell Brenton, why was I suddenly so worried about him liking me?

He cut off his conversation with a woman in a pantsuit to give me a sideways glance. She saw me too, offered a quick reassurance that they could catch up later, and let my estranged father turn his attention to me.

He stepped down the stage steps, and despite my inherited height, he still towered a full head taller than me. He raised his eyebrows in polite interest and waited for me to speak first, apparently unaware that he was looking at his daughter for the first time ever.

"Hi, um, professor? Sorry. Doctor," I corrected myself. My heart felt like someone had shoved an angry hummingbird inside my chest. It fluttered painfully against my sternum, and I stood with my hands behind me so I could take secret comfort in pulling at the skin around my thumb nails.

"Max is fine." His grin was kind behind his neat brown-and-gray beard. Despite the facial hair, I could see me in his bone structure. His cheekbones, the shape of his ears, the exact shade of brown in his hair— he'd given it all to me. The hummingbird behind my sternum kicked its fluttering up a gear. "I hope you aren't here to complain about my lecture."

"No!" I said, too aggressively. "It was fascinating, what I understood at least. I want to study volcanology, not paleomagnetism, though I'm sure I'll have to learn it anyway."

"You *want* to study?" he repeated. His grin turned curious, and he crossed his arms as he surveyed me. "You aren't a student yet?"

"I'll be a freshman here if I get off the waitlist."

"And you're sure about volcanoes? Paleomagnetists are the real rockstars of the geophysics world."

"That's a pun!" I blurted. His grin faltered, and I fumbled onwards, trying to redeem myself. "Because rockstars. *Rocks.* Get it? Although, it would probably be a better joke if you were a geologist."

His polite smile broke into a laugh that carried through the emptying auditorium.

"Oh, that *is* funny!"

My chest loosened, and I laughed too. He'd been so funny on stage, but now he thought *I* was funny.

My *dad* thought I was funny.

"It was technically your joke." I shrugged. He pointed a firm but good-natured finger at me.

"No, no, no. If you want to be a geophysicist, consider this your first lesson. Never, and I mean *never*, give anyone else credit for something you did."

I nodded, absorbing his words. I'd never received fatherly advice before. Or advice from a world-renowned geophysicist. It was hard to say which was more thrilling.

"Right. Sorry."

"Don't apologize. It was very clever."

"Thank you, uh, sir." I wasn't sure what to call him. "Professor" and "doctor" had felt wrong. "Sir" wasn't quite cutting it either, but "Max" was too informal. And I definitely couldn't call him "Dad".

But he was kind, charming, and good-humored—everything Mom had said he wasn't. So why had she been so dead-set on never letting me meet him?

"You're on the waitlist, you say?" A mischievous glint reached his eye, and he looked around conspiratorially. "Tell you what. You seem more serious than most of the incoming geophysics students I see, especially if you're here to listen to me rattle on for an hour about a field you don't care much for. Give me your name, and maybe I'll put in a good word with the dean."

"Oh, that's not—"

"It's really no trouble. Let me see if I've got pen and paper, so I can write it down." He patted at his pockets, and I steadied myself.

"I think you'll remember it."

"Oh?" He poked at his blazer, still searching for a pen. "Why's that?"

"Because it's Wren Warrender."

He froze with his hands over his blazer pockets and slowly raised his eyes to mine. He held my gaze, all signs of his previous mirth evaporated. His eyes roved over me a second time, and the lines around his eyes and mouth grew tighter as his frown deepened.

He took in a sharp breath, as if to say something, but then held onto the air, apparently at a loss for words.

"I'm sorry." I could salvage this. I could get us back on track. "I didn't mean to make it weird, but I'm here for an admissions interview, so I thought—"

"Does Eliza know you're here?"

I flinched at Mom's name.

"Technically? Yes. She just doesn't know you're here too."

"Okay." He nodded curtly, licked his lips as he glanced around for an escape, and then looked back at me with new determination. "So what is it you want from me? A recommendation to the dean?"

"No, I—"

"Money, then? Tuition?" There was a simmering anger beneath his panic, and I took a half-step back.

For a brief, shining moment, I'd almost had a dad. Kind of. Not really, but he'd been nice, at least.

As soon as I'd told him who I was, that version of him had crumbled.

"I don't want your money."

"Then why are you here?" A poorly contained snarl stained his tone. "I've told Eliza so many times—"

He cut off and shook his head.

"I have questions for you." My voice broke. I hated how meek and small I sounded. I hated how much I still wanted to turn this around, to convince him I was a worthwhile daughter.

"About the lecture? How about you wait and see if you get into the program first. There's no use in wasting both our time."

"Questions about Skalterra."

He froze at the name, and the knot in his brow loosened enough to let his eyebrows rise a fraction of an inch.

My heart hitched. Other than my run-in with Stanley earlier in the week, I'd never breathed a word about Skalterra to anyone, but the name alone had been enough to give Maxwell Brenton, PhD, pause. This conversation had gone south fast, but I could save it if it meant discovering my connection to Skalterra.

"I know about it," I offered, gaining confidence. He had answers. I could tell. I was going to learn why I was lucid as a Nightmare, and maybe even learn how to get back without Galahad. "I've been there."

"Skalterra?" he repeated.

"Yes."

"I don't know what that means." His eyebrows fell back into a scowl.

"Yes, you do," I insisted. He was lying. He had to be. "It's the reality that runs parallel to this one, where all the Magicians were banished four hundred years ago. Maybe you don't know it by its name, but—"

He put up a hand to stop me.

"I haven't read your mother's books." His words oozed disdain, as if the idea of picking up something written by Mom was making him physically ill.

"It's not—"

"I told Eliza almost two decades ago," he said, cutting me off, "and I've told her over and over again."

"Told her what?" Something inside me broke, and I felt like I was floating above the conversation, watching it happen to someone else. A numb buzz crept at the back of my head.

"I don't want this." He moved his hand in a circle in the air, palm facing me. "It's not fair. She made her choice, and I made mine. I respected her decision, so why does this keep coming up? When she called in June—"

"June?" I wasn't floating above the conversation anymore. I was watching from the base of a tree, curled up in the dark, alone and lost after being tricked by Linsey, wondering when the night would pass.

"She told me you were graduating and wanted to know if I would come." He looked so much like me. I'd never hated myself more. "You seem like a smart kid, and I'm sure you're great. Eliza says so anyways, when she reaches out. But this, this isn't for me, and quite frankly, I don't owe you anything. You're not *mine*. I mean, you are, but— well. You know."

"I know." My constricted throat made my voice hoarse, and I had to force the words out.

"Don't do that. That's not fair. Don't—" He took a steadying breath and looked around again. "Look, I'll talk to the dean and see what I can do. Okay? Just don't look at me like that."

I dropped my eyes to his tie clip, unable to continue looking him in the face.

"I wrote my admissions essay about you." The clip swam in my vision, and swallowing the lump in my throat felt like gargling glass.

"You shouldn't have done that," he sighed. "I'm not as great as my research would have you think."

"No, I know." I wanted nothing more than to raise my gaze to his, to tell him to keep his recommendation, that I didn't need shit from him. But I couldn't look away from his tie clip.

"This isn't my fault," he said. "Okay? I- I have people waiting for me, alright? I can't do this right now."

My jaw was clenched too tight to say anything more. I couldn't even raise my eyes to his before he walked away. I didn't want to see myself staring back.

His footsteps receded up the auditorium steps behind me, and I continued to stare at the spot in space where his tie clip had been.

He was a dead end for information on Skalterra, but worse than that, he didn't want me.

Not in any capacity. Not as a daughter, obviously. I'd always known that. But he couldn't even stand to talk to me.

I knew he'd abandoned me before I'd been born, but to learn that Mom had reached out over and over as I grew up, as recently as a month ago, and he had turned me down every time?

We weren't allowed to talk about him at home, not because she hated him, but because he hated me.

"I just passed the professor guy at the door. What're you still doing in here?" Liam came up behind me, and I kept my eyes forward. If I looked directly at him, he'd see the tears swimming in my vision. He came around to face me, and his shoulders fell, and his eyes widened. "Wren, what's wrong?"

I shook my head. If I opened my mouth, I wasn't sure I could hold back the sobs burning in my throat.

"Did he talk to you? What did he say?"

"He doesn't want me." The words were a soft, painful croak.

"Oh. That's okay, though. He's not the admissions officer. It's not his decision."

"No. He doesn't want *me*."

Liam's mouth dropped open, and I wondered if he'd put the pieces together yet.

"Wren, please tell me that wasn't your father."

I'd told him about my geophysicist father the day we'd paddled to the cove. There were a lot of geophysicists, though. It wasn't his fault he hadn't made the connection until now.

His take-out bag hit the ground with a soft thud, and then his arms were around me. I disappeared into the blue fabric and sandalwood smell of his Von Leer hoodie and cried.

Thirty-Nine

Seismic Design

Emotions no longer felt real, so I wasn't sure why I was still crying. A sort of self-preserving numbness had chilled my heart, but I stood in the corner of the dusty hotel lobby trying to sniffle through my tears as quietly as possible. In my periphery, the receptionist cast me concerned glances over Liam's shoulder as he checked us into our room.

He hadn't said anything on the walk from campus but had kept his arm around my shoulders, holding me close and letting me cry. I wondered if I'd ruined his trip, or if he was mad that I hadn't told him the truth about the lecture speaker.

"This way." Liam took my overnight bag off my shoulder to carry for me, and I dragged the heel of my hand across my face in a feeble attempt to dry my tears.

The kitschy wallpaper was peeling in spots, and the low carpet was worn thin beneath us, but there was something comforting about the cramped hall and yellowing lights.

I tried to compose myself in the elevator. My shoulders had stopped shaking at least, but tears continued to spill down my cheeks.

"I'm fine," I whispered unprompted.

"I know you are." Liam nodded, but his eyebrows knit in concern. The elevator door opened, and he offered me his hand before we stepped out into the hall. I accepted it, twisting my fingers in his.

A shuddering breath racked my chest, but I tried to pass it off as a shiver.

"This is us." Liam held a plastic keycard up to a door handle, and pushed into the hotel room.

It was at least in nicer shape than the aging hallway, with a fresh coat of gray paint and a clean white comforter stretched over the bed.

The single, king-sized bed.

Heat rose in my cheeks, and Liam groaned next to me.

"I'm going to kill your grandmother."

I gave a watery laugh as I released Liam's hand.

"It might have been an accident. She's not very good at using the internet."

"I know Ethel, and I watched her click on the double room. This was no accident."

"I can take the pull-out." I crossed the room to claim the couch, but Liam took me by the shoulders and spun me back around.

"Absolutely not. You go get cleaned up. I'll take care of it."

I scowled, but gave in, taking my bag with me into the bathroom.

The heat of the shower drew out the last of my tears, and while I would've loved to spend the night wallowing in disappointment and hot steam, I eventually forced myself to shut off the water and change into my oversized t-shirt and shorts for bed.

"I thought you might have fallen asleep in there." Liam had unfolded the couch into a lumpy bed that creaked under his shifting weight. He held up two plastic to-go containers. "Cake?"

"Where did you even get cake at a paleomagnetism lecture?" I made myself comfy on the edge of my bed closest to Liam. He'd changed into plaid pajama pants and a Von Leer Vikings t-shirt.

"It's a bakery across the street from campus. All the food goes on sale during their last hour every day, so I ran to see what they had left when you were talking to— you know."

"To my dad." I took the plastic tray of cake from Liam and studied the pattern in the chocolate icing. The shower had been refreshing, sure, but my eyelids still felt swollen and heavy from crying. Liam could probably see they were still red-rimmed.

"Why didn't you tell me he was your dad?" He sat facing me on the pull-out bed, his knees inches from my shins.

"It was embarrassing," I admitted. "And I didn't want you to say it was a bad idea to go."

"It *was* a bad idea," he frowned, "but I wouldn't have stopped you."

"Why not?"

"He's *your* estranged father." He waggled a bit of his cake on the end of his fork at me. "Why would I get an opinion?"

"I dragged you there without letting you know what you were walking into."

"I knew what I was walking into."

"Did you?"

"A *really* boring lecture."

I threw a pillow at him, and he dodged it with a grin.

"Watch the cake!"

"It was on sale. You're fine." I poked at my own slice of cake with a plastic fork. "I wish it *had* been boring, but he's a genius. And funny. Maybe I wouldn't feel so crappy if he had been crappy too."

"He is crappy," Liam said through a mouth full of cake. "And you know it. Didn't you say that you wrote your entire admissions essay on how terrible he is?"

I smiled in spite of myself.

"I did, yeah. And then they waitlisted me."

Liam set his dessert to the side and leaned forward with a new glint in his eyes.

"I want to read it."

"What?" I recoiled, drawing the heels of my feet up onto the bed.

"Do you have it on your phone?"

I pulled my overnight bag over from where I'd left it at the foot of the bed and pulled a folder out from inside.

"I have a printed copy, actually. For tomorrow. Just in case."

Liam abandoned his cake and his pull-out bed, pushing me over in his haste to take the folder. He sat on his knees next to me, and held the papers close to his face to read the essay in the dim light of the bedside lamp.

"'My father is a world-renowned geophysicist with research that has shaped modern understanding of continental shift, and yet I've never met a greater failure. Except, that's not entirely true, because I haven't actually met him.'" Liam slapped the essay into his lap and gawked at me with a massive grin. "You're kidding me. You submitted this, and they *didn't* immediately admit you?"

"They love him! And I'm pretty sure he donates to the geophysics program. There's an entire study room named after him in the science buildings."

"And someday you'll be a bigger deal than him, and they'll rename it after you."

"Or," I suggested, "they'll bulldoze the entire building, hire some ice-cream scooper to design a new one, and they'll name *that* after me."

"I like it. Tell me more about this ice-cream scooper. He sounds handsome."

I shoved him and retreated to lean against the pillows with my arms crossed. He flashed a devilish smile before returning to the essay. He read it under his breath, and I watched his lips move with the words, occasionally quirking upwards in a smile.

"This is amazing." He looked up at me with shining brown eyes when he reached the end. "Wren, you are incredible."

"It's just an essay."

He flourished the paper in front of him for dramatic effect and read from the pages.

"'Dr. Brenton may have made advances in his field that will continue to inform the study of geophysics for decades to come, but he was not there when his daughter was born. He did not see her first steps or hear her first words. He did not stay up late comforting her the first time a boy called her a bitch when she was twelve. He did nothing to make sure she had three meals every day for eighteen years, nor did he help provide the roof over her head, and at the end of the day, Eliza Warrender, Smut Author, is a household name while Maxwell Brenton, PhD, is not.'" Liam fell against the headboard next to me, still clutching my essay. "Wren. Are you kidding?"

"'Household name' was a bit of a stretch," I admitted. "But she's been searched on the internet way more times. I checked."

"You're amazing."

Mom had called me amazing. And Gams. And Orla probably would too. But Mom and Gams were biased, and Orla only knew the ideal, Nightmare-version of me.

No one who wasn't related to me had ever looked at me—the real me—and called me amazing. I felt myself blush, and I took a bite of cake so he wouldn't be able to tell how much the word meant.

"I told him I wrote my essay about him," I said.

"And?"

I rolled my head against the headboard to look back at Liam.

"And he assumed I'd written *good* things. About him and his research."

"Stop. No, he didn't." Liam laughed, then straightened up with sudden conviction. He laid the essay out on the comforter in front of him and held his phone over the pages to take a picture.

"What are you doing?"

"Fancy scientist like him, he's got to have a public email, and I think he'd love to read all the *good* things you wrote about him."

"No!" I lunged for the phone, laughing, and Liam tried to wiggle away, but I managed to pin him down with a move Ciarán had used on me once.

Unlike Ciarán, Liam didn't fight back, and he grinned up at me from the pillows as I held his hostage phone aloft.

"Please?" he said.

"He's friends with the dean," I said.

"Then I'll send it tomorrow after you get accepted."

I weighed the pros and cons for a moment, then rolled off to collapse on the pillows next to him.

"After I get accepted," I repeated, setting the phone down on his chest.

"Promise."

His face was very close to mine. He could probably see the red spots under my eyes from the capillaries I'd burst from crying too hard, and I wasn't wearing make-up. Eyeliner was my favorite weapon when it came to camouflaging my lack of eyelashes, but it probably wouldn't have helped at this close distance anyway.

The longer he stared, the more the laughter in his features faded into something more serious. I wanted to flinch away and hide, but my hand was still on his phone, resting on his chest, and I couldn't bring myself to draw it away.

"What happened to your eyelashes?" Liam whispered, his voice suddenly low and careful.

"That's a rude question," I whispered back.

"I'm a rude person."

I suppressed a laugh, afraid of breathing too hard in his face.

"No, you're not." I could feel his chest rising and falling with his breathing. "I pull them out. I can't help it. Most of the time I don't notice I'm doing it."

"Will they come back?"

"Yeah. And then I'll pull them out again."

"Does it hurt?"

"Sometimes," I admitted. "But not always. It hurts the most when I don't realize there's nothing left to pull on anymore, and I accidentally pinch my eyelid."

"Oh." He winced. "I'm sorry."

"You asked me a personal question," I said, "so now I get to ask you one."

He narrowed his eyes at me.

"That's not fair."

"Was it hard being on campus today without Riley?"

His heartbeat quickened against my hand.

"Yeah, but not for the reasons you probably think."

I waited for him to continue and froze when he rolled towards me, putting his arm around my waist and holding me close.

"It wasn't because you miss him?" I asked.

"He'll graduate next year. I have to get used to campus without him no matter what. But you," his thumb traced a circle on my back, "it kills me that he hasn't gotten to meet you yet. And that you haven't met him."

"He's not missing out on much," I promised.

"You're funny, you're clever, you don't care what other people think—"

"That's not true. I care very deeply."

"And you do a good job of hiding it." He smiled, but I was too close to his face to see his whole grin. "Because you are strong, and you remind me of Ethel."

"If you have a crush on my grandma, you should just say so, but if it works out, I'm *not* calling you Gramps."

"Wren Warrender," he teased, "what would you know about crushes?"

"Absolutely nothing." The corners of my mouth pulled upwards. Gams had said weeks ago that she was fine with Liam and me sharing a hotel room because he was "a good boy", and I "wasn't interested in those kinds of things". Something about the way Liam was looking at me and the way I felt curled up in his arms had me wondering if Gams was wrong about both of us.

Liam shifted forward and pressed his lips against the space between my eyebrows. He kept his mouth there to murmur into my skin. "You should get some sleep. Big day tomorrow."

A moment of wonderful panic made me lock up, but then I gave in to his embrace, burrowing into the pillows and nestling my head beneath his chin.

"You aren't the boss of me," I mumbled back.

"No, I don't think anyone is." His lips were in my hair. "Sleep, alright? I promise to keep the nightmares away."

I sighed against his chest, feeling for the first time all week that maybe everything was okay. Maybe Ferrin had failed, and I'd never see him again. Maybe I would do so well in my interview the next day that the admissions officer offered me admittance on the spot.

And maybe I would become a geophysicist so renowned that I would make Maxwell Brenton, PhD, cry over every day he had let pass without ever trying to get to know his daughter.

It was the best night of sleep I'd had since before graduation. I woke up to early morning light spilling from around the edges of the heavy window curtains, and I stretched, rolling away from the fingers of sunshine that spread across the ceiling.

"Liam?" He'd left his hoodie on the bed, and I rolled out from under the covers to search the bathroom for him. However, he wasn't in the hotel room anymore.

I was almost done getting ready for my interview, in my pencil skirt and blazer that was much too warm for the day's forecast, when a beep chimed out from the door, and Liam walked in carrying a tray of pancakes, bacon, and fruit.

"Where've you been?" I took the tray out of his hands.

"The lobby breakfast bar." He'd already dressed for the day, and his hair was still damp from a shower.

"I didn't even hear you get up."

He took a strip of bacon from the tray and bit it in half.

"I'm very sneaky. Are you ready for today?"

I grimaced and shoved the tray of food back into his hands.

"Mostly." My stomach churned as I said it. "I have to finish my hair and make-up still."

"I think you look fine."

"It doesn't matter what *you* think," I called from the bathroom. I leaned over the sink to get as close as I could to the mirror while I applied eyeliner. "You aren't the admissions officer."

I waited for a quippy reply, but Liam was quiet in the bedroom.

"What, no joke about me trying to seduce the admissions officer?" I poked my head out of the bathroom. Liam stood with his back to me and his head bowed, looking at something in his hand. "Liam?"

He turned around, still staring down at the crumpled flyer he was holding. My heart plummeted to my stomach. I'd forgotten about the stolen Riley posters I'd shoved into my backpack.

Forty
Synoptic Meteorology

A million excuses ran through my head, but none of them could explain away the stolen flyer in Liam's hand.

"Why do you have this?" he asked, still staring at Riley's wrinkled picture.

"Did you go through my backpack?" The anger that rose inside me was a defense mechanism. I knew that. If I was angry, how could I be guilty? But I clung to it. That was *my* bag, after all. Nothing gave Liam the right to go through my things.

"No. It was on the floor." Liam raised his eyes from the flyer to my face. "Why do you have this?"

"It's probably an extra from when I reposted the flyers a few weeks ago," I lied.

"It has Sabrina's lipstick on it."

My heart sank further. That first flyer we'd posted, Sabrina had stood on her tip-toes to give it a kiss, and Liam had laughed about her lipstick staining the paper.

I shook my head. I could feel my guilt written across my face, and Liam, who had only ever looked at me with kindness, even when I'd been rude, glowered back.

"I don't know what to say," I admitted.

"Say that you're the one who took down all of Riley's posters."

"I am." There was no use lying. He was holding the evidence in his hands.

"Who told you to do it?"

"No one." The lie was easy, but my delivery of it wasn't nearly convincing enough.

"You wouldn't do this, Wren." Liam held the flyer up. It felt like both he and the picture of Riley were glaring at me. "So who told you to do it?"

I shook my head. He loved Gams. I'd take the fall a thousand times before I ruined that.

"I told you. No one."

He lowered the paper and nodded.

"Ethel, then." My silence confirmed his guess, and his shoulders heaved with the weight of a sigh. "And when she told you to replace them, was that even real?"

His voice broke, betraying the hurt that lay beneath his simmering anger.

"Yes and no," I said. "I wasn't supposed to post new ones, but I did. Or I tried to. She took them down again after those girls came to the shop."

Liam dropped the paper and ran his hands over his face.

"She was trying to protect you—" I started.

"I didn't ask for that," he snapped. "I don't care how many people come to gawk at me if it means Riley is found."

"I know—"

"Then why did you take them down?" His voice rose into a shout, but he immediately retreated back a few steps and hid his face in his hands.

"I'm sorry."

"My best friend is gone, and everyone is rushing to forget he ever existed. The same way they did when my parents left."

I felt tiny and stupid standing in the entryway of the hotel room in my blazer and pencil skirt. I knew taking the posters down had been wrong. I knew he'd be hurt if he found out. I had no defense for myself.

"Liam—"

"Do you know how to get to campus from here?" He wouldn't make eye contact with me, staring instead at the door behind me.

"Yes."

"And you remember where College Hall was?"

I nodded, and even though he refused to look at me, he must've seen the affirmation in his periphery, because he nodded too.

"Okay. I'll be at the train station. If you get lost, you can call me."

He grabbed his hoodie and his backpack from the bed, and I stepped back into the bathroom to clear him a path to the door.

"Liam, I'm sorry," I said as he passed. He paused with his hand on the door handle.

"Don't overthink your interview." He pulled the door open, and finally looked back at me. His features were set in a stern frown, but his eyes were wide with hurt. "You'll do fine."

He stepped into the hall, and the heavy, metal door swung shut, leaving me alone in the hotel room.

I didn't even have the luxury of feeling sorry for myself, because no matter how I looked at it, I deserved Liam's anger. I knew it had been wrong to take the posters down and that it had been wrong to lie about it.

And it had been *dumb* to never get rid of the evidence. The flyer was now ripped to shreds in the trash basket of the hotel room, and every step I took along the sidewalk loosened the knot in my chest a little more as I put distance between me and it.

I wished Liam had been meaner. I wished he'd said something terrible that would put him on the same field as me. Instead he'd made sure I knew how to get to my interview and wished me luck.

He really was the worst.

He deserved better.

Von Leer University's campus was just as beautiful as it had been the day before, and as I traveled between the spots of shade provided by the oak trees, I kept my eyes on the squirrels, counting their tails and wishing Liam was here to help.

In a weird way, my blunder with the flyer was helping me. I was much more worried about Liam than I was my approaching interview.

I felt like a faker walking up the steep, stone steps to the massive double doors of College Hall, like the building itself knew I didn't belong there. The entry hall smelled like an old book, with a dusty quality that was more inviting than off-putting, and I took a deep breath, trying to let the cozy scent calm me.

A plain white print-out taped to a music stand that read "Admissions Offices" stood in the middle of the hall with an arrow pointing to the door on my right. The frosted glass of the windows showed several silhouettes already inside, though it was hard to make out much else.

I took another steadying breath, vaguely wondering if Liam was okay at the train station, and then pushed into the office.

"Name?" The woman at the front desk wore glasses on top of her head as she typed at her computer. She kept her eyes glued to her screen as I approached, seemingly unaware that her bun was already unraveling despite the bits of hair that hung in her face.

"Wren Warrender."

She typed a bit more and then exhaled heavily.

"Sorry, one of our admissions officers called out today, so we're running behind, but we can squeeze you in with someone else here in a little bit."

I waited for further instruction at the desk, but after another moment of typing, she finally looked up at me.

"Did you have a question?"

"Oh!" Embarrassment burned in my face. "Um, no. Sorry."

She gestured to the waiting area, and I pivoted on my heel, trying not to look at the other waitlisted hopefuls as I took a seat. A girl two chairs over repeatedly clicked on a pen. The boy in the seat next to me tapped his foot so rapidly that the floor beneath us trembled. He mumbled under his breath, apparently in the middle of a practice interview with an imaginary admissions officer.

I set my backpack between my feet and checked my phone, hoping for a text from Liam. I wouldn't have even cared if it had said that he hated me. Anything would've been nice.

I only had a text from Mom.

"Good luck and have fun today! I'm proud to be your mom!"

Fresh guilt frothed inside me. I'd betrayed her last night, and sure, I'd reaped the punishment for it, but I still felt bad. She'd tried to protect me. I'd ignored her.

A girl with her head bowed low hurried out of a closed door down the adjoining hall, clutching a folder to her chest and refusing to look up. She burst through the door I'd come in through, and disappeared into the main corridor of College Hall.

"Mr. Parker?" The woman at the desk looked at the boy next to me. "Office number three. Second one on your left."

The mumbling boy shot to his feet and staggered down the hall with short, nervous steps to the office the girl had just exited. His nerves set mine on edge, and I tried for another deep breath.

The thought of Liam alone at the train station made me choke on it, and I erupted in a fit of coughing as another prospective student came through the main door.

I closed my eyes. It would be fine. If I didn't get in, maybe I could go to community college with Sabrina. I was pretty sure she hated me, but so did most people. I would get over it. Carpooling would be awkward, but maybe we'd agree on some nice audiobooks to fill the silence.

And then I could transfer to Von Leer next year. There was a chance Liam would still hate me by then, but after a year of carpooling with Sabrina, I would be toughened up.

If I failed my interview, it would be a setback, sure, but I would land on my feet. I'd find a way forward.

But then I remembered the plastic mannequin Linsey had hung from the trees, and the look of anger on my father's face the night before when he'd learned who I was.

No.

I *had* to get in, even if it was just to spite them.

"Miss Warrender?"

I bolted to my feet, looking wildly at the woman at the desk.

"What?" My heart rate soared to the point of being painful. I hadn't even noticed Pen Girl get called back to her interview.

"Office Five?" The woman said it in a tone that implied she'd already told me this.

"Right." My voice was too high-pitched. "Yeah, that's what I thought you said. I was just making sure."

I got quieter with each word, and then after an awkward pause, I scooped my backpack up and hurried down the hall. The previous student had left the door to Office Five open, and the admissions officer stood with his back to me, messing with the filing cabinet behind his desk.

"Come in, come in! Please!" he called.

Summer sunshine poured through the large window to my right. That and the bookshelf full of old, leather-bound tomes and knick-knacks to my left made the office feel a little more inviting than daunting. I stepped in, steadying my breathing as I closed the door behind me.

"Sorry about the wait," the admissions officer said. He messed with the sleeves of his button-up that he wore under a wool waistcoat, rolling them up to his elbows. "Give me just a moment to pull your file up on the computer. Things have been a bit crazy this morning. What was your name?"

He turned around to take a seat, and flashed me a wide, assured smile that glinted white under his cockatoo-coiffed hair.

My breath caught, and my palms turned sweaty even as all the heat seemed to seep out of the office, leaving me frozen in place. For all the hours I'd spent going over practice questions with Liam, nothing in either of the two worlds could have prepared me for this.

My admissions officer, the only man standing between me and admittance to my dream school, was Ferrin Quillguard.

Forty-One
Transformative Properties of Matter

Orla and Fana were dead.

They had to be if Ferrin was here.

My legs shook, but I braced for an attack. Running was still an option, but I wasn't sure what good that would do if Ferrin had already broken through the Rift. I didn't have my Nightmare powers here, but that didn't mean I was going to let him take me down without a fight.

"Please, take a seat." He gestured at the chair across from his, but I stayed standing.

"You."

He looked up at me in surprise, his eyebrows disappearing into shadows beneath his coiffed hair.

"Yes, sorry again. You were supposed to meet with my colleague today, but she called out sick. Please." He pointed at the chair again.

He didn't recognize me. I hadn't thought my Nightmare form looked much different than my actual self, but maybe the blue hair had been pulling more attention from my face than I'd realized.

"You're an admissions officer." I thought he'd wanted the unlimited power allowed by our vast stores of Skal and all the creature comforts our advanced technology allowed, not a nine-to-five. It didn't make sense.

Who went through all that trouble, killing their own family and betraying everyone who had ever trusted them, just to live out their dreams in an office job?

I was missing a piece of the puzzle, but I wasn't sure what I was looking for.

"I am indeed an admissions officer." The chuckle in his voice set my teeth on edge. "There's no need to be nervous. I promise, if you've made it this far in the admissions process, there's a good chance this day ends well for you."

He leaned back in his desk chair and winked.

"Don't do that," I whispered. "Don't wink at me."

His smile faltered, and he cleared his throat.

"Right. On to the interview then. Did you bring a copy of your transcripts?"

"You've been here a while." I looked around his office. It was lived in. The knick-knacks on the shelves had a light layer of dust. There was a pin-adorned map of the coast on his wall next to the door.

"At Von Leer?" he clarified. "A few years, yes. But this is your interview, not mine."

I'd been wearing a Von Leer hoodie the night Orla and I had saved Ciarán in Vanderfall. When Ferrin had seen me, he'd been taken aback by it. I thought it was because he'd never seen a hoodie before. Now I wasn't so sure.

"A few years," I repeated.

He'd still been trapped in Skalterra just a week ago.

"It's a good school. Good place to work. Ah! There's your transcripts. The email just came through." He leaned in towards his computer screen, clicking and scrolling. "Again, I know we're a bit disorganized today. Sorry about that, Miss—"

He froze with his mouth slightly agape, and his eyes widened ever so slightly before he raised them to me. His look of shock slowly melted into one of cruel delight, and every instinct screamed at me to run.

"Miss Wren Warrender." He finished with a smile.

"Did you kill them?" I choked.

"You don't look like how I imagined you would. Your Nightmare was so…" He paused as his eyes roved over me. "So vivid. But this?"

"Are Orla and Fana dead?" I asked more forcefully this time.

He rolled his eyes and spun in his chair to rise to his feet.

"Come on, Wren. You can figure the answer to that one out. You're smart. Now *prove* it! This is your admissions interview after all."

He was playing with me.

"They're alive," I said. "You've been here too long. You—"

He leaned against his filing cabinet and grinned.

"Yes?"

"You're a Nightmare," I realized out loud. "This isn't your real body."

He made a show of clapping for me.

"Bravo, Just-Wren. That didn't take too long at all."

"But Orla said it's impossible to project Nightmares on this side of the Rift. She said not even Galahad—"

"And Galahad is dead." Ferrin shrugged. "He was good at his tricks, but he was stubborn and lacked imagination. Meanwhile, I figured out how to create a Nightmare of myself in Keldori decades ago."

"When you said you'd met another lucid Nightmare —"

"Surprise!" Ferrin gave me a salute.

"So Orla and Fana are—"

"Alive." He waved a dismissive hand. "I would love to rush to the Bay of Teeth, free the Frozen God, and open the Rift. Really, I'm impatient. I'm tired of living in Keldori as a sometimes-man. Or, I could do this right. I could figure out where the Rift lets out on this side, so when we free Saergrim, we have him surrounded from both directions and can subdue him before he becomes a problem."

"Then why are you *here*? Working at Von Leer."

He raised a lazy finger to point at the pin-laden map on the wall next to me.

"It took a while, but I've narrowed the Rift location down to somewhere within a five hundred mile radius of here. This is the most prestigious school in the area, so I sit in my office and go through college applications. Any hint of anything strange on an application, and I put them on the waitlist so I can meet them face-to-face and ask more questions."

"Anything strange?" I repeated.

"Sure." He shrugged. "It's not a perfect system, but every once in a while I'll get a student who started a lucid dreaming club at their high school, or a kid with close family that went missing one day never to be seen again. See, *those* provide good clues. Not the dream club kids, but the kids with missing family."

Liam had been waitlisted. He'd mentioned telling his admissions officer about his missing parents. But Liam was just Liam, and while his parents and cousin's disappearances were tragic, there was nothing supernatural or magick about them.

"You're wasting your time," I hissed.

"Am I?" Ferrin put a hand over his heart and leaned back over his desk to scroll on his computer again. "Because it looks like you submitted a finalized transcript after your graduation date, but the address doesn't match the one you initially listed. And the date, I mean, that lines up pretty dead on for when you showed up in Skalterra perfectly lucid."

I shook my head. This wasn't happening. It couldn't be.

"The town you listed, though, that's what's weird to me. It's the same town the orphan kid was from. Keel Watch Harbor. I remember it because I visited."

He crossed to his bookshelf and reached for a green chicken. I recognized Gams's brushstrokes in the paint, and I held my breath.

"It's a coincidence," I insisted. Gams had nothing to do with this. Neither did Liam, nor Keel Watch Harbor.

"I picked this up in the shop the kid told me he worked at. The cutest old lady was running the joint, but there was nothing special about it. Except for this." He turned the chicken in his hands, watching the light from the window bounce off the sheen of the glaze. "I know you aren't a Magician, so you aren't sensitive to Skal, but she had an entire shelf of these damn chickens. Each one buzzed with magick. I think it was in the paint, but the energy has long since worn off. Maybe it's time I went and picked up another one? Unless..."

Ferrin crossed the office in two long strides, and I recoiled with my back pressed against the door. He took my backpack from my hands and reached inside.

"Hey!" I lunged to take my things back, but he pushed me away with inhuman strength. He withdrew his hand from my bag, and the blue chicken Gams had gifted me at the train station gleamed in his palm.

"Skal," he hissed.

"But it doesn't glow!" I didn't mean for the words to sound so hysterical.

"Because Keldori is full of Skal. It's the same reason you can't see the stars during the day. Everything else is too damn bright." He crushed the chicken in his hand, and porcelain dust rained down onto the low carpet. "Shame. Guess I'll have to go buy another one. I've been meaning to go back ever since I found *this* in the town just north of there."

He slipped his hand inside his filing cabinet, and my breath hitched when he withdrew one of Riley's posters.

Ferrin grinned at the look on my face.

"Keel Watch Harbor has an issue with disappearances it seems. I'd ask if you'd believe that this kid is the cousin of the orphan boy, but looking at your face, I think you might already know."

I shook my head.

"You're wrong," I whispered. He had to be. And if Keel Watch Harbor did have a connection to Skalterra and the Rift, it didn't matter. All that mattered was that Ferrin would hurt Gams if he knew she was my grandmother.

"Tell you what, Miss Warrender. I'll let you into Von Leer if you tell me everything you know about Keel Watch Harbor, the orphan boy, and those funny, little chickens."

I lunged for my bag again, but he held it out of reach.

"You are going to stay away from my home," I growled, taking up a stance in front of his office door.

"You're going to fight a Nightmare?" He grinned. "I've been studying your tricks this last month, and I have to admit, I'm excited for the opportunity to try them out for myself."

His arm lengthened into a mantis-like spear, and I ripped the door open and ducked out just as I heard the thunk of Ferrin embedding his pointed arm in the wood.

The waiting room had filled with more students, and they stared at me as I sprinted for the exit and careened into the hall. The woman at the desk shouted something after me, but I couldn't make it out over the thundering of blood in my ears and the haggard breaths that worked their way out of my chest like sobs.

I ditched my blazer on the top step of the College Hall entrance. Even in the shade of the building, the July sun was hot, but I would not let it slow me down.

I was racing against Ferrin. He would hurt Gams and Liam and Orla and Fana.

I would not let him. I *could* not let him.

And I didn't know how Gams's chickens had become full of Skal, but I knew she couldn't have been who put it there.

As for Liam and his missing family, that was a coincidence. A bunch of random details were leading Ferrin in the wrong direction, and Keel Watch Harbor would pay the price for it.

My legs were painfully slow compared to those of my Nightmare form, but I forced them to sprint across campus. My pencil skirt ripped with the force of my strides. I needed to get to Liam. I needed to warn everyone.

My phone was in my bag with Ferrin, but Liam had a cellphone too. We could call Gams. We could tell her that Ferrin was coming. He was too powerful to physically stop, but if everyone got out in time—

I looked back over my shoulder. Ferrin was walking across the grounds after me, as if on a leisurely stroll. Up ahead, the forest whispered in the wind.

It was the most direct route to the train station.

My stomach clenched, and I watched my feet as I ran, unable to bear the view of the trees looming overhead. My shallow breath had nothing to do with the physical effort of running.

I forced my eyes upwards to find one of the trailheads I'd seen when we'd first come to campus. A breathless sob worked its way out of my chest as I sprinted past the wooden sign that marked the trail, and let the trees swallow me.

"Liam!" I cried. He wouldn't be able to hear me from here, but I couldn't help calling out. The trees towered overhead. The low vegetation made it difficult to see any farther than the trail allowed. Panic roiled in my chest.

But it should be a straight shot. A train whistled in the distance, hastening me forwards.

Something heavy collided with my side, and I hit the dirt rolling. I landed splayed out and flat on my back as

Ferrin stood over me rubbing the wrist of the hand he'd hit me with.

"You can't outrun me, Wren," he tutted. "And quite frankly, it's embarrassing that you even tried."

"I won't let you hurt them." I spat dirt out of my mouth.

"Forgive me for not taking you seriously. I've heard that line from you before, and it lost its punch after I killed Galahad." His arm morphed back into his mantis-spear. "Sorry about this. Honestly, I thought you would've died with Galahad, but if you insist on getting in my way, then this'll do just fine."

He drew his elbow back, preparing to drive his spear through my chest, but I grabbed dirt in both my hands and threw it upwards into his face.

He cried out and blindly jabbed, and I was able to roll out of the way and scramble back to my feet.

"You'll regret that!" Ferrin roared after me. "I was nothing but kind to you in Skalterra, Wren! I took care of you when no one else did, and *this* is how you repay me?"

I risked a glance backwards, and felt my face drain of warmth despite the hot air.

Ferrin had doubled in size and held two mantis-arms aloft, ready to strike, as he charged after me on beastly hind legs. His face elongated into a snout, and crocodile scales ran up his chest and neck.

I staggered to a stop, frozen in horror at the monster Ferrin had become. Was that how I had looked in Skalterra when I fought?

Part of my brain screamed to keep running, but the other, more rational part told me this couldn't be real. This was a bad dream, and if Ferrin killed me, I'd wake up in the hotel room, still curled in Liam's arms.

And if that were the case, then maybe I should get it over with and let him do it.

"Wren, don't stop!"

A hand wrapped around my wrist and yanked me down the path. Liam, in his blue Von Leer hoodie, dragged me after him.

"Liam!"

"Just run!" Liam's face reflected my own horror back at me as we sprinted hand in hand.

"How— why are you here?" I panted.

Liam shook his head.

"You called my name. Do you wanna tell me what the hell that thing is?"

Ferrin crashed through foliage behind us, and I bit back a terrified whimper.

"I told you," I breathed, "I have really bad nightmares."

I wasn't sure how he'd heard me call for help, but he'd come. Even though I'd betrayed him. Even though he was mad.

He was here, running from a monster with me.

I truly did not deserve him.

He looked back over our shoulders, and his eyes widened.

"Don't look back. Wren, keep running. Promise me you'll keep going."

"Liam?"

"Don't stop, Wren!" His voice, panicked and pleading, cut off in a scream of pain.

Blood sprayed across my face, and Liam's hand ripped away from mine. The forest tilted around me when I tried to stop too fast, and Liam's name tore at the back of my throat as I shrieked for him.

Of all the unreal, fantastical things I'd seen in the last month, the image of the bloodied spike driven through Liam's chest was the least believable.

Because he was *Liam*. He was constant, and kind, and wonderful, and brave, and Ferrin *couldn't* kill him.

"I said," Liam gasped, blood spilling from his mouth and down his chin, "keep running."

Ferrin threw Liam's body to the dirt path, pinning him to the earth. Liam twitched in the dust with his head lolled to the side like a broken doll.

Warm, wonderful Liam, now pale and lifeless.

"He didn't have to die." Ferrin's growl was inhuman. "You killed him when you refused to comply, the same way you killed Galahad."

"No!" I didn't sound human either.

"You can't beat me, Wren!" Ferrin roared. "I have given everything to make it this far, and I'll take everything you have too, if I must!"

My fingertips burned with a familiar, impossible feeling, and even though I knew I didn't stand a chance against this version of Ferrin while I was trapped as this version of me, I charged at him.

His lips drew back in a grinning snarl, but then his eyes widened, and heat burst in my arm.

A familiar handle took shape in my hand, and I brought my flail of Skal swinging upwards in an arc of dazzling blue.

My weapon hit Ferrin square beneath his chin, and it erupted in an array of blue sparks. His head jerked back, and a bone-crunching crack echoed through the forest as his spine broke in his neck with the force of my attack.

Ferrin, and all his monstrousness, disintegrated, falling down around me in a cloud of ash that clung to the tears tracing my cheeks.

Magick. I'd done Skalmagick. In Keldori.

And I'd killed Ferrin's Nightmare with it.

And Liam—

"Wren..." Liam's voice was a weak rattle.

"Liam!" I cried out as I fell at his side. Against all odds, he was still alive. Blood seeped into his hoodie through the gaping hole in his chest that I tried not to look too hard at, but he was alive. I just had to keep him that way. "Liam, I'm sorry. I'm so sorry. Hold on."

I pressed a hand over the wound in his chest and leaned over him.

"It's okay," he breathed.

"No, it's not." I shook my head. "But it's going to be."

"Did you...do magic?"

"I- maybe." Blue light sparked off my fingertips as I said it.

He stared past my face at the leafy canopy overhead. His eyes focused and unfocused, and a light sheen of sweat broke out across his forehead. I needed to get help, but I still didn't have my phone. I could yell, but who would hear me? My hand against Liam's chest was hot with residual Skalmagick and the heat of his blood.

"Riley..."

"That's right." I nodded. "We're going to find him, okay? But you have to stay with me, you have to—"

"He's dead."

"He's not, he's—"

"I saw his body. I only just remembered." He turned his head to look at me through eyes that fought to flutter shut. "You were there too, remember? On the night we met."

"No." I pressed my hand harder against the hole in his chest, refusing to look away from his face, refusing to see the hot blood I could feel soaking into his hoodie. "You met me in the morning, not at night. Riley is fine. *You* are fine. You have to be. You-you can't—"

If Ferrin took Liam away from me, I wouldn't stop at him and Caitria. I wouldn't stop until all of Skalterra had been reduced to Skal dust for rotsbane to sniff at.

Liam placed his hand over mine where I tried to stem the flow of blood.

"Don't worry about me," he rasped. "Blue, it's okay."

"No, I—" The forest froze and quieted, muted by the blood rushing in my ears. My head turned light, and my fingers shook against Liam's chest. "What did you call me?"

He reached for my face, and frigid fingers brushed my cheeks.

"Liam?" A new panic crept up my throat, and I pressed harder against the wound in his chest. "Liam, why did you call me Blue?"

Hot, painful tears rolled down my cheeks, and my chest heaved as I tried to catch my breath.

"Does he know?" Liam croaked. "Does Ferrin know where we are?"

"How do you know his name?"

"You have to come find us," he whispered. "If he knows..."

His hand fell away from my face, and his eyes lost focus, staring unseeing back at me. I tore my gaze away to finally look at his chest, but the blood that had bloomed across the front of his hoodie was gone.

I pulled my hand away from the wound and found my palm dirty with ash.

"Liam?" I searched his face, and there, in the half-second before he turned into dust in my hands, I saw him in the shape of his nose and the cut of his cheekbones. And when I was left with nothing but a dirty, torn Von Leer hoodie in my arms, I whispered his other name. "Ciarán?"

Something heavy shifted in the pocket of the tattered hoodie, and a blue chicken fell into my dust-stained lap.

Forty-Two
Glaciology

Nothing felt real anymore.

Not the trees that towered overhead.

Not the pile of dust in the dirt that had been Liam.

Not the blue sparks dancing on my fingertips.

The only thing I knew for sure existed was the tattered hoodie I clutched against my hammering heart.

However, Keel Watch Harbor, real or not, was in danger, and I needed to warn them. Ferrin would be on his way.

My legs shook beneath me, but I didn't have time to rest. I didn't have time to grieve or fall into a shocked stupor, even as reality seemed to strip away around me.

Liam was a Nightmare.

Wonderful, kind Liam who had turned to ash in my hands.

Thoughtful, sweet Liam who had been hunting me across a magic reality all summer.

As horrifying as the revelation was, I clung to it as tightly as I held onto the hoodie.

It meant that Liam wasn't dead. He'd died gruesomely, but he wasn't *dead*.

Had Liam known that he was Ciarán? I curled my fingers around the blue chicken that had fallen from his pocket.

No, he couldn't have.

He'd worried all summer about Riley. He'd never lost hope.

But Riley was dead, because Riley wasn't real and never had been. I'd watched Riley die my first night in Skalterra, with Ferrin's green Skalmagick bursting in his chest.

Except they'd called him Daithi.

Gams had known somehow. That was why she made me take down the posters. That and because she knew there might be someone like Ferrin, watching and waiting.

Which begged the question, who else in Keel Watch Harbor was a Nightmare? And more importantly, who was creating them?

I was halfway across a wooden footbridge that arched over the river when electricity coursed through my stomach and chest.

I cried out and fell to my knees. Fire danced along my every nerve, zipping back and forth across my skin and through my bones. Pain blossomed in my abdomen, and I coughed up blood-stained bile.

I pressed Liam's hoodie and chicken against my chest and extended my free hand in front of me with my palm facing up.

A tiny skalflame the same shade of blue as my Nightmare hair jumped in my fingers, and the burning in my veins subsided just a little. I didn't know what had happened to make Skal run hot in my blood, but it was tearing me apart from the inside.

I found Liam's backpack near the trailhead where he'd apparently discarded it. The train station was visible through the trees, and I stumbled out of the woods with the backpack, ripped hoodie, a torn skirt, and covered in dirt and ash.

Skalmagick continued to eat at my nerves, and I held it back like the sobs that suffocated in my throat. I couldn't breathe. If I did, everything would explode outwards, so I held my breath, allowing myself intermittent gasps that shook my body.

The tourists outside the train station parted for me as I approached. Someone asked if I was okay, but their voice was distant and garbled. I found the wherewithal to fish my train ticket out of Liam's bag so I could flash it at the platform officer as I boarded the train. The edges of the paper blackened and curled in my fingers, and I shoved it back into Liam's bag before the overflowing Skalmagick could light it on fire.

I settled into a window seat.

It would be another several hours before I got to Keel Watch Harbor. I searched Liam's backpack for his phone and found it near the bottom just as the train rolled away from the station.

I wouldn't be able to unlock it, but I should still be able to make an emergency call. The screen lit up, showing a wallpaper image of Liam, Riley, and Sabrina all posing for a selfie.

The energy in my hands pulsed, and a metallic pop rang out. The picture disappeared, replaced with a black screen that reflected my haggard face back at me.

"No." I hit the power button over and over and over again, until the acrid smell of burnt metal singed my sinuses and smoke started to stream out from under the phone screen.

I dropped it in my lap, and my fingers sparked with more energy. I shoved my hands in my armpits and bent over, trying to hold everything inside.

"Ciarán?" I whispered into the dark folds of Liam's hoodie. "Can you hear me?" No one answered. I wrapped my hand around the porcelain chicken. "Liam? Please."

Silence.

So I hid in the dark of my lap, held my breath and my Skal, and counted the seconds until the train ride was over.

The coastline outside my window looked too normal, like someone had forgotten to tell the sun and sea that the world might be coming to an end. The sun hung bright and high in a cloudless blue sky, and the water was calm and glittering.

I watched harbors and bays blur past in the final minutes of the train ride, bouncing in my seat.

There was a chance I had beat Ferrin to Keel Watch Harbor. I wasn't sure how his Nightmare abilities worked, but maybe he was unable to project himself directly to Keel Watch. Maybe I'd hit him hard enough with my flail that he needed to rest before he launched any sort of attack on sleepy, oceanside towns.

When the train finally came to a stop at Keel Watch Harbor Station, the platform seemed normal enough. I was alone, but that wasn't out of the ordinary. It wasn't a very popular stop on the train route.

But then an unshakeable cold settled over me despite the summer sun bright in the sky where it hung over the bay. Its heat was dull and muted, and I pulled Liam's filthy hoodie over my blouse to keep warm.

I stepped into the empty street between the station and the library. The train whistled behind me as it pulled away, leaving eerie silence in its wake.

A creaking sound broke the quiet.

The library's front door hung from its hinges, swinging slowly in the sea breeze.

"No," I breathed, and sprinted across the street to burst through the broken door. "Mr. Lane?"

The library was dark and empty. Mr. Lane wasn't at the front desk, and when I ran through the shelves, I didn't see him there either. I barreled around the corner by the printers and stopped at the sight of the two empty armchairs with a stack of magazines piled on the table between them.

My veins burned, but I ignored the fire as I took stumbling steps to the armchairs.

A pile of dust sat on each cushion, and my stomach twisted.

"Gladys?" I hissed. "Sarah?"

No.

It couldn't be real. It couldn't—

I turned heel and ran.

The cold air burned in my lungs as I sprinted down the hill towards the water with Liam's backpack bouncing against my back.

"Gams!" I screamed, not caring who heard me. Wind rolled over the tree-lined hill, blowing dirt up in my face. It stuck in my throat, and I doubled over in a blood-flecked coughing fit.

Dust and ash blew across my shoes, and I staggered backwards. It looked horribly similar to the piles of ash that sat in Gladys and Sarah's favorite library chairs. Horribly similar to the ash that Liam had dissipated into in my arms.

"No," I choked. "No, no, no!"

I flew around the corner onto Main Street. It was a Friday afternoon, and the shops should've been alive with tourists. Instead, the street was barren and cold despite the shining sun.

My dress shoes rubbed against the back of my ankles, but I ignored the burning in my heels and the fire in my lungs. I couldn't get to Gams's shop fast enough.

I passed through another pile of dust, and I screamed for Gams again, shrieking her name so hard that I tasted blood on the back of my tongue, but there was no one to hear me.

Keel Watch Harbor was empty, nothing more than a town of dust and deserted shops.

"Gams!" I shouted over the sound of the shop bell ringing out overhead. "Gams, please!"

She had to be here. She *had* to be.

The ceramic chickens stared at me from their shelf, and the wave of Skalmagick that rolled off of them, reaching for me, was nauseating.

"Gams?" I croaked. She wouldn't leave the shop unattended, but the shelves and the register were abandoned. I closed my eyes, afraid I would see more dust on the floor.

But Gams wasn't a Nightmare. She *couldn't* be a Nightmare, because I was real. This was my real form.

At least I thought it was. Fire burned in my hands. If I was using Skalmagick, then maybe I wasn't real at all. But then where was my body? Where was the real me?

A scratching sound brought my eyes snapping open, and the blue flames that tickled my fingers snuffed out.

"Gams?"

A yowling meow replied from the stairway to the apartment.

I scrambled behind the register and opened the door. Jonquil streaked across my feet with a puffed-out tail. She bolted for the back wall and disappeared through the open door to Gams's workshop.

I followed after her, shivering in the unfettered air of Gams's AC. I crossed my arms, trying to conserve heat inside Liam's hoodie.

"Jonquil?" I tiptoed down the wooden steps to the basement and turned the corner at the bottom.

A single ceiling light illuminated the concrete floor and barren walls of the workshop. A shelf of unpainted chickens stood opposite a wall of painting supplies, and the kiln in the corner radiated a meager amount of heat that did nothing to stave off the cold of the AC. A glaze-stained apron draped over a messy work table, as if it had just been dropped there.

"Gams? Are you down here?"

Jonquil meowed again, and lifted onto her hind legs to scratch at a supply closet door with both paws.

"What are you looking for?" I murmured. She turned her flat face towards me, and for the first time since meeting the cat, she seemed to stare at me with something other than total loathing. "It's just a closet—"

I pulled the door open, and a gush of frigid air washed over me, pushing loose strands of hair back from my face.

I was staring into the maw of an ice cavern.

Where there should have been closet walls, there were sheets of ice that arched upwards to form a barrel ceiling. The frozen steps that lay ahead radiated a soft light and spiraled downwards out of view.

I should've been shocked. Twenty-four hours ago, I probably would've been, but now I only felt something like resolved defeat.

My grandma was hiding an ice cave in her basement. Of course. Why wouldn't she be?

"Gams," I sighed. "What the hell?"

Jonquil stared up at me, as if looking for reassurance, and then led the way down the frozen steps. I followed her, bracing one hand against the icy wall. The cold air warred with the inferno that had been burning inside me since the forest behind Von Leer, and steam rose off my fingers.

The ice seemed to call out to me, reaching for my heart with invisible fingers of Skal. The electricity inside my veins jumped and sparked the deeper we descended into the mosaic of white and blue. I hugged myself, not just because of the cold, but in an effort to keep myself in one piece.

The stairs leveled off, and the glacial walls encased frozen, swirling patterns of light that got brighter the farther we went.

Muddled voices echoed through the icy tunnel. My breath crystalized in the air in front of me as I hesitated in fear and hope, but Jonquil, with her tail held high, ran ahead.

"Wait!" I chased after her, sliding on the ice but keeping upright.

The cavern twisted and opened into a bright well. The floor spiraled downwards around the open space, and at the bottom, two figures stood facing a wall.

Jonquil chirped as she raced down the ramp to reach the base of the well, but I froze.

Ferrin looked up at me from below, and his grin caught the green glow of the fiery blade he had held at Gams's throat.

"I thought you might be joining us soon!" His tone was casual and light despite the weapon he held against my grandmother. "Come on down, Just-Wren. I've got something to show you."

"Don't touch her!"

My words bounced through the cavern and were met by the echoing cackle of Ferrin's laughter. I held my hands up in surrender as I traced Jonquil's path down the spiraling ramp.

Something dark and shadowed lurked beneath the ice at Gams and Ferrin's feet, breaking up the bright glow emitted by the walls and floor.

"Go back, Wren." Gams's voice was stern. "Please."

"Oh, no," Ferrin called. "Wren's going to join us."

Jonquil ran across Ferrin's feet, but instead of going to Gams, she curled up in the middle of the ice, directly over the shadow, and laid her tail over her nose.

"Leave my grandmother out of this." Power pulsed in my palms, and I contracted every muscle I possibly could in an effort to contain it. If Ferrin saw me use magick, if he decided I was a threat, he might hurt Gams. "I'll do whatever you want, Ferrin. Just let her go."

I reached the bottom of the pit. Gams's frown sat heavy on her face, but she didn't seem bothered nor shocked by the glowing sword at her neck.

"My love," she said, "how do you know this man? What secrets have you been keeping?"

Ferrin tightened his grip on Gams's neck.

"What do you want from me?" I demanded. "Let her go, and I'll do whatever it is—"

Ferrin laughed again.

"Stop, if I laugh too hard I might cry, and it's much too cold for that," he guffawed. "You think *she's* the leverage? Against you? No. Your usefulness has regrettably run its course in all but one way. Precious Gams isn't the collateral. You are."

"You'll be okay, Wren," Gams assured me. "I promise. I won't let him hurt you."

My grandmother was strong. She had been strong my whole life, filled with fire and bite, and now all five-foot-nothing of her stood taller and stronger than ever.

Gams with her sleepy gift shop and Persian cat.

Gams with her Skal-filled chickens and her town full of Nightmares.

Gams with more secrets than I might've ever guessed.

"How long have you known about Skalterra?" I whispered. Gams's eyes wavered behind her glasses, and she shook her head.

Ferrin swung his sword away from Gams's neck to point at the dark shadow in the ice beneath Jonquil.

"How long?" Ferrin hissed. "She's known about Skalterra longer than any of us, Just-Wren. Since its very advent! She was, after all, the one who created it."

Forty-Three
Combustion Fundamentals

I waited for Gams to tell me that Ferrin was mistaken. He was lying. He had to be. He'd lied about so much already.

But Gams silently kept my gaze with her chin held high.

"You're the Frozen God," I said blankly. "The Saergrim."

Not Gams. It couldn't be Gams.

"To think I thought you were Galahad's nobody Nightmare," Ferrin laughed at me. "Oh, Wren! You took to your Nightmare form so quickly, I should've known. Too bad Galahad couldn't be here to see this. He'd never believe it."

"You turned my granddaughter into your *Nightmare?*" A careful anger simmered across Gams's face. She had the same look of indignant rage Mom had borne in the porch video.

"The old Lyrguard turned her into a Nightmare, not me. Don't worry. He's dead and rotting. But let's not get hypocritical, *Gams,*" Ferrin simpered. "You're a Nightmare too, and I'm guessing you're one of your own making."

"That's different!"

"Oh? And what about all the Nightmares you filled that cute little town of yours with? Was that different too?"

I stared at Gams, searching for signs that she was in fact a Nightmare. Her hair wasn't blue. Her skin was wrinkled with age. She was just Gams.

But she'd just admitted it herself. She, along with the rest of Keel Watch Harbor, were Nightmares. They were all *her* Nightmares.

"And Wren here!" Ferrin pressed onward. "You should have seen her the last few weeks. I thought she'd be useless when we first picked her up, but she was instrumental in getting the Divine Sovereigns here."

He beckoned at the curved wall that encircled the space. The Skal trapped in the ice made the walls blindingly bright, but shadows shifted behind Ferrin.

Gold and green Skal weapons glinted on the other side of the frozen surface, and my chest constricted at the dozens of cloaked figures held on their knees at sword point.

The two figures closest to the barrier brought my heart into my throat, and hot Skal threatened to burst from my veins. The frosted surface dulled their features, but Orla and Fana sat on their knees, bound and gagged on the other side of the ice.

The other side of the *Rift*, I realized.

"No!" I ran to the wall and pressed my hands against the barrier. Orla's eyes grew wide over the rag in her mouth. Caitria loomed behind her, golden knife in hand.

"Would you like to tell your grandmother what you've been up to all summer?" Ferrin asked. "Or should I?"

"Wren, I'm sorry. You were never supposed to—"
Ferrin pulled on Gams's hair to shut her up.

"I told you not to hurt her!" I cried, still kneeling next to Orla.

"Wren was such a good Nightmare," Ferrin said. "Not at first, mind you. She kept killing herself to get away."

"You should've told me," Gams whispered to me.

"Says the centuries-old Magician." Unshed tears burned behind my eyes like the magick swirling in my veins, but I refused to let Ferrin see me cry.

"Enough of this." Ferrin waved a hand. "I'll give you one chance, Saergrim, to open the Rift without me doing so by force."

By force.

He meant by sacrificing Orla and Fana.

"You don't want to free me, Quillguard," Gams said evenly. "Keldori isn't compatible with Magicians."

"I've been living in Keldori using your same self-projected Nightmare trick, and I promise, Keldori is plenty compatible."

"There's too much Skal," she continued. "Have you ever seen what happens to a Magician that uses too much Skal at once? It devours them from the inside out, and then it devours whoever it can find next."

"Rotsbane," I gasped. I thought I saw a flicker of uncertainty pass over Ferrin, but he shrugged it away.

"Lies," he grunted. "Rotsbane are Nightmares, not Magicians."

"Before Skalterra, Magicians were getting too greedy," Gams explained. "It spiraled into an epidemic. Rotsbane were ripping apart towns, cities, and countries. So Lyria, Quill, Fireld, and I put an end to it. We combined our magick to build Skalterra in a reality parallel to Keldori where the Skal is limited. Magicians can still use their magick, but in amounts that make it harder to turn into monsters."

"And you left the rotsbane in Keldori?" I asked.

Gams gave me a smug smile, as if proud of me for asking the right questions.

"We learned how to project ourselves back into Keldori as Nightmares, and we hunted them down until there were none left."

My grandma. Magician. Frozen God. Rotsbane hunter.

I looked back at Orla and Fana through the ice. Their ancestors had been my grandmother's closest friends. She had helped them create Skalterra. They'd risked their lives hunting rotsbane together.

"Then why did they trap you here?" I demanded. Ferrin must've wanted the answer too, because he waited patiently for Gams to answer.

"Because I asked them to." She frowned. "When we formed Skalterra, this glacier acted as an umbilical cord of sorts. It keeps Skalterra tethered to Keldori, but that meant Magicians could escape back through this ice cave. One of us had to seal the Rift, and Fireld, Lyria, and Quill, they all had families."

Her voice caught on the last word.

Gams had sacrificed everything, and she'd been rewarded with a reputation of evil and deceit.

My sweet, kind grandmother.

Skalterra didn't just hate her—they *feared* her.

"Why does everyone say you want to claim Keldori as your own and start a magick war? And why do they all think you're a man?"

I looked back at the silhouette under Jonquil.

"No one wants to release a power-hungry god." Gams's smile was sad. "And a frozen man demands more respect than a woman. The rumors my friends started kept us all safe. As an extra layer of protection, they bound me here with their blood. As long as their family lines survived, I would remain frozen in the Rift, and both realities would be safe."

"But you aren't frozen." I refused to think my grandmother was anyone other than the woman who stood in front of me now, and I refused to look at the shadow in the ice any longer.

"I grew restless, so fifty years ago, I created a Nightmare for myself in Keldori. Outside this glacier, on the Skalterra side, there is a colony of Magicians who have sworn themselves to protecting me." She glanced at the figures Caitria and her soldiers held prisoner on the other side of the ice. "It's dark and cold and not a life worth living. Keldori is so full of Skal, and I was lonely. So I built Keel Watch Harbor, and filled it with semi-lucid Nightmares made from the brave Magicians protecting me so that at least while they slept, they could live a comfortable life, and I could have their company."

"Semi-lucid?" Ferrin demanded. The way he cut in, I had the sense he'd only let our conversation go on so he could get answers to his own questions. "What do you mean?"

"You can't force a Nightmare to be completely lucid, but I discovered if I gave them Skal-filled totems, they'd retain their identities and Keldorian memories from day to day, though they rarely remember Skalterra while in Keel Watch." Gams shot Ferrin a scowl that she usually reserved for particularly annoying shop customers. "I've made thousands of chickens, and I've given out hundreds of them."

I held out my hand so she could see Liam's chicken in my palm.

"Oh, Liam." She frowned. "His family has dutifully acted as my most elite protectors for generations, but he is too gentle."

"Is gentle the word you would use, Just-Wren?" Ferrin goaded. "Didn't the Grimguard kill you?"

"Did he?" Gams tutted. "He didn't mean it, Wren. Liam's a good boy. If he'd known—"

"His name is Ciarán," I said. "And his cousin was Daithi."

"Riley."

"Riley wasn't real!" I didn't mean to raise my voice at Gams, but I couldn't help the sense of betrayal at it all. "And you knew he was dead, but you let Liam—I mean, Ciarán—"

"I tried to help him move on," she insisted. "The same I did when his parents died."

My stomach lurched with Skal and realization.

"Liam's parents," I said slowly, "they were Grimguards too."

Gams didn't reply, but the tight press of her lips told me all I needed to know.

"*You.*" I turned to Ferrin. "You killed them the night you murdered your sister. And you killed Riley!"

Heat flickered in my palms.

"And?" Ferrin shrugged. "This ends with me killing all of you. Don't waste your tears on Grimguards."

"This ends with you realizing this is a death-mission!" Gams snorted. "You'll let me, my grand-daughter, *and* my cat go back upstairs to our home where I'll call back all my Nightmare neighbors, and we'll continue to keep both realms safe."

"About the granddaughter." Ferrin put his arm around Gams as if they were old friends. "I didn't know Nightmares could *have* grandchildren. Or children for that matter."

"Nightmares are our ideal selves, and I was lonely," Gams said matter-of-factly. "So my ideal self became pregnant with an exact genetic copy of myself. I am a Nightmare, but the baby I had was real."

"Mom." My voice shook. "Does she know?"

But I already knew the answer. It had been Mom who first told me to remove Riley's posters.

And she had raised me away from Keel Watch Harbor.

Away from the town of ghosts.

"Nightmares can create life?" Ferrin mused.

"Only those who are also exceptional Magicians," Gams sniffed. "So a hack like you shouldn't get any smart ideas."

Gams had to be wrong though, because I wasn't an exceptional Magician. I scratched at my arms, thinking about the penicillium mold I'd spread across Ciarán's chest.

That had been life too.

"Why didn't you tell me?" I whispered.

Gams put her hands out to her sides as far as Ferrin's hold on her would allow.

"Look at us, Wren. This is not a world I ever intended to burden you with."

I stared through the ice at Orla and Fana with their mouths gagged and hands bound. Skalterra wasn't a burden. Skalterra was wonderful and full of wonderful people, and when I'd been there, I'd been wonderful too.

Ferrin pushed Gams away with sudden fervor and took a fistful of my hair to drag me back from the ice separating me from Orla. Her muffled cry called out, and her eyes widened in fear.

"And there it is, straight out of the Frozen God's mouth!" Ferrin shouted in triumph. "Skalterra is a *burden*, yet she would keep Keldori for herself!"

"Keldori is a mess. You should know that if you've been living there as a Nightmare." The green blade at my neck had brought a new edge to Gams's voice.

Ferrin shook his head. He had his arm around my chest, and I could feel his Nightmare heart hammering against my back.

"It's a mess because I'm living a half-existence there, splitting my time between two worlds. If I could come to Keldori as my real self, imagine what I'd be able to do with my magick and Keldori's technology."

Gams gave a derisive laugh.

"Spare me the savior act, Quillguard. We both know you only want power."

Heat singed the skin of my neck, and I let out an involuntary whimper. Gams's eyes softened behind her glasses.

"I'll kill her," Ferrin said. "You know I will."

"You need her," Gams asserted. "How else do you intend on controlling me if you break me free? If my granddaughter dies, do you really think you won't incur the Frozen God's immediate wrath? I've killed so many monsters, but it's weak men like you who always fall the easiest."

Ferrin breathed hot air against my neck and pointed his blade of emerald at the ice wall.

"Start with my niece, Caitria!" he bellowed. "I don't want her seeing what comes next."

"No!" I broke free of Ferrin's hold and collapsed against the ice. Orla cried out as Caitria undid her gag so Gams could better hear Orla beg for mercy.

But it wasn't Gams that Orla begged.

"Uncle!" she shrieked. "Please!"

Ferrin remained stony with his eyes on my grandmother.

"I'll kill her and the Fireld girl if that's what it takes to open the Rift. Or you can spare innocent blood and dismantle your prison from the inside yourself."

"You don't know what you're doing," Gams hissed.

"Oh, but I do, and I'm willing to kill my own blood for it, so don't lecture me about weak men."

Caitria grabbed Orla by her hair.

"Don't do this," Orla cried. "Uncle—"

"Is this a bet you're willing to make?" Gams said coolly. "That those are the only two Divine Sovereigns? Four hundred years, that's a lot of opportunity for secret children."

"I'm willing to try," Ferrin growled.

"Really?" Gams gave him a look of disdain. "Your own niece? You'd kill her knowing there's a chance it wouldn't work?"

Caitria looked at Ferrin, waiting for his signal to run Orla through with her knife. Tears streaked Orla's face, and her shoulders heaved with rapid breaths, and her muted words came through the ice.

"Don't look, Fana," she sobbed. "It'll be okay. Alright? Just don't look. I'll be waiting for you. You'll be okay."

Fana screamed through her gag, and I dared take my eyes off them long enough to look at Ferrin. He stared back at his niece, cold resolution etched into his face.

"If there are more, I will find them," he whispered. "Every last Sovereign. And I already promised to kill Orla first."

"Wren, thank you for trying." Orla's wide eyes found mine through the ice, and I pressed against the barrier, trying to reach her. "Your real face is so beautiful. I don't know why you changed it for your Nightmare."

She closed her eyes and braced for Caitria's killing strike.

"No!" I hit at the Rift, and the skin of my knuckles split, streaking the frost with flecks of blood. I looked to Gams for help, but she shook her head at me. "Gams! Please!"

"I tried, Wren. It'll be okay."

"No, *nothing* will be okay!"

"Caitria—" Ferrin's green sword flashed as he raised it.

I'd watched Galahad and Liam die in front of me. My entire world had stripped away over the course of the last twelve hours. Everything I'd ever known was a lie, and I'd lost all sense of reality.

I would not lose Orla too.

"I said *NO!*" I screamed, and every bit of Skalmagick I'd been holding back since destroying Ferrin in the woods exploded outwards.

Ice cracked and groaned, splitting Orla's image. The floor shook, someone was shouting, but now that I had released the Skal, I couldn't hold it back. It ripped through my veins, burning blue and bright, and I thought I might be dying, but through the pain and heat and light, I could see Orla as the ice around her fell.

And then as quickly as I'd combusted, I collapsed, shaking on the shattered floor.

Forty-Four
Collateral Risk Management

The glacier groaned as the ice settled. It hurt to so much as breathe, and I lay motionless as footsteps grew closer overhead.

"Well done, little Saergrim," a new voice crooned. I forced my eyes open to see Caitria standing over me, her dark face framed in frost-coated curls.

Rough hands yanked me to my feet, and pain radiated through every bone and muscle. Still, I fought back, digging in with the heels of my shoes and trying to gain purchase on the ice as I was dragged backwards with an emerald sword at my throat.

"Here she comes," Ferrin growled in my ear. "Stand still, and be good."

The walls separating us from Caitria's side of the cave were gone, and the light in the cavern had dimmed, but now I could better see the people in fur-lined cloaks held on their knees by Ferrin's soldiers. They stared back at me with scared faces, ruddy in the cold and cast in shadow by the light that streamed in through the cave entrance, but I recognized each and every one of them.

Siobhan, Teddy, Olive, Sarah, Gladys, Mr. Lane, and all the rest of Keel Watch Harbor sat on the floor of the ice cave.

The two closest to us kneeled just a few feet behind Fana, and my shaking limbs turned heavier at the sight of them. Sabrina's face held more freckles than it had in Keel Watch Harbor, and her nose had a more pronounced bridge, but the strawberry curls that hung limp around her fiery orange and black glare were exactly the same. Maybe if she hadn't had them hidden under her hood before, I would have recognized her when she'd chased us down on the frozen lake and put an arrow through Orla.

Ciarán sat next to her with his cowl down around his neck, a black eye that stood out against his pale skin, and a green sword held at his neck by one of Ferrin's men. He stared past me with a look that held none of Liam's warmth, but I could see my friend hiding in the shape of his face, easy to find now that I knew to look for him.

"Lady Saergrim!" he roared and lurched to his feet. The soldier guarding him grabbed him by his cloak and slammed him into the ice, but Ciarán kept his eyes up.

I shifted in Ferrin's arms to follow Ciarán's horrified gaze. My heart constricted when I saw the dust scattered on the ice where Gams had stood a moment ago.

"Gams?" I whispered.

Jonquil was gone too, and the ice where she'd lain was cracked and melted, a bright glow emanating from the crevice that now split the floor.

A shadow shifted inside, and Ferrin dragged me closer so we could look down into the broken ice together.

A young woman with long blonde hair stood in a pool of Skal with the skirts of her blue gown floating up around her waist on the surface of the liquid. She held Jonquil in one arm while the other fished in her dress pocket before pulling out a pair of thin-rimmed, circular spectacles.

She pushed them up her nose to better glare at us.

She really did look just like Mom.

"What a charming way to discover my grandkid is a Magician," she sniffed. Her voice was just like Mom's too, and the sound of it took my breath away. "Releasing me from my glacier when I specifically told her not to. How very like her."

"Saergrim," Ferrin chuckled darkly. "You look younger than I expected, based off your Nightmare."

"I went nearly four hundred years without aging. It was fun to try it out." The air around her rippled with blue heat, and Skal evaporated off her hair and gown in puffs of glowing steam.

"Out of the pool, Frozen God," Caitria jeered. "Your people are waiting for you."

Caitria approached Gams with her golden sword outstretched, leaving Orla to scramble towards Fana with her hands still bound behind her. The girl bowed into Orla's attempt at an embrace, and I wanted nothing more than to join them.

Gams's eyes flickered between my face and the sword at my throat.

"I'm sorry," I choked out at her. It was hard to reconcile the ethereal Magician in the pool with the image I had of my gray-haired, glaze-stained grandmother in my head.

"You were only trying to help your friend." Blue stairs appeared beneath Gams as she ascended out of the pool with Jonquil purring in her arms. "Don't worry, Wren. I'll take care of this. This fraud knows which of us is the more powerful Magician."

"Then you'll understand why I can't let you live." Ferrin's grip on me tightened. "You or your grand-daughter. One of you dies, so who will it be?"

I was helpless to defend myself against the blade under my chin. Even the tiniest movement hurt, and my arms shook with fatigue.

"Don't you dare hurt her," Gams hissed.

"You or her," Ferrin repeated. "I've got to be honest, Wren's been such a thorn in my side, I almost hope you pick—"

An orange blast knocked us sideways, and I sprawled out on the floor. Shouts echoed through the cavern, but by the time I gathered the physical strength to look up, Ciarán had already been subdued.

He'd almost made it all the way to Gams before Caitria had stopped him. He glared up at Ferrin from where she held him against the floor with his arms pinned behind his back.

"The little orphan boy." Ferrin still had his sword pointed at me, but he kept his focus on Ciarán. "I remember your admissions interview. The question is, do you?"

Ciarán scowled at the question, and Ferrin laughed.

"Is that a no, then?" He turned towards Gams. "I see what you mean about him being too gentle now. This will be my fourth Grimguard, and it feels a bit more like mercy-killing the runt of a litter than dealing with an actual threat. Still. Both can be fun if you do it right."

Ferrin pulled his sword away from me to hold it over Ciarán's neck.

"Ferrin, my pet!" A lilting voice called out, bouncing off the ice and wiping the triumphant grin from Ferrin's face. "You nasty liar. All that talk about preserving Skalterra when you intended on freeing the Frozen God yourself."

My vision swam with exhaustion, but the fiery red hair and the glint of a monocle at the entrance to the ice cave was unmistakable. Tamora stood in fur-lined boots with impractically high heels and a small army of Nightmares at her back.

Titus's hulking shape next to her blocked out the late afternoon sun that poured in from behind them.

Stanley had listened. Something I said had gotten through to him.

"The Baron?" Caitria hissed. "You said we didn't have to worry about her!"

"You're too late, Tamora!" Ferrin called. "Keldori is mine. Go home, and maybe I'll let the Grand Barony see the next great age of Magicians."

Glowing orange eyes caught mine, and Ciarán held my gaze where Caitria held him against the frozen floor. He smirked at me, and then drew his tongue along the glowing ice beneath him.

Skal sparked in his hands, and the air around him erupted in orange flames.

Caitria shrieked, and Ferrin brought his sword down, but Ciarán was already rolling out from under them. An orange spear burst to life in his hands as he leapt to his feet, and he drove the pointed end through Ferrin's Nightmare chest.

Ferrin roared in rage, and then crumbled into dust.

Red burst overhead as Tamora took advantage of Ciarán's distraction, and her Nightmares charged into the cavern, led by Titus. Gold and green Skalmagick rose to defend against Tamora's attack, and shouts and screams echoed through the cave in a disorienting clamor.

The floor shook, but I didn't have the strength to run. I was pinned to the ice by pain and exhaustion, so I closed my eyes, waiting for the battle to swallow me.

"Wren." Soft hands cupped my cheeks, and my eyes fluttered open. Gams, so young and ethereal with rosy cheeks and blonde hair that pooled on the ice, smiled behind her round spectacles as she knelt down with me. "My beautiful girl, I'm so sorry. I never meant for you to get dragged into all this."

She looked so different from the Gams I knew, but also just the same. Her brow creased with the same worry it always did when she fussed over me, and her lips drew down in the same neat frown.

"Did I ruin everything?" I choked. Tears welled in my eyes, and fatigue made the edges of my vision dark and blurry. "Is the world going to end because of me?"

Her frown melted into a gentle smile.

"I told you. I'm taking care of it."

A green and red blast sent more tremors through the floor, and Tamora's cackle rebounded off the icy walls of the cave. Caitria was shouting somewhere too, but I couldn't make out what she was saying through the chaos.

"Look at me, Wren." Gams's eyes swam with unshed tears. "I've created mountains and seas, but of all the things I've made, you have been one of the greatest. What an honor that I should get to look upon you with my real eyes."

Her hand lingered on my cheek for just a moment more, her blue eyes holding mine. Then her gaze snapped upwards, and she rose to her feet.

"Gams..." I reached out for her, but another explosion rocked the cavern and ice shards fell, forcing me to hide against the cracked floor.

"Protect her," Gams's voice, young and so much like Mom's, said overhead. "Please."

"With my life, Lady Saergrim." Arms wrapped around me as the cavern trembled. The floor dropped away, and a cowl-covered chin swam in my vision.

The fire in my veins burned, and the porcelain chicken pulsed in my hand where I held it against my chest.

"And take my cat!" Lips pressed against my forehead. "I love you, Wren. Tell your mother when you see her that I love her too."

"No..."

I fought through my blurring vision for a final glimpse of my grandmother, but then Ciarán was running and lights were bursting overhead as I called for Gams. Ice groaned and cracked, and a massive chunk of ceiling fell. Maybe telling Stanley to warn Tamora was a mistake. She'd been a useful distraction, but she wanted the same thing Ferrin did.

Screams echoed through the cavern, and blue lightning flashed in the enclosed space, sending fissures spiderwebbing across the frozen surfaces of the walls.

"Ciarán!" The cavern was collapsing, and from my vantage in Ciarán's arms, I could see the ice above us crumbling.

"I've got you," he panted.

"But Orla and—"

"Worry about yourself for once, Blue."

The cave opened up overhead, revealing a fog-laden sky. Skalterran sun percolated through and bounced off the icebergs that floated in the water around us. Everything was in shades of white, blue, and gray, and Jonquil mewed somewhere nearby.

I was meeting Skalterra for the first time, in the light of day with my real face and my real self.

I'd made it back, but I wanted to go home. I wanted my mom. I needed my grandma.

"Gams..."

An explosion of yellow and green rocked us sideways, and the sun snuffed out.

Forty-Five
Intro to Storm Chasing

Everything hurt.

A dull heat throbbed in my muscles, and sweat slicked my brow. I could feel it pooling beneath my back too, but I shivered, impossibly cold despite the heavy blankets that covered me. Nausea and pain roiled in my stomach, and a metal taste tinged my tongue. My ribs were the worst, though. Each breath I took sent shooting pains up my sides and across my chest.

While the purring weight on my ankles was familiar, the musky pillows beneath me were not, yet there was something cozy and reassuring about their smell.

But I didn't know where I was. I didn't know if Gams was okay, or if the world was still in one piece. I felt like a dying fire, crumbling to ashen embers in my borrowed bed, used up, dried out, and turning cold.

I pushed myself up, forcing my way through the agony spasming through my ribs. Fur pelts insulated the wooden walls, and the lack of windows made it feel like a cave. A lantern that flickered with an orange flame cast long shadows up the pelts and across the ceiling beams.

Its light illuminated the dark sheen of Ciarán's hair where he stood with his back to me in the doorway. I wondered where his cloak had gone, especially with how cold the room was, but then I recognized its tattered folds across my lap.

Jonquil blinked at me from the foot of the bed, curled up next to Liam's backpack.

"Water?" I croaked. My tongue felt like sandpaper.

"There's a skein next to you." Ciarán kept his back to me.

I prodded at the shadows of my quilts until I found the leather container. I uncorked the mouth, and gagged on the liquid when it seared my raw throat.

"Careful," Ciarán murmured.

"Where are we?" I demanded. "Where's my grandmother?"

"We're at an outpost in the foothills."

"And Gams?" I pleaded. He was silent, as quiet as he was immobile. "Ciarán?"

"My Lady?"

I recoiled at the title.

"Don't do that."

"Do what?"

"Call me lady."

"I'm bound to the service of you and your family. To call you anything else would be improper."

I was sitting in a torn collegiate hoodie and a ripped pencil skirt. My hair was knotted, and my eyelashes patchy. I'd been rejected by my biological father, tanked my school interview, and released an imprisoned Magician so powerful they called her a "god", putting two separate realities at risk of collapse.

The title "Lady" was anything but proper.

"If you're bound to my service, do you have to obey me?"

"Yes, my Lady." He emphasized the title just to annoy me.

"Then I demand you call me anything except that."

His shoulders heaved.

"Such as?"

"Anything you like. Just not 'Lady'".

"Ever-enduring pain in my ass, then."

Heat rose in my face, and I brought the water skein back to my lips.

"It's a bit of a mouthful," I said between tentative sips. He fell silent again, dutifully watching the hall outside my room. I studied his back, wondering if the man in front of me could really be the friend who had comforted me on a paddleboard and held me as I cried over my father. "Look at me."

He ignored me, and I set the water skein down.

"You have to obey."

He pivoted slowly, turning his bright orange gaze on me. His pale skin was still bruised around one of his eyes, and a cut on his chin had been bandaged.

For the first time, after a month of fighting in this world and finding comfort in each other's friendship in the next, we took each other in with our real faces.

I tried to find Liam in his, but it was harder up close with his dark hair and black sclera that looked like the eyes of a monster.

"Do you remember me?" I asked.

"It's going to take more than a new hair color for me to forget you, Blue."

"I don't mean my Nightmare."

He blinked slowly, and I thought he'd fallen silent again, but then he lifted a hand and unfurled his fingers.

Liam's chicken glowed a dull blue in the dark of the room.

"What is this?" He kept a serious frown fixed to his face, but the tiniest hint of panic laced his tone and shook his voice.

"It's a chicken."

"I know." He broke off, still staring at the little statue. "I've never been to Keldori."

"But you remember it."

"Pieces." His eyebrows knit.

"Like what?" I needed him to remember. I needed Liam.

"A steamcart."

"We rode one recently." I nodded. "What else?"

"A man. Some sort of leader, I think. Everyone respected him. Except me, for some reason." He was talking about my father. These were all memories from his last few days as Liam, things that had happened after Gams had given him the chicken when we left Keel Watch.

"A good instinct, honestly. What else?"

"You." He raised his glowing eyes from the chicken to my face. "And needing to protect you. It was my purpose, I think."

How many times had I joked that he was only hanging out with me because Gams was forcing him? Liam had always denied it, but he wouldn't have been aware of any secret directives Gams had built into his Nightmare.

My friendship with him hadn't been real, but Liam hadn't been real either.

"Why do I remember these things?" Ciarán asked. "And why do I miss it?"

"You were a Nightmare."

"No, I wasn't." He shook his head.

"Your name was Liam."

"I died."

"Not an uncommon experience for a Nightmare."

Ciarán stared at the chicken with his orange and black eyes. Liam had been blond, tanned, and perfect. Every difference between him and Ciarán highlighted everything Ciarán wanted to be.

"I knew the Saergrim in Keldori," he murmured. "I remember seeing her."

"My grandma." I nodded.

"So that's why I was never able to summon your Nightmare without you yielding," Ciarán said. "I swore an oath to your family. I cannot control you without your permission."

I remembered his arms around me as he stopped me from turning into a rotsbane. I remembered his arms around me in the hotel bed outside of Von Leer.

"You still haven't told me where my grandmother is," I said before I could let myself get confused over my feelings for Ciarán. Or Liam. I still wasn't sure they were the same person. How could they be if Liam didn't exist and Ciarán did? "And my friends too. Where are they?"

"The other Sovereigns are downstairs."

I pushed my blankets off, and a new chill rolled over my body. I ignored it.

"My Lady—"

"No." I pointed a stern finger at him, still trying to fight my way off the mattress. Everything was sore, and the tiniest movements threatened to lay me out with pain. "I told you, none of that."

"You're injured. You should stay in bed."

"Then I demand you help me *out* of bed."

Ciarán sighed.

"In over four hundred years, no Grimguard has ever forsaken their duty."

"So?"

"So you are tempting me to become the first."

The cold wood of the floor against my bare feet sent a fresh shiver up my spine. My ribs ached, and I held a shuddering arm over them, as if to keep myself in one piece.

I bit down on my tongue to keep from crying out when I tried to stand.

Something heavy settled over my shoulders, and I flinched away from Ciarán as he draped his cloak over me.

"I'm fine," I lied.

"Your body isn't used to using Skal, and you used a lot to free the Frozen God." He let me lean into him as I staggered to my feet.

"Stop calling her that."

"Is that another order?"

"Yes."

"And what do you prefer I call her?"

"Ethel. Or Gams. I don't think she'd mind if you called her Gams."

He was sturdy beneath me, and his armor smelled of fresh leather.

"I'm not going to call the Frozen God 'Gams'."

The hallway was narrow, and he lit a fire in his free palm to light the way down a set of wooden steps. Jonquil chased after us, purring at Ciarán's heels. I hated that I needed his help, but I was grateful to have him to lean against.

"Sorcha said you broke your ribs, and you vomited blood, so she thinks you have an ulcer," Ciarán said as we navigated the stairs. "Holding in too much Skal can do that."

"I never had that issue before."

"You were a Nightmare before. You were made of Skal. It was different."

Holding in Skal would break my bones and rip open my stomach. Using too much Skal would turn me into a rotsbane.

I wasn't sure I was cut out to be a Magician, much less the granddaughter of one of the four most powerful Magicians to ever live.

A fire crackled in a massive hearth that overlooked the narrow, vaulted hall of the ground floor. Yellow and orange light bounced off the contours of haggard faces. Two old women ladled liquid out of a steaming pot into mugs made of some sort of animal horn, and an old man shuffled to deliver them to the three girls sitting at the table.

Fana's dark curls were immediately distinguishable, and she looked up as we came down the bottom step.

"Just-Wren!" she cried.

Orla's head jerked up next to her.

"Wren!" Orla leapt from the table and barreled into me. Pain shot through my ribs, and I cried out. "Oh, no. I'm sorry—"

"It's okay," I insisted. And it was. I was back with Orla. Ciarán released me, letting me lean into my embrace with my friend. She shook with sobs, and I held her as tight as my aching muscles would allow. "Orla, we're okay."

"He tricked me." Her whisper was a heartbroken hiss. "A week ago, Ferrin said he had a special mission for me. I didn't know he was taking us to the Frozen God. Galahad and the others don't know. I didn't even have the chance to say goodbye before we left."

I pulled away from Orla, and the firelight caught the streams of tears that fell from her face.

"Orla," I croaked, "Galahad's dead. Ferrin killed him."

Her eyes filled with fresh tears.

"No, he didn't," she whispered. "He wouldn't. Ferrin wouldn't—"

"He was going to kill you."

"I know."

Her chin quivered as she tried to remain strong, but then something in her expression broke, and she fell into fresh sobs that racked her body.

I buckled under her embrace, and Ciarán steadied me. Familiar strawberry curls rushed to Orla's side to help her back to the table.

"Sabrina?" I asked.

Sabrina's head snapped towards me, and her eyes, black and orange like Ciarán's, caught me off guard.

"My Lady Saergrim." She knelt down on one knee. As if that wasn't mortifying enough, several others in the room followed suit.

"No." I shook my head. "Don't do that. You tried to shoot me."

"It was a misunderstanding," she growled, and I got the sense she loved kneeling for me just as much as I loved being kneeled for.

"What are you doing out of bed, girl?" One of the few who hadn't knelt bustled over. "Ciarán, you should have called me."

The woman's floor length robes of leather and fur weren't something she'd ever worn in Keel Watch, but the sharp nose and chin were unmistakable.

"Sarah?" I asked.

"It's pronounced Sorcha here." Sarah prodded at my side, and I yelped in pain. "Back up the stairs with you. Ciarán, you might have to carry her."

"I want my grandmother," I pressed. "Where is she?"

"Ethel is fine," Sarah grunted.

Ciarán tried to lead me away, but I held a hand up.

"You called her Ethel," I said.

"All those decades, and all those Nightmares in Keel Watch Harbor." Sarah smirked. "One of us was bound to be lucid."

"Two of us." The other woman still stood over the pot of stew. She waved the dripping ladle at me. The white hair she kept so short in Keel Watch was long and braided into a crown that wrapped around her head here. "And who else was going to keep Ethel updated on Skalterra?"

"Gladys?" I asked.

"Aoife is my name here, my Lady." She shuffled over and shoved a horn full of steaming red liquid into my hands. She nodded to a man standing by the hearth. "And that's Ronan, but you know him already too."

Ronan, who looked an awful lot like Mr. Ronald Lane the Librarian, bowed his head to me.

"Please, sit. Drink." Aoife-Gladys pointed to Orla's table. "You'll feel better."

"I'll feel better when someone tells me where my grandmother is."

Sarah, or Sorcha, frowned.

"Go ahead then." She shrugged at Ciarán. "Show her. And then it's straight back upstairs. I don't care whose granddaughter you are. You have a fever."

"Show me what?" I demanded. Ciarán helped me forward to the low-framed door past the tables.

Night was heavy outside, but the stars shined bright in the bitter cold. I still didn't have shoes on, and I held Ciarán's cloak tighter around my shoulders as I stepped out onto the snow-covered path.

Despite the clear night, thunder rolled in the distance, and a sharp wind tugged at the cloak.

"Careful, Blue," Ciarán murmured.

The building we'd come out of was made entirely of wood with few windows and a steeply-sloped, multi-tiered roof. It stood at the top of a hill nestled against a cliff face. Ahead of us, the landscape flattened in the distance, before giving way to a bay of massive icebergs. Either side of the bay was dotted in firelight ranging in hues of red, greens, and golds.

A storm raged at the bay's center. Heavy clouds sat low over the water, and blue lightning forked at its heart, flashing against the icy faces of the surrounding icebergs.

"What is that?" I asked.

"The Bay of Teeth, where your grandmother's prison used to be," Ciarán said. "But her prison has been broken, and now she's doing what she can to hold both Ferrin's and the Barony's armies from entering Keldori."

I shook my head.

"That storm is...Gams?" I remembered the flashes of blue lightning that had brought the cavern caving inwards as we'd made our escape. "But then how do we get her out?"

"We don't." Ciarán's arm tightened around my shoulder, but I pushed him off.

"I'm not leaving my grandmother in the middle of a storm!" I snarled. "She's my grandma! She's— she's—"

Wonderful. Fiery. Compassionate.

Everything I wasn't.

My legs shook beneath me, and I couldn't feel my toes in the cold, but when Ciarán took a step towards me, I took a step back.

"We aren't leaving her in a storm," he promised, but his furrowed brow and strained frown didn't do much to put me at ease. "The original Divine Sovereigns froze her in the Rift four hundred years ago, and Sorcha says we can do it again."

My heart plummeted, and I turned to look back at the distant storm. My knees buckled, and I let Ciarán catch me this time.

"We have to re-imprison her?" I said.

"We have to try," Ciarán conceded. "We don't have a Tulyr, but we have you."

"You want me to do it?"

Freeing Gams had put both Skalterra and Keldori at risk, but there was something cruel about refreezing my grandma and condemning her to a life in a town full of phantom people.

"I'm sorry, Blue," Ciarán said.

My grandmother had opened her home and her arms to me for the summer. She had cared for me. She had given me a job. She had made sure I had friends.

And now she stood at the vortex of a storm, holding off two armies, not necessarily because of me, but I'd played a role in bringing Fana and Orla north. I'd been Ferrin's missing puzzle piece in finding Keel Watch Harbor. I'd broken the glacier in an effort to save my friends.

And now I was the one who would have to lock her away again.

"How much Skal does she have?" I asked. "She can't last forever in there."

"I'd give her three months, give or take," Sorcha sniffed behind us. I twisted around to watch her shuffle down the snow-covered path. "Lucky for us, she's a better Magician than she is a backgammon player, but you need to go back upstairs and get better because you're headed in there to fix this before it's too late."

She pointed a wrinkled hand at the storm in the distance.

"Leave her alone, Sorcha," Ciarán sighed.

"'Heal her ribs, Sorcha'. 'Fix her ulcer, Sorcha'. But then it's 'leave her alone' as soon as you don't need me," Sorcha snorted. "I'm only out here to let the Lady Saergrim know there's someone here to see her."

"Who?" I demanded.

Sorcha already had her back to me as she retreated back into the building.

"No, don't worry. I'm leaving!"

Ciarán helped me after her, and while I had no idea who might be waiting for me inside, my heart hammered painfully in my chest.

"Sorcha, the Nightmare isn't very happy," Aoife hissed as we came back inside.

"I can hear you, Gladys," a woman's voice said from the hearth. "But no. The Nightmare *isn't* very happy."

The flames of the hearth dyed the newcomer's blonde hair in shades of orange and gold. She turned her head to watch us enter, and my stomach flipped.

"Wren, my love," she said, "what did your grandmother tell you about poking around Keel Watch Harbor?"

I gave a strangled cry and broke free of Ciarán to stumble across the hall, unable to reach her fast enough through the pain that lanced my sides.

She leapt up from the bench to help close the distance, and I collapsed in her arms, crying.

It wasn't her real body, but she smelled just like herself. Warm and floral and perfect.

"Mom," I sobbed and squeezed her tighter as we held each other on the floor.

"Hello, my love." She tucked hair behind my ear so she could press a kiss against my forehead. "Welcome to Skalterra, my little Magician."

494

Acknowledgment

For being a book about sleep, I gave up hours of mine to get this story into your hands. I'm now four books into my career, but this is the first one I've written while also juggling being a full time Stay At Home Mom. While I could only write when she was asleep or, much like Wren, hanging out with either of her grandmas, my beautiful daughter inspired me every day. More than ever, I wanted to write about daughters and moms and grandmas, and I hope someday she'll enjoy reading this story as much as I enjoyed writing it.

My own mother and grandmother are hiding in the pages of this book as well. While my mom would never write smut like Eliza, and though my grandma wasn't very fond of cats like Ethel is, either one of them would happily smash lawn gnomes for the people they love. I'm proud to come from a line of ferocious women, especially ones who raised me to love stories and fantasy worlds. So thank you, Mom, and thank you, Gaga, for loving me, for teaching me, and for inspiring me.

Speaking of mothers, so many stood with me through the process of creating this book. Sally, who is one of many women to prove they don't need the Maxwell Brentons of the world to raise badass daughters, not only do you dutifully help me test and proof all of my books, but you inspire me in everything you do. Melissa, my first reader and Ciarán's first fan, you are the ultimate cheerleader, somehow finding the time to raise your girl while holding my hand through my daily bouts of imposter syndrome. Liz, you thought you were auditioning to narrate a superhero book and now not only are you my forever narrator, but a forever friend who showed me it's possible to be a mother and pursue your literary dreams at the same time.

However, not everyone who helped this book come to be is a mom, but their contribution to both my creative endeavors and personal life deserve just as much note. Madi, not only did I name Sarah, Ethel, and Gladys after your cats, but you looked over my early draft with the care and diligence (and sea star enthusiasm) I would expect from one of my oldest friends. Jess, not a day goes by that I don't thank the universe we stumbled back into each other's lives, and I'm so grateful for the time and effort you put into proofing and editing Wren's story. Maria, I don't know why you keep agreeing to create beautiful book covers for me, but I'm going to keep on asking you until you stop. Joe, also affectionately referred to as British Joe, your unending enthusiasm for anything I write (as well as your colorful commentary) keeps me motivated and reminds me that there will always be an audience for my stories- even if that audience is just some kid in Liverpool.

I love and appreciate all my friends equally, but while writing this book, no one did more for me than Hailey. Hailey who helped me at multiple conventions and events (including one where we had to stay in a tent for three nights). Hailey who let me ramble and rant my way through the writing process in her voice messages (though Melissa also supported me in this way, so let credit go where credit is due). Hailey who champions my books without tiring across the internet. Thank you for being my friend, my unofficial publicist, and my number one fan.

And finally, Connor. My business partner. My love. My husband. None of this would be possible without you, your enthusiasm, or your patience. As the dedications in my previous three books hopefully make clear, you are my superhero, my inspiration, and my best friend. You were the first to tell me to write, and I'm going to keep going until you regret those words. I caribou.

Character and Pronunciation Guide

Keel Watch Harbor

Wren - A recent high school graduate who has been waitlisted at her dream school. She's staying with her grandma for the summer, but every night her consciousness is dragged into Skalterra to aid the Riftkeepers.

Jonquil - (zhon-QUILL) Gams's Persian cat who shares a room with Wren.

Ethel - Wren's grandmother. She owns a small shop on the marina of Keel Watch Harbor and spends her free time painting and glazing ceramic chickens in her basement.

Eliza - Wren's mother. She's abroad for a book tour.

Linsey - Wren's former friend and current mortal enemy.

Liam - Wren's new coworker. He's just finished his freshman year at Wren's dream college, and he lives with his aunt and uncle above their bagel shop.

Siobhan - (shuh-VAWN) The owner of the local tavern.

Sarah - A friend of Ethel's and local town gossip. She's more cynical than her counterpart, Gladys.

Gladys - A friend of Ethel's and local town gossip. She's a bit more friendly than her counterpart, Sarah.

Teddy - Liam's uncle and owner of the local bagel shop. His son, Riley, has gone missing.

Riley - Liam's cousin who has recently gone missing.

Sabrina - Liam's friend and the daughter of the local tavern owner. She's friendly unless you give her reason not to be.

Ronald Lane - The local librarian.

Olive - Liam's aunt and owner of the local bagel shop. Her son, Riley, has gone missing.

Maxwell Brenton - Wren's biological father who has never met his daughter. He's a well-known geophysicist.

Skalterra

Ciarán - (keer-AWN) The Grimguard working for the Frozen God. He is hunting the Riftkeepers to free the Frozen God from his prison.

Orla - (OR-luh) A Quillguard and the youngest member of the Riftkeepers at 18-years-old. Her mother was killed by Grimguards.

iv

Tiernan - (TEAR-nan) An Eldguard and the Riftkeeper directly in charge of keeping Fana alive. He may be young, but he takes his job very seriously.

Galahad - (GAL-ah-had) An old Lyrguard in the Riftkeepers and the nocturmancer in control of Wren's Nightmare.

Fana - (FAN-uh) A young girl and the last Divine Sovereign. If she dies, the Frozen God will be freed.

Ferrin - (FAIR-in) A Quillguard and Orla's uncle. He is the unofficial leader of the Rift-keepers.

Caitria - (KATE-ria) An Eld-guard who is killed by the Grimguards when they attack Fana's home.

Dathi - (DAH-hee) A Grimguard charged with serving the Frozen God. He is hunting Fana with the help of Ciarán.

Saergrim - (SAYER-grim) The Frozen God. One of the four Magicians who built Skalterra before he turned against the others, forcing them to freeze him in a glacier.

Tamora - (tah-MOR-uh) The Baron of the Grand Barony. She's greedy and practical, but cunning too.

Titus - (TIE-tus) Tamora's bodyguard.

Iseult - (ISS-ult) Galahad's granddaughter and a Skal-breaker who can undo the creations of other Magicians.

Urian - (UR-ee-an) A Lyrian knight, though his combat skills are lacking.

Balin - (BALL- in) Galahad's long deceased brother.

Cade - (KADE) Orla's brother and Ferrin's nephew.

Sorcha - (SUH-ruh-kah)

Aoife -(EE-fuh)

Ronan- (RONE-an)

Locations

Cape Fireld - (CAPE fur-ELD) The home of the Fireld Family.

The Second Sentinel- The home of the Quills and Quillguards. It hides in the hollowed peak of mountain that overlooks the Frozen God's domain.

Vanderfall - The capitol of the Grand Barony.

Riverstead- A river port city.

The Umberdust Plains - An expansive plain of tall grass on the border of the Wisting Wilds.

Tulyr - (too-LEER) The fallen city where Skalterra was born and where the Tulyrs once lived.

The Bay of Teeth - The lagoon of icebergs that hides the Frozen God's glacial prison.

About the Author

M.T. Zimny is a young adult author in the Pacific Northwest, where she subsists off of rainy days and ungodly amounts of overpriced coffee. She lives with her husband, her daughter, and her golden retriever.

Other Works by M.T. Zimny

THE APEX CYCLE

A YA SUPERHERO TRILOGY